CW00524429

The Fossil Artist

The Fossil Artist

Graeme Friedman

First published by Jacana Media (Pty) Ltd in 2010

10 Orange Street
Sunnyside
Auckland Park 2092
South Africa
+2711 628 3200
www.jacana.co.za

© Graeme Friedman, 2010

All rights reserved.

ISBN 978-1-77009-924-1

Set in Garamond 11/14
Job No. 001330
Printed and bound by Ultra Litho (Pty) Limited,
Johannesburg

ISO 12647 compliant

See a complete list of Jacana titles at www.jacana.co.za

By the same author:

Madiba's Boys, New Africa Books/Comerford & Miller, 2001

The Piano War, David Philip, 2003

For Tracey, David, Matthew & Asha,
who make my life bountiful

We carry with us the wonders we seek without us: there is all
Africa and her prodigies in us.
    Sir Thomas Browne, *Religio Medici* 1643

But here the walls have teeth, the roof is low;
And suddenly a deep and silent river
Looms out of nothing, and into nothing flows.
    Ruth Miller, *Sterkfontein* 1965

1

RUSS SAT ON A WICKER chair in Rebecca's studio, wishing he could page back time. He would be able to continue his Sunday morning ritual, the lazy reading of worldly gossip, of death in strange lands and imperfect love at a remove from his own. Or he might simply look up from the *Sunday Times*, to where his wife was busy at work. He might take a sip of his coffee and watch the dance of her sculpting knife, the flecks of clay caught in the downy hairs of her forearms. He might listen to her mumble '*Fuck it!*' as she struggled to get something right, knowing that she would eventually get it right. He might breathe in the smell of moist clay mingling with the salt air coming off the sea, and feel at peace.

But this Sunday he could do none of these things. All he could do was shift uncomfortably in his wicker chair and gaze at the article with its accompanying photograph and accusations of murder.

MUMMIFIED MASS MURDERERS
DISENTOMBED

It was an odd headline for an odd story. The photograph, in colour, showed two sunken, parchment-like faces, russet long hair on the one and crisp, short-cropped curls on the other. The mummies – a male and a female – had apparently been found in a cave on the Atlantic coast, along with a collection of human bone fragments, the physical remnants, according to a police spokesperson, of their victims. The killers, the police officer said, referring to them as 'the Bonnie and Clyde of the West Coast', had used chopping and cutting implements to dismember their victims and had then fallen foul of Mother Nature when the entrance to their cave hideout collapsed. Evidence discovered with the bodies suggested that the grisly events had occurred many years ago.

Left here, the article would have been a curiosity for Russ. He might have wondered how it was that the bodies came to be mummified under wet coastal conditions, or how ancient these crimes were, or what might have led a man and a woman to such a violent end. He might look up from the picture of these mummified heads to watch Rebecca working on her sculpture, her focus shifting from the clay head to the preparatory sketches pinned to a large board, detailed studies of the face, a vein caught in mid-throb at a temple, a mole with wiry hairs sprouting from its dark mass. He might take another whiff of that soothing mix of moist clay and sea air.

But he could do none of these things because the newspaper article had identified the male mummy as one Barak Codron – and this just happened to be his father's name, Russ's father, the man who had disappeared more than forty years before.

'My God,' said Russ, his voice a hoarse whisper. 'Beck, look at this.'

2

'THAT'S THE FRIDGE of the unknown dead.' An air of unpredictability escaped Captain Morkel's speech, as if he might weep or fly into a rage at any moment. 'You'd be surprised how many bodies are never identified or claimed. You'd think *somebody* would miss them.'

After making enquiries Russ and Rebecca had been directed to the police head of the state mortuary, and now they were here, in Salt River, following the police captain along his haunted corridors.

'And this is the receiving fridge. You might want to hold your nose. I hope you don't mind me bringing you here. We usually have identifications in the viewing room, after we've done the autopsy. But your relatives are a special case. They're so brittle they break every time we move them.'

'They're not my... only he...,' said Russ, and then gave up. He glanced towards Beck. She had been holding a handkerchief over her nose and mouth since they walked through the front doors of the building but he could see her eyes. She was excited. She can't help herself, he thought, she's gathering material, picking up little nuggets. This place was ridiculous. They should do tours, like those to the townships.

The rubber frame of the door gave a sucking sigh as the captain opened it. The stench hit them first, then the sight of three decks of steel sliding trays that lined the room, then the cold air. The rack was made up of a network of pipes that were bolted to the floor. Emerging from the shadows of this scaffolding were the splayed-out soles of rows and rows of feet. Tied to a big toe of each pair of feet was a numbered manila tag, hanging like limp flags of surrender. The trays, as far as Russ and Beck could see, were full, which explained the mound of corpses on the floor against one wall of the cold room, a tangle of naked body parts, strangers caught in a stiff embrace. A little behind them lay two shrouded figures on a pair of gurneys.

Beck gagged.

'Yes,' said the policeman, 'it is bad! Stinks to high heaven.' His mortuary humour seemed unintentional but Russ found himself choking on a nervous laugh. 'My predecessor installed fridges instead of freezers,' the captain continued. 'Not so clever, hey? The bodies freeze, then thaw, then freeze again. Just the thing to help them decompose. The bacteria love it. I always tell the family not to worry. The coffin will keep the smell inside. But your guys have got no body fluid, so that means no bacteria. Of course, there're plenty of maggots hatching in these other bodies here, so we've tried to keep yours separate.' He smiled grimly, pointing them towards the two metal gurneys alongside. 'Your people seem so fragile. I don't know how they're going to cope with these conditions.'

The mummified corpses were covered with white sheets, which Morkel folded back to reveal first the woman's head, then the man's. Rebecca's forehead had begun to bead with sweat, despite the cold. The handkerchief was useless in here and the smell clung to their tongues. She gripped Russ's hand as he stared at the man's burnt-orange face, some of which was covered in a film of fungus. In patches it looked like charred meat, in others tanned leather. The eyes had become dried apricots staring up at the ceiling.

The mould on the woman's face appeared to have been

wiped away on one side to reveal skin that was more evenly blackened. The tip of her nose was missing but her nostrils survived, flared. Her jaw hung open, as if unhinged, the mouth frozen in a rictus of pain. The man's face, in contrast to that of the woman, looked composed, his dark, cracked lips fused shut. Although it now hung loosely, there was a dirty rag tied in a clove hitch on the top of his head, which seemed to have been used as a jaw strap, holding his mouth closed.

Russ nodded. He spoke in a daze. 'It's my father,' he said, stammering. 'It really is my father, Barak Codron. My father. I don't know who the woman is. Maybe she was working with him. A university student? He used to have assistants but they were always African men. Shona or Masai usually. They made the best fossil hunters. Could spot a hominid tooth standing up, in direct sunlight, from five paces.'

'Well, this is definitely not a man,' said Morkel, pointing back to the body alongside the man. 'I wonder how long they'll hold together.' He showed no curiosity concerning Russ's reference to his father, nor to fossil hunters. His expression as he stood regarding the two leather people was one of awe, or perhaps fondness. He had given them star status in his horror show.

'I want to see the rest of him,' said Russ, surprising himself as much as Rebecca and the captain. He stepped forward, lifted the sheet for a moment, then let it drop. There was stillness in the room, the three of them absorbing what Russ had done.

Beck touched the captain's arm. 'How long would they have been like this? I mean, how long would they have been dead?'

'Dead before they were mummified? Mummified after they were dead?' The policeman lifted the bottom end of the sheet and took the manila tag on Barak's blackened toe in his hand, examining it as if it were the label on an item of clothing instructing him in the required laundry procedure: *Wash separately, do not tumble dry.*

'I don't know, Mrs Codron,' he said. 'It's not every day we get mummies in here. I've never seen one before. None of us has. We're really not qualified to handle them.'

What more was there to be said? Morkel thanked them for coming in to identify Russ's father and saw them out, a look of pained sympathy on his face, which seemed oddly not to be for their benefit at all. They drove away with Beck at the wheel, through Salt River's semi-industrial plume of panel beaters, sign manufacturers and garment warehouses and on to the motorway that would take them around the city and the mountain that cradled it. Russ took in little of the return journey. It was his father's withered remains, a skeleton wrapped in crumples of tanned hide, which rode home beside him.

'I should be feeling something,' he said.

Rebecca said nothing. Not in the usual way she said nothing, with that air of having given up trying to engage a man who refused to explore his own history. This was a differently charged silence. For once she was also numbed into it. For a while, she rested her hand on his leg. The familiar markers of their homeward journey floated by the air-conditioned cabin of the car: harbour, outstretched hands of homeless children, beachfront, old aquarium and the final glide into the automated garage of their Clifton home. They came in through the kitchen, Rebecca walking down the passage towards the children's bedrooms.

Russ sat down at the kitchen table. There had been a moment in the mortuary cold room, walking towards the pile of bodies on the floor, when he'd first seen the pair of figures on the gurneys and known it was them. For an instant the angle of sight had the white shrouded figure of

Barak hovering over the mound of naked bodies, as if he lay on top of the pile, the other bodies acting as a bier, servants slain to accompany Pharaoh into the afterlife.

Russ's mother might have offered tea right now, the English lady's therapy for shock. Russ didn't feel like being English. Perhaps a new tradition – a tranquiliser? As if sensing his master's need for comfort, Dali, the family's Alsatian, ambled into the kitchen, his nails clicking on the tiles. He dropped to the floor in a graceless collapse, raised his head and stared with rheumy devotion into Russ's eyes. Russ reached for him, for the reassuring, everyday touch of the dog's head, the contact almost, but not quite, releasing the tears that were building up within him.

Salt River, salty tears. Where better to house Cape Town's mortuary? The pile of bodies heaped on the ground spoke of the city's shame, its inability to look after its dead. Russ had been unable to claim his dead, let alone look after it, and his shame seemed now to be without boundary.

3

RUSS WAS SIX YEARS OLD when his father started taking him to work. No other boy in the mining town of Krugersdorp had a father who did work quite like this.

His father would wake him before dawn and the two would drive out to the hills of Sterkfontein. In those days, it was quite a walk from the car to the caves and Russ's little legs struggled to keep pace as his father strode ahead through the dawn mist. There would be time to rest later, when Russ would curl up on the canvas tarpaulin his father would spread for him on a level shelf above the cave floor and doze to the tap-tapping of the old man's rock hammer.

The boy had his own bag of tools. As he walked along the craggy ground, trying to keep up, the strap bit into his shoulder and the tools jostled proudly against his bare thigh. Barak, his mood unfailingly buoyant at the start of a day's dig, would launch into his chosen topic, Russ straining to catch his words before they disappeared into the grey morning, as if they were precious puffs of candyfloss drifting on the breeze.

On the first day Barak took the six-year-old Russ excavating, he began his son's apprenticeship in the art of fossil hunting with one of his maxims. 'If you want to find a hominid fossil, lad,' he said, his East End accent like a familiar blanket to the boy, 'head for the caves.'

Barak, old enough to be Russ's grandfather, was fitter than most men half his age. Keen to start the day's work, he was, for the moment, oblivious of Russ's battle to keep up. 'Take the bloke who dies out on the savannah. Scavengers pick up the scent of his death. They rip him apart, devour his flesh and muscle. The organs are a tasty treat. They crush his bones in their jaws. The little that's left gets bleached by the sun and in a few years, poof! The poor chap's disintegrated completely, leaving nothing for you and me to find.'

Here the old man finally stopped to allow Russ to catch up. His father had a gaze that Russ would later come to understand as the scene from his imagined time-travel, that the view he now saw of these dry, dolomitic hills was as they would have been five million years before: a verdant landscape roamed by sabre-toothed cats, pigs as big as hippos, and little groups of vigilant ape-men.

Barak touched a hand to his face, his calloused fingers scratching at the white stubble, then ruffled the child's hair. 'But if that chap's remains had ended up in a cave – well then, he might live forever.'

'But he'd be dead!' said the boy.

'There's death and there's immortality. Let's say he got taken by a sabre-toothed cat and dragged into a cave. That carnivore and her family's going to eat what they can. But they'll leave some bones behind. The bigger chunks like your skull or the unappetising bits like your jaw – ' Barak broke off to cup his son's chin ' – those lie about the cave for years, getting buried by debris. Or better still, the cave roof collapses. That chap's well and truly buried, kept snug and warm. Just waiting for us to dig him out. Got it, lad?'

'Yes, Dad,' said Russ, none the wiser but keener now to begin digging.

They slipped through the cavern's narrow entrance. Soon Russ would be working alongside his father, the smooth skin of his face becoming coated with a fine dust as he wielded his hammer in his soft hands, tapping at a chisel held against the rock – the same tool that would, two years later, slice his finger to the bone.

And five years after that little trauma would come a bigger one. Barak, acting on his theory that the tip of Africa was the birthplace of modern Man, would pack his bags and decamp for the fossil beds of the Cape – then would disappear forever.

4

Inspector Toka's voice on the telephone was warm and relaxed. The case had been assigned to him, he explained, and he wondered whether the son of Mr Barak Codron would attend an interview at Caledon Square police station.

'*Doctor* Barak Codron,' said Russ. 'And my father is not a murderer.'

'Personally, I'm well disposed to agree with you,' said the inspector. 'And I hope you'll be able to clear things up for me. When would be convenient for you?'

Well disposed? Who was this bloke? 'What about this morning?' said Russ. 'I can be there in less than an hour.'

'Good.'

There was more Russ wanted to say but Inspector Toka had gone. Still, he seemed amiable enough. Russ would explain, the matter would be cleared up, and that would be that.

It was school holidays and Beatrice, the housekeeper, was on leave. Savannah had arrangements to meet friends at the Waterfront. At sixteen, she was old enough to look after herself. Luc would need to be dropped at Rebecca's elderly Aunt Julia, known by the family as Tante Julia, in the colonial language of her birthplace. Tante Julia and her sisters – Beck's late mother was the youngest – had grown up in Elisabethville, in the Belgium Congo, part of a closely-woven community of Sephardic Jews. Julia was one of the few people who could be trusted to look after Luc.

11

Russ went to get Luc ready. Dressed in a baggy long-sleeved shirt and jeans, the seven-year-old was standing in the middle of his room, his arms and open palms outstretched, his head tilted towards his feet, surveying a little white, yellow and brown city he had built with Lego bricks. He looked like Christ the Redeemer gazing protectively over his plastic Rio.

Luc became aware of Russ's presence, or at least a disturbance to his solitude, his body turning rigid, as if the statue his posture resembled had been of putty and had now become stone. Russ felt his patience running thin. He wanted to get to his appointment with Inspector Toka and clear up this stupid misunderstanding about his father being a mass murderer. He didn't have time to go at Luc's pace, to coax him back from whatever world he had entered. My poor, mad son, Russ thought, and then, horrified for a moment, wondered whether he had said it aloud because Luc turned towards him, the dark lines of his eyebrows raised over eyes made larger by his narrow, delicate face. He turned his head away from Russ, glaring over his shoulder towards the bed.

'What?' Luc said. 'What? No, I… it's impossible. *C'est impossible.*' His tone was impatient, as though he were an adult telling off a child, the blood of his face collecting in his lips, red and full against pale cheeks and chin. His skittish eyes settled on Russ's chest for a moment and then were gone. Whoever it was he imagined to be on the bed did not want to let him go. *'C'est impossible! C'est impossible! C'est impossible!'*

'Luc!' said Russ, immediately regretting his reproachful tone. Anger was no answer to panic. It wasn't going to get him to the police station any sooner.

'C'est impossible!' whispered Luc over his shoulder.

Russ left the room, closing the door behind him. Beck was walking hurriedly down the passage. She must have heard his shout.

'I can't,' said Russ, shrugging his shoulders.

'You never can,' she replied, opening the bedroom door.

Russ saw her kneel in front of Luc. The boy's palms were pressed flat over his ears, his eyes screwed shut, his teeth showing between urgently moving lips. He was muttering to himself: '*Pisgado, pisgado, pisgado*', the words emerging in a fast-moving train of articulations: *pis* – the toothy grimace and hiss of the 's', *ga* – the mouth opening to spew out the guttural 'g' from the back of the throat, *do!* – the pursed lips spitting the final syllable into the world with an urgent breathy jet of air.

'*Pisgado!*' It was Ladino – the language of the Sephardim – for hindrance, deadweight.

They sat in a cool corridor inside Caledon Square police station, staring at the dull cream enamel of the wall opposite. Russ was thinking about Luc. When it first became evident that he was an unusual child Rebecca had dragged him from one specialist to the next, Russ had thought the answer might lie in his eyes, something he, as an optometrist, knew a lot about. Beck agreed. They might 'read the poetry of his eyes', she mused. But if Luc's eyes were writing poetry, it seemed to Russ to be a series of disconnected, hopelessly repetitious haiku: staccato movements of the brow and upper cheeks, the compression of lids against a smile or grimace, the rapidity of blinking that others might have called a tic. Still, he embarked on a study of his three-year-old son. He kept notes.

> *25th May: woke chirpy, communicative (for Luc, that is), unsmiling, eyes bright, sclera clear…*
>
> *5th June: Sav takes toy, Luc has tantrum, rigid body tone, irises luminescent, pupils dilated…*

17th June: at dinner, constructing Table Mountain with strips cut from fish fingers! lids droopy, almost ptosis-like, neovasc. right sclera? (NB: keep checking), tear sacs inflamed...

After five weeks he gave up. There was no discernible pattern. If Luc's eyes were expressing something, it wasn't in a language Russ could understand.

The dreams of a mother and father for their young son were torn slowly over months of doctors' appointments. Russ would find Beck in the doorway to Luc's bedroom staring fixedly at the beautiful face with those haiku eyes that should have been enthralled by the delights of the universe, or raging against its unfurling frustrations, but seemed not to be seeing any of this, showing life only inasmuch as they were surrounded by a face that twitched dispassionately. It was as if he was looking into a parallel universe he found mildly annoying in the way one might flick at flies buzzing too close. It wasn't natural. Russ would come up behind Beck as she trembled in the doorway and try to touch her shoulders, only to have her turn on him, until the fierceness in her eyes gave way to tears of despair. He was stuck, unable to cry, and the less reaction he showed, the more furious she became, until finally one day she ignored him and left him feeling shattered in a way her distress never did. She had been expressing the sadness of two and when she turned from him, he was left without a mouthpiece.

'This bench would be quite valuable,' Rebecca said, jolting him back to the present, 'if it weren't quite so battered. It's Georgian. God alone knows how it found its way in here.'

Russ looked at the bench. The seat cushions were lumpy. He sneezed, removed a small wad of tissues from his trouser pocket, peeled one off and blew his nose.

ppp

'I feel like a kid sitting outside the principal's office,' he said.

People walking past made a wide berth around them, not so much because of the narrowness of the corridor but because of Russ's bulk. In a crowd Rebecca would make use of this, keeping close to him while oncoming waves parted before them. He broke six foot by a good two inches, his brown hair often unruly, and wore his parentage in his face: his mother's Anglo-Saxon bone structure, his father's dark Sephardic eyes. He was, they joked in the early days, a mongrel, a crossbreed whom Beck, with her ambivalence about her own claustrophobic Sephardic background, found irresistibly sexy.

Luc's difficulties changed that. Beck began to accuse Russ of short-changing her, of having promised a combative strength he could not, or would not, deliver. He looked so much like a real man, she complained. A real man would take his son by the hand. But Luc shrank from Russ's hand and Russ didn't know what to do. When the child's uncanny ear for languages became apparent, it confused Russ even more. Luc seemed so intelligent, absorbing the French of his aunts and uncles and cousins, and a smattering of Ladino, still used by the older generation of the family. They worried he might mix up the languages but their concern proved unfounded. Russ was perplexed by Luc's intelligence: if the child could keep the complex world of language in order, how come Russ couldn't hold a conversation with him?

'We mustn't forget to ask about your father's possessions,' said Beck.

'What? Yes, yes, of course.'

'And the private pathologist.'

He nodded.

She leaned down to adjust a strap on her sandal, her short auburn hair bobbing forward. Russ had recently noticed strands of grey flecking the richness of it. She had that teasingly amused look on her face, an invitation to enquire about a thought she wished to share with him.

'What?' he said.

'Remember that fight we had a few days ago? In bed? About getting help for your problem?'

He winced. 'I try to forget those fights.' He hated clashing with her and that particular argument had been repeated too many times. Now he took her raising it as an opening salvo, a rekindling of hostilities.

'I accused you of being dried up.' Her eyes were smiling, head tilted in sympathy.

'So?'

'So now your father comes along after all these years and he's all dried up.'

'Beck, this isn't helping. What's your point?'

'Well, no, wait, sweetheart. Maybe this is your chance to do something about your relationship with him. Resolve something.'

'Ah, shit, Beck. What's there to resolve? It all happened so long ago. It wasn't like he neglected me. He loved me. His disappearance wasn't his fault. He had an accident. It happens. Children lose their parents.' He got to his feet. 'I'm going to find out how much longer this bloody cop is going to keep us waiting.' He didn't need a debate. He needed to see the fucking cop, clear up the misunderstanding about his father, and go home.

But now his feet didn't want to take him anywhere. He looked one way up the corridor, then the other way down. He felt as though he was inside Sterkfontein caves, standing beside a visible section of the underground river as it flowed from darkness, and back into darkness. He sat down again, cupping the sides of his head in his hands. Barak wouldn't put up with this. He would sniff out his man. Would *have* sniffed out his man. *Past tense*, remember, he's dead, hasn't sniffed out anyone in decades. He's just decaying leather and bone. Where's he going with a body in that kind of shape?

Russ turned to face Rebecca. 'Will you come with me to the cave? I want to see it, see what he was doing there.'

Yesterday Beck had phoned the *Sunday Times* journalist, who had been very helpful, although not to the point where he was prepared to drop the story's murder angle. The cave was a few hours' drive up the coast from Cape Town, in a demarcated military area, an artillery testing ground. The entrance had been blocked for years by an old rockfall, until two local boys from a nearby fishing village stumbled onto it. The village held the area's police station. The journalist told her of the local policeman's theory: it all happened a few years ago. The 'couple' lured or forced their victims into the cave, killed them in some fashion or other, then carved them up and devoured their flesh. Satanism. And cannibalism. They'd had trouble with this type before.

'Mr Codron? I'm Inspector Toka.'

Startled, Russ rose off the bench to shake the detective's hand. 'Ah, Inspector Toka. There's been a terrible – '

Toka dressed his diminutive frame well. A sombre suit, yellow silk tie, boots with elevated heels, silver cufflinks peeking from the arms of his jacket glittering in contrast to the dark skin of his hands. He had a manila folder tucked under his left arm. As he shook their hands, his mouth spread in a friendly grin that managed not to touch his steady brown eyes.

'I am sorry you had to wait. I've been busy with a bank robbery. Please, this way.'

They followed him down the corridor to where they were shown into a small office with two pairs of chairs facing each other across a wooden table. Beck and Russ sat down on one side. There was nothing on the walls. Toka dropped his folder on the table top, removed his jacket, placed it over the back of one of the vacant chairs, and sat down in the other. Russ stared at the folder, and then at Toka's jacket. He had the peculiar feeling that they were facing two detectives, although the one was headless – an effect of the jacket encircling the wooden backrest of the chair, as if it were a man's torso. Maybe, he thought jokingly to himself, Toka's going to play a budget 'good cop/bad cop' with the chair-man.

'If you don't mind, Mr Codron, I would like to ask you some questions. It's routine, really.'

'Sure,' said Russ. 'I can clear this up for you very quickly.'

'No doubt you can. And that is why we are here. When last did you see your father?'

Russ hesitated.

'Over forty years ago,' said Rebecca.

'I was thirteen,' Russ said. 'It was November, 1963.'

'So you were a child. Were you with your mother?'

'When I saw him?'

'No. Were you living with her?'

'Yes. I was a child.'

The policeman smiled. 'Not all children live with their mothers. Did you have brothers and sisters?'

'No, I didn't have any.'

'And why did you not see your father after that?' Toka's accent told of an upbringing in England, the son of exiled ANC activists, guessed Russ.

'He disappeared.' Christ, why should he feel guilty for not seeing his father? He was only a child.

'Just so? Was there an investigation?'

'Not at first. He often went away – for his work, on digs. Excavations. We used to go with him. I spent my early childhood roaming East Africa. But then we settled in Krugersdorp so I could go to school and my father could

18

excavate the Sterkfontein caves. But then he went on a dig to the Cape, and that time he never came back. The police couldn't find him. He was listed as missing. I think he's probably still listed as missing.'

For Russ, traces of his nomadic early years – in the primary care of his gentrified English mother – were left behind in his accent, a BBC diction that defended itself admirably against the chafed Krugersdorp inflection.

'Well,' said Inspector Toka, 'he's been found now. It must be quite a shock for you.' It seemed to Russ that the inspector's eyes hardly blinked, that he may have a thyroid stare – the infrequent blinking indicative of hyperthyroidism – or had trained them to become an interrogator's lamp shining unflinchingly into those of his subject.

'Yes, I suppose it is a bit of a shock,' said Russ. 'Look, I know how this thing must look to you, but – '

'Indeed,' said Toka. 'It's rather unusual, isn't it, to appear after who knows how long, as a mummy, *and* in the company of human remains.'

'But it's the nature of those human remains,' began Russ, and then stammered. 'It's that, well, they're probably really old. You must understand, you have to see...' While Russ was talking Toka had picked up his manila folder and a photograph of Barak's body *in situ* had slipped out onto the table. Beck would later insist that it was a mistake, that there was little in Toka's manner to suggest anything tactical, only an overworked, diligent man going about his business. The inspector quickly picked up the photograph and inserted it back into the file.

'My apologies,' he said as he flipped through the contents.

Russ felt a terrible anxiety well up. The headless cop didn't seem such a joke anymore. He was struck by the feeling that this really was an interrogation, and that it was going badly, and within moments the inspector was going to summon his underlings to handcuff Russ and lead him away to the cells. He had hoped to muster a piercing tone that would skewer Toka's unflappable demeanour, that would embarrass him with the knowledge of how wrong the police had got it but the unbidden appearance of Barak in the room had undone him, and his words registered in his own ears as an insipid protest, the *plop* of the cork from a child's fagged-out popgun.

'My father…,' he said but had no breath to continue.

'So I guess,' said Toka, 'you being thirteen when you last saw your father, that you didn't know him all that well? I mean, what does a thirteen year old know of his parent's business?'

Russ's own gaze kept darting from Toka's eyes to the manila folder that held the photograph of his father's burnt face, which Russ imagined might now be grinning in agreement with the policeman. His breathing was rapid and shallow. For the first time since this mess had spilled over into his life, he was losing control. He glanced at Rebecca, wanting help.

She rested her arm on the back of his chair. 'Inspector,' she said. 'You have a point. In fact, it's the very point I was making to Russell while we were waiting for you outside. But, please understand, this has been a shock, and while you may be right about my husband not knowing his father, it's not in the way you might think.' Beck's skin had repelled the effects of aging in an epidermal act of rebellion reflective of her personality. But lately and quite abruptly, as she entered her early forties, it was giving ground, creasing atop her upper lip and at her eyes, and opening a deepening trench between her brows. It made her look more commanding as she leaned forward to deliver her judgment. 'I don't know what sins my husband's father committed, but I doubt they included murder. Those bones you found with him must be fossils, perhaps hundreds of thousands of years old. Dr Barak Codron was a fossil hunter and he probably dug them out of the cave walls.'

Russ stared at the inspector's jacket. It seemed to be mocking him.

Toka chuckled knowingly. 'And does being a fossil hunter exclude a person from also being a murderer? What other professions are exempt to killers? What do you do for a living, Mrs Codron?'

'I'm a sculptor.'

'Ah, so has no artist of one kind or another ever committed murder? Adolf Hitler was an artist. Look, you're good, moral people, I can see that. But I should tell you something you don't know. We've managed to keep this piece of inflammatory information out of the press but I doubt it will stay out for long. In 1965 two local teenagers disappeared from that area and now their relatives are sure it is their remains that have been found. I have to investigate this fully. Especially a race crime. White male suspect, coloured teenage victims. You know how it is.' He paused. 'And black female suspect.'

Russ and Beck exchanged glances. 'You mean, the other body?' she said. 'The female mummy?'

'Yes, oh, I suppose you might have assumed she was white? No, seems they've found some old ID. An old apartheid passbook, strangely enough. Her name was Nombeko Nondula.'

'Hold on,' said Russ. 'You say the teenagers went missing in 1965. My father disappeared in 1963.'

'He disappeared from *your* life in 1963. That doesn't mean to say he disappeared from everyone else's lives too.'

'But...' Russ didn't know how to phrase his objection. What was he to say? Barak *must* have died in 1963, or at least early 1964, within months of leaving Krugersdorp. If he had lived much longer, he would have come home.

The inspector hesitated before opening the folder again and this time they caught a glimpse of what he was looking at, photographs of bone fragments against a light background. He studied the photos for a good few minutes and then raised his head.

'One or two of these do seem a little odd. Not quite human, in fact.'

'If you let me take a look,' said Russ.

Toka handed them over. Countless times Barak had handed Russ pieces of bone, saying, 'what do you make of this, lad?' And the young Russ would examine the piece, eager to get it right. Now – after a hiatus of more than forty years – his father was handing him another test.

He studied the photographs. A partial femur. A vertebrae. A segment of jawbone. The pieces were tagged with strata and grid reference numbers.

'These labels are my father's method of noting the exact location where the pieces were excavated.' Fuck, the bones did look human. Old, but human. Modern human even. Not human ancestor. Not australopithecine, as he had hoped to be able to point out, or even better, a chunk of ancient giraffe or antelope. Russ looked up hopelessly.

'I don't know… it's been a long time,' he said. 'I'm not sure. You'd need to have the piece in your hands.'

Toka leaned forward with his elbows on the table, his fingers interlocked, eyebrows raised politely. He blinked.

'But they might be human?'

'Yes, they… might be human.'

Toka leaned back again.

'But they're not your missing teenagers,' said Russ. 'If they are human, they're old, much older than forty years. More like forty thousand! And my father dug them out of that cave.'

'Inspector,' said Beck, 'do you have any other evidence to suggest that these bones belong to your missing teenagers? That a crime was committed here?'

Toka smiled, this time with his eyes.

'Look, to be honest,' he said, 'I haven't had much time to get acquainted with the case. There are some notebooks. Not in good shape. Mouldy. There're also some chopping and cutting implements. My colleagues up the West Coast believe these to be the murder weapons. Also some other bones, which weren't photographed. They only took pictures of the sample bones they sent for analysis. Pathology's a little overwhelmed at the moment. They didn't want them all at once.'

Russ's voice was low. 'Your so-called weapons are probably his digging tools.'

'The notebooks sound interesting,' said Beck, the tilt of her head causing a fan of hair to half-mask an eye. 'Can we see them?'

'At the moment,' said Toka, addressing himself to Rebecca, 'everything is State's evidence. If your husband's father is cleared, all his personal effects will be returned to you. Then you can do with them as you wish.'

'For God's sake!' said Russ. 'My father was a pal-, pal- .' He was shaking now and couldn't get his tongue to co-operate in the pronunciation of palaeo-anthropologist. 'He spent his whole bloody life looking for the origins of man. There's no doubt he was excavating that cave. He hunted fossils, not teenagers.'

Rebecca put a hand on Russ's arm. 'It's okay, darling. Inspector Toka understands this.'

'Quite so,' said the inspector. 'You should calm down, Mr Codron. It's not good for you to get so upset. The bones are at the state pathologist. If they are not the bones of the missing teenagers, or any human being who recently walked this earth, then we'll know soon enough.' He rose to his feet, scooped the photographs back into the folder, and extended his hand across the table. 'Mr and Mrs Codron, you have been very helpful. Thank you for coming to see me.'

'What an arsehole,' said Russ as they came out of the building into the midday sunshine.

Beck laughed. 'Oh, come on, Russ. He's a cop who's been handed a murder case. At least he's trying to investigate it. Isn't that what we want from the police? How would we feel if it was Savannah who was one of those missing teenagers?'

Russ ignored her. 'We forgot to ask him about getting my father out of the mortuary.'

'I thought he answered that question. Your father is State's evidence.'

5

'Why was the Egyptian boy confused?' It was Luc, his voice too strident for the joke he intended to deliver. Breaking off their conversation about Barak and the woman, Rebecca and Russ looked up from the couch they were sitting on.

'I don't know, sweetheart,' said Beck. 'Why was the little boy confused?'

'Because…' Luc stopped, darting a glance towards his father before continuing in a raspy tone, 'his daddy was a mummy.'

'Luc,' said Russ, 'that's not the kind of mummy we're talking about.' When used by Russ, the boy's name lost its French accent. Perhaps that was it. The boy responded only to the rolling sound of a French syllable. *Llllluuuke.*

'Oh, come on, Russ, it's a joke. And it is the kind of mummy we're talking about.' Beck was battling to keep a straight face. 'That's a funny joke, Luc, but Daddy's upset because it's his father that is a mummy, and he's just found out about it.' Her own words proved the tipping point in the battle to suppress her giggles, and it was some moments before, wiping the tears from her eyes, she was able to say, 'The thing is, it's a sad thing for Dad and so we shouldn't really joke about it.' Luc stared at her, willing her to say something. She raised her eyebrows hopelessly.

'Mummia,' he said, and walked towards the door.

'What's that, sweetheart?' said Beck, but Luc had left the room.

'You know what I don't get,' she said. 'If Inspector Toka is right and the notebooks have been damaged by mould, how come your father and the woman didn't decompose? Does that make scientific sense? What would preserve bodies like that?'

They had driven mostly in silence, a strong wind chasing great, brooding banks of cloud after the Mercedes as it sped north. With the opening of her Johannesburg exhibition only a month away, few events could get Beck to put aside her work on the final piece. She was going to place a series of heads, each cast in silicone, inside infants' incubators, the glass sides of which she had coated with one-way film. The viewer would reach inside the darkened case and try to 'see' with their hands. Small electrical elements inside the heads would heat them to body temperature so that the experience would be of touching a live, human face. After two minutes' touch, spotlights inside the incubators would be activated, illuminating the sculptures. She was not interested in the obvious, clichéd effect of these works, of giving the sighted a glimpse of what it was like to be blind – but rather in the very moment at which awareness shifts, the transition from a state of knowledge assembled by one sense – tactile – to that provided by another – sight – and how the surprise of new knowledge forces the viewer to retrieve her own projections. She called the series 'Outsight'. She would have to arrive in Johannesburg at least a few days before in order to assemble the parts of each composition. There was little time left in which to finish sculpting the last piece, make the cast, set the polymer face and fix it to the armature. This one was bald. At least she wouldn't be worrying about getting the hair right.

Russ was reeling. Luc's mummy joke was true. He *was* the Egyptian boy, confused as all hell. He kept thinking of that moment in which his comfortable life was ruptured. What if he hadn't seen the *Sunday Times* article? If he had inadvertently skipped the page, or simply glanced at that moronic headline and looked no further? Or read the damned thing and still paged on. It was they who had contacted the police, willingly gone off to the mortuary as directed. Without Russ and Beck, the police would have eventually realised there was no foul play afoot, and in all likelihood not bothered to track down the relatives of the long-dead couple. God knows, there were enough recently dead corpses that needed claiming. Barak and the woman's bodies might have been passed on to one of the universities or museums. And Russ might have gone about his life, unaware of this movement of mummies about the city.

He had *tried* to go about his life, examining eyes, writing scripts, fitting frames, but all the while his father's Cockney voice kept up a narrator's patter, somehow managing to disturb him just as it filled him with nostalgic warmth.

'If you want to find a fossil out in the open, Red,' the old man would say, the nickname 'Red' coming from the Old English derivation of Russell's name, 'you have to walk. *Walk, walk, walk.* And then walk back again. You went left at that bush an hour ago? Now you must go right. The sun was at your back this morning? Walk towards it this afternoon. Feel the ground. When you see the piece of bone, it'll be as if you'd always known it was there, in that place.'

Barak's voice was coming back to him, telling him to get going. Finally Russ could bear it no longer and again asked Rebecca to go with him to the cave. They'd be there and back in one day, he promised.

With Dali looking quizzically up at him, Russ gathered some rain gear and, rummaging in the hall closet, found an old pocketknife and a torch. Together with two water bottles, he placed these items in a backpack. Rebecca made arrangements with Beatrice, who had returned from leave. The housekeeper evinced a hurt, reproachful air. It was unnecessary to tell her what to do. She knew the contents of the refrigerator and the children's tastes better than Rebecca. Beatrice would collect Luc from school, and Savannah would make her own way home. Tante Julia had promised to be on call. In any case, they would have their cell phones and could get back within a matter of hours.

Russ phoned his receptionist to reschedule his patients.

'Mrs Oxtoby isn't going to be happy,' said Barbara Robertson. 'She's sat on her specs again. And this is the third day this week you've taken off and disappeared for hours on end. Monday afternoon you went off and didn't come back. Then yesterday you only got in at midday and now you're taking off the whole of today. What's going on?'

'Anthea can see Mrs Oxtoby if she isn't happy to wait,' said Russ, knowing full well that Mrs Oxtoby wouldn't settle for his assistant. Barbara had that clipped, irascible tone in her voice. Her Crohn's Disease must be playing up. Over the fifteen years she had worked in the business, she had grown accustomed to her reason winning out over what she interpreted as his sluggishness. You should lose weight, she chided him. Her own body was rake-thin, her colon eaten away by her illness. He told himself that he was all she had, and so he paid her generously and let her give the orders. Not this time. She had hung up with a surprised goodbye.

Now the wind was tailgating them up the coastal road, pushing memories at him, flinging his childhood in his face. Barak was carrying him. There was music from the gramophone. Russ's face was wet. Barak danced with him in his arms. The boy didn't understand the music, but he knew that it touched his father. Barak was crying. Those were his tears on Russ's cheeks. The old man swayed to the music, and broke into a dance step, a fast one – Russ felt jolted – and then slowed his time again. He was sobbing and gave a start when suddenly the boy's mother was there in the room.

The road matters, only the road, not the memories. The road to the fishing village, to the cave. They passed Koeberg, the nuclear power station. He looked to their left, beyond Rebecca's profile, towards the sea. Choppy white water broke in wave upon wave against rock and beach, obscured now by a bank of dunes. Reeds and long grass that sprouted from the fine white sand bent and waved. A young boy darted out from between the reeds and ran across the road in front of the car. Russ braked hard.

'Shit!' he said. 'Did you see that?'

'What?'

In the rear-view mirror Russ glimpsed movement and colour disappearing into the dunes, the boy dressed in shorts and a faded red T-shirt. A ghost-child conjured by the wind. The little bugger must be cold, so poorly dressed in this weather.

'It's a bloody good question,' he said.

It had taken him so long to reply to her – almost an hour of the journey undertaken with each coated in their own thoughts – that she didn't know what he was talking about. 'What's a good question?'

'Why didn't they decompose? They should've been skeletons. The cave must be full of organisms, worms, God knows what. And it's not like it's in the middle of a desert where it's dry and hot. I'm damn sure a wet body – even a moist body – wouldn't mummify here. Christ, we're made up mostly of fluid as it is, and where there's fluid, there's bacteria… Unless the salt water – no, surely not enough dry salt to preserve anything.'

The clouds had them now and the raindrops began to break on the windscreen, first one, then another. These are like my memories, he thought, they come slowly at first but soon they're going to pour down in torrents. I have no cover.

He turned the wipers to their intermittent setting.

Rebecca said, 'The way the woman's mouth lay open reminded me of *The Scream*.'

'The painting? The one that got stolen? I thought she looked a little like your head.'

'No,' she said, shaking her head. 'In my sculpture, the mouth is open in anger. *The Scream* is not about anger, it's about horror. That woman's jaw is unnaturally open. It's as though she died in terror.'

He thought about that for a while. 'My father doesn't look like he died in terror. He looks... sort of... like he's contemplating the universe. But then, his jaw was tied shut. Why was that? Do you think he had toothache?'

'I'd have thought he had bigger problems than toothache.' Beck laughed and then, considering Russ's face, said, 'You've hardly ever spoken about him. I remember trying to get you to talk. You'd tell me one or two stories about your outings with him – nice, sweet stories about a dad and his son looking for bones in the ground – and then you'd clam up, as if you were scared to carry on in case the stories turned sour. It left me thinking he'd stuck a claw out from his grave and was holding onto your ankle. I've disliked him for that.'

'He never had a grave. And anyway, there weren't any sour stories to tell. He was a magical father.'

'There's nothing magical about a father who disappears.'

It felt as though she'd slapped his one cheek with her remark about Barak and then the other with the implication about Russ's disappearance from Luc's life.

'He didn't do it on purpose.'

'How do you know what he did on purpose? That's

what I mean. You don't want to think about it. *Really* think about it.'

'You don't understand,' said Russ, his voice breaking, sounding like the pubescent boy he was when Barak left, 'for years after he didn't return home from that dig I *never stopped thinking about him*. I didn't do *nothing* – I mean, I did do something… I tried, I tried to find him. I used to picture it all the time: the journey… packing for the trip, the one I'd take to go in search of him.' He laughed bitterly. 'I had these scenarios I'd play out, over and over, in my mind. I'd take the old Ford *bakkie*. I suppose it didn't matter that *he'd* taken the Ford. I'd pack supplies, maps, rope, everything I'd need. At nighttime, I'd lie in bed for hours, planning these trips down to the smallest detail. I'd go over all the equipment I'd need to save him from any one of a range of dire situations I could think of. I'd need a torch in case he'd been trapped in a cave. Lots of food because he was somewhere deep in the interior, starving. Water supplies, of course. Spades and pick-axes and dynamite to dig him out of an avalanche, a stretcher and rope for when he'd fallen off a cliff, a compass because he'd lost his way in the mountains, a rifle to deal with the leopard who'd dragged him into a tree. For each of these scenarios I'd need medicines: Grandpa headache powders, bandages, Vaseline, splints. Fuck, I made myself into a surgeon who'd operate and save his life. Lying in bed I packed that first aid kit every night for the rest of my teenage years, item by fucking item.'

The last of these words came out with a sob. The windscreen was thick with water, the road ahead blurred and rippled. He could barely see, and turned the wipers on full. He slowed the car, looking to pull over. The Merc's wipers were of no use clearing the film of tears over his eyes.

'Honey,' she said carefully, after they had rolled to an idling halt on the shoulder of the road, the wipers' motion gently rocking the car, 'all those stories are about how you were going to rescue him from some tragedy that had befallen him. Something that had happened *to* him. Something *beyond* his control.'

He looked away from her, out of the side window at the blurred shapes of cars speeding by. 'Christ, Beck, I was only thirteen. Other kids were doing their homework or playing rugby and I was packing and re-packing that fucking rescue kit. Okay, it was in my head. In reality, I didn't know where to start. The days stretched into weeks and then months and then it seemed the natural thing was to be waiting for him. And that's where things got stuck. I was *waiting*. That was my activity. I know this is hard to understand, waiting as an activity, I mean, but it was. For years and years I never stopped thinking about him. Thinking was holding me back. Then I met you and I didn't want to think about him any more.'

He wiped his eyes, put on the indicator and, looking over his shoulder, began to edge back onto the road.

They were close to the fishing village, according to a signpost with a few bullet holes in it, and had spoken themselves into a silence. It had stopped raining, leaving the sky a satisfied, heavy grey.

'I hope Beatrice remembers to check the towel,' said Beck. She had draped a dampened towel over the unfinished head to keep the clay moist.

'She never forgets anything,' he said.

'You know,' Beck's voice was pensive, picking up on their unfinished conversation, 'I've blamed your father for your emotional limitations, but I've blamed you for not doing something about them. The funny thing is, now that I've met him, I think I'm beginning to like him. There's something romantic about him and his mummy woman –

sorry, his student, or whoever she was to him. Still, there's something quite thrilling about the two of them.'

Unlike me, thought Russ. Nothing romantic or thrilling about me. He fell back into a more familiar silence he had begun, in recent years, to recognise as self-pitying. His only defence against Rebecca's disappointment was that, if anything, he was as he had always been: immovable. It was rather that her requirements of him had changed. When they met, she was slipping over the edge of her life and he stopped her. In those days, his solidity was a good thing. It began literally. She was on her way to the docks. A southeaster ripped into the Foreshore, channelling through the dry beds formed by the city's rows of buildings, picking up speed and pedestrians. Women flailed in helpless modesty, grasping at skirts that rose up against their torsos like the wings of stingrays. Shopping packets spun past at head height, cars rocked on their suspensions. It was the worst wind in years. She had been working on a painting called 'Docklands Girl', depicting a young coloured child sitting on an iron bridle, the oxidised links of the chain mirroring the plaits in her light brown hair. A ship's taffrail suggested prison bars, and beneath this its barnacled hull cried tears of rust down its faded black and red cheeks. Walking menacingly towards the girl were lone figures of Taiwanese sailors each seemingly intent on doing her no good, while dusky Cape whores, some with the Oriental eyes of their fathers' generation of seamen, looked on. The painting failed to capture her idea of the misplaced object. Despite its inherent danger, Rebecca felt unmoved by it. The girl looked oddly at home.

Beck did not understand why it wasn't working, how to grasp the tension between girl and harbour, and her tutor's gushing comments, confused by his wish to seduce his sultry young student, were no help. He had been unable to state the obvious, that the painting was autobiographical. The girl was Rebecca, too defiant to show vulnerability in the face of male threat. She had originally created the tableau by consulting photographs of derricks and ships, and using models for the figures. The actual docks, she now believed, held the answer. She was nineteen. People warned her against venturing down there but the only precaution she would allow was to conceal her camera in an OK Bazaars packet. She hoped to flirt her way past the customs official at the gate. The southeaster was an unexpected impediment. The howling wind pushed her across the pavement. The only way to prevent a headlong fall was to keep running faster, to throw her legs and feet out ahead of her upper body. It was frightening and exhilarating. Russ's act of grace was less heroic than it was clumsy. He couldn't get out of the way of her uncontrolled flight and she ploughed into him. Cape Town's tempestuous breath had brought them together.

Now, over twenty years later, that breath was blowing them away from the city, up the West Coast, towards a cave that all this time had held his father's remains.

'Your bones are inside the cave, that's wonderful,' Barak would have explained, his hand in Russ's as they walked along a dirt track through the veld that bordered their house, 'but that's not the end of it… There are the shifts and shakes of the earth – all this ground dumped on top of you, then some few thousand quakes or so, maybe the earth spits you out again, or delivers you by erosion, kind of being born of the earth, uh? Rain, wind, and two million years later, there's nothing between your bones and the sky.'

Barak had somehow managed to become the subject of his own field of study, to be born of the earth. Not quite turned to stone, but preserved nonetheless. But, Russ fretted, for how much longer? How long before those brittle bones and tissue disintegrate like dry leaves underfoot, taking their pieces of forensic evidence with them? Barak needed to be examined. He should be on a pathologist's table, with sluice-ways for the draining off of fluids, of which his dried-up prune of a corpse had a singular lack. He thought at first that Barak might enjoy the idea of his body parts being examined, that it would be far less an insult than being paraded before the nation as a murderer of two adolescents. But then he had a rogue thought: Barak wouldn't have been embarrassed by the mix-up – he would have enjoyed the joke, and then enjoyed being studied for the unique mummy he was.

Is this what Beck meant, this thinking about his father?

The dunes gave way to the village and the blue casing of the police station's signature light. The tyres crunched across a gravel patch scattered with pools left by the rain. The police station was so small Russ wondered whether it contained a cell. Was one required? Maybe drunks and mummies were the only criminals this place saw.

Inside the low perimeter fence, patches of grass struggled to take hold. A brick path with borders of *vygies* led to the door. Sand, blown off the tips of the dunes across the road, lapped at the outside edges of the fence. Wet gulls huddled on the lee side.

'This is beautiful!' said Rebecca, unbuckling her seatbelt. 'Do you think there's anyone home?'

'There's a van. Although I'm not sure it's capable of going anywhere.' The police van's rear end was jacked up, the wheel on the driver's side missing.

They walked into the charge office. A young man in police blues lounged over the counter, cleaning his handgun. Behind him in the small room was a desk, its top bare apart from a telephone and a dull grey blotter. Against the wall was a single steel cabinet and alongside that, several posters sporting attractive policemen and women. The word 'community' smiled out from around the haloes of the figures. The live policeman behind the counter seemed barely twenty years old, his moustache looking like something from a dress-up box.

Russ cleared his throat. 'Hi, I… I wonder if you can help? I'm the son of the man whose remains you found here.'

The boy's moustache crimped in recognition. 'Oh.' He looked down at his disassembled weapon. '*Wat doen u hier, Oom?* I thought they were handling everything from Cape Town.'

'They are,' said Rebecca. 'But we thought we would come and have a look at the cave for ourselves.'

'The cave?' He giggled nervously. 'Sorry, lady, it's in a restricted area. Defence Force property. Your father shouldn't have been there in the first place.'

'Yes,' said Russ, 'just as he shouldn't have killed all those poor old fossils.'

The young man gave them a look of sympathy. 'Listen, you mustn't be here. There's gonna be trouble. Some people here are very angry.'

'We understand that,' said Beck. 'But my husband's father has nothing to do with the disappearance of those teenagers. Those bones you found with him are very, very old… older even than Van Riebeeck's time. They do not belong to the missing teenagers.'

He stared at Rebecca's chest, as if the hidden recesses of her cleavage might provide some clue to what she was talking about. He shook his head. 'I can't help you.'

'We're not leaving until we see the cave,' said Russ.

'If you trespass on Defence Force property, I will have to arrest you.' The policeman sounded more confident now that he had found a law to stand on.

'In that case,' said Beck, throwing Russ a meaningful

look, 'I think we'll get in our car, and just go and talk to the boys who found the cave, then drive straight back to Cape Town. That's not against the law, is it?'

'The *klonkies*?' The policeman thought for a moment. 'Ja, well, I suppose there's no law against speaking to them. But if you get into trouble, you mustn't say I didn't warn you. They are from here and this is the place of the kids who your father murdered!'

'Firstly,' said Russ, 'shouldn't that be *allegedly* murdered? And secondly, those bones found with my father don't belong to those kids, so there's nothing to link him with their disappearance!'

'Well,' said the young man, 'it's your skin, not so?'

'Yes,' said Russ, 'it's our skin.'

6

THE POLICEMAN'S USE of the word 'klonkies' was enough to tell them where to find the boys, and so they parked the car and walked to the old part of the village, up on the hill, where the houses were roughly plastered, whitewashed with green stable doors and tin roofs. The sky was lightening, the sun's rays picking out the whitewash.

There was a dry-stone wall, tumbled down in places. It must have formed the boundary between what was the coloured part of the village and the white. They passed through one of the wider gaps. They heard and then, walking over a rise, saw the surf breaking on the beach. A fishing boat was coming in, its slack net draped over the side, a lone seabird hovering above its mast. There was no sign of an angry mob ready to lynch the son of their children's killer, only a few women going about their daily chores. Two of the women sat chatting on the edge of a concrete stoep. Rebecca asked them where they might find the boys who discovered the bodies.

'You mean the brothers Petrus and Bartholomew,' said one, the tan folds of her grandmother's face pushed up against one another like those of a pug. 'It is that one, there by the blue jeans hanging.'

By the blue jeans hanging, thought Russ. If Barak had stayed over in this village, would he have seen it as home or anthropological heaven?

The boys were outside, kicking an empty cold drink can

across the rocky ground. They both looked under ten years of age. Their mother came to the half-open door, emerging from the darkened interior.

'Hello,' said Rebecca. 'We're from Cape Town. We've come to see where my husband's father was found.' And then, mindful of the young policeman's warning, added, 'The police have made a mistake. He had nothing to do with the teenagers who went missing from this place. He was a doctor who studied very old bones that he dug from the earth.'

Petrus and Bartholomew's mother wore a faded pink cotton overall, an old maid's uniform with one of its large opaque buttons popped open to reveal the fold of a wrinkled breast, a sagging yellow sack. She studied Beck with a steady eye, waiting for this white stranger to make plain her business.

'We were wondering if your boys could take us there? To the cave?'

The woman folded her arms. 'They were naughty,' she said finally. 'They know they mustn't be there.'

'Yes, yes, but we're so pleased they were. It has been forty years that my husband hasn't known what became of his father. If not for your boys, we might never have known. We'd like to give you something for your trouble.'

'They must be in school, but they don' wanna go. Bart! *Julle twee*, go with the *wit mense*.' She took the small wad of notes proffered by Beck, shrugged unsmilingly and turned to go back inside. Her two sons followed the white couple to their car.

'Isn't this weird?' Beck's voice was quiet, meant only for Russ's ears. 'That she should let her boys go with us, just like that? I'll bet it's not because she doesn't care for their welfare. It's because she trusts us. We know we're trustworthy but how does she know that? Because we're white and look like rich people to her? How fucked up is that?'

After stopping at a café in the town to buy sweets and Coke, they set out for the artillery testing range. The brothers ran their hands along the upholstery, their cream palms caressing the leather. Bart, who seemed to be the older of the two, discovered the electronic window. Petrus leaned over him to take control of the button. The boys wrestled over it until Petrus found that his door also had one. It seemed to lose its value and he leaned over Russ's shoulder and pointed at the radio.

'Play it,' he said. Russ turned it on. The radio cracked and hissed, a wavy, living presence inside the car, until the automatic tuner fixed on a station, a pop song that felt vaguely familiar to Russ. The boy stayed leaning over the edge of Russ's seat. He smelled of dank soil. '*Daardie kant,*' he directed, his breath warm against Russ's neck. Russ turned the car onto a dirt road. A sign informed them that they were entering a nature reserve and that this was a private road, no entry allowed.

Rebecca half-turned in her seat to face the boys. 'How did you get to the cave?'

'*Ekskuus?*' said Petrus.

'*Hoe het julle by die... die...*' said Russ, 'what the hell's a cave?' He looked past the boy's face towards Rebecca for help. '*Grot! Hoe het julle by die grot gekom?*'

'*Boot,*' said Petrus. '*Dis nie ver. Jy kan mos swem.*' He looked around at his brother, who laughed. He spoke with an emphasis that made Russ think, if fish could talk, this is how they would do it. Everything comes out with a lyrical, drawn-out *pah!* as if the words formed in a bubble just behind blown-out lips, and then popped out of the mouth when they became too big. But for all their strangeness to him, these two brown boys were well adapted to their world.

Russ and his father would begin *their* journeys when it was still dark and his mother lay in bed, the blankets under her chin held tightly by hands white-knuckled even in sleep. His child's arms struggled in the dark with the equipment, out to the tray of the Ford pickup truck, peering around the baggage he was carrying so as not to trip over the steps. Did she hear them leave? Should he have wondered how it was for her to be left behind? They were going to spend the day with their whisk brooms and excavating picks and maybe, just maybe, a piece of bone sticking out of the rock. Despite his naturally pale complexion, his skin, darkened by sun and dirt, got to be almost as brown as these young boys'. He never thought, until now, of what his mother did all day. He never dreamed of how she spent her time, and never wondered why, when they came back, she was still in bed.

She only came into focus once his father had disappeared and by then what he saw all too clearly was a drunk whose nostalgic tales of her childhood amongst the English nobility repelled him. 'It was another life, Russie,' she would begin her tale, perhaps about the early mornings of her childhood, when the rest of the family were still asleep, and she would sneak down to watch the kitchen-maids sweating in front of the hot ovens, preparing the brioche. 'Oh, Russie, that gorgeous aroma as the rolls were taken piping hot from the ovens!' She would speak of the fastidious preparation of the tea trays that were to be brought up to the bedrooms, each with flowers in a little vase, and how one day horror descended upon the kitchen when the brioche burned and the maids had to serve Marie biscuits instead.

It sounded to Russ like the world of English fairy tale, a ridiculous place his mother had dreamed up from storybooks. If that world of privilege, that Krugersdorp antipode, really existed, why had she left it behind? Why hadn't she married a duke, or better yet, a prince? Why had she descended to the lowest rung on the English social ladder, upon which rested the feet of a Sephardic Jew?

Becoming a middle-aged drunk in a dusty South African mining town surely wasn't what she had in mind.

Bart thumped the back of Russ's seat. '*Ry vinnig!*'

'*Ja*, fast, make it go fast,' said Petrus.

Russ, happy for the distraction, smiled, and turned to Rebecca. 'Should we ask them about the missing teenagers?'

'Why not? It was long before their time but they come from a small village and there would have been talk since the mummies were found. They may know.'

And so Russ asked the boys, his questioning prompting a series of giggles that, in the idiom of laughter, suggested the boys' knowledge of something sexual between the teenagers.

'*Het hulle weg gehardloop?*' Had they run away? And – he tried to think of a delicate way of putting it – were they man and wife?

'*Ja, Oom.*' Bart giggled. 'They ran away to Cape Town.'

'So much for the chopped-up teenager theory,' said Russ, then, seeing the irony of it, added, 'There's only one chopped-up teenager in this story and that's the thirteen-year-old kid I was.'

The boys had grown quiet and Russ concentrated on the road, which was becoming increasingly difficult to navigate. There were deep erosion scars and at times the low suspension of the Mercedes scraped along the bottom.

They lurched into a pothole. 'The Ford we had could've tackled this easily.'

'Maybe we should have come by boat.'

'If *they* came by boat,' Russ said, motioning his eyes towards the boys sitting on the backseat, 'how do they know this is the right road?'

Rebecca shrugged her shoulders. They were going at a crawl now, Russ worrying about getting stuck.

'Do we have reception?' he asked.

'One bar,' said Rebecca, glancing down at his cell phone.

'You're not the only one who's getting chopped up, you know.'

Here was their other big argument. Luc. Sex and Luc. He wasn't man enough, and he wasn't father enough.

They had come to a part of the road that was more gravel than compacted soil and the tyres slipped, as if in response to Beck's grievance. Russ took his foot off the accelerator until he had regained control.

'I lost my father,' he said.

'And Luc has lost you.'

'I wish I could connect with him. I don't know how to. I don't feel like I'm his parent, not like I did with Savannah. At least at that age. Do you remember? People used to joke that I was her mother and you her father.'

'Yes, I remember. I wished you had breasts, so I didn't have to do all the feeding.'

'You couldn't keep yourself from your art.' If Russ was home, he would be the first to respond to Savannah's cries and would take the baby to Rebecca, in her studio, to be fed. Then he'd take her away to wind and change her, and in the morning went out into the world to earn a living.

There was a high fence ahead, topped by razor wire. The gate across the road was padlocked. More warnings, painted on large boards, told them to stay away, this was Defence Force property.

DANGER! GEVAAR!

She was quiet for a moment. 'It wasn't just that, you know. I think I escaped to my art, and when you brought Sav to me, you helped me mother her. You were so sweet with her. It made it so hard for me to accept that you couldn't be the same way with Luc.'

'Luc is different.' The words had slipped from between his lips. Or maybe propelled. That phrase – *Luc is different*

– was their little artillery testing ground. Poorly aimed and indiscriminately explosive.

They parked the car and followed the boys to a hole in the fence. Russ passed his backpack through the hole but his pullover snagged as he tried to wriggle through on his back and the boys had to bend the wire to free him. Rebecca slipped in easily.

'Is it far?' she asked.

'*Nee, Tannie*,' said the younger brother over his shoulder, '*dis nie ver nie.*'

They made their way over open ground toward the merged blue of ocean and sky. There were no paths. The beauty was wild, scattered and unconventional. The stark, rocky land seemed hardly able to sustain life, and then suddenly there was the lavishness of a protea bush bursting from the surrounding *fynbos*, the fingers of the flowers' red hands thrown open. A little further, a few grey rhebok darted shyly away, like quicksilver ghosts of the dry bushveld. Russ tried to picture the artillery shells dropping amongst them.

They scrambled over some rocks and entered a small valley where they lost sight of the sea. The sound of the waves' pounding below and the smell of their salty fragrance could still reach them. The boys, whose bare feet whizzed across the ground, often had to stop and wait for the couple. They wore grey shorts of a school uniform and long-sleeved white shirts under their faded jerseys. They laughed but were not impatient. Petrus had eaten all his sweets. Bartholomew had been more careful than his younger brother, hoarding his and taking them out of his pants pocket every fifteen minutes or so to break one from the packet.

The wind picked up, dragging itself across the bushes. Russ had to keep his eyes on the ground to avoid stumbling which is why, when finally he saw them, he was almost on top of them. He stopped short. Dark shapes blotted the edges of his vision. Not ten feet from him were two baboons, their beady brown eyes on him. Several others appeared, dotted all around. They had walked into a troop of them.

'Christ,' said Russ, gripping the strap of his pack. Smiling nervously, Rebecca reached for his arm. The boys were respectful but seemed unafraid, and passed by. One of the females went about her business, picking fleas and ticks off one of the others, and then the baboons began to saunter off, their tails arched stiffly in the air.

'I've never been that close to one of them,' said Rebecca. 'Except at Cape Point but then we're always in the car, and even when they jump on the bonnet, it feels safe inside.'

'We kept a baby once, for a few weeks. I must've told you,' he said. 'There were lots around Sterkfontein. You shouldn't smile at them. You don't want them to see you baring your teeth.'

They came out on the back of the peninsula and stood on a spine that made its way into the ocean. A gust of wind hit them from below. The jutting land lay down with its nose in the water like a giant reptile, its backbone the ridge from which at first gradual slopes, then steep cliffs, fell away on either side into the sea. Down below, in the mist that hovered over the shoreline, cormorants wielded themselves across the water, darkening the white cusps of the waves. This was the type of terrain his father would stride across while Russ fought to keep up, fearful of falling behind, convinced that if he were to lose sight of his father he'd fall into the sea.

They made their way down to the beach where the mist enveloped them. Here the rocks were wet and it was hard to find steady footing. One of Beck's shoes was wet. She had stepped in a puddle. They were both breathing heavily, and had removed their pullovers, stowed by Russ in the backpack. She looked over her shoulder at him.

'How much further?'

There were caves but so shallow they were more like indentations in the rock face, and none showed evidence of a dig, or of having been closed up by a rockfall. The brothers were purposeful, moving on. And then they had to climb again, until they were half-way between the water and the horizon formed by the peninsula's ridge. It was here that the boys led them to a crop of loose boulders and showed them the entrance to the cave that lay behind.

It wasn't difficult to get inside. The ground looked freshly turned where the policemen must have widened the hole in order to get the bodies and the trunk out. They slipped through the opening feet first into a place of cool darkness. Everything echoed, the drip-drip of water over the lip of the cave entrance, the agitation of the ocean, the sound of Russ's backpack dropping to the ground. The shape of things slowly emerged from the gloom.

Russ reached into the backpack for the torch and switched it on. For all his forethought, he had forgotten to check the batteries and the beam bounced weakly off the thin cloud of dust particles made airborne by their footfalls on the cave floor. He cursed himself, anticipating an irritatingly accurate interpretation from Beck concerning his ambivalence towards his father – *you're turning a blind eye*, or some such comment. But Rebecca said nothing.

He felt dizzy and sat down on a rock, sweeping the near useless torch about the cave. At his feet, stretching into the darkness, he could make out the criss-crossing of slackened twine which he imagined as much as saw was fastened on four sides by large nails driven into crevices in the rock. Another grid of twine dangled down one wall, the drag in the middle giving it the look of a web spun by an inept spider. Otherwise the cave appeared devoid of human artefact.

Beck came over to sit next to him. 'The coolness feels lovely. How on earth did he know to look in here?'

Russ grinned at her pun, clearly unintentional. 'How on *earth*? Head for the caves, he used to say. You see, if your bones get left out in the open, the chances of them surviving long enough to become fossilised are just about nil. You'd need to sink into some mud, maybe at the side of a lake. And then you'd need the soil to have the right chemical balance. It shouldn't be too acidic.'

The boys sat proprietarily on a ledge on the other side of the cave opening, Bartholomew sharing his last sweets with his brother. Between the boys and the couple, a shaft of sunlight picked out footprints in the dirt that covered the floor.

As Russ and Rebecca cooled down, the wet air made them shiver.

'Beck, do you want your top?'

'Mmm, thanks.' She took the sweater he pulled out of the backpack. 'Do you think it was suicide? He was old, maybe dying...'

Russ was pulling his own sweater over his head. 'And the woman?' he said, his head emerging from the neck of the pullover, 'why would she go with him?'

'Well, she wouldn't have been the first. The Pharaohs were buried with their wives. In some Indian sects you find the same thing. Some were even buried alive.' She smiled and touched him on the arm. 'If you died, darling, I would want to be buried with you.' Her look was playful, mischievous. She was trying to lighten things, help him. He could see that, he just couldn't do anything with it.

'That woman wasn't my father's wife,' he said.

'True. But was she his lover?'

'It was probably an accident... a rockfall.' His breathing was coming in gusts now. 'Maybe a storm, boulders

47

loosened by erosion, that sort of thing. He came down here, started excavating. There was an accident. He couldn't get back home.'

Russ got to his feet, dizzy. He had to stop talking, catch his breath. He began working his way around the perimeter of the cave, panning the increasingly weak torchlight along the walls and floor, the beam throwing up shadows that undulated and curved. He had directed the torchlight past it by the time he realised he'd seen something. He panned back. Yes, he hadn't imagined it. The light was creating a cluster of small, jagged shadows out of place with the erosion pattern of wall. It was in a place where the twine grid fixed to the wall sagged. He stood in front of the irregularity. The patch of rock showed signs of excavation: even in the poor light, the cavities and indentations left by Barak's hammer were visible. Russ swept his fingers lightly across the surface of the wall, feeling for the ridges and valleys that might define something alien to the rock. He remembered the time he found a femur and the excitement on Barak's face. It had been easy. The bone had been blackened by fire almost 600,000 years before and stood out against the breccia like a firefly against the night.

In the light of the dying beam he touched the protrusions, the dents of Barak's hammer blows, the cold pockmarks of the rock face. He heard the chipping of steel against rock. He saw the little beads of sweat trickling down his father's forehead, becoming trapped in his bushy eyebrows. He saw his eyes blink away the dust and sweat, the prominent wedge of his nose pointed towards its target. He felt the sharp edges of the fossil jutting from the cave wall. He felt the thrill of discovery bolt through his body.

'No!' he said exultantly. 'It wasn't suicide. He'd never have gone before he'd gotten this thing out.'

7

THEY ARRIVED HOME to find Beatrice clearing up after dinner, and Luc at the kitchen table, gluing breadcrumbs onto a piece of paper to create the mane of a lion he had drawn. Savannah was next door visiting Temba Cohen, a boy from her class at Camps Bay High.

Luc smiled and accepted a kiss and hug from his mother.

'That's a beautiful lion,' Beck said, leaning over his shoulder.

Russ went off to draw a bath. Beatrice had kept dinner for them but he wasn't hungry. Barak had touched that fossil and now Russ had rested his fingers there, where the old man's had been. It allowed a touching of Barak, as if only moments had elapsed between his father's hammer blows and Russ's examination of the exposed fossil. He clicked on the CD-player in the bedroom and stepped into the bathwater, only to realise that Savannah had been listening to one of her CDs, and now he was trapped with the voice of an African hip-hop artist beating its way into the bathroom.

His fingers retained a memory of the cave wall, the small hollows left by Barak's exploration. The sound of rock coming away. And suddenly, unbidden, undesired, Inspector Toka's voice saying 'You didn't know him all that well? What does a thirteen year old know of his parent's business?' But Toka was wrong. Russ knew his father, knew his business. He had been with him countless times, tummy to the ground, shifting sand with brush and broom, compacted earth with pick and putty knife, rock with cold chisel. He could pull the right tool like a master caddy the perfect golf club. And now, he was convinced, he could pull the right explanation for the old man's death. It was simply a matter of objectivity. Barak had taught him that. The old man would look at a piece of evidence, say, the pattern of holes that had been found in fossil skulls. 'My colleagues,' he'd scoff, 'would have us believe these are a result of some elaborate burial rite. But they bring their own desire for religion to the evidence. I say these holes in the head were made by the talons of eagles, or the canines of sabre-toothed cats!' And he'd position his downward-pointed index fingers in front of his mouth and snarl at his son. *'Grarl! Grarl!'*

'Make room.'

Beck was standing naked beside their oversized bath, a foot hovering above the water. Russ followed the line of her leg up the smooth curve of her thigh to her hip and beyond, unsettled by a feeling that her breasts were suddenly unfamiliar. Perhaps it was just the steam from the hot bathwater, or the angle of his view. They were no longer quite the audacious breasts of Beck's youth – their generosity now embracing the gravity of years – but they looked more beautiful than ever. She was voluptuousness incarnate. He was used to other men sizing her up and felt envious of them, wanting to see her through their eyes so that he too could devour her. They seemed to see her so much more clearly than he did. Following Luc's birth, whenever he saw her naked, he felt as though it was not him watching her, but someone else, and he was an observer, looking at a man looking at his naked wife. He had misplaced his desire. Beck had become so frustrated she had accused him of *not* having a wandering eye.

'Russ!'

'Sorry,' he said, and shifted his body.

The bath had an old hospital tap, with a long arm that swung away to the side, leaving space for her head to rest against the lip of the bathtub. She settled into the warm water. The tangle of their legs comforted him and he began to drift off, satisfied with his conclusion concerning his father's death. No matter how many times he added up the evidence, he could picture only one equation:

> *blocked cave entrance + half-excavated fossil + no return to Krugersdorp conclusion: arrives at cave → excavates for a few weeks → gets trapped inside by accidental rockfall*

'Weird!' It was Savannah's turn to interrupt Russ's abstraction. 'Aren't you guys too old for this? Are you trying to save water?'

'Hey, Sav,' said Rebecca. 'Very funny.'

Savannah had turned to face the mirror above the basin and was examining her flawless complexion for blemishes. She was wearing her customary black, a mini-skirt over stockings, loose cardigan that was longer than her skirt, sleeves pushed back to the elbows, and bare belly with cotton top. While her brother had the haunted beauty of a grimy waif from the streets of 18th century Paris, Savannah's looks were those of her three-quarters Sephardic ancestry: olive skin, dark hair, brown eyes, precocious womanhood.

The African hip-hop didn't sound half bad. The beat made him sleepy, his eyelids closing. He felt the press of Rebecca's legs alongside his, heard the distant drone of her conversation with Savannah. He floated back to the cave, reconstructing a picture of Barak, his meagre possessions packed neatly into the trunk, working at the rock to summon forth its secrets, the woman – was she his servant?

– cooking a meal, while outside the South African Defence Force punched the air with artillery shells that dropped down on small herds of rhebok.

'Some cop phoned this afternoon.'

Russ opened his eyes. Savannah was squeezing her cheek between the nails of her forefingers.

'Inspector Toka?' asked Rebecca.

'Inspector Talker, that's it.'

'No, Inspector *Toka*, sweetheart.'

'Well,' said the teenager, her mouth stretched into a sickly smile, 'Inspecter *Toka* wants to *tok* with you.' Savannah did not like to be corrected.

'Did he say anything else?'

'No… well, something about fetching the stuff. Can I go to Temba's for supper tomorrow night?'

'No, it's Friday night – we're going to Tante Julia's,' said Beck. 'Did he say we were right? About the bones?'

'I dunno. He said he'd phone tomorrow morning. Oh, something about getting someone to examine the mummies. How weird. Can I go *after* supper?'

'Let's see how late it is.'

Savannah let her hands drop to her sides in an exasperated huff, and left the bathroom.

'Bah!' An involuntary bleat escaped Russ's half-submerged mouth, spraying water across the bath. He could barely give voice to the thought that suddenly trespassed on his reverie. 'Shit, do you think she's… you know, having a relationship with him?'

Beck laughed. 'Honey, where have you been? She's been with him for months.'

'Jesus, is she, I mean, are they…?'

'She's on the pill, Russ.'

'But what about…?'

'He's madly in love with her and they were both virgins.

And just because he's black doesn't mean to say he's more at risk of infection.'

'I never said that.'

'Yes, but you thought it.' She lifted herself to her feet, the water cascading down her body, and stepped out of the tub.

Russ shut his eyes, hoping to take himself back to the cave. But the music was intruding and now all he could see, to the pulse of the African hip-hop, were uncontrolled flashes of his daughter and Temba Cohen *in flagrante delicto*.

8

THE LAST TIME DR BARAK Codron's scarred, rock-mover's hands touched his son was when he held the thirteen-year-old Russ by the shoulders on the day he left. His grey hair had grown long and as he leant towards the teenager it fell into his bloodshot eyes. His old man's bladder had him up at night, but these last two years his life's fever had reached a new high, and his sleep was far more fitful.

'Off on an expedition, Red,' he said. 'The "Tip of Africa" theory I've been working on since they kicked us out of Sterkfontein. It's time to put it to the test. When I get back, it'll be with the evidence. Sorry I can't take you with me. I'll be gone too long. You look out for that schoolwork now.'

Then he'd picked up his old army duffle bag, heaved it over a shoulder, and walked out of the house. He was wearing his heavy boots, the ones he wore in the field when he knew he was going to find something big. Russ heard the *thunk* of the duffle bag landing in the back of the old Ford, then the slam of the driver's door. His mother said Barak would return in three months.

He counted off the days on the calendar that hung behind the kitchen door, the blue ink crosses forming neat, hopeful rows beneath the picture of a grazing elephant. Three months to the day his father left he said to his mother: 'Dad's coming back today, Ma. It's been three months.'

'Not today, dear,' she said.

'When, Ma?'

'When he's finished his work, darling,' she said.

A week later, he asked her again. 'When's Dad coming home?'

She smiled at him. That tired, half-brave smile. 'Darwin left England and his family to sail with Captain Fitz-Roy on the Beagle,' she said. 'He was gone five whole years. Can you imagine the set-back to twentieth century thought if he hadn't?' They both knew Darwin had not yet married when he sailed on the Beagle.

A few weeks later she was dishing some peas onto his dinner plate when her serving spoon stopped in mid-air and she said quietly, 'Men of genius sometimes have to go away to do their work. If Gauguin had not left his family and taken off for Tahiti, the world would never have known his most beautiful paintings.' The serving spoon in her hand was shaking and the peas began to scatter.

It was the day Russ had come back from school with a black eye after a fistfight with one of the Afrikaans boys whose curled lips proclaimed knowledge of Russ's father.

'Your father,' he'd said, 'sleeps with kaffir women in the bush.'

'My father hunts fossils!' Russ had screamed tearfully. 'He *works* in the bush.'

Arnoldus van Schalkwyk clearly had no clue what a fossil hunter was – the Nationalist Government had banned any talk of evolution in the schools – and neither did any of the other boys; even if they had, Russ's defence of his father was no match for Van Schalkwyk's jibe about Barak's 'kaffir women'.

Inspector Toka was on the phone. Dr Barak Codron, he informed Russ, was no longer a person of interest (to the police, that is, the inspector added).

'You've discovered the truth, then?' said Russ.

'The truth?' Toka laughed genially. 'What is the truth? What I do have is the pathologist's report on those bones found with your father. They are indeed ancient. So if you mean that the bones are not those of the missing teenagers, or any other recently living person, then that certainly is a scientific truth... but is your father a murderer?' He paused. 'In my experience, Mr Codron, everyone is guilty of something. But there's no evidence of foul play here, no reason to suspect your father was either perpetrator or victim. I do apologise for the anxiety this inquiry has put you through.'

Taken aback by the genuine tone of the inspector's apology, Russ could only stammer a 'thank you' and make arrangements to meet at Caledon Square an hour later.

At the police station, Toka's convivial greeting further disarmed Russ. He'd had the sour aftertaste of that first interview in his mouth, of having been held hostage to the police's version of events. Now he felt an odd feeling of gratitude, even an affinity for the man. They both seemed a little displaced, sharing the influence of England in their language and accent. But it was Russ, the white man, who had grown up in Africa, while Toka, the black man, appeared to have been raised in England. The world was a little mixed up.

There was some paperwork for Russ to sign, stating that he was in receipt of Barak's belongings, listed as 'various personal effects' and 'work items'.

'What do you intend to do with his body?' Toka asked.

Russ looked up from the document he was signing. 'Have it properly examined.'

'Look,' said the inspector, 'the pathologist I spoke to was pretty impressed that two mummies have come to light. Apparently you don't get naturally occurring mummification in South Africa. Not the right conditions. He's given me the number of a professor at the University of KwaZulu-Natal.' He pulled out a Blackberry and scrolled to a note, scribbling down the details for Russ. 'Here it is. Physical anthropologist. Teaches anatomy at the medical school. Professor Leila Naidoo. She's the country's top expert in mummy studies, although given the scarcity of subjects, I doubt she's got too much competition.'

'That's very kind of you,' said Russ, accepting the piece of paper with the professor's contact details.

Toka hesitated before saying, 'With regard to the woman… We've contacted as many Nondula families as we can find on the database but so far nobody's claiming Nombeko. If one of the universities is involved, I'm pretty sure I can get Captain Morkel to release her as well. He's worried the mummies are going to disintegrate.'

Russ wasn't sure he wanted anything to do with the woman but thanked the inspector.

'Oh, and one last thing,' Toka said, 'I had a call from a young constable up the West Coast. Says he had a visit from a couple wanting to go exploring on restricted Defence Force property.' He smiled. 'I wouldn't advise that couple going out there again. Not without the right permit.'

He had two constables help Russ haul Barak's trunk and army duffle bag out of the evidence room and down to the car. Once home, with help from Rebecca and Beatrice, these were transferred to the studio, where Russ sat staring at them.

'Time we took control,' said Beck, and suggested they contact the *Sunday Times* so that the newspaper could do a follow-up story clearing Barak of any suspicion. Russ, immobile in front of his father's things, asked her to do it.

The journalist was unhappy with her. He had already completed his article, now linking 'Dr Codron and the Nondula woman' to the disappearance of the two teenagers.

Sexy stuff, he informed Rebecca. He was hoping it would make the front page under his suggested headline, 'Mummies the word for teenager killers'.

'Well, now you know it's all bullshit, you'll have to rewrite it,' she said. Ending the call, she turned to Russ. 'Either open them and get on with it, or go to work. Barbara's probably tearing her hair out and I need the studio to myself.' She looked exhausted. Unable to sleep, she had spent the night in the studio, her hands on the clay face.

'I want to look. I just don't seem able to.' What had he said to Beck on the way to the cave? About waiting as an *activity*? He wasn't sure he was really ready to stop waiting. His father's body was Russ's to claim. He had the duffle bag and trunk. He knew where to find the cave and Barak's half-excavated fossil. He had possession of his father's story. Or, at least, as many of its elements as he was ever likely to have. So why this agitation? Why this reluctance to look? To fit the pieces together?

He had spent so many years waiting for Barak and now it was as though his father had come home to him, wanting to explain the circumstances of his disappearance. Suddenly, he wasn't sure what he was going to hear. Stymied by the puzzle of his own contradictory self, Russ drove to work.

It was only during the early afternoon that he remembered the piece of paper in his pocket, handed to him earlier in the day by Inspector Toka. He took it out and stared at it. He could hear Toka's voice – 'Everyone is guilty of something' – as a memory fell from a hidden perch at the back of his mind. Barak *had* been accused of a crime before. His colleagues had suspected him of illegally selling fossils to foreigners. They had never been able to prove anything, as far as Russ knew, but – now it was coming back to him – isn't this why the old man was banned from excavating at Sterkfontein?

He remembered the letter in Barak's angry, trembling hands. 'What's the bloody point?' he had said, or something to that effect, 'you can't publish without exposing your crime and if you don't publish, what have you got? Contraband fossils are bloody useless!'

Barak's logic, as Russ recalled it, left him feeling unsettled. You could make a similar point about stolen art – that it would have to remain secreted away – but the trade flourishes. Why shouldn't someone get a kick out of owning a piece of a three-million-year-old ancestor?

He telephoned the Nelson R Mandela School of Medicine at the University of KwaZulu-Natal. Professor Leila Naidoo was on leave. He had to get hold of her urgently, he said. The mummies are disintegrating.

'Excuse me?' said the young receptionist. 'Is this a joke?'

'I'm sorry,' he said, and explained himself. 'There was an article in the *Sunday Times* about them, did you see it?'

'No, I didn't,' said the receptionist. 'If I had, I might have phoned Professor Naidoo myself. We don't get many mummies in South Africa.'

'I know,' said Russ, a feeling of relief that he was making headway outweighing the growing irritation at being told, yet again, what a rare specimen his father was. He could hear the tap-tapping of the receptionist's keyboard in the background. She could have been carrying on with whatever she'd been doing before his call, but he had the feeling she was running an internet search for the article.

'Yes, I see it here,' said the receptionist. 'Wow. They look well preserved, don't they? Wow. Look at them! Professor Naidoo's going to be totally stoked. Hey, she's on holiday in Malawi. She's got her cell, but I can't give the number to you. I know what. I'll call her, tell her the good news. Then I'm sure she'll call you.'

Russ gave her his contact numbers and, having needlessly

extracted a promise from the now breathless receptionist to call the professor right away, hung up. How odd, he thought, the number was sitting unnoticed in my pocket for hours and then when I remember it I can't wait to get hold of the woman.

His impatience was rewarded. Within five minutes of his discussion with the receptionist, Professor Naidoo was on the phone. After quizzing him for fifteen minutes about the circumstances of the discovery, she said, 'Where are they being kept?'

'They're in the State Mortuary.'

There was a groan. 'Don't tell me... in one of the fridges?'

'Yes, with a heap of bodies.'

'Oh goodness, that will not do. Don't those silly people know anything? They're not fresh corpses, they're desiccated! They don't need refrigeration, they need a climate-controlled environment. They need fumigation. They need *care*. You've got to move them. You've got to protect those bodies. I'll see what I can arrange with my colleagues at UCT. I'm due to fly back from Lilongwe on Tuesday. The flight lands in Johannesburg, 17:25. I'll come straight to Cape Town or failing that, first thing Wednesday morning. I'll try and get back sooner but it's probably not possible.' She stopped for a moment. 'Do you know, Mr Codron, there have been only two mummies discovered in sub-Saharan Africa? The one is a skull found in bushveld near Randfontein, and the other a 2,000-year-old Khoisan burial in a rock shelter in the Kouga Mountains.'

'Professor Naidoo?'

'Yes, Mr Codron?'

'Are you going to be able to tell me when my father died?'

There was a pause. 'I am sorry, Mr Codron. I was getting carried away. This is your father and you must be wondering all sorts of things. We'll see what we can do. In the meantime, the mummies are fragile. They must be protected or they will crumble to dust and we won't be able to tell anything.'

Barbara was motioning to him. Mrs Oxtoby had arrived with her broken spectacles, a little huffy about not having seen Russ earlier in the week. It was, surprisingly, a welcome distraction. Russ shifted back into work mode, staying at the practice longer than necessary, unpacking a new consignment of frames that had arrived from China.

'Anthea can do it in the morning,' Barbara Robertson said, by which she meant that Anthea, the junior optometrist, should work for her salary.

By the time he got home, it was too late to open the trunk and duffle bag. The Sabbath dinner at Tante Julia's was due to start. Distracted, Russ tagged along. But towards the end of the evening, with most of the extended family already gone, he found himself lingering, so that it was, unusually, Beck, and not he, who had to herd the family out the door.

9

THE BOY NEVER COMPLAINED but jeez those early starts were cold. They didn't always dig inside the Sterkfontein caves. Sometimes they'd be out in the open. With his little broom in his hand, Russ would mimic Barak: father and son crouched down on their knees sweeping dirt as the sun rose in the morning sky, at first warming them, then baking them. They might rest on a haunch, propping themselves up with one hand, freeing the other to work. But there were places where Russ could not follow his father. During a difficult dig in the Karoo, Russ looked on from below as Barak tied himself to the rock face because the ledge he had to support himself on was so narrow. It turned out he was standing on the cheekbone of a *pareiasaurus* – a fearsome cross between a hippo and a crocodile. Anything they suspected of being a fossil would end up in a box. Over the midday period they would go back to the camp, carefully tip the contents onto a trestle table, and sort through the pile. Russ took his job very seriously. As far as he knew, his father never checked his sorting, and he was terrified of throwing a piece of Adam's tibia or Eve's jaw onto the reject pile.

'My lad,' Barak said one day, leaning over the trestle table, 'what we're engaged in can be compared to the policeman trying to catch a thief. You find evidence, you examine it for the smallest clue. Here,' – and he passed his son a fossilised joint – 'what can one glean from this?'

Russ could see his father was barely able to contain his excitement. He had to be holding something important.

'It's a knee joint,' he said. It could only have been that, or perhaps an elbow joint, or a heel, or... but he'd guessed correctly. Barak didn't say much, just smiled and Russ could see how happy he was.

Finally Barak said, 'Good! Now, what can you tell me about this knee joint of yours?'

'It's old?' said Russ. 'I mean, very old. Millions of years.' Well, it had to be.

'Yes! We've got a bloody beauty here. What else?'

Russ examined it more closely. Gingerly he tried to manoeuvre it but of course it was stuck fast. Barak sat patiently, a smile on his full lips, waiting for the boy to finish. Russ held it next to his own knee. It was about the same size. 'This fossil was ten years old,' he said.

'No,' his father said, as if he was a game-show quizmaster and Russ a hapless contestant about to go home with a month's supply of budgie seed. 'This joint belonged to an adult. You're taller and bigger than he would've been at ten years of age.' He told Russ the fossil was two, maybe three million years old. An Australopithecine, same species as Dart's Taung child. They didn't grow very tall. What he had wanted Russ to say was that you could tell by the joint that this ancestor of ours walked upright.

It was, for Russ, as though he was taking lessons at the right hand of a god. He knew most sons felt this way about their fathers, but this was special: they were uncovering the very nature of Nature.

'Dad?'

'Uh?' Russ was mixing a vodka tonic. He should be celebrating this day of vindication. The story of the 'Mummified Mass Murderers' had been put to rest.

'I'm going to Temba's.'

'Okay, sweetheart.' He downed the drink, then repeated

the procedure. Fortified, he headed for the studio. He didn't get there, deciding instead to look in on Luc. Rebecca, having come to settle the boy into bed, was now asleep, nestled against Luc's small, wakeful form. Russ tried to catch his eye but he was off in that dimension-hopping way of his. He seemed to reach the best part of his day at the end of it, like this, in bed, the duvet pulled up to his chin. It was here, with the real world held at bay by the borders of his mattress, that touch was most welcomed. Book in hand, Rebecca – or 'Becca', which is what he called her – would lie down next to him. During her periods of frenetic creativity, this might be the first sustained contact he had with her all day, Beatrice having seen to his needs. Beck's body would emit her very distinctive odour, the smell of her sweat – absorbed in a binge of work, she could go two or three days without bathing herself – mingled with the particles of the materials that clung to her clothes and hair and skin; wood shavings, resin, clay, paint, iron or plastic filings layered over the ubiquitous base of turpentine must. Lying that close to her meant you could literally taste it all. Luc didn't seem to mind, not even when the particles stung his eyes or irritated the soft inner-membrane of his nose. It was, Russ supposed, far sweeter than any perfume. It was the smell of Becca.

She would read to him. When he was younger, it was *The Little Prince* or *Winnie-the-Pooh*. He was Owl, she said, her wise young Owl. By the time he was five, she was reading him *Watership Down* and *The Chronicles of Narnia*, which stretched her ability to stay awake, but pleased him. He insisted on the French translations. Beck was intrigued by his love of French and had come to the understanding that it was not the pitch or cadences so much as what these signified – the fact that the language was of another place. English, on the other hand, was the language of his reality and his bad dreams.

Gazing at the peaceful expression on her face as she

spooned against a watchful Luc, Russ had the peculiar impression that, wrapped in the circle of his mother's arms, it was Luc who was her protector. The boy had soothed his mother to sleep. And now Russ remembered that he, too, had enjoyed such times with his own mother, sober enough on occasion to read bedside stories to him, and after she had finished, kissing him on the neck, behind his ear, a warm, shadowy tingle pelting down his spine like a squirrel down a tree's trunk.

'Good night, Luc,' Russ said quietly, and left the bedroom. Whoever was protecting whom, neither appeared to need him.

With Sav next door at Temba's, the house was quiet. He could go to bed. He could watch TV. He could read. Or he could go to the studio, and open the trunk and duffle bag. He heard himself blurt out a silly phrase, repeated sonorously in Hollywood genre movies. '*It is time*,' the actor intones, trying vainly to inject gravitas into the ridiculous. Well, it *was* fucking time.

On the floor in the studio were Beck's preparatory sketches for the first head in the series which, along with all the others bar the last one, was already waiting for her in finished form in Johannesburg. She must have hoped to see something in the beginning of the series that would enable her to finish it. The face was open, eyes round and honest. In some of the pictures the jaw hung slackly, parting the mouth in an expression of bewilderment. It was a young face, but whether it was that of a boy or a girl, Russ couldn't tell.

He stood in front of the window, the reflection of his face imprinted on the dark night. The sea was out there, an unflagging vessel of life and death. After Barak disappeared, Russ would stand in his bedroom at night looking at his reflection in the window pane and beyond it, at the veld. He had not been so aware of the veld until he was hardly ever in it. When Barak was around, it seemed to be part of both of them, some sort of bodily extension; after he disappeared, it became separate and unfathomable. There had been a brief period during which Russ had extended his imagined searches into the real world, walking the hills for signs of his father. But even then he knew Barak was not anywhere in the Transvaal, and Russ kept his distance from the veld. Like the sea now lurking massively before him, it was deadly.

He felt his finger where the chisel had sliced him when he was eight years old. The ridge of scar tissue had flattened and spread as his finger had grown, but it was still there, as was the memory of a young boy inside a cavern with teeth and bits of bone protruding from its dank walls, and blood oozing from his wound. He could still see the colour of the Sterkfontein rock, the cross-hatching and wrinkles that looked like elephant hide, the crystals hanging from the roof, the columns of stalactites and stalagmites amputated by the men who had mined the cave for lime in the 1920s. His father had bathed his bloody hand in one of the underground streams, the icy water numbing the pain. Then Barak had taken out his medical kit and told the grimacing, screaming child the story of the greatest scientific fraud of all time, each stab of the needle into the little digit punctuating a minor climax in the tale, each drawing through of the thread accompanied by a build-up of narrative. It was the story of Piltdown Man and despite his yelps of pain, Russ heard it all.

There had been a punishing row that night, his mother's stifled wrath roused by the sight of her child's pale face and damaged finger, and enveloping the father who had presumed to treat the injury himself and then had the temerity to carry on digging for the rest of the afternoon.

Russ brought his finger up to the light. The severed nerves had not grown back properly and the top third of his finger had been left deformed and with little feeling. Pretty much like the rest of me, he thought.

His father's possessions lay to his right. He went back down the corridor to make another drink, and then brought it to the studio where he stood in front of the trunk and the duffle bag, gulping the vodka, remembering. 'Look at this, Red,' Barak might have said, holding a skull in his hands, 'see the sloping forehead? Small brain, maybe 550 cc's. This chap was great at swinging from the trees but he'd never have lit a fire. The forehead had to go up and out. It had to accommodate the evolving cerebral cortex.'

Russ's head pounded. This is not a headache, he thought, this is something else. This, he imagined, as though it were a flower opening up through the lens of a time-lapse camera, is a growing, aching brain, the forehead bursting forward to make room for an expanding universe of cerebral power, the ape-like face morphing into its human counterpart. With a bigger brain our ancestors harnessed fire. Fire changed everything. We could keep ourselves warm. It frightened away predators. Cooking became possible. The earliest pyromaniacs roamed the earth.

Russ knelt down, wobbled, managed to regain his balance, and took hold of the duffle bag, dust sloughing off the mildewed canvas as he lifted it up. Despite all the handling it had received – the lugging from hand to hand, the police opening it up – it was still dislodging layers of cave dirt. He loosened the drawstring, the oxidised eyelets separating in an open sesame that released a fetid smell of earth and metal. Russ grunted with satisfaction as he tipped the contents out. Barak's tools were there, rusted rock hammer, whisk broom and paint brushes, cold chisels, awls, the now-mouldy velvet bag that surely contained the set of scalpels and dental picks. The look and heft of the tools, as familiar to the child Russ as his father's hands, lay before him, the past served up on the floor of Rebecca's studio. He lifted each in turn, holding it in his grown man's hands, the touch of a friend he'd not seen in decades. The hammer's warm wooden grip, the bristles of the brushes drawn across his open palm, each particle of wood, steel, horse's hair triggering a sense-memory. The velvet bag he remembered being burgundy, or perhaps grape, was now covered in a dead bluish-white mould. He fumbled with the tie, his dexterity hijacked by the vodka, finally managed it and with a thrill of recognition rolled the bag out. Each implement had its own individually sewn pouch, the sharp end of the tool protruding from the top for easy selection.

These items he would have expected to find. What the trunk contained was another matter. He shifted over, lifted the catch and pulled. It wouldn't give. The rust had cemented it closed. He tried to loosen the sides of the lid but his movements were clumsy, and he succeeded only in scraping his fingertips. There were indentations around the catch, signs of the lid having been crow-barred – the police breaking in. But now that he had decided to listen to its secrets, the trunk wouldn't reveal them. His father's weighty ghost was sitting tight-lipped on its rusty lid.

Russ reached over for one of Barak's cold chisels, inserted it under the flange of the trunk's top, and prised it open. If ghosts have a sensate presence, perhaps this would be it: the crackle of the lid coming away, followed by the fetid blast of rotting clothing.

Resting on top of a pile of mould-caked dresses and women's underwear was a bundle wrapped loosely in an oilskin rag. It had to be the notebooks. Russ picked it up and separated the folds of oilskin. There were two hard-backed shorthand notebooks and a child's A4 school exercise book. Even before he made out the faded red crest of a lion, with the words 'Lion Brand' below it, he knew the first two were

Croxleys, his father's favourite for taking into the field, the spiral-binding at the top allowing for ease of entry. The one Croxley, at least externally, was far better preserved than the other, whose cover had patches of a scaly crust. The exercise book was a surprise. Perhaps Barak, having run out of his preferred shorthand Croxleys, had had to make do.

The cover, which must originally have been of a flexible, tinted board, was, like the poorly preserved Croxley, marked by mould, warped and brittle. It had a distinctive range of brown- and orange-hued swirls, and expanses of grey fungi, reminding Russ of the mummies' skin. It tore as he tried to open it. He'd had to use his strength to get the trunk open, and his hands had retained the need for brute force. He felt as if he had ripped the skin from his father's face. He moved the cover back in a wish to undo the damage. He was going to have to be more careful. He reached for the velvet bag he'd held moments earlier and selected a scalpel with a long blade. Inserting it gently between the brittle pages and, in a slow cutting motion that scythed forty-five degrees from the spine of the book, he managed to separate several of them. Some of the ink had faded, some had rotted off the page, and that which had remained was unintelligible to his eyes. He picked up the Croxley with the scabby cover. It, too, refused to talk. Barak had written on both sides of the page but one was more impenetrable than the next, and as he flipped the pages over the spiral binding, care gave way to desperation, his fingers tearing at the fragile paper. He tossed it aside and with the desperation of a man who knows he has one last hope, picked up the second Croxley. The cover opened, the pages turned but he could not pick out a single word. Toka was wrong, they weren't just in bad shape, they had been destroyed altogether. Barak had closed his mouth against his interrogators without as much as a murmur escaping.

'Bugger it!' said Russ. He began rummaging through

the rest of the things. Maybe there were more notebooks. But there weren't. What there was, apart from some moth-eaten clothing – the woman's, as well as Barak's – were the fossil fragments the police had mistaken for parts of the missing teenagers, now crammed together in a *Sergio Rossi* shoebox. Someone in the police department had good taste in footwear. He discovered three of the larger pieces wrapped in a mouldy red polka-dot dress. The police must have taken them from whatever wrappings Barak had kept them in. Russ laid the fossils out in front of him. He counted 37. There were chips the size of a fingernail to a few larger pieces, the biggest being the partially intact femur Russ had seen in one of the photographs Inspector Toka had shown him. The fossils ranged in colour from a light stone to the dark appearance of several cranial fragments, stained, Russ knew, by manganese salts seeping into the bone during the fossilisation process. He picked out the vertebrae and jawbone, the other pieces he had seen in Toka's pictures. Their reference tags were still attached.

Here was something he could do. He could identify the other pieces. But it didn't take long to realise that the detectives had sent the only easily identifiable pieces to their pathologist for analysis. He started with the other bigger pieces, thought one might be part of the jaw of a giraffe-ancestor. The more he examined it, the less sure he became. It might be an ancient zebra. There were no teeth in the jaw but, in any case, whatever he once knew of giraffe and zebra dentition was long forgotten. Who was he kidding?

He slumped back against the wall of the studio. It was useless. If he couldn't tell the difference between a chunk of giraffe or zebra, what chance did he have with the smaller fragments?

10

HE MIGHT HAVE PASSED out. He was curled up on the studio floor, shivering from the cold, Rebecca nudging him gently on his shoulder. He sat up groggily, the strewn-about contents of the trunk and duffle bag yanking him into the present.

'Can't make head or tail of them,' he said, his words coming out in a slur of vodka and disappointment.

'Of what?' Beck asked, surveying the items scattered about her studio space.

'Can't tell the difference between a fucking zebra and a giraffe.'

'The giraffe's the one with the long neck.'

'There's no bloody neck. It's just a bit of jawbone.'

'Russ, you're an optometrist.'

'And,' he said, lifting his chin towards the notebooks, 'they're bloody well ruined. I can't make out a word. It's like someone's playing a game with me. Here're your father's last words but hey, sorry you can't read them, we've arranged to have them smudged out.'

'Oh,' she said, picking up the good Croxley and fitting on the reading glasses which hung from her neck. He had chosen them for her, had enjoyed the way they softened her face. She refused to wear them whilst sculpting, preferring to find a natural focal length. She must have been using them to read to Luc.

She sat down next to him on the floor and paged

carefully through the notebook. When she'd finished, she took up the other two. Finally she slipped the glasses off her face and looked at him.

'A regular trunk of Babel,' she said.

'Yes.' But he had misunderstood her. He picked up one of the bones, so obviously showing a frontal sinus. The bone was dark, almost black, the system of cavities above the nose a crucial clue that differentiated hominids from Old World monkeys. Why hadn't he seen it before? He began to cry. It was a hominid!

'What is it?' She received no answer. 'Russ. You've been drinking.' Later she would refer to the pieces of bone as a gift from Inspector Toka. Technically they would belong to the Department of Defence, since it was on the Department's land that the bones were apparently – and illegally – excavated. Toka would not have included them by mistake. If the collection represented a significant find the policeman must have known it would be placed in the right hands.

'I can do the French,' she said, 'that's easy. The Ladino, well, we need an old Sephardic soul for that. Tante Julia will be perfect. She's been depressed, it'll help her. The English you'll just have to battle through.'

She was cradling the exercise book, the brittle, burnt-orange cover becoming more and more suggestive of his father's face, so that it was as if she held Barak's head in her hands. It took him a while to understand that she was talking to him.

'Wh-what did you say?'

'Jesus, Russell. A lot of its illegible but it's clear enough in places. It's just that he's used different languages. And in this one he's flipped the book around and written in the space between the lines. He must have run out of paper and needed to double up. Can't you see that? Look here.'

She held out the notebook for him, upside down. He stared at the page. There were lines of cramped script running in one direction and in between, upside down, handwriting running in the other. And then, advancing from within the bowels of the book, marching towards him, were words in formation.

'Arriver comme un cheveu sur la soupe.'

He understood little French, but could, now that Beck had pointed it out, recognise its printed form.

'Christ, what's he saying here?'

'It means, "to arrive like a hair in the soup". It's the French way of saying "to turn up like a bad penny".'

Russ grabbed the book from her, paging through again, snatches of French words clear this time. 'I couldn't see it before. What languages did you say?'

'English, French, Ladino. Here…' She picked up the exercise book, paged through, and passed it to him. 'This is Ladino. People have used different scripts over time and place, but he's used the one that's most common these days. It's a Turkish script, I think.'

Yes, he could see it now, obvious enough to be at least mistaken for some sort of European dialect. His eyes had a desperate look. 'And English! You said English. Where?'

'Maybe we should get you some coffee.'

'No, show me.'

She found a passage in the mouldy Croxley. *'Motorbuses and motorcars'*, he read, skipping a few smudged words, making out *'streets'* and *'London'* and then a clear run through *'it was still possible to catch a horse-drawn bus of the London General Omnibus Company. In those days the city had about it an air of grandeur –'* It was near the bottom of the page, where the ink had become a light pale blue sea, and the page fused with the next one. He reached for a scalpel and separated them carefully but the pages had turned to paper-mâché, and the top page came away with the bottom part of the next page still attached. The top few lines of the next page had escaped immersion in the sea. '... *some of the landmarks you will see now had not yet been built. Even the arch at Hyde Park Corner had not yet received its quadriga. Well-heeled visitors stayed at the Hotel Cecil, gentlemen dined at their clubs in Northumberland Avenue, Londoners were soon to take to the Underground where they would move about like moles beneath the city. It was –*'

It was the end of that section's surviving script.

'Fuck,' said Russ. 'The fucking old bastard! Yes!'

It began as a laugh but within moments he was crying, his tears flowing with impatient haste, little inmates rushing for an unexpected gap in the prison wall. Rebecca put her arms around him, reluctant at first, then tightened by the pull of his sudden intensity. She kissed him on the lips.

'Beck?'

It took only seconds for her to switch off the lights and remove her clothes, and help him out of his. Her nipples were hard against the chilly air, the flesh of her thighs and belly pale and goose-bumped in the moonlight that shone through the large studio windows. In the early years, she would take every appendage of his body into her mouth, including his toes. He had felt as though she was puffing air into a blow-up doll, her breath giving him form. Now she had given him life again. She had given him his father's words. His sense of gratitude laced with excitement, he ran the fingers of his hand across the braced swell of her stomach and the dark patch of her sex and then, his cock stiffening, went down on her.

His face was between her legs, his tongue picking up a half-forgotten pulse, the sweet tangy fluid in his mouth, the disregard for the coldness of the studio floor and the press of the fossil's facial bone – the one with the hominid-differentiating frontal sinus cavities – that had somehow become trapped under his thigh.

'Oh, God, Russ,' she moaned as she swung her leg over him, 'that's quite a fossil you've got there.'

But Russ's hard-on had been the minor part of the issue. Her legs were folded at the knee, calves against the sides of his torso, her arms outstretched, hands pivoting on his shoulders. His right hand lay palm up in a tangle of their pubic hair, the tip of a finger against her clitoris, stroking apace with her quickening breath. They opened their glazed eyes, almost simultaneously, their timing for once in sync, and laughed, a man and a woman who have shared their lives for more than twenty years, taken aback by this sudden re-discovery of something they'd thought lost.

She was coming. Her breasts jostled in front of his face, goading him. He felt as though he might join her. She went still, arching her back, shuddering against him. Her moans, he was sure, would wake Luc. Hell, they might even be heard by Savannah and Temba next door. This thought did not help him.

The cry coming from him was one of pain. It had been like this for years, and it was this that had her urging him to get help. He reached the point of climax and then seemed to skip the edge, and miss it entirely. The pressure deadlocked inside him. He could not come, pounded away in frustration, tried to slow down, retrace his steps to the lower reaches – and quickly grew flaccid, his balls throbbing as though kicked. He slumped back on the floor, the blow-up doll deflated. She collapsed on top of him.

'Hey, it's okay,' she said. 'Let's go to bed.'

He turned his head towards where she had put the good Croxley and reached out for it. Holding it up, he said, 'Will you read me a French bedtime story?'

'Okay, one more. But then it's sleepy time.'

They both laughed. It was something he used to say to Savannah after she'd beg for one more story, and then say it again after he'd given in to her request for 'one more, one last one'.

11

THEY LAY IN BED WITH Barak's mouldy towers of Babel. Three notebooks seemed an awful lot of field notes for the short time Barak had been excavating before his death. But then, Barak had found 37 fossilised pieces of bone. That's a massive haul for a few months' work.

Russ tried to read more of the legible English sections from the scaly Croxley. These were not field notes at all.

In those teeming narrow streets of Whitechapel and St. George's, of the Jewish steam baths and bookmakers and workshops and seducers preying on young virgins newly arrived from Eastern Europe, it should have been to the socialists that I was drawn. These agitators – Russian Jews in love with the idea of a classless society – found fertile ground for their ideology amongst the seamstresses packed like sardines into sweatshops. But I wanted no part of a Jewish struggle. The place disgusted me. I was far more excited by another group of rabble-rousers: Mrs Pankhurst's militants. I went window smashing with the women.

They were notes about his earlier life. It was some sort of memoir! *Window smashing with the women!* Beck would like that. Or maybe not. *I was far more excited…* Barak was more horny bugger than pioneer feminist, that much Russ knew. But the father he remembered didn't put much store on personal reflection, even of the dramatic, titillating kind. Where were his field notes? And why would he write a memoir in the field? This blurring of the boundaries did not fit Russ's picture of his father, of the old man of science. It was too sentimental. On the topic of past digs he was effusive; but of his personal life he never spoke.

You didn't know him all that well? Christ, when was Toka's voice going to leave him alone? But the bloody voice had a point. Russ was so certain he was investigating a period from November 1963 to early 1964, so sure his father must have died within months of leaving Krugersdorp. But what had Toka said? *He disappeared from your life in 1963. That doesn't mean to say he disappeared from everyone else's lives too.* Those notebooks could have been written *later* than 1964. Impossible. Toka was just speculating. Barak would have come home. More likely the notebooks were begun *earlier*, prior to his departure. Russ couldn't recall seeing these books, but then four decades had intervened, and his father's study had always been so full of books, files, reference works, survey maps.

Russ's balls were still aching but worse was the vodka boring into his temples. He put down the notebook – the poorly-preserved Croxley – and sat up.

'Here, let me.' Rebecca moved behind him, propping herself against the pillows, and with his head leaning back against her chest, she massaged his throbbing head.

'I keep getting these flashbacks,' he said. Her fingertips seemed to be caressing his brain. 'It's like he's been out of my life for so long, and now he's come flooding back... especially stuff about the digs he took me on. Ouch! That was sore.'

'Shut up,' said Rebecca, but her tone was gentle and she softened her touch. She was quiet for a moment. 'What was Piltdown again?'

'Piltdown?'

'There're a bunch of references to Piltdown in the passages I've just read. Technical stuff, mostly. Comparing this jawbone with that one. That sort of thing. Teeth that should be this, but aren't. But he's not exactly dispassionate about it. Here, pass me that one.'

He handed her the good Croxley. She searched through some pages, muttering to herself in French. Haltingly, she translated the passage for him: '*They would never listen to me about Piltdown. They should have listened.* And then again, where's it… oh, there're some lines I can't make out. But here, it's only a bit later: *Lord, how could they have been so taken in? The* – let's see, what word would fit him? – *stubborn! The stubborn fools! And for such a long time? For their part in the Piltdown affair they all got knighted – except poor old Dawson. Had to distinguish between the scientific class and the amateurs, of course. Sir Arthur Keith, Sir Grafton Elliot Smith, Sir Arthur Smith Woodward. What a bloody joke!'*

'Funny,' said Russ. 'I was thinking of Piltdown earlier. He first told me the story when he was stitching this up.' He raised his scarred finger. 'Piltdown Man was the scientific fraud of the 20th Century, maybe of all time. It took about forty years to finally prove that it was a fake, although Barak was one of a small number of European scientists who dismissed it from the start. Someone concocted a fossil man by combining a modern human skull with an orang-utan jaw, chemically aged the bone to make it seem really ancient…'

'Sounds like an artist.'

'More like a con-artist.' He smiled at his joke. 'Anyhow, this faker buried his made-up fossil at Piltdown – that was around 1912, 1913, I think – in any case, just before the First World War. Then he organised to have the bones "discovered" in good old authentic fossil-finding style. It was supposedly the biggest find yet made. The science was only getting going and it was taken off track for more years than it had been around in the first place. For decades the Brits thought they'd found earliest man in their own backyard. That's what fossil hunting's really all about, you know. See who can find the earliest man. Barak was as obsessed as the rest of them. It was only in the fifties that Piltdown Man was finally proven to be a fake – by a South African, Joseph Weiner. Actually, he called himself *Veiner*, to try and hide the fact that he was a Jew.'

'Who planted the fake?'

'God knows. Lots of suspects, lots of theories…'

'They should've consulted Sherlock Holmes.'

'Ah yes, well, he was one of the suspects, as I recall.'

'Sherlock Holmes planted the Piltdown bones? That's fiction, sweetheart.'

'Not Holmes. His creator, Sir Arthur Conan Doyle.'

12

'HAH!' RUSS EXCLAIMED, pouring ice into a glass bucket. Darwin took leave of England, Gauguin of France, and Barak... Barak took leave of Krugersdorp. He sighed and shook his head.

Jelly Roll Morton's piano filled the dining room and Russ began to hum along. Morton's swing at slow tempos was just the thing to go with the muscle relaxant he'd taken for the pain in his back. He laughed – where did *that* sound come from? – then gasped as he bent to reach into the dining-room dresser for the liquor. Leaning over to look into people's eyes, despite the ergonomic arrangement of his chair and the patient's, had not helped him. Today, during a routine test, he'd picked up a possible occlusion to the central retinal artery of a patient's left eye, and arranged for an emergency consultation with an ophthalmic surgeon. The young man was in danger of losing vision in that eye.

Dali lumbered into the room after his rickety fashion, nails clattering on the wooden floor. Russ couldn't remember whether he had given him his heart medication.

He started humming again. The investigations were going well. He was, it suddenly struck him, assembling a team of professionals. Naidoo. Shaw. Even Toka now seemed to have taken up a position in his team of helpers, albeit as the Devil's Advocate. Someone should be making one of those awful reality shows, narrated by an American who would imbue his lines with a breathless urgency:

Professor Leila Naidoo is the country's top expert in mummy studies. Russell Codron picked up the phone and dialled. Would she be in town? Time was running out fast! If they didn't act soon, the mummies would disintegrate and they'd have no way of knowing what happened to Russell's father!

Well, as it turned out, Leila Naidoo wasn't in town but that didn't stop the Caped Mummy Crusader! She had already arranged with a trusted colleague for the transfer of the mummies to the Medical School at the University of Cape Town, she'd informed Russ earlier. It was due to take place tomorrow, and merely required Russ's written permission, which he lost no time in faxing to Captain Morkel at the State mortuary. Russ chose a white wine from the fridge and placed it in the wine cooler.

Professor Naidoo, cutting short her holiday in Malawi for this unique scientific opportunity, is booked on an early morning flight to Cape Town on Wednesday. By then the mummies will be x-rayed and ready to be examined! Brief dramatic pause from the American narrator. *In the meantime*, the narrator says in a cleverly timed narrative switch, *Dr Trevor Shaw, a young Englishman who has fast become one of the world's foremost palaeo-anthropologists, is due to arrive at the Codron house for dinner!*

Russ laughed again. Why was it that even one's own life seemed exciting on television? And ridiculous, of course. But he needed someone to examine Barak's fossils, those from the trunk as well as whatever was still sticking out of the cave wall. And it wouldn't hurt to have an expert from the University of Cape Town expedite the required permit. Russ knew of Shaw. The fossil hunter was forever popping up in the news for some discovery or other. Russ had made two calls to the University and was put through to him on the third.

Savannah had put her nose in the air when she heard who was coming for dinner. 'Some boring old scientist?'

she had said. 'Oh, Dad!' Luc appeared, as usual, to be incurious. But Russ was beginning to wonder. Maybe that bland expression *was* an expression after all. Maybe it was like silence, boundless in its possible meanings.

Rebecca had invited her agent who was down from Johannesburg. Ulrike, a former East German Olympic marathoner now in her late forties, had enlisted Rebecca as a client after seeing, and buying, one of a series of brass vagina sculptures that had so embarrassed Russ and prompted the only attempt he would ever make at censoring his wife's art. Beck saw these works, created in the months around Savannah's birth, as issuing forth her '*vagina dentata*' phase – and bit back at Russ with accusations of misogyny and double standards. 'You've never objected to Michelangelo's *David*. There's a penis in all its glory. Why should a sculpted vagina be seen differently? Or are you embarrassed because it's *my* vagina?' He'd had no reply and she had added, 'Pussy got your tongue, Russ?' Her playful smile took the edge out of her tone, but the cat had indeed got his tongue – and kept it long after the sculptures fetched a good price on the overseas art market.

His focus returned to Shaw. The scientist had been excavating a site up the east coast and – the American narrator's voice came back to him – *Russ had been lucky to catch him in town*. Shaw had laughed about the police's confusion surrounding the bone fragments and, after hearing that the bones were excavated by Barak Codron, had grown excited. 'I came across his work when I was writing my doctoral thesis. Your father wrote some brilliant papers which everyone thought were ridiculous at the time. Then he disappeared. In *Digging for Darwin* I called him the dark horse of palaeo-anthropology.'

'Sorry,' said Russ, '*Digging for Darwin*, is that your book? I don't know it. I've not followed the field of late.'

'Oh, well, it reached a pretty wide audience. I'll bring you a copy.'

Over the weekend, Russ had struggled to re-open the notebooks. There had been so little time. Beck was cloistered in her studio, leaving him to chauffeur Savannah around and look after Luc.

But who was he kidding? He would have found the time. His resistance to look had him by the throat. That first night with the notebooks, he'd joked with Beck about reading him a French bedside story, but it was no joke. He desired her company. He was afraid. And she was shut away with her sculpture. He was like Luc, needing someone to read this bedtime story to him. And he was gathering people around him to do just that.

Finally, he sat down with his father's notes. Although long passages were clearly readable, the poor state of some of the pages tipped his precarious mood, as if the fungus had sent its spores to break open inside his intellect, sending out its hyphae to soak up what life there was left in him. He could, he reasoned, begin with 'the Good Croxley' – his term for the most well-preserved of the books had become capitalised, along with 'the Bad Croxley', and the exercise book, which had become known to him, in a flash of irony, as 'the Mummy's Notebook' – but a very brief survey of the English sections of the three books suggested to him that Barak had written them in a particular order, which he noted down as:

1. *the Bad Croxley*
2. *the Good Croxley*
3. *the Mummy's Notebook*

The evidence for such an ordering was sparse – a few snippets of Barak's youth in the Bad Croxley, a mention of

Sterkfontein in the Good Croxley, and a story about a boy and his drumstick confirming the location of the cave in the Mummy's Notebook.

The chronology of Barak's notes, Russ would later discover, was more random than this or, at least, followed an order suggested not by historical sequence but rather by a need to bring together in a climax the revelations of his past and present. But the exercise of naming and ordering the notebooks had served a purpose, allowing Russ to feel he'd faced the task.

The doorbell rang. Russ hurried to receive his guest.

Shaw could have been a reincarnated Richard Burton setting out in search of the source of the Nile. Tall, clean-shaven, his wavy black hair pulled tightly into a pony tail, daring eyes reading Russ's face as if for the tell-tale shadow of a fossil piercing his cheek. He wore the dress of the young cutting-edge scientist-explorer: jeans, scuffed leather hiking boots, a suede jacket over his T-shirt, a canvas sling bag hanging from his shoulder.

This young Englishman is going to lead me to my old English father, Russ thought. Even Sav's going to be impressed with this bloke. He ushered Shaw into the lounge. 'Drink?'

'Thanks. Soda water.'

'With whiskey?'

'No, plain soda water. No ice.'

'Warm soda water?' Russ shook his head and went to pour.

'Break a leg,' said Russ. One of his father's injunctions was *never* to wish a fossil hunter good luck.

'I'd rather not,' said Shaw. Maybe this generation of fossil hunters wasn't superstitious.

'My parents were English, you know,' Russ said. 'Mother from Hampstead, father from the East End.'

'Opposite ends of the world.'

'Yes, well, they were opposites. In class, religion, age. She was a lot younger than him.'

'Will she be joining us?'

'Who?'

'Your mother?' Shaw swept a rogue strand of hair from his face.

'Rebecca's agent Ulrike will be here. Mom might join us if Ulrike holds one of her séances.'

Shaw smiled. 'Sorry.'

'Oh, don't worry,' said Russ, although Shaw didn't look in the slightest bit worried. 'She died a long time ago.' This was not going well. Where was Rebecca?

Shaw took a book from his bag. 'Here, this is for you.'

Russ opened *Digging for Darwin*. On the title page, Shaw had written:

> *To Russell, the son of a genius who dug his ideas from the earth.*

'Genius?' said Russ. 'He dug in the earth for over fifty years. Lots of animal fossils but the few hominids he found never rewrote the tree. Half a bloody century on his hands and knees.'

Shaw looked insulted. 'It's not so much *what* he found. It's what he *wrote* about those finds. He was the best fossil interpreter of his generation. And that's the amazing thing. There's no mention of him in the historical literature. In fact, right from early on his colleagues seem to make a point of *not* mentioning him. Hooton doesn't include him in *Up From The Ape* – but then he leaves Dart out as well. And Leakey leaves him out of *Adam's Ancestors* which was published much later, in 1934. But then Leakey also omitted any mention of the Taung Child. Your father shared Dart's earlier fate, but not his later recognition.' Shaw sipped his soda and nodded towards the book in Russ's hands. 'Turn to page 67.'

Russ flipped through the book to page 67.

> *Perhaps the greatest theoretician in the field since Darwin was an enigmatic figure who has been all but forgotten: Barak Codron. As a young man Codron studied at Oxford with Professor Clement Oldfield and, after graduating, worked under Sir Arthur Smith Woodward, Keeper of Geology at the British Museum of Natural History. While he is not credited with any great fossil finds, Codron's was a mind of genius. He anticipated almost all the current debates in the field. In a paper, published by Nature in 1933, called 'Evolution: A Continuous or Stepwise Process?', he hypothesised…*

Russ looked up. 'I remember his fight with *Nature's* editors. He felt they'd supported him and then run for the hills when the flack hit.' He knew the theory Barak had put forward, that evolution did not necessarily occur at a slow, steady pace, as Darwin had anticipated. Early ape-man might have hung out in the trees for millions of years and then, within a few hundred thousand, become bi-pedal simply because the forests disappeared.

Shaw smiled. 'You have to understand the context. What your father was suggesting was iconoclastic. He seemed to have made a career of debunking prevailing thought. He was against Piltdown Man from the start. For an Englishman, that was a bit like Copernicus telling the rest of the world that the Earth isn't at the centre of the universe.'

'Ah, but then he wasn't quite English enough, was he? He was a Sephardic Jew –'

'From the East End, yes. The same could be said about Raymond Dart, although not about the East End, of course. His crime was to come from the colonies. But if he hadn't been seen as an impulsive Australian upstart, the Taung child might have been accorded the recognition *it* deserved, instead of being dismissed as a young ape because it didn't fit with Piltdown Man.'

'My father took me to see Professor Dart a few times.' Russ took a sip of his drink. This was going much better. 'I'm not sure Barak liked him much but maybe he recognised a kindred spirit. Taking me along was an excuse to see him. You know, *the boy wants to see your fossils, Raymond, that all right with you?* I was only six or seven – no, it must have been later – but I was still in primary school.'

'*That* must have been interesting.'

'During one visit – I suppose I remember this because it was so frightening – he and my father were having a heated debate about something or other. Dart suddenly began to weep. Just like that. It was bloody disturbing. He had sparkling blue eyes, and he'd stammer when he got excited, but that time he started crying... He'd had a nervous breakdown a few years before.'

'Who had a nervous breakdown?' Rebecca was at the door, smiling, her hair wet from the shower.

'Ah, Trevor, this is my wife, Rebecca. Beck, Trevor Shaw.' He turned to their guest. 'Beck's always interested in nervous breakdowns. In fact, she's the Automobile Association of broken-down nerves. She thinks either she can fix them or if she can't, at least she can sculpt them.'

'Hello, Trevor. I see you're being introduced to Russell's caustic sense of humour.'

Russ watched Rebecca extend her hand and Shaw draw her towards him for a kiss on both cheeks. He could imagine the effect Shaw's smile would have on a room full of *National*

Geographic sponsors, the women wanting to bed him and the men wanting to be him.

They went through to the family room where the children were watching television.

'This is the boring old scientist, Sav,' said Russ. 'Trevor – Savannah and Luc.'

'Savannah,' said Shaw, 'named in true fossil-hunting style.'

The teenager stared at the Englishman.

'Sav,' said Rebecca, 'it's rude to stare, sweetheart.'

'I'm not staring. I'm *appraising*.'

'That's fine,' said Shaw, 'I'm a scientist. We're used to being appraised.'

Ulrike arrived, her colourful caftan billowing about her body like an avant-garde circus tent. She can conduct her séance inside there, thought Russ. We can hold hands in a circle around her steroidal thighs and call up the dead. He had never liked Ulrike.

They seated themselves at the dining room table.

'Russell,' said Ulrike in her thick accent, smiling provocatively, 'you must tell me all about your father's mummy.' *She* had never liked *him*.

It was safe for Russ to ignore her. Beck had gone into the kitchen.

'Is dynamite still used?' he asked Shaw.

'I don't like to,' said Shaw.

'We used dynamite,' said Russ, 'not like Broom. We did it in a much more controlled way, if the brechia was particularly hard. My father was a dab hand at it.'

'*Sooo* exciting,' said Ulrike. 'Mummies, *mein Got!*'

'We'd plant very small charges around the perimeter of the find and blow the piece of rock from its surroundings, then take the whole thing home to the garage, pick away using dental picks and acid baths.'

'Drilling is more effective,' said Shaw.

'And a female mummy. *Sooo* romantic!'

'We couldn't have drilled – no generator. We did once light a fire around a very large rock and then in the early hours of the morning poured freezing cold water from a river over it. The rock cracked but in unpredictable ways.'

'Barak says there's something magnificent out there,' said Rebecca, coming in from the kitchen with a soup tureen in her hands.

'What?' said Russ. He had touched the fossil in the cave, knew it held promise. But Beck had said nothing about a reference to it in the notebooks. 'What does he say?'

'"The greatest find ever",' she said.

'Where? When? I thought you weren't reading any?'

'The school book. French bit.'

Shaw's intense explorer's face opened up. 'Greatest find?'

'He left some notebooks behind,' Russ said. 'Not field notes, though. More like notes for a memoir.'

'Does he say what it is?' said Gore, 'the *find*?'

'Not that I've been able to make out,' said Beck, passing Shaw a bowl of pumpkin soup. 'I haven't read that much yet.'

Luc, who had been sitting quietly, suddenly piped up, 'Mummia!' He was looking at Shaw.

'Mummia?' Ulrike repeated. This was her territory. Russ shot Luc a glance.

'It is Arabic for bitumen,' said Luc, his eyes darting from Trevor's face to the tablecloth and back. 'The people who went to Egypt thought the Egyptians were using it on the dead bodies. They saw them smearing a dark oil between the layers of mummy wrappings. But it was not bitumen. It was resin from the trees.'

'Jesus, Luc. Where did you learn that?' said Russ, knowing as soon as he opened his mouth that he wasn't going to get an answer.

'Vot a clever boy!' roared Ulrike.

Luc's stare returned to his plate. He hesitated a moment, then pushed his chair back from the table, stole an exchange of looks with his mother, and left the dining-room. Shaw gazed after him.

Russ sat at the table staring at the after-dinner clutter that awaited Beatrice's attention in the morning, the ribbed blue ampulla that held the salad oil, the pewter candlesticks, the dark sediment in the wine glasses. He drained the cold coffee from his cup. The guests had left, the children were in bed and Beck had returned to her studio.

He felt tired from having gone over the history of his father's disappearance, the years of waiting for his return, the decades of not knowing his fate, and the sudden flood of information since the find of the mummies. Russ could see Shaw mining the story for nuggets that might help him make sense of Barak's fossils. After dinner, Russ showed him the fragments. A cursory look was enough to convince Trevor that there were several pieces from the same skull, and when he left he was carrying them with him.

Russ promised to keep him updated on any significant revelations in the notebooks and Trevor promised to apply for a permit to excavate the cave. 'It won't be a problem,' he said. 'I know someone in the Department.' He grinned, almost apologetically. 'In this place, everyone knows someone. Or at least knows someone who knows someone.'

Now Russ brushed some crumbs off the tablecloth. *Mummia becomes mummy*, he thought. Words are like species, they evolve accidentally. It was foreigners who gave an accidental name to a sacred process, the belief of the ancient Egyptians in an afterlife, and the practice of preserving bodies required for that afterlife.

But aren't beliefs themselves the result of accidental evolution? Was anything not an accident?

Barak had an afterlife, Russ thought. Only not the kind the ancient Egyptians believed in. He lived on in Russ. It wasn't Barak who had needed his body. Russ had needed it. His mother had needed it. It had been impossible for the two of them to mourn without it.

13

RUSS PARKED HIS CAR AND entered the house. Luc was sitting at the dining-room table, reading a book. Russ said hello, was greeted with the boy's silence, and was going to go through to find Rebecca when he noticed what Luc was reading. It was one of Barak's notebooks – the Bad Croxley.

'Careful with that, Luc.'

The boy looked up. Russ couldn't place the expression on his face. It seemed to be out of his usual repertoire, as if he was beginning to view Russ as someone to be pitied. He returned his attention to the notebook.

Russ peered over Luc's shoulder. He could make out the faint French script of Barak's writing hand. Even before Luc began to read aloud, translating almost as fluently as his mother was able to, Russ felt inept, regretting having admonished him to be careful with the notebook. The boy's strange intellect seemed to hold the book with a greater respect than Russ himself would ever be able to muster.

'*I was a young man,*' Luc read, '*I wanted to… to be important. I was lucky. They did not like… people like me… at Oxford. My father had flour covering his beard and…*' He looked up. 'That stuff you make bread with?'

'Dough?'

'*Dough under his nails. On Rhodes, where he was… born, he was not Greek, he was not Turk. He went to London…*'

Luc broke off, unsure. Russ gripped the back of Luc's

chair. The cloistered voice of his son carrying his father's words swept over him.

'... *because they were poor. But the Christians said he was a Jewish thief. And his* Ash-ke-nazi *– Ashkenazi – brothers said he was a... spic, that the Sephardim were not Jews. He fitted nowhere and spent his life trying to fit somewhere.*'

Luc turned the page, hesitated, then inserted a bookmark and put the notebook down. The bookmark advertised an optometry conference Russ had attended three weeks before – had it *only* been three weeks, a time before this tearing of normality? A time before he would be sitting at a table having Luc read, no, *translate*, from a notebook written by his father?

'Wait,' said Russ, wanting to add, *read more*, but Luc, without looking at his father, had already got up from the table and was leaving the room. Russ followed the path of his delicate frame, an odd sensation of needing his son. How had things come to this? When Luc was a toddler, he would flap his hands, his fingers splayed out, his wrists pivoting furiously, his arms almost unnaturally still. It was this symptom that finally had them calling for help and, together with his facial tics and emotional rigidity, had the medical profession proffering a terrifying smorgasbord of diagnoses: Autism, Asperger's, Tourette's, FLK. They were familiar with the first three but not the last – 'FLK' – which they'd not been given formally but had overheard being muttered by an intern psychologist in the corridor of a clinic they had attended. When they enquired, the flustered but candid neophyte replied, 'It's a bit like the birdwatcher's LBJ – "little brown job". FLK is an unofficial catchall meaning "funny looking kid". I mean, Luc is a beautiful child, but unusual...' They never went back.

The intern's remark had galvanised Rebecca. 'Fuck it,' she said one morning after a sleepless night. 'Luc is Luc.

He is who he is.' She started seeing a psychoanalyst. To prepare a space in my mind for him, she told Russ. She went to conferences, studied the remedial therapies on offer, choosing the parts that she felt suited Luc, and discarding the rest. She turned her studio into an activity room for Luc, and for three years did not make a single piece of art, other than the primitive forms she and Luc worked on together. Beatrice, who'd had to bear the pain of her own children being raised by others far away in the Transkei, was already on board, having treated Luc matter-of-factly from the start. The make-up of his personality seemed of little concern to her. He was a child worthy of love, and anything he brought with him into the world was to be seen as a gift. Russ didn't understand her attitude. He wished he could idealise it, but his childhood had been steeped in his father's practical views of anthropology. Perhaps Beatrice simply felt that the gratitude of a family living together under one roof should overlook such small things as Asperger's Syndrome, or whatever it was that Luc actually had. In time, Savannah, too, joined the project, and Tante Julia as well. One day Russ came upon Luc in the company of all four of these nurturers, all of whom were laughing uproariously. Luc's peculiar hybrid giggle – a cross between a whimper and a joyous cry – seemed at home amongst the women's tears of happiness. Instead of evoking the wonder he knew he should feel, the scene made Russ utterly miserable. He could gain access to the joke as little as he could join the greater project. He had never felt such an outsider.

I am a son without a father, thought Russ, pressing his face against the mildewed cover of the Bad Croxley, *and a man who cannot father his son.*

He opened the Bad Croxley to the bookmarked page. The rest of that page had been swallowed up by the swirling blue ink of a weak sky. Russ wondered whether Luc would have read on if it had not, and decided, to his surprise, that he would have. He carefully teased apart the next two pages, stuck together at the edges. In small print just below the spiral binding, as if the words had bubbled out from the holes made rusty by the decaying wire binding, Barak had inserted a startling statement, in English, as if something was pressing at him, something that did not belong amongst the reminiscences and observations of his baker-father's lack of place, but had to be noted.

There are those who would claim that I committed a terrible crime. I have this to say in response to their judgement: look to the men who were about me, look to their actions and ask yourselves this: just who in damnation were the real pigs of the piece?

Pigs of the piece? Terrible crime? For a fleeting moment, before logic could show him the error of his conclusion – for one thing, the timing was all wrong – Russ's head thudded with the thought that the police and *Sunday Times* were right after all: Barak was a murderer of teenagers. No, he had to be talking about something else. The illegal selling of fossils? But even illegal fossil deals – despite Barak's protests, he could easily have sold off less valuable fossils, keeping the academically more interesting ones for himself – are too insignificant and shabby to warrant the descriptor 'terrible'. Barak seemed to be shifting the blame onto others, the *real* pigs of the piece. This crime, whatever it was, had at its heart a moral transgression that involved several others at whose feet Barak was laying the blame. His action – and he *was* owning up to an action – would be exonerated as a justified response. He was looking for atonement.

The script on the page, though, reverted to, or rather continued, the story of Barak's youth, before bleeding back into the page. And then, hidden between the warped pages as if to compensate for the loss of Barak's exposition of his 'terrible crime', Russ found two small photographs. Unlike the pages of the notebooks, the photographic paper had withstood the deleterious effects of exposure to moisture, and gave up their images without a fight. The first was a formal, sepia portrait: a young man, dressed in a suit, stands behind a handsome, full-cheeked woman with dark hair. She is seated. To her right are two boys, perhaps nine and twelve years old. To her left are two younger girls, of similar height, perhaps twins, or sisters born close to each other. The woman holds a toddler in her lap. The child's dark hair is framed from behind by her mother's white, or perhaps cream, lace bodice. The older of the two boys is staring into the camera, as if daring it to capture his soul. Could this be Barak as a boy with his family? The adult man – the father in the picture – certainly looked like he could be Barak's father.

The second photograph was taken at the beach in a much later era: Barak is in his early sixties. He poses in his bathing trunks, his hands on his hips, smiling a wild, enigmatic smile. The hair on his chest and legs comes out white against the dark photographic grain of his tanned skin. On a towel at his feet sits a woman with light hair and fine features, her legs curved beneath her. A shadow defines her cleavage. She is quite beautiful. She holds the hands of a baby boy as he stands one foot on the towel, one in the sand, scowling into the camera. This child, Russ knew, was himself.

The grainy photograph of his wildly smiling father took him back to the grainy sand of the beach where he found his mind's eye gazing at a row of brightly coloured bathing boxes: yellow, blue, red, green, all raised on stilts so as to accommodate the high tides, when the waves surge forward, sweeping water under the bathing boxes, leaving puddles behind in the cool, heavy sand as they withdraw. But in this image it is low tide, and children play in the gentle surf. Some boxes have people standing on the little landing, lounging over the railing. Umbrellas dot the beach. Adults suntan on deck chairs, chatting and eating roast chicken prepared by the women. Wicker picnic baskets lie scattered about. The mountains across the bay are turned blue-grey by the light, the deeper waters home to some of the biggest sharks ever seen.

This was Muizenberg, in Cape Town, a beach of Jews. They came from Johannesburg and the smaller towns – Springs, Worcester, Kimberley. At night they visited one another, or fell exhausted into bed, or on occasion went to the drive-in, the kids already in pyjamas, dressing-gowns and slippers, ready to be carried sleeping from car to bed. On Friday evening they packed into the shul where the men talked business, the women fashion and children, breaking off to intone Hebrew prayers. Barak didn't belong amongst those people, with his young upper-crust English wife. He never went anywhere near the synagogue, and he hated the other holidaymakers.

The photographs in hand, he went to find Beck in the studio. She was wearing jeans and a loose vest. There was a time when he would have had to stifle an impulse to grab hold of her vest and pull it over her head. Or not stifle the impulse. But that was a time when he could let her have what was inside him, and he seemed to have lost the desire to make love as quickly as he had found it on Friday night.

Beck's concentration was broken. She raised her eyebrows in an irritated arc. He had come to show her the photographs, but grew wary in the face of her annoyance, and instead he said, 'D'you remember about tomorrow morning? Professor Naidoo?'

14

'HERE, DEARS,' SAID Professor Naidoo, proffering pairs of surgical masks, caps and gloves as if they were on a plate of sweetmeats. 'Put these on.' A diminutive woman in her early sixties, Professor Leila Naidoo filled out her white coat like a jolly grandmother would her kitchen apron.

'I don't care about the dust,' said Russ. 'Nor the smell.' The odour given off by the mummies – now wrapped in acid-free paper and lying on dissection tables in the University of Cape Town's Anatomy Building – was musty, tinged by an acrid sweetness, the lingering scent of their erstwhile mortuary companions.

Professor Naidoo shook her head in a gentle reproach. Her soft cheeks gave way to small lips that seemed to pucker up permanently in a friendly kiss. 'I'm not concerned for you, my dear, although ancient detritus can be rather aggravating. It's the mummies I'm worried about. They've been treated atrociously up until now and they're not faring well. Even the smallest amount of moisture in your breath can add to the decomposition process.'

'Oh,' said Russ, reaching for the mask. 'I'm sorry.'

When they had spoken on the phone, Professor Naidoo had been a little surprised at, but then happily agreed to, Russ's request to be present during the examination. Rebecca was more than willing to accompany him, despite the pressure to finish the final sculpture. Russ didn't doubt her desire to support him, but more compelling for her, he knew, was the opportunity to accumulate knowledge about the human body for use in her own work. They had spoken little in the car on the way here, he breaking the silence only to double-check which exit he was to take from the Eastern Boulevard to the Medical Campus. For the second time, she assured him it was the Groote Schuur Hospital turnoff. From there they had travelled the short distance to the Main Road, then turned up again towards the spire of Devil's Peak, and been lucky to find a parking space not far from the Anatomy Building, where they met Professor Naidoo in the foyer.

'My dears, you have no idea what this means,' said Professor Naidoo, now securing a mask over her face. 'Home-grown mummies in South Africa! My word. What odds they have overcome. I have examined many mummies overseas but only a handful exist in South Africa and, I think I told you Mr Codron, only two of them were home-grown. The rest are Egyptian. It's very exciting.' Her glasses reflected bright images of the fluorescent operating lights above the room's dissecting tables. She must have seen something in their eyes because she soon added, 'Oh, there I go again. I mustn't forget, this is a shock for you.'

'Oh, no,' said Beck, 'please don't let that stop your enthusiasm. Really. It's so nice to be with someone who is passionate about their work. And we're here to learn from you, so don't hold back. Right, Russ?'

'Yes, yes, of course,' said Russ.

'My colleagues have prepared x-rays for us,' she said. 'We'll want to do other investigations, of course – CAT scans, histology, dental studies.'

Now she pulled the x-rays from their oversized envelope and placed them on the light boxes against the wall. The head and upper chest area of both mummies appeared in shades of ghostly grey and black. The woman's open mouth and the shadowy, large flat sacs of what were once enormous breasts made it easy to tell the sets apart.

'Hmmm. They've only done the upper bodies and the heads. Never mind. We'll get the rest done later.'

From her coat pocket, Professor Naidoo produced a collapsible pointer – it looked like it once did service as a car aerial – and with a deft little tug extended it. With their backs to the mummies, Russ had the eerie sensation that Barak and the woman might at any moment brush their wrappings aside, raise themselves into a sitting position, and peer over the shoulders of the live human beings at the x-rays.

'Let's see what we've got. The internal organs are rather well preserved. Look at this.' Inside Barak's skull lay a discernible pouch. 'He was reclining after he died, but at a slight angle – certainly not flat on his back. You can see by the way the brain has settled in the base of the skull after it dried out. Remarkable.'

She spent some time pointing out the different organs, and the small and large fractures in the bones. Eventually she turned to the bodies, carefully unwrapping them, folding back the layers of paper, petals opening up to reveal their precious innards. Barak's penis was hiding in the shadows, retracted into a carapace of dirty matted pubic hair. Or maybe it wasn't there at all. His ribs stood out above his hollow belly like the separated planks of a sunken galleon. Professor Naidoo leaned over him.

'Moths,' she said resignedly, pulling a dead one out of a cavity in the hollow formed by one of Barak's clavicles. 'It's one thing to find a mummy, but to keep it intact is something else altogether. Moisture, fungi, microbes, vermin… it's open season once the body emerges from whatever conditions had preserved it in the first place.'

'We'd love to know –'

'Fuck!' The Professor shook her head angrily.

The sudden outburst from their grandmotherly guide had Beck and Russ avoiding each other's gaze for fear their surprise might dissolve into a fit of giggles.

'Look how clean this break is! There's no grime on the exposed bone. And this one!' The physical anthropologist's right hand hovered over the body as she glanced back at the x-rays, locating the fractures one by one. 'And here!' Barak's right arm was attached by what looked like a twisted strand of dark leather. 'Ah, those stupid bloody policemen. These have all been sustained *since* the bodies were discovered.'

She hung her head quietly, breathing deeply. Then she looked up, a beatific smile on her face, and went on with her examination, her hands – even when they were still they radiated energy – poised over Barak as if she were massaging him.

'How interesting... see the crease mark here on the top of the male's head?' Beck and Russ moved in closer. 'It's from the knot of some material tied around the head. You can even make out the lines of the material coming down either side of the cranium. As the body begins to decompose, gases build up, the tissues expand and this causes bloating. So the head swells up and the strap digs into the scalp. Then when the corpse dries out, the pressure decreases, the bloating subsides, the strap slackens, leaving this crease here. I've seen it before, on bodies that have been purposefully embalmed. The chin strap is used to prevent what we call "mummy gape" – it's the typical yawning mouth that you can see on the female here.'

'But nobody mummified them,' Russ said.

'Yes,' she nodded her head. 'Very curious.'

'Is it possible that he knew his body would be preserved and didn't want to have a gape?' Rebecca's eyes had her sculptor's look, an agitation that mirrored the Professor's hands, ready to explode into action and manipulate some part of the mummy to fit a shape in her mind.

'I doubt it,' said Russ, 'his vanity was of the intellectual kind. It didn't concern his appearance. Maybe he just had a toothache – an abscess or something – and the pressure of the bandage relieved it. In any case, how would he have known that his body would be preserved?'

The Professor smiled. 'Oh, my dears, these bodies can tell us a great deal. Perhaps even about their last moments on this earth. But we can only infer the abstract from the physical, and so we must patiently gather the evidence.'

'But will you be able to work out what mummified them?' said Russ. 'And *when*?'

'Mummification, especially accidental mummification, is an intriguing process.' The Professor's words came more slowly now, a practised spiel that allowed her to continue her examination of the furrows left by the chin strap around Barak's head. 'It's not easy for a body to get preserved naturally, *especially* in a coastal cave environment such as the one in which these were found. Insects are quick to arrive and lay their eggs, and when they hatch, hungry maggots devour the flesh. Bacteria start the putrefying process inside the body. Within twenty-four hours or so, your body will turn a greenish colour. Gases form, the body swells up.' She stopped what she was doing and straightened up. Her words seemed to have excited her into giving them her full attention. 'Within a few weeks, the skin will split open. The bloating exerts pressure on the lungs, forcing the blood there out of the nearest orifice – the mouth. That's why, in the old days, people in search of vampires who dug up bodies thought they'd found the evidence they were looking for – blood around the mouth, as if the dead were rising from their graves and sinking their teeth into the living. Science has a way of taking the romance out of life, doesn't it?' She chuckled.

'In all but the rarest of cases, the internal organs will eventually dissolve, as will all the flesh. That leaves the skeleton. Now your father would have been interested in the next process – how a skeleton becomes fossilised. But we want to know how his body avoided reduction to its skeletal form. Caves are good places for mummification, although I've never heard of a body being preserved in conditions such as in the cave where they were found. If it was deep enough underground, I suppose the temperature might have remained consistently cool, which would have helped – but in that part of the world they would certainly not have been frozen, which of course would be the simplest way to preserve a body. There are cave mummies that have been preserved by dryness, along with cool temperatures and salt present in minerals in the rock and soil, which helps to suck the moisture out. The body is made up mostly of moisture. I'm sure you know this. Desiccate it and you may preserve it.'

'I'd been thinking of him as a prune,' said Russ.

Professor Naidoo gave him a searching, concerned look. 'Yes, just so. You start with a plum and you end with a prune. There have been many bodies that were dried in the sun, or placed on platforms and had fires lit under them to smoke them. Some Australian aboriginals preserved their special dead for a time by doing this. But it seems no one took that kind of trouble over your father. You'd think the water would seep into the cave and the micro-organisms and insects would have a field day.'

'That's pretty much what we thought,' said Russ.

'Although not quite in that kind of detail,' said Beck.

'Are there other minerals or chemicals that might have been present in the cave?' asked Russ.

'There have been instances of all sorts of chemicals doing the job. In the fens in north-western Europe, bodies were preserved by lime. Three thousand years ago, the

Danes used to bury their dead in hollowed-out oak trees. When water seeped into these natural coffins it created a solution of tannic acid. That's used to make leather. Those bodies were turned into leather people. Sometimes you can tell the cause of preservation from the look of the mummy. Bog bodies have dark brown skin, the same colour as the peat, which contains tannin, and their faces aren't shrivelled like you'd find with Egyptian mummies. The skin and muscles of Egyptian mummies are usually brittle because of the resin used in the embalming process. This resin, by the way, is how mummies got their name.'

'Yes,' said Russ. 'Mummia. Luc – our son – taught us that.'

'Quite. Bog mummies are pliable because they've been in a water bath for a few thousand years. Often the bones have been dissolved by acid, leaving behind a bag of skin. These two are brittle, as you can see by this.' She pointed to Barak's tibia – the trigger for her earlier anger – the bone snapped in a neat break.

'But I'm afraid, looking at these mummies now, I can't come to a definitive conclusion as to the cause of mummification. We will need to do further testing. Gas chromatography might help. The same goes for a date of death. I'll remove some tissue samples and send them for analysis.'

'You' had become 'we'; Professor Naidoo seemed to have merged with the Codrons, and they with her, standing and working alongside her, Beck slightly taller, Russ a good head taller still, but seeing through her eyes as she kept up a commentary. The mummies were patient, and time was distorted. Professor Naidoo made measurements, took photographs, and they weighed the bodies – in itself no easy task, entailing as it did the painstakingly careful insertion of a long metal tray beneath each body, and then a weighing of tray and body. They weighed pitifully little. 'Most of our body weight comes from the fluids inside our bodies,' she said.

Finally, like the sublime dramatist Russ and Beck had come to appreciate their new teacher to be, Professor Naidoo pulled a magic wand from her box of tricks: an endoscope. She inserted the instrument's slender tube into an existing hole in the woman's chest cavity, below the sternum and in between the two sacs that were her breasts, sagged to either side of her ribcage. A surprisingly vivid image from the endoscope's tiny camera was thrown up onto a flat-screen monitor above their heads.

'My God, now this is interesting,' said Professor Naidoo, going back to the light box to re-insert the woman's x-rays, which she had some time before taken down. 'Yes, I thought I hadn't seen any sign. It hasn't shown up here because they didn't x-ray that far down. Silly me. I should have noticed that her lower abdomen is not as concave as it should be. We will get it CAT scanned for a clearer picture, but there's little doubt. What we're viewing now is the remains of her uterus. Can you see what those are, those five tiny objects, and the curve here, leading to this. Those are five little toes, and this is the heel. This woman was in the throes of childbirth when she died. The infant is still here, inside her.'

15

I HAVE SPENT OVER HALF A century studying the handiwork of the process others call by one of many names: God, Allah, Yahweh, Brahma. The list is endless but each name on it speaks of the same thing, of the creation of Modern Man. When finally I knew where to look it was all too obvious. This is where they – the people to whom all living humans owe their ancestry – were waiting to be exhumed: Adam and Eve.

The words were flowing. It was the Good Croxley.

Russ was adapting. He had to ignore the inverted French script running in the space between each line of English. He pictured the old man sitting outside the cave in his singlet and shorts, fountain pen in hand, notebook on his bare thigh. The sea is before him. It is a new, pristine Croxley shorthand notebook. Barak flips the cover, the red-crested Lion somersaults backwards. He steadies the book in his left hand, his fingers clamped around the edge, his earth-encrusted cuticles at variance with the white, lined paper. He begins his entry. *I have spent over half a century...*

There followed several pages of argument, some of which was illegible, the decay and the interference of the capsized French proving too much. But Russ knew enough to fill in the missing words. *Africa is the world's greatest primate evolutionary hothouse,* Barak wrote, laying out his theory of evolution, travelling in time from the great Miocene rain forests of 15 million years ago to the climate change that occurred 10 million years later, triggering a retreat of those abundant forests before advancing grassland, and with it the need for at least some of Africa's primate species to evolve. *The ability to scurry across the savannah is rewarded with survival, and leads to bipedalism; bipedalism frees the hands; freed hands make better tools; better tools provide better nutrition. The brain grows in size.*

This, Russ knew, was all about the transitional species between the apes and the Homo line. But Barak's search was for the first ancestors of Modern Man. He was looking for that turning point that signals the *very beginning* of humanity as we know it. He was looking for the first human parents, lovers, artists, fighters.

Barak was, according to so many of his colleagues, like an idiot child playing hide-and-seek: while everyone knew the hider was in the front garden, Barak Codron was the lone child searching in the back yard. Prevailing thought had it that our ancestors became modern humans in the new world of Europe and Asia. It was here that God chose to grow the Garden of Eden, not Africa, that primitive place of the ape. Barak was having none of it. He was looking for it in Africa, in that great continent's southernmost tip, the furthest feasible place from Eurasia.

When the theorist is a man who believes his own race to be at the pinnacle of evolution, there is even more cause for doubt. The European-Asian theory fits too well with jingoist White men desiring a more 'cultured' birthplace for ourselves. It is Piltdown all over again. They cannot imagine Adam as a primitive black man from Africa.

The presence of the Neanderthals in Europe and erectus in Asia is proof of a first wave of migration out of Africa but there is no proof that those hominids evolved into modern Homo sapiens. *It is just as likely that* Homo sapiens *evolved in Africa and that a second wave of migration into Europe and Asia saw these modern men competing with more ancient* Homo *lines (including the Neanderthals) for resources, a conflict which eventually led to these less-evolved competitor species' extinction. I can hear the guffaws of my colleagues. Go on, laugh all you want. It is as likely a hypothesis as any upon which you readily stake your dearly-held reputations.*

Jesus, thought Russ. I've heard this second wave theory before but not from Barak. Surely Trevor would have written about it in *Digging for Darwin*? He found the book, paged to the index, located what he was looking for. During the 1980s geneticists at the University of California devised a model to measure the rate that a particular kind of genetic material – mitochondrial DNA – which is inherited only through the female line, mutates over time. They then found that current populations in Africa show greater variation than any other population on earth, proving that Africans have inhabited their continent significantly longer than any European, American or Asian has inhabited theirs. Ergo, modern humans evolved in Africa. Their data led the geneticists to a further conclusion: the entire population of the world is derived from a small group of physically modern *Homo sapiens* who lived in Africa between 100,000 and 200,000 years ago. Even more startling was the implication that we are all the descendants of a single female within that group. Had Barak intuited a theory geneticists were proving twenty years later? Russ paged back through the Good Croxley and found the part he was looking for; it was a reference to the *Nature* article Shaw had cited.

I knew that Darwin was wrong about the consistency of the evolutionary process. There were spurts, and the spurts were controlled by the species' environment, by climate, and by predator and competitor species. I had to find the place where the coalescing of these four factors provided the spurt for the beginnings of modern Homo. *I might have come to it sooner, had my colleagues taken my correspondence more seriously. Obtuse little men! But in the end, those two years of concentrated, uninterrupted study showed it to me. The logic is ineluctable.*

Barak had spent the two years in his study poring over maps and data he had elicited from archaeologists, palaeontologists, geologists, geophysicists, biologists, climatologists – Christ, just about every kind of *blah-blah*-ist from California to China. Russ bit his lower lip as the thought struck him: if the answer had been different, he might not have lost his father. *Fuck.*

Where did I begin this quest? It was this: what conditions would lead to the evolution of Homo sapiens? *Something would need to spur an increase in brain size. Random mutation? Natural selection? Possibly. But what helps us grow strong? Food! I am the son of a Jewish mother and a father who baked for a livelihood. Surely I should know the importance of nutrition? But exactly which nutritional element were we talking about here? The answer can only be PROTEIN.*

The competition for meat in the forests or the open plains is high – and Australopithecus *or* Homo habilis – *if we accept Leakey and Tobias's very recent 'Handy Man' taxon – was no match for the big carnivores. There is one place where the carnivores would not compete with a clever little near-man: the sea! Big-brained modern* Homo *evolved because he was eating protein-rich marine life! Fish!*

And what magical place would force our ancestors to make sea creatures his staple? The answer is again obvious: where he is trapped by geography on the shoreline and where the plant life offers a miserable alternative.

After looking at dozens of regions, I kept coming back to one that might have been home to a little hominid group that, with the expansion of the deserts in the interior of the country, had become trapped along a shoreline whose plant life was nutritionally poor. It is a bleak hothouse but by jiminy it is that very bleakness that forces our little group of archaics to turn towards the generous sea. They roam the shoreline, scavenging, digging, harpooning, coming away with mussels, scallops, crabs, beached seals! Keep eating those for thousands of years and see how your brain size fills out! I had to go there, my theory told me, along the rocky shores of the Western Cape, to discover the Garden of Eden.

16

I⟟ WAS FOUR DAYS SINCE meeting Trevor Shaw, and Russ hadn't heard from him. He dialled the fossil hunter's work number, only to be told by the secretary of the Department of Anthropology that Dr Shaw was away, and not contactable.

'No cell coverage,' she said helpfully.

Russ was curious about the fossil pieces he had handed over to Shaw but in the middle of conducting an eye test it suddenly struck him that he was curiously not as curious as he should have been. After all, those fragments could be Barak's claim to the 'greatest find ever'.

And then there was the matter of the translations. On Monday Beck had given the Mummy's Notebook to Tante Julia – and she had barely started on the French passages in either of the Croxleys. Russ had felt no urgency to hurry them. He was still struggling through the English sections, drained by reading his father's words, of hearing the old man's voice, of peeping through his own almost-closed hands. The cave was in his head, crowding out everything else.

His need to return was becoming more urgent by the day, and Shaw's promise to procure a permit was the key. Russ was, after all, his father's son. The tactile lure of the cave had colonised his mind. For one last time he could be the child at the side of the father as the secrets of the past were revealed. But even this explanation did not satisfy him. There was something else, he finally decided, and it had to do with a feeling that *he* was urgently needed and unless he got there soon, all would be lost.

Barbara's interruptions – 'Russell, Mr Richards is here for his fitting' – became unbearable. Why had he consented to Anthea going off to that conference? A young man wanted a pair of sports glasses made up. Russ had recently received a new range from an Australian company. He used the lensometer to read the script off the patient's old lenses but the Snellen test indicated a need for an adjustment. He took refraction measurements and tested the young man's peripheral vision. The entire process must have taken twenty minutes but at the end of it Russ felt as though he'd awoken from a dream, and wasn't sure whether he'd finished examining the patient's eyes or was about to begin. Looking down at his notes, he found the measurements were all there. But were they accurate?

A woman presented with severe pain – her one-year-old daughter's sharp little fingernail had caught her in the eye. After dilating her pupil, a slit lamp examination confirmed his initial diagnosis of a corneal abrasion. The little girl's fingernail had scratched away the thin sheet of protective cells, exposing the sensitive corneal nerves. It was a common enough injury, for which he managed to harness some compassion, remembering his own searing pain when Savannah had done the same thing to him fifteen or so years ago. In his work he was rarely presented with medical emergencies – most people went to their GP, or straight to hospital or to a specialist. But it was as if the universe was conspiring to focus his attention on the frailty of the human body. He kept his composure, too, with an elderly Jewish man whose sudden, painless loss of vision in his right eye suggested a central retinal artery occlusion. There was no way of telling what might have caused it – it could have been atherosclerosis, an embolism, inflammation or a number of other causes – and the chances were that the patient would suffer a permanent loss of vision in that eye unless the blood flow could be restored within the retinal vessels, and very soon.

'When did you first notice this?' Russ asked.

'On Friday,' said the elderly man.

'You mean, today?'

'No. Friday last week.'

Russ was incredulous. 'You've been blind in that eye for *one week* and you never came for treatment?'

The old man shook his head. 'I thought it would get better.'

How the fuck could anyone be so stupid? Russ organised an emergency referral to an ophthalmologist and saw the man out of the examination room, half-expecting to see a middle-aged daughter or son ready to receive him. There was no one. 'I came by taxi,' the patient explained. Two of his children lived in London, the other in Hong Kong. His wife had passed away last year. Russ asked Barbara to phone the taxi service, and breathed in deeply as the man shuffled towards a chair.

Jesus, poor old Raymond Dart had to wait decades – and the discovery of adult australopithecines by Robert Broom – for Sir Arthur Keith to issue his gracious apology and, along with it, a final vindication of his claims for the Taung Child. And he, Russell Codron, optometrist of Sea Point, could not wait a few days for Shaw?

Russ's precarious hold on his emotions slipped, finally, with a well-dressed young woman whose response to every frame he showed her was to exclaim indignantly, 'Shit, that's expensive.' He could see she had spent double the amount on her shoes. There was nothing new in this for him. He understood that for some people purchasing spectacles was a grudge buy. They considered the need for glasses a weakness and having to dish out money to rectify a weakness was adding insult to injury. He usually responded by showing the person his cheaper range. Often, their impulse to protest satisfied, they would return to the more expensive frames. Today he had no patience for the process, and to this woman he said, 'I'll bet your shoes cost twice as much.'

'So what!' she said, catching Barbara's eye as she walked past the display cases of frames. 'Shoes are different.'

'Damn fucking right they're different,' said Russ. 'They're far less important than your eyes.'

Barbara appeared suddenly at his side, taking the young woman's arm and turning her to face a mirror.

'People see your face first,' said Barbara. 'And you've got the kind of face that can carry a stunning pair of glasses.'

The customer's face was in no state to carry anything other than a reddening expression of disbelief and umbrage. Bugger this, thought Russ, but smiled sheepishly at Barbara. Waiting for Shaw and the permit was costing him too much. He should go to the cave. But to go alone? The same apprehension that gripped him as a child standing at the sorting table, petrified he would throw one of Adam's ribs into the bin, now chilled him.

'We hardly ever find ribs,' Barak once explained. 'They're too fragile, too easily chewed to pulp by a scavenger.' No spare ribs on the palaeo-anthropology menu.

Russ left the customer, who had entered into league with an equally angry Barbara, and went into the back room, a cramped little alcove that housed a sink, some yellowing cupboards and a microwave mounted at eye level. He caught sight of his broad face, a copper-brown on the tinted glass of the oven's door. He examined his reflection, turning his head one way, then another, trying to catch a view of his profile, of a forehead that slanted back, of bone that protruded above his eye sockets.

'Eyebrow ridges,' he mumbled. 'Sloping forehead, not much room for a big brain: 1300, maybe 1400 cc. Christ.'

He walked out, past the customer, who had – surprise, surprise – been drawn back to the expensive range he had first shown her. Barbara glared at him. Fuck her, she can deal with it.

He left work and drove home. His cell phone rang.

'You called,' said Shaw.

'You've been away,' said Russ, sitting down at the dining room table in front of the two Croxleys and *Digging for Darwin*, fidgeting with them until they were lined up to form a neat pile.

'My dig. Klasies River. It's a promising site.'

'And my father's cave isn't?'

'Of course it is. If your father says he's found something big, I trust his judgment. But there is the Defence Force to contend with. I've applied for a permit but we don't yet have permission to excavate. You've waited years to find out about him, what's another few weeks?'

With a sense of déjà vu about this conversation – he had repressed the insight it had brought earlier in the day when he'd had the debate with himself – Russ found himself picking up the other role.

'What if vandals get into the cave?' he said. Shaw was a fossil hunter. He of all people should understand the dreadful stretching of time waiting to go into the field. It didn't matter that the fossils had been in the earth for thousands of years, there was always that feeling, *if I delay, they'll be gone* – or worse, *someone else will get to them first*. The coloured boys found the cave, why shouldn't others? Whatever else Barak left behind would disappear forever.

'It's unlikely,' said Shaw. 'If you're going to search for fossils, you're going to have to learn to be patient.'

Russ's voice was that of a splenetic teenager. 'You don't understand.'

'But I think I do,' said Shaw, and fell silent. Russ said nothing. Eventually Shaw spoke. 'When I was a boy I had a tortoise that disappeared. His name was Eugène, after —'

'Dubois.'

'Yes, that's right. Every day I'd put food out for old Eugène in his usual place. But I never went to look for him. The food just went rotten.'

'I, well, I don't know if that's the same thing —'

'I mean about the waiting,' said Shaw. 'I felt like I was doing something for the tortoise, but I wasn't really doing anything.'

'So what happened to the tortoise?'

'I found him a few weeks later. He'd fallen into a ditch and couldn't get himself upright again.'

'It's not the same thing,' said Russ. 'You could've gone to look for your tortoise.' The fully-laden Ford had gone, Barak had gone, his Shona helpers had gone, as if a dust devil had picked them all up and hurtled them across the veld, over the hills of the Western Transvaal, somewhere to the south. The tip of Africa was a big place. Where was he, a thirteen-year-old boy, to look?

'Yes, I could've,' said Shaw. 'But I was waiting for *him* to return to *me*. And weren't you doing the same thing? Isn't that what you told me the other night? You waited all that time after your father disappeared, but you never really tried to discover what happened to him, did you?' Russ was about to object but Shaw anticipated him. 'Even when you were old enough to do it.'

Russ's eyes were fixed unseeingly on the floor, his face grown ashen. Shaw had conjured up an accusing ghost, Barak come in out of a sandstorm and standing in the doorway, looking gaunt. Shaw was right. Russ and his mother had sat back passively, leaving the police to make their obligatory enquiries.

And suddenly Russ knew why it was that he had never properly conducted his own search, that deep inside his thirteen-year-old being Russ had *known* – rightly or wrongly – that Barak had chosen to go away and not come home, that Barak was too big, too strong ever to fall foul of a leopard, or an avalanche, and that Russ's rehearsal of the various tragedies that had befallen his father were merely bricks in the wall of his own denial. Barak had abandoned him.

17

IN THE PLACE OF HIS OWN family history, Barak spoke of the great men of his field as if they were far-flung relatives. Darwin was a great-grandfatherly sage, Raymond Dart a clever cousin considered by the family to be a little bonkers, and Sir Arthur Keith a haughty great-uncle who felt morally justified in stealing the family inheritance. Eugène Dubois, the young Dutchman whose radical thinking led him to make the groundbreaking *erectus* finds in Java in the early 1890s, could have been Barak's twin brother, there to be teased affectionately, a fellow spirit, misunderstood and eventually at war with the rest of the family.

In the evening of their first day in the Krugersdorp house, a tired father and son sat on the stoep, Russ playing with Barak's hand, twirling his wedding ring around his cracked, leathery finger. The day had been hot as hell, with no afternoon thunderstorm for relief. Russ was six years old, and had chased about for hours trying to pick up boxes too heavy for him.

'Tell me a story about old Dubois,' said Russ, pronouncing the Dutchman's name 'Dew Boy', which was how he had heard it. He knew about Java Man, that Dew Boy thought he'd found the missing link but that he'd been wrongly disabused by Sir Arthur Keith, and that Dew Boy had taken to hiding his fossils under the floorboards of his dining room.

'Be a good fellow,' said Barak, 'and fetch a chocolate and I'll tell you the story of how Dubois ended his days.'

Russ's official designation – ordained by Barak – was the *Keeper of the Chocolate Cupboard*. Earlier that day he had gone into the kitchen where his mother was cleaning and had told her, 'Ma, this drawer is going to be the Chocolate Cupboard.' She had looked up from her feverish business, wiped the back of her hand across her forehead, and nodded wistfully.

She was still in the kitchen, preparing dinner, when he ran in, opened the 'Chocolate Cupboard', grabbed the only item there, and ran back to his father.

'Ah, John Cadbury's! Good choice, my lad. Remember to suck it, now.' Barak took his time opening the wrapping and handing Russ a piece. He put one in his own mouth, making a show of swishing it around before swallowing it. The boy could hardly contain his impatience.

'Come on, Daddy, tell me about Dew Boy!'

Barak cleared his throat. 'I have it on good authority that Dubois's days ended rather interestingly.' A dog, a neighbourhood mutt, clambered onto the stoep and took to licking at the boy's chocolaty fingers. 'My source, a scientist of great standing – I will not mention his name – asked me one day whether I'd heard the latest about Eugène Dubois. I said no, I hadn't. He said that Dubois had returned to Java where he'd gone to live in the jungle with an orang-utan.'

Barak paused for effect, peered into his son's eyes. 'Male or female? I asked. "*Female*, of course!" said the scientist, "there's nothing queer about old Dubois!"'

The boy laughed because his father was laughing, and maybe because he thought that a man living in a jungle with a great red ape was a very funny thing.

The Good Croxley wasn't on the dining room table where he was sure he had left it. He searched the house, the rhythm of his heart building to that of a drum roll, the frantic heart inside a parent racing up and down a beach in search of a lost toddler. *Jesus, Barak, where are you?*

There were the children's rooms. The mess in Savannah's would itself need excavating but there was little chance the notebook would be there. Luc's room was always tidy, and the more likely option. The order here was of Beck's design: opaque plastic containers of various sizes each bore a label – 'puzzles', 'Lego', 'computer games'. The book shelves were categorised – 'classics', 'fantasy', 'science', 'humour' – so that Luc wouldn't have to feel overwhelmed by a chaotic array of stimuli. The screen saver on his computer, the only disturbance he seemed to tolerate here, sent effigies of dead physicists into the room. The one item out of place was the Good Croxley lying on the bed.

Russ picked up the notebook and went to the kitchen to make tea. He took his cup to Rebecca's studio, and rapped his knuckles against the closed door. He imagined her inside, her fingers working slavishly on the last head's features, rolling a small pellet of clay between finger and thumb, applying it to the head, smearing it with the ball of a thumb into the contours of the face, her hands moving quickly, the pellet merging completely with the face, lifting a cheekbone or defining the nose. He could hear her moving about inside. There was no answer to his knock. Obedient to her wish for privacy, he turned on his heel, thought better of leaving altogether, and sat down in the passageway just outside the door. If he couldn't be inside, he would wait for her here.

It had been a trying weekend. When he wasn't talking about a return to the cave, his uncharacteristic volubility turned to something else he'd been unable to rid himself of: the image of those five little toes.

'Just because she was giving birth, and they were found together, doesn't mean the baby was his,' he told Beck over breakfast that morning. 'There could be a dozen other, more plausible explanations. She was a large woman. He might not even have known she was pregnant. Maybe she was local, and brought him food when the accident happened.'

'And she just happened to have a trunk load of red polka-dot dresses with her,' was Rebecca's comeback, her right eyebrow raised dramatically. 'Russell, you're going to drive yourself to distraction. You're going to have to take this a little more calmly. *Breathe.*' If she got to hear that he had sworn at a patient on Friday, she would put this a lot more strongly. How long would it be before a colonic spasm urged Barbara to inform on him?

But she hadn't understood. If the baby was Barak's it meant that he was busy starting another family at a time when he should have been fathering Russ. After the discovery of the mummy's pregnancy, he had asked Professor Naidoo to take tissue samples for a DNA test. He needed to know.

'Do you know,' said Beck – she was reading the arts section of the *Sunday Independent* – 'that Munch painted *The Scream* after he studied some mummies? There was something about the woman's face that kept reminding me of the painting, and so I looked it up. That horrible, yawning mouth in *The Scream* is actually a mummy's gaping jaw. The very moisture of life is being sucked out of that mouth. I thought I understood its power. Now I know I hadn't.'

'You know what really gets to me?' The *Sunday Times* lay next to Russ. He had already scanned it for mention of the murder mix-up but there had been no article since Beck's phone call to the journalist. The piece the journalist had prepared for last week's paper linking the mummies to the missing teenagers had been pulled but nothing had taken its place either in that edition or this week's.

'Mmm?'

'These fucking arseholes won't ever apologise.'

'Which fucking arseholes?'

'The *Sunday Times*.'

She had given him a knowing grimace. 'It's of no consequence. No one cares whether your father was a murderer, and those who do will know he wasn't. It has nothing to do with him. The mummy murders were simply a means to sell more newspapers. It's all a fiction, and if you weren't connected to it, you'd think it funny.'

'I don't care! It's still not right. It's a question of honour.'

'Calm down, Russ. Since when are you so concerned with honour?'

So often in the past Beck had exhorted him to feel. Now that he was feeling, he was in trouble for not feeling the right things. It was maddening. Beck herself never held back, evidenced most dramatically, for him, in her vagina sculptures. When she fell pregnant with Savannah, Beck spent hours in front of her canvas trying to express the emotion of her new state. Frustrated, she painted over canvas after canvas, until the angry covering up of her efforts began slowly to evolve into a new form, a gradual transition into a third dimension: she began to stick things onto the canvas, first using thicker and thicker paint to cement on extra layers, and later melding bits of children's dolls, stalks of wheat, pieces of military uniforms. Her sculptures literally grew out of her paintings. Her transition from young woman to young mother paralleled that of painter to sculptor. The vagina sculptures she created prior to Savannah's birth gave way to a post-natal series expressing the moment of birth, the cresting of the baby's head, the umbilicus, a tear from vagina to anus.

When he'd bring Savannah into the studio for her feed, Rebecca would lift her t-shirt – already showing damp little ponds around the nipples, her let-down response having been triggered by the baby's cries piercing through the house. And now this virago, this fierce, mad warrior-woman who had to be woken to nurture, was telling him to calm down.

Sitting now in the passage outside the studio, Russ closed his eyes, and heard Rebecca stomping about inside the studio. It wasn't a happy stomping. She would be pissed off if she came out and found him there. But he was too tired to get up.

He opened the Good Croxley. A Christmas beetle clattered metallically against the naked spotlight above his head, carapace against hot glass. In his reading, he had begun to page ahead, wanting advance warning. Was he going to struggle to make out the words, was the upside-down French going to scramble the English, or was this section preserved enough to ensure a more flowing read? He smiled. This passage was going to be easy.

It was the best and worst night of my life. Wednesday, 18th December 1912. The date is imprinted on my brain –

The Christmas beetle left off its attack on the light and buzzed around, slamming up into the whiteness of the ceiling, then falling to the ground in a mad fit, until it came to rest on its back, pathetic little legs circling helplessly. What was it doing here anyway, this long before Christmas? Must be a lonely insect.

A loud crash from within the studio had Russ struggling to his feet. He opened the door. Rebecca stood like an exhausted boxer over her fallen opponent, her right hand balled into a fist, knuckles smeared with clay, the kinesis in her body hovering still. She had smacked the head off its plinth. The injured clay face now rested on its nose, the armature having preserved its overall shape.

'Jesus, Beck!' Russ was looking down on an ear, distorted by the concave imprint of Rebecca's fist. With the feeling of a medic on a battlefield he knelt down to examine it.

She turned on him, her features contorted with rage. 'Get out! Get out!' Her clay-encrusted hands gripped the neck of his shirt, dragging him away from the sculpture. Pulled off balance, he fell on his arse, and looked up in dumb surprise.

'What –' He staggered to his feet.

She shoved him towards the open door. 'Get the fuck out of here!'

There was a silence in the passageway, broken only by the rasping of the Christmas beetle's wings against the floorboards. Slack-jawed, Russ stared at the little brown upside-down insect. The sound grew fitful as the creature weakened.

Russ sat down again, trying to reflect, his breath in contrapuntal rhythm with the dying beetle's wings. That glimpse of the damaged head was enough to register a hint of recognition, but too fleeting to be sure, and the head's fall had left its mark: the chin had a flattened edge, the nose was skewed and small pieces of clay had been torn from the tips of nose and chin like burnt flesh shredding off a wound.

It must look ridiculous, Russ thought, a man of his bulk pushed out the door by his wife. But there had been frenzy in her eyes, and a hint of something else. Guilt? Fear? He wasn't sure. It was as if he had caught her in the act of something shameful. His usual response to her episodes of pique was to write them off. It was simply her artistic temperament. But lately his usual responses to things weren't working all that well.

At these moments of spousal impasse there seemed only a maddening noise in his head, with two discernable escape routes, the one framed by the words 'I'm leaving', the other by something physical, primitive, violent. The latter was as abhorrent as the former. It was useless. He couldn't understand how someone capable of such sensitivity in her art, such compassion for her children, could act so brutally towards the man who shared her bed. But then, did he truly share her bed? And with that thought, he opened the notebook at the section he had begun several minutes earlier, before the interruption of the clay head crashing to the floor:

It was the best and worst night of my life. Wednesday, 18th December 1912. The date is imprinted on my brain. Burlington House in Piccadilly, in the meeting room of the Geological Society. The leather benches are laid out parliamentary style, two rows facing one another. In the middle is the lectern behind which the speaker addresses his audience. White marble statues along the walls, paintings, the oils dark and sombre. It was a cold December night and I was shivering. We had received notice reminding us of the limited seating and so I arrived early. I should have been more cautious; the room was already almost filled to capacity. An old codger in a very unfashionable suit and a red handlebar moustache reluctantly made room for me and I managed to squeeze in at the end of the row. As we shifted over the elderly Victorian dropped his cane and I bent to pick it up for him.

The place smelled of perfumed men and wore an air of great expectancy, one such as you sometimes find in the House of Commons – say, on the eve of the breaking of some scandal or other. There was – how shall I put it? – a veritable buzz.

The meeting was due to start at eight o'clock and shortly thereafter the Society's president brought the room to order. At first Strahan attended to regular business. I am sure I was not alone in wanting to shout out, 'On with it!' But I must confess I knew something of the direction the evening's presentation was going to take. Above the measured tones of a scientific lecture we would soon be hearing the cry, 'I have found earliest Man!'

Finally, his chubby cheeks resting on his wing collar, Dawson got up to show us his fossil remains. His bald pate reflected not only the electric light but the light of all those intellectual minds sitting in his audience. He buttoned and unbuttoned his suit coat to good effect. On his solicitor's wages he could well afford the expensive suits he wore. Then he launched into his presentation and very erudite it was. The listeners were agog.

He told us that he had recovered his fossil from a field near Piltdown Common in East Sussex. With the aid of lantern slides he described the distribution of the flint-bearing gravels in the central Weald and went into matters of the fossil's age. Lower Pleistocene, can you believe it?

It was by now much warmer in the meeting room. The old codger next to me had not stopped tapping his cane against the bench in front of us and I felt some nervous laughter threatening in my throat. To suppress my laughter I looked up at the ceiling, away from the awed silence of the gathering. There are strong wooden beams that criss-cross and cut the ceiling into several segments, each perhaps five foot by five, each with its own intricate mouldings. In partition after partition, for some reason beyond my imagination, I saw the white heat of my father's ovens. All the while the most distinguished of His Majesty's scientists sat enraptured. Dr Arthur Smith Woodward, Keeper of Geology at the British Museum of Natural History, took the lectern. He carried a silver tray which bore a form covered by a white cloth and with great pomp he placed it upon the ledge of the lectern. He proceeded to review each of the nine cranial pieces they had found, as well as the fragment of the lower jaw. That jaw! By God, it had taken them in. He gave his rationale for piecing them together in the simian form that he had. The audience was riveted. He stroked his white goatee; he too was almost totally bald. And he went further. He told us that there had been two divergent evolutionary shoots: the Neanderthals, which he referred to as the 'degenerate offshoot', headed for extinction, and this new fossil – Piltdown Man – which he said gave rise to modern Homo sapiens.

And then he ripped the cloth off the form in front of him, unveiling the reconstructed skull.

'Here it is!' he exclaimed. 'I have named it Eoanthropus dawsoni, *in honour of its discoverer.'*

There, he had done it! And I could have convulsed with laughter to hear him create both a new genus and species. Dawn-man! Forefather of modern man. Ha!

It was the turn of Grafton Elliot Smith, professor of anatomy at Manchester University. It was his honour to comment on the neurocranial endocast. I thought with great relief: at last, here we have it, the voice of reason, an anatomist of note, surely he will dissent? I sat next to the fidgety Victorian, my hand clasping my chin in expectation.

Elliot Smith adjusted his pince-nez and cleared his throat. 'Piltdown Man,' he intoned, 'is the most primitive and most simian human brain so far recorded.'

That was it then. Someone later asked him the obvious question as to why the jaw was so ape-like. He explained, as if to a child, 'The growth of the brain preceded the refinement of the features and of the somatic characters in general.' How can I not remember his exact words?

I stared at the pillars along the white walls, at the tables, inlaid with green leather tops, at the old and wise men seated around the place. It was immensely satisfying to witness this debacle, to see such grand men as these making such asses of themselves.

But it would eventually have to be put to rights.

The door opened and Rebecca stepped into the passage. Was this the same woman who had given birth to Luc in the bathtub, whale music playing in the background and three women, Tante Julia included, urging her on in a chorus of New Age song, 'Breathe, breathe, pu-u-u-sh'?

She sat down next to Russ. 'I'm sorry,' she said.

He grunted. He wanted to ask her whether his eyes had deceived him inside the studio but she might round on him again. Her thighs were drawn up alongside his, almost touching. The moment arched between them like an expansion bridge with a toll neither could afford. The Christmas beetle was within reach of his shoe. He lifted his foot and moved it across to put the insect out of its misery but instead pushed himself to his feet, scooped the beetle up in his fingers and walked down the passageway to let it out the kitchen door.

18

FROM CORRESPONDENCE exchanged with the geologist Johan Hesse (British Museum archives), it is clear that Codron pegged the San as being of 'Eve's people', the progenitors of modern humans. For this he was roundly criticised. They were a modern version of the Neanderthals, some detractors scoffed, an evolutionary cul-de-sac. Others scoffed at the scoffers. The Neanderthals, they claimed, were no one's cul-de-sac; they were the direct ancestors of Homo sapiens.

Russ was seated at the dining-room table, reading *Digging for Darwin*. Palaeo-anthropologists, he mused, are like a bunch of geeks fighting it out at a science competition. My fossil is the earliest, the best, the species archetype, the most missing of the missing links.

Beck, one track-suited thigh pressed up against her body, her chin at rest on her raised knee, sipped her mug of tea, staring past the lounge furniture and the gridlines of the large bay window at the sea, undulating beneath a laden sky. Russ tossed *Digging for Darwin* onto the dining table and got up to scan his CD collection, housed in a cabinet between the dining area and the formal lounge. He considered Jelly Roll Morton since he had been playing the great jazz pianist when he first received Shaw and he'd begun to hope the fossil hunter might locate Barak amidst the dry gangrenous body parts the old man had left behind.

Both children were also seated at the table, Luc's hands cupped at his temples, giving him the impression of a blinkered foal. He was reading the Good Croxley. He, Beck and Russ had finished an early Sunday supper of pizza. Savannah had come in from watching Temba play soccer, had a shower, dressed in pyjamas, and was now eating a bowl of muesli, the backbone of her diet.

'He was nuts,' she said. 'Why don't you just leave it at that?'

'I still think he did it,' Rebecca said. 'Whether he set some sort of explosive device that brought the cave entrance down, or whether he chose not to get away from some natural disaster. Passive or active, he put them in harm's way. It was murder by gross negligence. He killed the woman and himself and the foetus.'

Savannah raised a spoonful of cereal to her mouth. 'That's why we're all a bit nuts, 'cos Dad's father was so screwy.'

'Jesus, where's the logic in all that?' said Russ. His fingers were moving automatically across the jewel cases. 'They were camping in the bush! How does that become family murder?'

Savannah's jaw tensed up. 'Yeah, like everyone camps in a bomb site.'

'Not a bomb site, a testing ground,' Russ said, as if it made a difference.

Savannah shrugged. 'Whatever. Would you take us there for an optometry conference?'

Now that was a question worth considering. Would he? What if an Edenesque paper was being presented on a new cure for blindness? You might blow your family to bits but the good news, folks, is that you'll be able to cure their sightlessness. Russ shook his head.

'You're right, Sav,' he said into the rows of CDs, 'I wouldn't take you there. But my father thought he was invincible.'

And maybe his helper elected to stay with him. She was black, it was the sixties… was she so servile as to risk death for him? Or was it love? Where was the line between servility and devotion? He thought he could understand the wish to stay with Barak in that cave, that both Russ himself and the black woman might have chosen this. His mother would have – she left behind a gentrified life to follow Barak to the loneliest spots in Africa. Wasn't that the same thing? He could see now that they had all been inducted into the church of Barak's omnipotence, believing the old man too strong to fall to a leopard or an avalanche.

Russ had scanned the entire CD collection without taking in a single title, and returned to his seat. Christ, he could do with some of Barak's self-belief to help with his own mental avalanche.

'My father wasn't a violent man,' he said.

'Russ,' said Beck, 'he left you and your mother! What kind of man walks out on his family? That's a kind of violence, isn't it? You loved him! He left you! He ripped the family in two.'

Savannah smiled at him. 'Nice try, Dad,' she said, getting up to take her empty bowl to the kitchen. Her pyjama flannels sat low on her hips, the evening light catching the downy hairs in the hollow at the base of her spine. What secret alchemy had transformed her once little form into one suddenly so womanly? Temba Cohen's dark fingers now owned that space where Russ's soothing hand had broken the infant Savannah's wind, or cuddled her as a toddler, or applied sunscreen to the girl. Russ didn't seem to mind so much at the thought of it.

'Sav, wait,' he called after her. 'You guys should take a look at this.'

The photographs had suddenly come to mind. He hadn't shown them to anyone yet. He slipped the two pictures out

of the photo pocket in which he'd been keeping them, and
gave the one to Savannah.

'Guess who that little kid is?'

'That *you*, Dad?' said Savannah. 'Aah, how cute! Look at
this, Luc.'

'And this?' Beck had the older photograph in her hand.

'Must be Barak as a boy.' Russ pointed to the older child.

Beck waited for Luc to finish, then examined the two
photographs side-by-side. She shook her head. 'No, I don't
think so. These two men are the same man.'

'What? No, can't be. That's his father. Familial
resemblance.'

'No, Russ. That's Barak Codron as an adult in both
pictures, only they're taken years apart. Here he's maybe late
thirties, early forties, and in this one maybe sixty or so.' She
hesitated before adding, as she turned away to reach for her
tea mug, 'I've been studying his face.'

He didn't understand her and wasn't sure he wanted
to. He got up again and this time, settling on the classical
section of the CD collection, withdrew *The Lark Ascending*
from its place on the rack. An English composer for an
English riddle. And Ralph Vaughan Williams's great-uncle,
Russ recalled from some deep recess in his trivia vault, was
none other than Charles Darwin.

The riddle could be distilled to one stark contradiction:
how could the father on the stoep, or in the cave, the father
who so generously shared his love of stories, his passion for
hunting fossils, be the same man who would abandon his
son? How could the same body house two such fathers?

Russ sat down. Rebecca had gone, leaving the silently
reading Luc, his hands now so cupped about his eyes that
they resembled make-believe binoculars. Russ fingered
the latest addition to his enquiry, a two-volume set he had
found in a rare book dealer's shop the previous morning,

after dropping Savannah at a friend to complete a school project. The stacks had reminded him of the rows and rows of Barak's library. It was his mother who laboured with a yellow dust-cloth, on and off the wooden three-step ladder, wiping and blowing dust from each individual book. As a child he'd not given this much thought, simply taking her behaviour as homage to Barak's learning. After the old man disappeared he saw in her now careless, furious dusting the expression of what had only formerly been hinted at: a hapless, pathetic attempt to communicate with Barak, to tell him how desperate and pissed off she was. It was as if she was massaging his mistress with sandpaper. After she died, the library, along with everything else in the house, was sold to second-hand dealers to settle debts.

Russ ran his palm over the covers of his two newly-acquired volumes, the revised second edition of the most popular palaeo-anthropological text of its day, published in January 1929, *The Antiquity of Man* by Sir Arthur Keith. Volume One came to rest, closed, its spine snug against the crease of his palm. He closed his eyes and ran the fingers of his other hand along the edges of the pages. The paper was cut roughly, and it felt as though his fingers were taking a journey as they ran into bumps and troughs and extra strips that still attached themselves like skin tags to the book. Williams's orchestra supplied the backdrop of a lush, green, peaceful English countryside, the solo violin beginning its long, slowly rising cadenza, the lark's gentle ascent. This pastoral England had not been Barak's England. Barak's was the England of the East End, an industrial, Cockney scramble for survival. Pastoral England was where they found Piltdown Man, an impression of whose skull adorned the cover of each of the two volumes of *The Antiquity of Man*. Since they were his works, Sir Arthur had naturally chosen his own rather more human-like reconstruction before

Woodward's original simian version. The volumes were bound in biblical blue and on each the skull was embossed in gold, with the words *Piltdown Fragments* appearing below it. The actual fragments were shown in shaded and solid gold, the reconstructed parts in outline.

Russ eased open the cover. There was a musty smell, the peculiar rotting peach-skin fragrance of a book not read in decades. The heavy bond pages were cream-coloured, almost the texture of blotting paper, only thinner and somewhat smoother; and on the inside cover, in dark, soft pencil, in the book dealer's hand, were inscribed the details of date, edition, and the fact that this was part one of a set of two. The remains of a squashed fish-moth, perhaps more than seventy years old, rested there, the tiny strands of antennae and feet threading out from the blotch of a body that had become part of the fibres that made up the page.

He found mention of several expeditions, the names triggering memories. Did Barak say he'd actually taken part in these? Ghar Dalam cave in Malta, La Chapelle-aux-Saints in France? But there was no reference to the young Barak Codron, neither in these sections nor elsewhere in *The Antiquity of Man*. Sir Arthur did mention Raymond Dart, 'the young and able Professor of Anatomy in the University of the Witwatersrand'. But this was in connection with Dart's examination of a relatively modern Boskop-type skull, believed to be the ancestor of the Khoisan, found in a rock-shelter at T'zitzikama. Not a word was written on the subject of the Taung skull, found five years before the appearance of this revised edition. This didn't surprise Russ. After all, it had been Keith's authoritative dismissal that had finally sunk Dart's claims for the Taung child. Sir Arthur Keith backed Piltdown Man as the quintessential fossil. But while Piltdown Man had the brain of a human and the jaws of an ape, Dart's Taung child had the brain of an ape and the jaws of a human. The Taung brat upset Keith's meticulously argued theory. The juvenile skull, held Keith, belonged to a young ape. Ergo, *Australopithecus africanus* did not exist, it was a figment of the young Dart's fertile imagination.

The garlic from the pizza announced itself in an involuntary burp. Barbara was going to have something to say about his breath in the morning. 'You can't go peering into people's eyes with breath like that,' he could hear her admonishment as she goes off in search of breath freshener. What would he do without her? Only right now it wasn't breath freshener he needed but antacid. He walked through to the en suite bathroom. Rebecca was in the bedroom with Luc.

'But I don't get the joke.' Luc was sitting on the bed, looking up at his mother. 'Why does the little boy blush when he sees the salad dressing? And why is that funny?'

'Well, darling, the little boy blushes because, when he opens the fridge door, he sees the *salad dressing* – that has a double meaning. "Salad dressing" as in balsamic dressing *and* as in he's opened someone's bedroom door and caught them in the act of getting dressed.'

'But why would that make him blush?'

'Ooooh, well, some people get embarrassed when they see other people without their clothes on. It makes them kind of curious and excited all at the same time, but that makes them feel guilty, and so they get embarrassed. So, the joke is playing on that fact. Do you get it now?'

'Yes,' said Luc, 'I get the joke now. But I still don't see why people get embarrassed when they see other people without their clothes on.'

Russ didn't understand how Luc had gone from his intense study of Barak's notebook to telling Beck the joke, which is probably how their conversation started. But then Luc was in the habit of entering rooms with a riddle or a joke, a somewhat bewildered Johnny Carson kicking off his show. Russ popped the antacid tablet from its foil packaging, placed it on his tongue and walked back to the dining room, returning his own attention to palaeo-anthropology.

Death is naked – Barak wrote in the Good Croxley – *it is the final humiliation. The moment when people stare and you cannot stare back.* This entry, Russ found as he read on, turned out to be the pithiest of a collection of fragmented philosophical ramblings that were turning into a blur of black print floating before his eyes. Perhaps, he thought, his eyes drifting to the photo pocket with its picture of a bare-chested, bare-legged Barak, death is only semi-naked. He laid the two photographs side by side. Maybe the oldest boy in the formal portrait wasn't Barak after all. There was something very wrong about the cheekbones, and the chin. The expression on the man's face – was there a hint of forbearance? – was at odds with Barak's reckless smile on the beach. But the bone structure, the spacing of the eyes, the high forehead, that nose... Beck's insistent claim: *these two men are the same man.* But –

If –

Fuck –

Can't be –

If that's Barak –

Then –

The woman is –

And the children are –

And Inspector Toka saying, *What does a thirteen year old know of his parent's business?*

And then it came back to him. His mother's drunken claim. Made from lips loosened by drink – and dismissed by him because of the drink.

19

It had happened three years after his father's disappearance. Russ was sixteen years old. He had come home from school to find her on the front stoep staring out toward Sterkfontein. His suspicion aroused by the buoyant greeting she had given him, he'd dropped his schoolbag in his bedroom and gone out to the backyard, rummaged in the garbage bin, found what he was looking for, then trudged back through the house, his school tie swinging angrily.

The house was no longer on the outskirts of Krugersdorp. A row of red-tiled roofs now blinded their view of the veld, more lebensraum for barking dogs and barefoot blond children.

The mug grasped in her hands had an inch of wine still in it.

'Ma!' He was holding one of the empty wine bottles he had found hidden in a wad of newspaper at the bottom of the bin. She looked up at him from behind her fringe, flicking at it with an irritated hand, the strands falling back over her forehead, fanning out into a blond curtain.

'Don't look at me like that!'

The skin of her face, freckled by the African sun, thinly lined, had remained remarkably taut apart from the dark patches under her eyes that some mornings verged on the purple, as if her face bruised itself each night and with the day's advance would set itself to healing.

She usually avoided looking in the direction of the caves.

She did enough of it when Russ was a little boy and she would wait to see the dust trail of the Ford, for her 'men' to return. In the car Russ would be fighting sleep, his head lolling against the inside panelling of the door as they bumped along the dirt road, wanting to tell her about the day's search and – if luck had favoured them – about a find. She would take him inside, draw a bath and sit with him as he washed himself, listening to him tell of their digging in the earth.

'I used to wait here for you and your father,' she said, turning away from the accusation in his right hand – the empty bottle held by the neck. 'I'd sit and watch for the dust cloud. The road hadn't been tarred yet. It was often dusk and in winter it was always cold. But the sun going down would cast a golden glow over the veld.' As she settled into her story, her voice took on a wistful evenness. 'I told myself you would arrive before it got unbearably cold and that there was no need for me to go inside for a cardigan. Sometimes you'd be really late and it would be dark before you got home. No longer comforted by the golden veld, I'd stay nonetheless. I'd know you'd found something, and that Barak hadn't been able to tear himself away. Knowing that would warm me up.' She laughed bitterly and, foregoing her alcoholic's cloak of secrecy, lifted a wine bottle – hitherto hidden from Russ – from the side of her chair and filled her mug. 'Then just before I couldn't take the cold any longer, you'd come riding out of the cloud to save me.' Russ wondered whether she was making this up – or perhaps the drink had romanticised the story for her. His memories were of coming home to find her in bed, passed out.

'Each Saturday I couldn't stop myself from recalling my own childhood,' she said. 'In the afternoon the family would come together in one of the drawing rooms for tea, in front of the blazing fire the house butler would have made earlier on. "William," my father would say to my older brother' – she gulped her wine – "'William," he'd say, "come and read to us. I do believe we had reached the pivotal moment of Mr Polly's history when we find the unfortunate man facing bankruptcy and preparing for his suicide." He'd always remember the precise point at which William had stopped reading the previous Saturday.'

It was odd. His mother seemed to become more articulate the more she drank, a building of words when a slurring should've occurred. That is, until she reverted to stereotype, rose with effort, and staggered off to bed, an outstretched arm steadying her against the passage walls.

'One day William told Father that his eyes were sore and that he didn't think they could tolerate the strain of reading. He suggested to Father that I read instead. By that time I was thirteen and could read well – I'd been reading *Decline and Fall*, which had just been published, in the privacy of my bedroom. Father would've had a fit had he known. He gave his approval only to books in which the hero triumphs in the end. He used to say that the novel's protagonist must be a worthy subject of the King. Come to think of it, he must not have understood the subversive nature of Mr Polly to have allowed it.' She was quiet for a moment. 'When William suggested that I read, the mood in the drawing room took on an air of nervous expectation. You have to imagine what it was like. My two younger sisters and little Lindsey would sit attentively on the ottomans in front of the fire. Mother and I would be on one of the couches doing our embroidery. Father always sat in his wingback. With hindsight it is clear that my brother William was being provocative, but how could I know it then? Then I could only look down at the embroidery in my hands, blushing, waiting with pounding heart for Father to give his approval to William's suggestion. No one spoke. I could hear the fire crackling and feel the heat coming off my reddened cheeks. I remember Mother letting out a nervous laugh before saying, "What a splendid idea, William. Emma has such a beautiful voice. You really should hear it, Father." I imagined – I had to imagine it, I just couldn't bring myself to look, to raise my eyes from my embroidery – everyone looking away from Father, but not that far away that they wouldn't be able to see his response out of the corners of their eyes. Finally, after an awful age, Father spoke. "No, Mother, I should think not," he said. "If William's eyes are not up to it, we shall have no reading today. The revelation of Mr Polly's fate will simply have to await another day.'"

She was silent for a long time. Russ expected at any moment the uncertain rise to her feet, the stumble to the bedroom. She reached down to fill her mug again. 'I suppose I am still awaiting the revelation of Mr Polly's fate.'

'You've got to stop, Mother. You're ruining your life.'

'I don't care. I have no life. You don't need me any more.'

'Of course I do.'

'You'll leave,' she said, the words almost swallowed by the wine at her lips.

'Mother!'

'No! You don't understand! It's in your blood. You're *his* son, goddamit. Heaven knows, I tried to make you mine. I really did. Put that bottle away. It's enough, Russell. Enough! Throw it out! I don't need reminding.'

Russ fidgeted with his school tie, staring at the veins that quivered a delicate blue at her temples. He held tightly to the neck of the bottle. 'We've gone over this a thousand times, Ma. Something must have happened to him, he would never have just left.'

'Yes, he *would* have,' she said tearfully. 'He did it before.'

'What? When? He never! I would remember. I know I would!'

She put her face in her hands.

Something dropped inside him. 'When, Ma? Tell me! Tell me!'

She dragged the back of her hand across her nose. Her knuckles came away glistening with mucus.

'Tell me, Ma. What are you talking about?'

She looked down at her hands, then back into his face. 'With his first family, the one in England. Oh, don't look so shocked. Yes, he had another family, a wife and children before he met me. You have some siblings, Russell. Let me see now.' Her tone changed, the weariness giving way to sarcasm. 'Two half-brothers and three half-sisters. Much older than you, of course. The youngest would be a good twenty years older than you. Deborah. He never spoke about them. Oh, for Heaven's sake Russell, put that bloody thing down.'

Russ threw the bottle into the garden. She carried on talking.

'The Viscount's spinster daughter running off to Africa with a married Jewish scientist in search of ape-men. It's quite comical, really. Perhaps we should produce a farce. But we're not laughing, are we, Russie? Neither, I'm sure, was his first wife. Poor darling. I suppose I was as culpable as your father. Although they were *his* family. Do you know that I actually had the audacity to introduce him to my father? What got into me, I don't know. But I never spoke to him again. My father, that is. He came out onto the front steps. He looked at Barak, closed his eyes and went straight back into the house. I've never seen his shoulders so stooped. His spine looked like a question mark.'

She took a gulp of wine. 'For years they'd trotted out eligible young men they wished me to marry. I suppose I wanted to show them what kind of man I was interested in. On the boat from Southampton to Cape Town I don't know what made me more nauseous, the fear of Nazi U-boats or the sickness I felt at losing my father. Or the morning sickness. I don't suppose I know what was more scandalous – that I was 28 and Barak 53, that I was pregnant, that he was married, that he was Jewish? I lost the baby. And three more after it. When I realised I was pregnant with you, I was sure I was going to lose you too. Oh, don't carry on with that look on your face!'

They never spoke of these revelations again and in the days that followed he managed to persuade himself that they were the spiteful claims of a bitter drunk. Two years later she was dead, worn out at fifty-three, the same age Barak was when they met.

20

HE TURNED OVER. BECK moaned quietly next to him, a sleepy complaint. He cuddled up to her, wanting to Velcro his body to her warmth. His cold foot came to lie against an ankle. She moved away. He rolled onto his stomach. A lump in the pillow against his cheek annoyed him and he raised himself onto his elbows and fluffed the pillow, tried again. He couldn't find a place for his left arm – under the pillow was no good; neither was down along his side. He heard a noise in the house and grew suddenly alert. The house was creaking. It did that, the floors and roof seemed also to suffer from the occasional insomnia, not able to get comfortable for the night, and then it was as if the family lived in an irritable house that moaned and quivered and couldn't settle down.

The house creaked again. He must have slept because it was growing light. He could hear the sounds of Beck taking a bath. The sloshing as some part of her body broke the surface tension of the water sounded like sighs of exasperation. He lay on his back, listening to her. How is it that a man can hear criticism in the sounds of his wife's bathing?

For so long she had accused him of absence, of becoming an emotional illiterate. Yet at work he wasn't simply an optometrist who treated eyes, a corrector of sight. He had an ability to choose frames that suited the faces and fancies of his clientele. People said of him, *Russ Codron? Darling, he took one look at me and pulled out the perfect pair. You must go and see him!* He had learned well at the side of his anthropologist-father: he knew the structure of the face. But even more important than this was his knack for grasping his patient's vulnerability, what it was she didn't like about herself, and how a pair of glasses might compensate for this. In this, he had learned well at the side of his mother: he knew the structure of a vulnerable mood. He knew where to find the hidden wine bottle, and how shame could be concealed.

But Beck was right, he had long ago given up looking out for her.

Not in the beginning. The wind brought them together and swept them along with it, and for a few years they were able to keep moving. With Savannah, he was able to deliver on his promised strength. While Beck battled to marry her art with motherhood, it was Russ's ear attuned to the baby's cries. Was it not he who got up in the middle of the night? Was it not he who brought the hungry baby to her? Did he not soothe the mad artist *and* the needy infant? Bring them together to both their satisfaction? My god, he knew how to do that! He was the fossil hunter's apprentice, anticipating Barak's needs, having the right tool in the old man's hands even before he'd asked for it. He simply did the same with Rebecca. He replaced Barak with Rebecca. No wonder he fell so deeply in love with her!

But then as Savannah grew, so did Beck's comfort, and Russ began to feel more and more redundant. If he couldn't play the apprentice, what was there for him? By the time Luc was born, Russ was slipping from view. And when Luc showed needs Russ had no hope of understanding, and Beck gave up her art for those three years in order to understand her son, Russ all but disappeared. Dried up, as Beck put it. Luc had become a kind of inverted Barak, a presence dominant and powerful, not as Barak was in his flamboyance, but in his singular remoteness. And Russ didn't have a clue how to apprentice himself to that.

'If you're excavating out on the savannah,' his father used to say, 'don't go looking when the sun's high in the sky. At midday you can be staring straight at a two-million-year-old cranium and not know it because it looks just like the piece of granite next to it. You need the shadows, they're your friends, they'll tell you what's there.'

That's what he had to do. He had to use the shadows. He had to look for his own shame. And for that, he had to disentangle it from his father's.

I was not the only one to know the secret of Piltdown. The anatomist Franz Weidenreich, for one, was of the opinion that the jaw and skull did not belong together. But he was German and a Jew to boot and therefore held to be anti-English – sour grapes and all that. Piltdown Man sinks the Neanderthals!

The anti-Piltdown camp lost even more ground in early July of 1913 when Dawson and Woodward unearthed more fragments of their precious skull: the left and right nasal bones and splintered pieces of the turbinals. And then in August they found the all-important canine. Imagine the cooing!

It was Darwin who said that false views, even though they may be supported by some evidence, do little harm to the progress of science, for everyone takes salutary pleasure in proving their falseness. False facts, on the other hand, are highly injurious, for they often endure long. So after these new bones made their appearance in the gravels of Piltdown, I knew I had to act. I requested an audience of the Royal Society. I had to work through my mentor, Professor Oldfield, in order to achieve that modest goal. I was granted an audience at the next meeting, to be held one October afternoon. I remember stepping out of my lodgings just before noon. Oldfield had invited me to lunch at the Savoy and was going to fetch me in his new motorcar. Quite a treat, to ride in a motorcar. The streets of London were still populated by horse-drawn traffic; you had to be fairly well-to-do and a modernist to purchase a horseless carriage.

I was waiting for him outside the tobacconists on the corner of my street as arranged and I was thinking 'what inclement weather!' That adjective – inclement! – kept up a steady barrage inside my head all the way to King's Reach and on through lunch. I remember this odd little incident, you see, because the weather was in fact rather fine, particularly for an October afternoon. Not a cloud in the sky! Perhaps I should skip ahead in order to clear up this little mystery. I must take you twelve years on, to the very day, an October evening which in actual fact was particularly inclement, to an address for a lay audience I was fortunate enough to attend. I was in Vienna, taking part in a symposium, and managed to find time for a little diversion. The speaker was the psycho-analyst Professor Sigmund Freud. As he spoke I felt as though someone was walking upon my grave. It was absolutely prescient. With rather a startle I realised what the nether reaches of my mind had been up to. Freud had been talking about his concept of parapraxis – including das Versprechen or slips of the tongue – when suddenly I remembered the pre-meeting lunch with Professor Oldfield and the words 'inclement weather' running as if on a treadmill through my mind. It was clear: despite the royal treatment, the ride in his motorcar, lunch at the Savoy, I had a premonition of the good Professor's imminent betrayal of me. The old bugger was fattening me up for the slaughter. Inclement! How clever of my unconscious mind. You see, Professor Oldfield's first name was Clement. Professor Clement Arthur Oldfield. Rather rich, don't you think?

Back to the meeting! The attendance was good, the lecture hall stuffy with cigar and cheroot smoke. I waited nervously for my turn and when it came I laid out my carefully constructed argument. Of course, I did not have the original fragments to use in evidence, only a cast. Almost everyone had only had the opportunity of examining casts and not the originals, the British Museum having been rather cagey about exposing Piltdown Man in the flesh, so to speak. And even though I was employed by the BM, Woodward had caught wind of my thesis and forbade me access.

Graeme Friedman

I said to them: you cannot see them in the casts, but if you look at the original molars, there are striae on the surfaces (naturally, I was well acquainted with the originals). These teeth have been tampered with! There were loud coughs and several men cried out indignantly. In order to understand the unmerciful response my revelation received, you have to realise that, firstly, the arguments put forward thus far against Piltdown Man had been about the association of the jaw and cranial fragments – that they didn't actually come from the same specimen – or about the antiquity of the bones, or, as in the Keith-Woodward debate, about the nature of the reconstruction and, secondly, that my accusation was tantamount to blasphemy: that anyone should make claims of this nature against a colleague, never mind the inference, given the location of the find, that it would be an English colleague!

Having questioned the integrity of the Dawson group, I went on to cast aspersion upon the broader assembly's scientific competence. If this is the jaw of a man, I insisted, we can no longer claim any ability to distinguish between the mandible of an ape and that of a man! The jaw, gentlemen, is that of an orang-utan, broken in just the right places.

I had brought along an orang-utan jaw which I had previously broken – as far as I was able, and I was able, I might tell you – in the same places as the Piltdown jaw, and then lightly glued back together. I held my specimen aloft. Behold, I said, the jaw of an orang-utan! I snapped it in two and compared it to the Piltdown cast. The coughs and scattered objections were rapidly turning to a loud rumbling as anger infected the crowd. My dear gentlemen, I cried out, can't you see how it has been broken in just the right way so as to fool you? People began talking loudly to their neighbours. I hastily proceeded to the next piece of my argument: the molar teeth. I went into some detail about the comparative features of orang and human dentition, why in fact it had to be an orang if anyone was to be fooled, and not a large chimpanzee or a small gorilla, and showed them orang teeth, then showed them molars that I had filed flat. Look, these are now more human-like! That is when they started hissing and booing. Someone shouted out, 'Flat earth!' Most ungenerous of a Royal Society audience. I looked over at Professor

Oldfield for support, only to catch sight of him leaning with his lips in a mocking curl towards his neighbour, and whispering something in the man's ear. His neighbour was none other than Sir Arthur Keith. Keith smirked in agreement. But I was determined and I pressed on, against the growing uproar. The canine, I shouted, it has also been fiddled with! Look! So that it would seem to have erupted early in life, as in humans, rather than as the last of the adult teeth, as in apes!

Looking back now, I do not think I finished that last sentence. Certainly it seems too long and determined a phrase for a young man to have managed in the face of such hostility. I do know that I stormed from the podium in a helpless rage.

The next day I resigned my new position at the BM and made plans to join an excavation in China. I had done all I could. The persistence of false facts would be on their heads.

21

HE PUSHED THE DUVET away, swung himself off the bed and walked heavily to the kitchen, the wooden floorboards yielding unhappily. The early morning light was diffused by a cold, low sky. He put some bread into the toaster. One of the children was busy in the bathroom. It had to be Luc, Savannah had to be dragged from her bed in the mornings. But it was Savannah who first appeared in the kitchen, followed by Rebecca, who made herself a mug of tea and sat down at the table.

'I thought I'd be able to do it all in one trip,' said Beck, 'but I'm going to have to go and come back again.'

'What? Where?'

'Oh, for Christ's sake, Russ. To Jo'burg, for the exhibition.'

'Oh.' He sat down next to Savannah who was spooning muesli into her mouth whilst reading over some English material for a test she would be sitting in a few hours. Russ felt very tired. His body ached. If he lay down now, perhaps he'd never be able to get up again.

Beck sighed. 'I can't let them set up without me, it's too complicated. I was going to stay up there for a week before the opening, remember? But under the circumstances, I think I'd better not. And besides, I've decided to do this additional piece. I'll need the time to finish it.'

From where he was sitting, he could see through the cottage panes of the back door into the garden. Elephant ears, delicious monsters and other jungle plants crowded in on one another.

'When are you leaving?'

'I'll go on Friday, and come back Monday. Then I'll go up for the exhibition on the tenth.'

'What's the last piece?' It was disingenuous, he knew. It would bring to both their minds that little knockout scene in the studio the morning before, the sculpture fisted to the floor.

He thought she'd be angry but when she spoke, her tone was conciliatory, betraying her own concerns for *his* anger. 'Russ, please leave it. When it's out of my head and into its own, you'll see it.'

Russ paced in the garden, waiting for Shaw. He stepped in a turd left behind by Dali and swore as he realised what it was, then tried to get it off by smearing his shoe along the grass. It didn't quite work – he was wearing running shoes and the soft mess – at least Dali's bowels were working – found a stubborn hold in the grooves of the sole. He grunted and gave up.

Quite suddenly he felt the need to pee. He unzipped his fly and directed a long unbroken stream into the rockery where the urine hissed against the ends of a Medusa's head, the stems of the plant quivering under the impact. He hated those bloody succulents anyway. They reminded him too much of having to get by on nothing.

The telephone conversation he'd had with Shaw was perplexing. What was he up to? He had sounded like all the other fossil hunters Russ had known, in love with melodrama. *Russell, wait until you see what I've got!*

Russ had hoped it was the permit to excavate Barak's cave but Shaw said he had something that may be more exciting than anything they would find in the cave. And that was it, apart from agreeing on the time the young scientist would bring his surprise round to the house.

And now Russ, pulling in his stomach slightly, one hand on his belt, the other on his zip, jerked the zip closed. He shivered. It was getting dark. The house loomed over him, its stone façade, coldly awesome when they moved in fifteen years ago, was now softened by drapes of ivy and by the replacement of the small steel windows with large wood-framed ones. The wood had been a triumph of their desire for warmth over the reality of the corrosive sea air and, despite regular sealing, was beginning to rot.

Russ heard a car door slam. Shaw had been lucky to get a parking directly outside and was now at the gate, a cardboard wine box held against his body. On its sides were printed thick red arrows and the words 'THIS WAY UP'.

'You'll be the first to see it!' said Shaw.

Russ beckoned him towards the house, slipped his faeces-encrusted shoes off, leaving them outside the front door – whoever wanted to swipe them was welcome – and showed Shaw through to the lounge. The Englishman placed the box on the coffee table and sat on the couch. Russ sat next to him. A row of miniature mons pubis sculptures peered down from the mantelpiece. The fire was lit, and spat and crackled, sap bleeding from the wood. Shaw opened the flap and began to remove layers of shredded paper. He put his hands inside the box and gently scooped out the contents.

In his pale cupped hands Trevor Shaw held a bronze-black skull of the strangest proportions. The cheek bones were enormous, so that without the lower jaw, which was missing, the face was almost as wide as it was long. The braincase was small, the forehead low and sloping backwards, and starting between and above the eyebrow ridges, running over the top of the skull where it formed a warped bony keel – the sagittal crest.

'It's not a monkey,' said Russ.

'No.' Trevor laughed. 'Apart from anything else, there's

the frontal sinus.'

'What is it?'

Shaw pointed to the skull with a shaky finger. 'Well, that's what I've been trying to work out. Nothing's quite right. The face is almost what we would expect of *boisei*. But then we've got this.' He tapped the ridge of bone on top of the skull. This is the oddest bloody sagittal crest I've seen on any hominid. It's as big as *aethiopicus's* crest but the shape is all wrong. Wasn't much to go on for the reconstruction – a few slivers, really – but this seems the most sensible fit, and it accords with your father's reconstruction.'

Carefully, Russ took Barak's fossil from Trevor and ran his fingers along the crest, which was made up of bits of bone and the filler material palaeontologists used in their reconstructions. 'It is not the ability to recognise the pieces in his hands that makes the anatomist truly great,' Barak would say, hunched over a reconstruction, 'but the ability to surmise that which he does not hold in his hands.' Any two scientists might reconstruct an incomplete fossil skull in two subtly but crucially different ways, depending on the significance of the missing parts.

The bone was cold to touch. Russ brought it up to his face and stared into the hollow orbits. They stared back. A faint smell of... what was it? Hairline cracks and other, much wider fissures covered the entire skull. There was that smell again. Ah, it was the glue, the scent of it made him happy – perhaps even at his age he had the makings of a glue-sniffer. The glue took him along an olfactory memory tract that ended in his father working at the large baize-covered table in the garage he had taken over for his laboratory, while the Ford stood outside and got battered by hail: Barak is piecing together a skull. He peers into a microscope, turns two bits of bone this way and that, and then carefully glues them together.

Russ let out a flippant laugh. 'Maybe it's the progeny of some horny old *aethiopicus* and his *boisei* mate. Miscegenation in the Pleistocene.'

Shaw frowned. Russ's idea was an interesting one – since the single species theory had been demolished, and the concurrent existence of more than one hominid species had been proved, there were those who postulated cross-species mating. But Russ's tone was irreverent, and Trevor seemed unsure – was his host issuing an insult?

'It's possible,' he said. 'Although *aethiopicus* is thought to be ancestral to *boisei*. The colouring is so beautiful, it's like another Black Skull. It's the manganese salts – penetrates the bone during fossilisation. Where on earth did he find it? Not in the cave where he died.' He shook his head. 'No manganese. Doesn't he say?'

'Say what?' Russ's thoughts were back in the old Krugersdorp garage.

'Say what? Where he found this beauty!'

'Not so far. Not a word. He doesn't mention it at all. How did you sort this out from all those other bones?'

'It was easy. They were the only dark pieces. They were also the only pieces that weren't tagged. Which makes sense since your father had already reconstructed the skull, only somehow it got broken up again. Most of the sections with very small pieces were still intact. There were also useful traces of glue and filler material, as well as several recent hammer blows. Look: here, and here, and here. Your father put the skull together, then someone smashed it up again. I just followed the lines of his reconstruction – it took a couple of days but it wasn't difficult to put him back together again.'

'Unlike Humpty Dumpty.'

'Russ, you – you seem disappointed! This could be the find of the decade.'

'Oh, no, it's just – oh, I can't explain it. It just doesn't make sense. It must have taken him months to re-construct it. It's not like *he* had any pattern to follow. He'd never destroy a fossil, *never*. Especially one he'd reconstructed.'

What – Inspector Toka's insistent prosecution ran through his mind – *does a thirteen year old know of his parent's business?* Oh, shut up, Toka. This, at least, I know of my father!

'Well,' said Shaw, 'it could have been an act of madness. Why else would he do such a thing?'

Russ got up. 'I don't think madness would make him crazy enough to do it. Do you want a drink? Soda water?'

'Put some whiskey in it, please,' said Shaw, ignoring Russ's non sequitur. 'We're celebrating.'

There was no soda water in the dresser. Russ would have to collect it from the pantry. Probably he should open a litre bottle – it looked like Shaw might be in for a few refills. Pouring the drinks Russ imagined his parents together, as strange a fit as the head and sagittal crest of this black fossil, and yet he couldn't imagine them not being together. He was despondent and felt himself grow sulky, like a wronged child. He should be ecstatic. Trevor Shaw was. But there was something very wrong. Fossils were not recovered in this manner. Not from Barak.

He turned from the dresser. Luc was sitting next to Trevor on the couch.

'This is the foramen magnum,' the scientist was explaining, pointing to the large hole at the bottom of the skull. The boy's eyes were shining with interest. 'The spinal cord enters the skull through this hole and connects with the brain. If you were an ape, it would be at the back, which allows the spine to attach itself at a more horizontal angle. You know what that means, Luc?'

Luc took the skull from Trevor, who released it hesitantly, looking to Russ for confirmation that the boy could be trusted.

'Yes,' said Luc. 'I understand. In human beings and people like this man, the foramen magnum is closer to the front, so that the backbone will fit upright. Otherwise we'd walk like Dali.'

'Quite right!' Trevor's jaw looked as though it was going to go the way of the fossil's – missing. Russ smiled and handed over the whiskey.

Luc, cradling the skull in his lap, explored the pitted surface with the tips of his fingers, seemingly unaware that his mother had entered the room and was standing in front of the couch.

'What is it?' she asked.

'A black skull,' said Luc.

It was the fossil itself, Russ decided. There was something horribly wrong with it. Whatever professional shortcomings Barak might have possessed – and Russ was prepared to accept the old accusations that he had dealt in contraband fossils – he would never, ever have destroyed a genuine fossil. Mad or not, the old man would have sooner crushed his own skull.

'Not a black skull.' Russ's tone was sotto voce. 'A red herring.'

Shaw frowned and returned his attention to Luc. 'The skull is the most important part of any fossil. Most of the features that will identify a skeleton are to be found from the neck up.'

Russ's impatience was growing. The cave beckoned. There was a rocked forefinger at its mouth, flexed, motioning, urgently summoning him. It wants to swallow me, he thought.

'Hello, Trevor.' Savannah, who had been doing homework with Temba in her room – the flush on her face attested to homework of a different sort – stood at the door, half-masking the figure of her boyfriend.

'Good evening, Russ,' Temba said confidently.

Did he used to call his girlfriends' fathers by their first names? Russ wondered. Ah, but then he never had many girlfriends and by the time he did, they, and he, were long absented from the homes of their parents.

'Hello, Temba,' said Russ. 'Have you met Dr Trevor Shaw?'

The scientist and the teenager greeted each other and Russ's thoughts about his father were submerged in the general hubbub of the little group huddled around the fossil in Luc's lap.

'Russ,' said Shaw, looking over to where he was standing. 'This fossil must have come from an earlier dig. What sites had your father worked?'

'All over the bloody place.'

'Where, exactly?'

Russ sighed. 'He says he was at La Chapelle-aux-Saints when they found that arthritic Neanderthal in 1908 – the one that had everyone thinking the Neanderthals walked with a stoop. Where else? In Malta. China – before the First World War. But he had to get out. Didn't get much of a chance to dig. That was one of his more dramatic stories. Broken Hill in the early 1920s. And then I don't know, God knows what he did during the next couple of decades – back in England starting a family with his first wife – my mother was his second wife, by the way.'

He caught Rebecca's gaze. They hadn't spoken about the photographs since she'd first insisted that those two fathers in those different families were the same man.

'After I was born we moved around a lot. We were in Zanzibar and Tanganyika before independence.'

'So, Trevor,' said Rebecca, 'does our illustrious dinner guest have a name?'

'Ah, now that's the interesting part. Who is this chap? Our problem is that he has features of two different species:

Australopithecus boisei and *Australopithecus aethiopicus*. Russ thinks this chap's parents might have been from different species, rather like what would happen if a mixed-race couple today has a child.'

Temba shifted uncomfortably. For once, the smooth Dr Shaw had slipped up. Fuck, thought Russ, throwing a panicky glance at Rebecca, expecting her to take his comment about miscegenation as evidence of his objection to Savannah's boyfriend. I don't care that he's black, I just don't want my sixteen-year-old daughter pregnant – she's not, is she?

'The bone running along the top of his head,' said Luc, pointing at the specimen's sagittal crest and unknowingly rescuing Shaw from his faux pas and Russ from his discomfort, 'is like the big bump on a gorilla's head.'

'Too true, Luc,' said Shaw. 'This bony ridge is known as a sagittal crest and it is as big as a gorilla's. When the creature was alive, it acted as an anchor for the muscles that worked its massive jaw.'

And then Russ knew. Shaw's casual comment had given him the words to describe the idea floating unwanted on the edge of his consciousness: the crest wasn't simply as big as a gorilla's, it *was* a gorilla's. Or, at least, it *wasn't* a *boisei*'s. Shaw was going to be embarrassed – far more so than any faux pas about miscegenation in the Codron household – and Russ didn't know how to tell him without losing him as an ally.

22

IT WAS PERHAPS A *month or two before we had enlisted that I received a letter from Isaac Rosenberg, delivered to me by a geologist colleague at Chou Kou Tien. I held no truck with the moralistic high-handedness that held up Asia, not Africa, as the birthplace of man. I was nonetheless lured by the region's 'dragon bones' – as the fossils are known in China, where they are put to profligate cannibalistic use as traditional medicine. So I arrived at Dragon Bone Hill at a time when the not-yet-famous Davidson Black was still working in Elliot Smith's laboratory, caught up with his supervisor in examining the Piltdown fragments.*

Chou Kou Tien, or Zhoukoudian as it is now spelled – Russ had read in *Digging for Darwin* – is a famous *Homo erectus* site in China. In the early 1930s Davidson Black was hailed for having found the missing link there. As it turned out, Black's fossil was of the same species Dubois had found in Java, only, unlike Dubois, Davidson Black knew how to work a crowd, and had diplomatically sent advance notice to Elliot Smith of his find. In the process he also managed to upstage Dart's presentation of the Taung Child in London.

Isaac's letters were those of a poet. 'Across the bay,' he wrote from Cape Town, 'the piled up mountains of Africa look lovely and dangerous. It makes one think of savagery and earthquakes – the elemental lawlessness, but the people! I am in an infernal city by the sea. This city has men in it – and these men have souls in them – or at least have the passages to souls. Though they are millions of years behind time they have yet reached the stage of evolution that knows ears and eyes.

But these passages are dreadfully clogged up – gold dust, diamond dust, stocks and shares, and heaven knows what other flinty muck.'

Russ felt as though he were sitting at the old man's knee, after they had cracked a coconut together, chewing on the white flesh, listening, playing with Barak's wedding ring, looking up at his craggy face. *Across the bay*, he thought, as he raised his eyes from the Good Croxley to catch a glimpse of Beck dashing past towards the studio, stuffing the remnants of a sandwich into her mouth, *the piled up mountains of Africa*. Was Rosenberg describing the view across False Bay of Hottentots Holland mountains?

Russ's first memories of Cape Town were not of an infernal city with men whose passageways were clogged with the stuff of their greed, but of a seaside resort and a father whose object of compulsion – for the holidays anyway – was his son. It was these memories that brought Russ to live here: playing on the beach at Muizenberg, the bright bathing boxes, the white sand and across False Bay, the mountains a dreamy blue in the distance. His mother waits up the beach, watching them playing in the shallows, the husband tackling the son, racing with him chest to chest into deeper water, limbs flailing in excitement. Raucous laughter rises up with the falling of the waves. They half-disappear, submerged by the white froth and then pop up giggling, both boys for now. And then covering Barak with sand, spading it over his body, calling her to join in. She shades her eyes with a hand and smiles but you cannot see her teeth, her lips do not part; it is not a smile after all, merely a dim reflection of the joyful grin on your face. And Dad lies so still inside his sarcophagus of sand. And then it is too much, and you hastily uncover him, lest he stay buried forever.

Poor Isaac. It would not be so long before we were to meet up again in the ranks of the First King's Own Royal Lancaster Regiment, Sixth Platoon, B Company. We were trained in field tactics that had changed little since before the Boer War: the entire battalion was to form into sections, advance, deploy in open order, and attack with bayonets at the ready. 'Remember that every Boche you fellows kill is a point scored to our side; every Boche you kill brings victory one minute nearer. Kill them! Kill them!' It all seemed gung-ho on English soil but on the bloody fields of France it was another matter altogether. Bayonets? We could hardly get within thirty yards of the Boche because of the machine guns.

So piercing was the odour of mustard gas and shell fire that we never noticed the whiff of men shitting in their pants as we waited on the tape-lines. Weighed down by our packs, by the lice that crawled over our bodies like some living undergarment, by this unwanted suicide, we advanced in successive waves towards the grey coalscuttle helmets, line after line, feeding ourselves to the hungry machine guns of the enemy and the cretinous pride of our own commanders as if we were courses on a dinner plate.

We were driven to strange acts of heroism by which we hoped to regain our humanity. One night as we slept fitfully, a heavy bombardment opened up, followed by an infantry attack, and those of us who survived the onslaught scrambled back to our reserve line. Having gained their fifty yards, the Boche fell back and dug in, leaving our trench in no-man's land. One of our comrades had taken his false teeth out and laid them down beside him, where they still lay, in the abandoned trench. He looked wretched, his mouth puckered as if it was a shell crater. Without exchanging so much as a word, Isaac and I crawled over the top and out to the trench, felt about in the icy mud and found our friend's teeth.

There was more, and as he read Barak's description of the battle death of his good comrade Isaac Rosenberg, Russ kept thinking, *what a brave reflection on war. Only bloody trouble is, it isn't true.* According to Russ's mother, her husband had never been anywhere near the Western Front. After fleeing the Chou Kou Tien dig he'd spent the duration working in his father's bakery, had avoided service because the army needed bread. Barak himself had never, as far as Russ could

remember, told him a story about the Great War. Surely
if the old man had been there, he would have rejoiced
in regaling his son with tales of daring-do? Russ turned
the page and was confronted by three lines that had been
vigorously crossed out, a rare sign of regret on his father's
part. He held the warped page up to the window's light,
squinting at the smudges.

'Fuck this,' he said.

He'd had enough of this crap. Trenches and poets and
false teeth. It was all false, not just the teeth. Barak was
a fabulist, a maker of tales. He lived his life in a sea of
falsehood, a kind of False Bay. Russ's mother was the one
with the truth, but he had dismissed her drunken aspersions
on Barak's integrity, especially the story of adultery. He
could see now the source of his own denial. If he had
accepted that Barak could leave one set of children, why
wouldn't he leave Russ? Why would Russ be so special as
to keep his love? The story of Barak's tragic disappearance
shortly after he left in November 1963 would shatter. He
might have lived well into 1964, or 1965, or 1966. It would
mean that Barak had not simply gone on a three month dig;
it would mean he had chosen to stay away.

He could see now that his mother had – wittingly or
otherwise – given him the means to slay his father, to free
himself of his false hero. It was as if she was offering up the
errant offspring of Excalibur in her pale, dripping arm, rising
from the murky green-brown water of Muizenberg Lake.

Toka was both right and wrong. Thirteen year olds *do* know
their parents' business. The evidence was all inside Russ. He
was a thirteen year old who had been exposed to all he needed
to know. But he couldn't interrogate himself. He didn't have
the maturity, the strength to face the terrible disappointment
that knowledge would bring with it. He laughed, an edgy,
fragile shaft of sound. Barak was looking for Eden, and Russ

was trying to preserve an Eden before the snake of knowledge made its appearance. He tossed the Good Croxley across the room. It hit the wall and bounced off, landing in a twisted and curled muddle of French and English.

It wasn't enough, this burial in a paper pit where there were only paper worms. He wanted more, He wanted the cutting of his clothing at Barak's funeral, the skullcap on his head, with the hairclip to keep it from blowing off. He wanted the reading of Hebrew prayers, the walk between the rows of cold graves, the thud of soil against coffin wood. He wanted the washing of hands. He wanted something he could touch, something he could rely on, something corporeal. He wanted it done, so that he could get on with his life.

He knew what he had to do. He had to bury his father. And if the child belonged to Barak, he would simply bury the little half-sibling along with him.

He telephoned the Jewish burial society. The *Chevra Kadisha*'s Rabbi Moshe Levy, to whom he was referred, heard him out, was silent for a moment, and then in a measured tone proclaimed 'two points' upon which he was equally adamant: Barak was to be buried without delay, and the half-born child was not Jewish – even if it was Barak's – and could not share his coffin.

But Rabbi, listen: like all Homo sapiens, *Rebecca's people originated in Africa five thousand or so generations ago (perhaps not very far from Cape Town, if my father's theory is more reliable than its author). Over thousands of years they made their way up the continent, eventually finding themselves in the Holy Land, from where, in far more recent times, they left for Spain, and from there, after the persecutions, sought sanctuary elsewhere in Europe, finally settling in Belgium. Chased by Hitler they returned to Africa, to the Belgium Congo, then on to Kenya. The Mau-Mau rebellion hastened them south, to Southern Rhodesia where they later fled the Chimurenga and ended up here, in Cape Town. Like all Capetonians of a paler complexion, they have come full circle, traversing the length of Africa and on into Europe before making the return journey to the place of their African ancestors, to the place, my father would argue, that you call the Garden of Eden.*

But wait, the point is this: things have been put to rights. My father was Sephardi, my wife is Sephardi, my children are Sephardi. So we skipped half a beat, a delicate Englishwoman and a sturdier African in the spic pile, what does that matter? We are all African under the skin and the African child is but a small collection of bones. It looks like the remains of a fish. Why can't my father be buried with a fish?

This is how a man would have expressed it. But when Russ opened his mouth, it was to stifle a sob, and only the sound of sucked air came out.

'You are upset, Mr Codron,' said the Rabbi. 'And you are not making sense. The child was not born of a Jewish mother, not so?'

Russ gasped and hung up, angry tears falling like wet hammer blows on his cheeks.

23

I HAD ONLY JUST ARRIVED *in the area when evidence of the richness of the deposits began to emerge. This was December of 1963 –* each line of English was beating a rhythm, cap to toe, against its French brother – *and I had started on the beach to the north of the peninsula, having been directed there by a young coloured boy. I should say, by the fossilised tibia he was using as a drum stick. I came across him at Simonstown harbour, where I had come to buy fish off the boats. I had been in Cape Town for several days, double-checking my calculations with geologists, etc, and stocking up for the West Coast dig. Can you imagine my joy at finding this evidence on the eve of my departure for that very same area? Serendipity, you might say!*

The boy was sitting cross-legged on a concrete breakwater, sand sticking to the cracked soles of his feet, banging with great gusto on a tin drum, making the most awful din and upsetting the seagulls who had gathered in the hope of catching scraps from the boats. Their screams only made things worse. At first I thought the fishermen were using the young drummer to signal to prospective buyers that the boats had returned, although I had been down several times and couldn't recall ever having seen the little musician. The morning sun shimmered off the scales of steenbras, tunny, hake. An octopus was entangled in one of the nets, its skin, despite the glint of light in the droplets of water that clung to it, already having lost the sheen of life. The fishermen were throwing their catch off the boats on to the wharf, where the fish landed with a wet thud. Here they gathered in their stranded mass, some still flapping valiantly about.

The smell of the fish and the salt and the burning of the boats' diesel engines washed in waves over the concrete harbour walls. One of the men – I thought perhaps he was the boy's father – shouted at him and the boy stopped his drumming. As he began again, slowly, quietly to tap the drum – rather, I thought, like a dying bee asking to be put out of its misery – I caught sight properly of the instrument he was using as a drumstick. He told me, through an interpreter since my refusal to learn Afrikaans rendered me unable to understand, that he had received the 'been', which I understood to mean 'leg', from an uncle who trawled in waters up the West Coast. He seemed happy for the attention and happier still for the fifty cents I gave him for the bone. The tibia, I could see immediately, was that of a species of buck, extinct for a hundred thousand years or more. There were striations on the bone, evidence of cut marks from a hominid-wielded flint. I tracked down the uncle and he took me by boat to the beach where he had found the specimen. It cost me a few quid, I can tell you, or rather, rands, since they had become the new Republic's currency.

Buffeted by fierce southerly winds that picked up grains of sand and hurled them as if they were pellets from a shotgun, I began to search the beach that very day. I grew used to those winds – and thankful for them, since they did so much of my digging for me. In winter, they changed direction and came in from the north, but were just as stinging. The early Europeans had good reason to call this place the Cape of Storms. But the beach, oh, bless that glorious blanket of sediment. It revealed a tale of richness, a glory now wiped out by radical climatic change: tropical rainforests, swamps, lagoons and an abundant wildlife.

When I realised the depth of the fossil record, I couldn't help recalling my first excavations as a child on Brighton beach. My father would take the family for our annual holiday to Brighton. 'Our beano,' my parents used to call it, one of their sad, misplaced attempts at being English. They were celebrating the survival of another year. I remember it well, the buggy ride to the station, the steam locomotive, our excitement at crossing the countryside, my mother, in that thick accent of hers which always embarrassed me, instructing my youngest brother Charles to speak in English and not the Ladino our young minds had so nimbly picked up from them. And me calling out the stations on our way to the coast — and all the while my wretched father worrying about the weather and the survival of the bakery in his absence. We would stay for a week in a boarding house belonging to an horrendous woman by the name of Mrs Tilburn, whose drunken husband was all too fond of pestering my older sister Sara. It is there, as a ten year old, with one of the Tilburns' foster daughters, that my taste for Gentile women first took root. The couple fostered some twelve children in all, and were in the habit of beating them to within inches of their lives. 'God is all-knowing,' my father would say, lifting his eyes to the heavens, although whether he was looking for the Almighty or checking the weather, I'm not sure. 'Do you think that pisgado brother of mine has remembered to have them bring the flour?' But those were the happiest times of my childhood, because I could indulge my other nascent taste: I could search the shore for fossils.

Russ closed the notebook on this rare glimpse of Barak's childhood. The Croxley was bulkier where he'd tried to repair the pages that had torn and crumpled after he'd thrown it against the wall. Beck had hit her sculpture, and he'd hit the Good Croxley. What were they turning into, a boxing tag-team?

The spotting of the coloured boy's drumstick was serendipitous all right, the kind of story fossil hunters loved to tell. They called it chance, or luck, or serendipity, but what they really meant was this: *I have been chosen to excavate here.* And for this reason, Russ did not believe the story. The fossils themselves, however, were another matter. Russ could not give up his belief in Barak's loyalty to the science of description. 'Honour them with accuracy,' the old man used to say.

The cave was singing a mournful Siren's song, inviting him to share its secrets. That place, at least, was set in stone. And stone does not lie. In Russ's mind he crossed the rocky threshold, the sunlight in his eyes as he slithered through on his back, his legs and crotch inside, his waist and heart bridging the entrance, that place between light and dark. He shuddered. Perhaps it was but a black hole soaking up light and him along with it. But he could manage that, could he not? He was a manipulator of light, was that not what he did for a living? Did he not correct vision by bending light through a lens? The higher the prescription, the more light must be bent, and the cave called for a high prescription. He could bend light into that cave. He had done it before. He had looked into his mother's grave and it had brought him relief. He would no longer have to search her hiding places, dilute her wine, negotiate her passed-out form from bathroom to bed after finding her asleep on the toilet. A boy should not have to do such things. Most times she would have passed out before taking off her pants; sometimes – and he hated these times – she had managed it – and he would wrap a towel around her waist so as to protect the tattered remains of her dignity. And no wonder her humiliation had reached such depths. If Russ's classmate and tormentor Arnoldus van Schalkwyk had known that his father was sleeping with 'kaffir women in the bush', then the whole of Krugersdorp, including Barak's aristocratic English wife, must have known it. And in those days, in that place, there could have been no greater humiliation.

Then came one morning in Russ's matric year when he found her in a coma. He telephoned for an ambulance and she was taken to hospital. She woke only once. He was smoothing down her dirty blond hair, staring at her once-beautiful sore face, skin peeling off dry lips that he had unsuccessfully tried to moisten. Her eyes opened and looked into his face.

'Russell, keep the house clean for when your father gets back.'

He took her hand, silent in his confusion. She slipped back into her coma and died that night.

Rebecca had a new theory and as she began to expound it, Russ had a theory about her theory: that it bore the signature of Luc's wayward logic. It struck him that the two of them had been talking about the mummies all this time, that Luc had been consulting with his mother in the same way that he sought her clarification on the puzzling matter of humour.

The new theory was that Barak had *intentionally* mummified himself and the woman.

'Don't be ridiculous.'

'Why? Eleventh century Japanese Buddhist monks mummified themselves so they'd be around when the new Buddha came.'

And then, as if on cue, Professor Naidoo phoned to say that the lab results had been returned. The tissue samples revealed unusually high levels of sulphur and sodium. Sulphur, she told Russ, is found widely in nature, in minerals and ores, in plant and animal protoplasm, and in volcanic regions (in which the cave was not) or large underground deposits, often concomitant to coal and natural gas. It's what fire-breathing preachers refer to as *brimstone*. Sulphur dioxide is used as a food preservative but she doubted this could be the main factor in the mummification of the bodies. Sodium, on the other hand, was essential to the most common preservative in the world: sodium chloride. Salt. Embalmers used it to suck out moisture and to discourage micro-organisms. An ancient Egyptian wanting to do it on the cheap used natron salt; the South American Palomans dried out their dead with salt; and nature does it too: the mummies of Taklamakan Desert of northwestern China were perfectly preserved for 3000 years because of the dry, salty, hot conditions.

'Quite fantastic,' said the professor, ending her salt and brimstone lecture, a woman, Russ reckoned, having the time of her academic life. 'I suspect, given the unnaturally high levels of sodium and sulphur, that the bodies became mummified quickly. I've arranged to do CT scans. They'll show if I'm right. The more we can see of the sub-cortical structures, the more likely it is that an event mummified the bodies quickly, before any insects or micro-organisms could get hold of them. Once the bodies are desiccated, it's like leaving an old leather shoe in a dark, dank place. It'll get pretty mouldy, but its basic structure will remain intact for a long, long time. I doubt very much that the agent of mummification was natural to that cave, at least not in the required quantities. I see in this the hand of man.'

'That proves it,' said Beck after Russ relayed the conversation. 'At the very least, he *knew* they were going to be mummified. That's why he tied his jaw shut.'

'Maybe, maybe not,' said Russ. She got up to return to the studio. Russ followed her. At the closed studio door she turned to face him, waiting for him to leave. She was not going to allow him another glimpse of the sculpture.

He went back to the Good Croxley.

On the north beach where the fisherman left me, I was picking the bones of extinct animals off the sand, just as I would as a child find shells and crustaceans under Brighton Pier. This was the stuff most of us can only dream of – short-necked giraffe, a four-tusked elephant, a horse with three toes, buffalo with a horn-span of twelve foot and pigs three times the size of your average warthog. But search as I might, not a splinter of human ancestry surfaced. I had been seduced away from my maxim by the impossible riches of the beach. It was clearly time I returned to it: head for the caves! And that is when I happened upon this site but by an amazing stroke of luck. The natural place to look for a cave was in the rocky outcrops of the peninsula, but scour as I might, I could find no trace of cave or fossil deposits. The granite boulders were not in the least bit promising. I had stopped to rest one morning and was watching a dassie make its way across the ground, when suddenly it disappeared between two rocks. This is hardly extraordinary for a dassie but some time later when it still had not re-emerged and since any surface route was in full view of my position, I began to suspect that it had a burrow there. I went over to investigate. The sediment between the boulders was loose and there was an opening just big enough to accommodate the little animal. The lie of the boulders around the opening suggested an avalanche, perhaps dating back a few thousand years at most.

Now, you know I do not easily turn to Robert Broom's methods, but I was feverish with excitement. I was interested, remember, in the period 100,000 to 200,000 years ago, in what might be hidden behind the outer layer. I could see that if I placed the charge correctly, it would only blow away the more recent landfill.

The blast revealed a cavern in which I could easily stand to my full height. I was to discover that the cave is a book of many chapters, its roof having collapsed at various points, only to be opened up again by thousands of years of wind and water erosion. Oh, those early, glorious weeks. As I uncovered layer after layer, my digging began to turn up a range of animal fossils as impressive as those of the beach below, including the cranium of an antelope with two neat holes from the teeth of a sabre-toothed cat. But the most enlightening were the pigs, evolution's beautiful chronometers. Their remains allowed me to date my finds.

Listen, lad, – 'lad'? was Barak addressing him? who else would he call 'lad'? one of his *other* sons? – *you know how it is: bone fragments from one species can look just like those of another; if you do not know what you are doing, you will not know what is antelope, hominid, or pig. Not only that, but you have to contend with extinct forerunners of each species. If you know all this, and you're lucky, you can turn it to your advantage; like the pigs, son: they evolved with such clockwork regularity that we are able to use their changes to date our finds. If you know what a species' lineage looks like, and the date when each form appeared and disappeared, you can use this as a measure of time. Anything else you find in the same tuff will be of the same age. The pig genus* Metridiochoerus, *for instance, shows a change in the chewing surface of its teeth over the millennia – you find a tooth, match it up to the known record, and you've got a marker as reliable as if someone had left a note. It is the only way –*

No, let me stop this babbling.

There is something I have to confess.

But it was the end of the Good Croxley and, if his father had continued this passage in the Mummy's Notebook, Russ would have to wait. Tante Julia had the Mummy's Notebook.

24

THE PHONE WAS RINGING him back to reality. He should have been getting ready for work. Instead he had been frozen in front of the bathroom mirror, a toothbrush in his hand. He picked up the phone.

'Russell?'

'Trevor?'

'I've got bad news. Well, it's bad, but perhaps not news to you. The fossil's a forgery, a bloody composite.'

Russ was quiet.

'The whole fucking thing's a fake. I can't believe I was taken in by it. He must have cast a real *boisei* fossil, sculpted that oversized crest, thrown in a convincing looking stain using I don't know what because I've never seen a cast look so much like the real thing. What was he doing, Russ? Playing a child's game? I can't believe it fooled me. I was so much in awe of him that I just assumed it was genuine, that I was dealing with bits of fossil and filler material.'

'I tried to tell you,' said Russ, his voice flat, apologetic. He held the telephone against his dulled face.

'Christ,' said Shaw. 'How are we going to be able to trust anything he's done?'

Russ was quiet.

'Russell, are you there?'

'Do you know,' said Russ, 'whenever I see a chicken on the boil, which is not very often – maybe once a year, for *erev* Yom Kippur, the start of the fast – you know, for Beck...

well, actually, I join her in fasting – when that chicken's in the pot giving off that awful sweet smell of boiled meat, I'm reminded of him. He used to boil the heads of dead people on the stove – to get the flesh off. Or he'd get his helpers to bury bodies in the garden, in a shallow grave, so that the worms would clean the skeleton, then months later he'd send one of them out – the workers, not the worms – to exhume the remains. When one of his workers died my father bribed the burial society to bring the body back to him. He was interested in comparing Shona skulls with those of the San. The first I knew Witness – my father's assistant – was dead was when I saw his head floating face-up in my mother's big soup pot.'

'Fucking hell, what's your point, Russ? Apart from the fact that your father was out to lunch?'

'Well, that's just it. Was he? Broom used to do the same thing. They weren't sitting in some stuffy laboratory in Oxford. They were in the *field*. My father was a complex man. He had a passionate interest in science. The normal rules of social behaviour didn't come into it. He believed that science, the pursuit of truth, shouldn't be hampered by notions of morality.'

'How on earth could false evidence aid in the pursuit of truth? It makes him no better than the Piltdown forger.'

'Look, what makes you think he meant that composite to be found by anyone? You said yourself he'd broken it up after he'd constructed it.' There was a sulky silence on Shaw's end of the line. Russ pushed on, his words speeding now. 'Maybe he was exploring a hypothetical branch of the evolutionary tree. Maybe he was making a statue for his… for the woman. Maybe it wasn't his.'

'I don't think so,' said Shaw. 'Hell, I'm sorry, Russ. I should've listened to your scepticism. It was just so damn seductive. The whole thing is absurd. Why would he explore hypotheses like this? None of us would waste our time sculpting hypothetical fossils. We'd rather be in the field finding the real ones. It's too time-consuming. That's what fossil artists do but they're *artists*, not scientists.'

'He found something out there,' Russ said, trying to keep the plaintive edge from his voice. 'He didn't have enough time to get it out of the cave wall. I felt it.'

'I don't know, Russell. I think you're being hopeful. You said yourself the cave was too dark to make anything out clearly. No disrespect intended, but you haven't excavated since you were a kid. Not even Kamoya Kimeu could identify a fossil simply by feeling it.' He was invoking the famously eagle-eyed Kenyan leader of Richard Leakey's Hominid Gang. 'We could well be wasting our time. Your father was a maverick genius and like all maverick geniuses, pretty damn unreliable. It was you who said he'd never made an important discovery in his life. Why should he have left us anything after his death? I don't know. I don't know what to say. I have a responsibility to the university, to the trustees of the National Geographic Society. I have to go up to my East Coast site.'

'Better to dig with the devil you know, huh?'

'My devil is geology and time,' said Shaw. 'Yours is human.'

It was Russ's turn to lapse into a leaden silence. Any utterance he might make now would be that of the over-burdened mule.

'Russ, we'll investigate the cave. Of course we will. It's just going to have to wait. There's nothing we can do without the permit anyway. I'll have to speak to you when I get back.' Before ending the call he added, as if reading Russ's thoughts: 'Don't go out there again, Russell. They're very sensitive about issuing these permits. If you're caught, you'll compromise our chances. They'll give it to someone else.'

Shaw hung up. Russ sat on the side of the bed, the receiver in his hands. He wanted to go to the cave. There was something there for him, he knew it. There had to be. And as for Shaw, well, it only took him a week to discover the fraud. That's a damn sight better than the four decades it took to expose Piltdown Man. He returned the phone to its cradle.

Rebecca walked into the bedroom. 'Who was that?'

'Trevor. That skull of Barak's is a fake. He's pissed off. He thinks he's wasting his time.'

'A fake?'

Russ stared at his toes. 'He's embarrassed that he was taken in by it. He was so in awe of my father, all he could see was the puzzle, this brilliant Christmas gift my father left for him. He never stopped to look at the individual pieces.'

'Sounds like someone I know,' she said.

'Knew,' he corrected her. 'I'm looking at the pieces now.'

25

ONE DAY I ENCOUNTERED *my father outside the bakery greeting one of his Gentile customers. The man could have been a lord for the deference Papa showed him. The conversation between the men, having been struck up in a civil manner, began to heat up, or should I say, the man addressing my father began gesticulating angrily. I have no idea regarding the substance of the customer's complaint but that of my father's response was all too clear. My father, pious Jew that he was, kept his head covered at all times but he seemed to shrivel up in the face of the Gentile's growing rage, his shoulders turned inwards like the rollers of a Torah being brought together, his gaze locked onto the man's boots as if he wanted to lick them and, worst of all, my beloved father removed his hat, leaving his head bare to the heavens. It was not his Judaism over which I felt protective but his pride. Had he none? To what ends would he go to fit in? I felt sure that whatever offence the customer alleged, it would have been no more deadly than a flattened weevil in a loaf of bread, hardly cause for such humiliation. Wherein, therefore, lay the cause for the man's complaint and my father's grovelling?*

Thus began my political education at the tender age of thirteen.

26

RUSS PEERED OVER LUC'S shoulder. The child was on the Internet, gazing at the screen as if he was peering through a window at a distant landscape. A Google search list repeated the word 'sulphur' in bold blue type.

'You're researching sulphur.' It was more a statement than a question. *Well,* said Russ's tone, *of course Luc's researching sulphur, what else would he be doing?*

Luc clicked on a link, Wikipedia's entry for 'Sulphur mustards':

> *The sulphur mustards, of which mustard gas (1,5-dichloro-3-thiapentane) is a member, are a class of related cytotoxic, vesicant chemical warfare agents with the ability to form large blisters on exposed skin. Mustard gas was originally assigned the name LOST, after Lommel and Steinkopf, who first proposed the military use of sulphur mustard to the German Imperial General Staff...*

LOST. Was Wikipedia playing a joke on him? He stared at the screen. *The sulphur mustards, of which mustard gas...* Jesus, yesterday he'd read Barak's account of his experience – *claimed* experience – during the First World War. The synchronicity was too much. Or perhaps it wasn't synchronicity at all. Luc had already read about the trenches and he must have heard Russ discussing Professor Naidoo's feedback about the high levels of sulphur. Luc scrolled down the page.

… Mustard gas was dispersed as an aerosol in a mixture with other chemicals, giving it a yellow-brown colour and a distinctive odour. Mustard gas has also been dispersed in such munitions as aerial bombs, landmines, mortar rounds, artillery shells, and rockets.

Mustard gas may have caught up with Barak half a century after it decimated the young men of Europe, as if the universe was making true his claim to have fought in the trenches. But this irony would not have been what alerted Luc. Luc did not get irony. He would have got here via another route. He would have been alerted to the fact that men built chemical weapons, would have put this together with the artillery testing ground and the information from Professor Naidoo, and come up with the simple explanation Russ had hitherto missed:

- *the cave entrance was hit by a bomb*
- *the bomb released a chemical mixture that spread into the cave*
- *Barak and Nombeko were gassed to death*
- *intense concentrations of sulphur and sodium in the gas preserved their bodies*

Russ squeezed Luc's shoulder. 'Thank you.'

Professor Naidoo's number was stored in his cell. He pulled the phone from his pocket.

'Hello?'

'Professor Naidoo. Hello. Russell Codron here. I have a question.'

'Fire away, my dear.'

Fire away was right. 'Well, here it is. Let's say a missile was launched carrying chemicals. High concentrations of sulphur, sodium, whatever. Something like mustard gas.

The shell hits the cave entrance, there's an avalanche, the entrance is blocked. The explosion propels the gas inside where it's trapped. Kills my father and the woman. And then snap-dries them.'

There was a silence, followed by Professor Naidoo's considered tone. 'Chemical weapons are not my field, Mr Codron. But I suppose that is not what you are asking. You are asking whether airborne supplies of sulphur and sodium would be sufficient to mummify a dead body. Hmm. Trapped in the cave. Why not? If the temperature was right, if the air was dry enough, if parasites and maggots were somehow absent or neutralised, which they may well have been by the chemical blast – sulphur just happens to be a very effective fumigator. The quicker the mummification, the more tissue will be preserved. Then it's like that leather shoe I was telling you about. It'll get mouldy, but stay pretty much intact for years. It fits. This may be the event I was speaking of, a horrible death followed by rapid desiccation. Those apartheid artillery men would have been pleased with their handiwork.'

Russ, who had been pacing Luc's room, sat down on the bed. He looked up. Luc was standing in the doorway now, his expression blank.

'Thank you, Luc,' said Russ. 'That was a brilliant idea.' He grinned in appreciation and thought he might have seen, an instant before Luc turned and walked down the passageway, a faint, skew smile flit across the child's face.

Thus began my political education at the tender age of thirteen. The passage was in the Bad Croxley, in French. Without a word, Beck had walked up to the dining room table where Russ was seated and handed the translation to him on a piece of paper. God knows when she'd had a chance to do it. Her cheeks were flushed with satisfaction. She had yet to wash away the day's spattering of clay. The sculpture, he thought, she's got it right. And then, the crease of her smile saying, *here it is, you see I haven't forgotten my promise to translate the French*, she pulled the sheet out and dropped it in front of him.

Thus began my political education. What was the old man talking about? Russ flipped back through the Bad Croxley to the English passage about Mrs Pankhurst's Suffragettes. *I was far more excited by another group of rabble-rousers: Mrs Pankhurst's militants. I went window smashing with the women.* Barak was born in 1890, and if he was thirteen at the time of his father's bare head incident, this would have made the year 1903. This is what comes of being the son of an old man, a century has since passed. Surely Barak hadn't joined the marches at the age of thirteen? But perhaps this was not the point. Barak was talking about his immigrant father's grovelling response to an Englishman. The smearing of shame like shit-streaks staining underwear.

Barak had left a trail of mysteries that had spawned public investigation: Inspector Toka's murder inquiry, Trevor Shaw's pursuit of his fossil discoveries, Professor Naidoo's mummy examinations. These mattered to Russ inasmuch as their explanations might assist him in his private quest, the one that had occurred to pathetically few people, perhaps only to Barak's wives and children: *why had Barak abandoned them? Who was he really?*

Thus began. Of all Russ had read up until now, this short passage about Barak's obsequious father, nondescript as it was, struck him as true simply because it was too insignificant to be worth making up. It hinted at an inner life beneath the curious gaze of strangers. It was nothing like trench warfare, or finding evidence of early Man. Barak's father embarrassed him. Big deal. No one gives a shit about that.

Except Russ.

... *at thirteen*. Russ had also been given an education at thirteen. Only it wasn't political. It was an education in betrayal. And Russ had refused to take it. Now that he was learning his lessons, Russ might say that Barak had lived longer than the three month period following his departure for the Cape. He had lived long enough to find at least 37 fossil pieces, and to write the three notebooks. He had lived long enough to impregnate Nombeko, and to see the baby grow to term. He had lived long enough to turn departure into desertion.

27

'REBECCA HAS TOLD ME, your father's woman was pregnant there in the cave. A little mummified foetus. Zat is wonderful. Such exquisite sadness.'

It took some moments before he realised who was talking, despite the Zeppelin of an accent. He looked over at the clock. Not yet six. Jesus, only Ulrike would call this early.

'Fuck it, Ulrike,' he said. 'Last I checked Jo'burg was in the same time zone as Cape Town.' He handed the phone to Rebecca. 'It's for you. The agent who never sleeps.'

And then the dream came flooding back to him. It was set in the world of Krugersdorp. Russ was sixteen. The dream was specific on this point. He is walking home from school. He sees a stooped figure on the corner watching him. He goes into the house, makes himself a sandwich for lunch and then wheels his bicycle out of the garage. He is going to meet some friends for a game of rugby. There is the man again. He is very thin, his khaki pants and shirt dirty and torn, a filthy felt hat on his head. He looks like a tramp, perhaps one of those soldiers still shell-shocked from the war, his eyes deeply recessed into his face and his past.

Russ bicycles toward the soldier-tramp. The man needs a shave. On either side of a pronounced nose, his eyes are red, as if he's been crying. He raises a hand, his forefinger pointing limply toward Russ. His lips are cracked. His skin is a pale brownish-grey, the colour of moths.

'Hello, Red,' says the man. His voice is hoarse, a voice that has fallen into disuse.

Russ carries on cycling.

'Place your chin over here,' he said, indicating the chin rest of the slit lamp. He went through the motions of explaining the biomicroscopy procedure – the slit lamp projects narrow beams of light onto and into the eye, using powerful magnification to provide cross-sectional pictures of the eye tissue – and was distracted as his patient spoke of her studies. She was a young woman he had not seen since she was a teenager. Her family had immigrated to Vancouver. She was back in the country to conduct research for her doctoral thesis on cross-generational transmission of trauma. The previous day she had interviewed a twelve-year-old boy, the son of an ANC cadre who had spent three years on Death Row. The boy was a veteran car hijacker by day and secret bed-wetter by night. When she told Russ about this, her voice thick with the poignancy of a child's response to the violent doings of adulthood, he let out an involuntary 'pah!'. The young woman was taken aback.

'S-sorry,' he said, 'nothing to do with you or the boy – I was just … it just reminded me of something.'

The patient leaned forward and steadied her head on the chin rest, her forehead against the machine's top strap. She looked into Russ's eyes, her expression one of interested pity. He must have appeared vulnerable. In avoiding her gaze, Russ found himself peering around the structural arm of the slit lamp and down the scoop of material created by the fall of her blouse. Her breasts, barely supported by a loose camisole, were small, perfectly curved, the nipples dark in the shadow of her shirt. He could easily reach inside and cup one in his hand. Jesus, he was getting a hard-on. He focused the narrow beam of light onto her eye. The magnified image of her cornea bored into him, as if it was not her eyes – nor her breasts – that were being exposed to him, but his mind to her, sliced into neat cross-sections, layer upon layer: anger, grief, excitement, shame. His cock strained against his pants. Most confusing of all, he felt as though it would take the merest touch from her to make him come. Did she know? He couldn't tell.

Anthea was there to cover for him and so he went home early. He had promised to take Rebecca to the airport. He wanted to tell her about the young woman from Canada, about the feeling that he'd be able to come. He could parody himself. *The slumbering giant awakes* – something like that, a shaggy-dog story to defuse the reminder of his sexual desiccation.

At home, he watched in silence as Beck took out her clothes and placed them in a suitcase, the zippered flap peeled back like a layer of burlap skin patiently awaiting the conclusion of an abdominal procedure. She pushed a wad of G-strings into the side of the case, a frown forming a ridge between her eyebrows like a bulge of thought protruding from her brain. *Setting up the pieces*, they said to him. He looked at the clock. Just enough time to run. Once outside the house he stood Nike-clad on the slasto of the patio and stretched his bulk into the air. He clasped his hands behind his head and swung his upper torso from side to side, then stood, feet apart, hands on his hips, rolling his head around on his neck. *The Colossus of Clifton.* Damn vertebrae aren't even clicking, they're creaking. He set off.

He and Beck used to run regularly to Llandudno, or the other way, through Sea Point to the Malay Quarter. They did the Two Oceans a few years after Savannah was born. Now in the stretching of his muscles, the pounding of the pavement, the patterned jarring that shot up his legs as his heels hit the ground, was an old recognition, the delicate balance between pain and pleasure – only his limit seemed to be one kilometre from his starting point. Ridiculous. And so he pushed further, following the stone parapet that bordered the cliff road, suddenly aware of the smells about him: the sea, dog shit, fumes from the passing cars, and the relief of something that didn't quite fit, a whiff of turmeric.

His body parts were clattering into one another. They seemed not to be made for running at all. Yet he had inherited a body that had striven so hard for bipedalism, a few million years of evolution geared towards walking and running. Conquering the savannah had been a prelude to marathon running. What was he doing? Was this sudden urge to exercise triggered by his attraction to his young patient and an urgent need to shed the excess of age? He didn't mind being a cliché, at least it would herald his return to the human race. He had to be alive to have a mid-life crisis.

Sweat beaded out from his overheated mass. He began to imagine himself from above in a flickering sequence of black and white pencil drawings, and then imagination broke its mooring with reality and he was riding his bicycle and the soldier-tramp is in front of him, at the bend in the road, pointing limply at him, a weak, old man's gesture, the soldier-tramp calling out brokenly, 'Red! Red!' Only one person ever called him Red, the person who named him Russell, the only person in his life whose quirky mind would have been interested in the Old English derivation of that name and its meaning. *Rut! Rut!*

The old people said *rut* when they wanted to describe the colour of rocks.

He stumbled, picked himself up, wobbled uncertainly, managed a few more metres, and then staggered towards an opening in the adjacent wall where the cement blocks had been removed to allow access to an excavation machine for the building of a new seaside mansion. He fell head first through the opening and tumbled down the side of a ditch, dug for the foundations of the new house. He was in a trench of the First World War, he was a soldier wishing to return to the valleys and fields of his home in time to plant the crops, in time to find a wife, in time for a child's birthday, in time to hold a dying mother's hand, only to find himself back in a world of mud and mustard gas and misery. Perhaps it was not a First World War trench after all, but the gravel pit at the side of the road outside Piltdown and he was there looking for pieces of the great Piltdown Man, anything, anything at all, if only God would make him famous: a tooth, a fragment of tibia, a chunk of skull, glory resting on the discovery of a few inches of ancient bone.

In the ditch near his home in Clifton, Russ rolled over onto his side, drew his knees towards his chest, his head trembling in his hands as a wave of shame broke its way from his throat. The dream he had woken with this morning, of himself as a sixteen year old cycling past the tramp, was not so much a dream as a recount of an actual event. It *had* happened. He had been that boy. And the tramp had been Barak.

Arriver comme un cheveu sur la soupe. It had been the very first thing Russ had read in the notebooks, translated for him by Rebecca. *To arrive like a hair in the soup*. Barak must have been talking about that incident, he was referring to himself as the bad penny, turning up suddenly. And the sixteen-year-old Russ had been unable to acknowledge him. Russ had treated him as if he were an hallucination, or a ghost. The boy had been waiting and waiting for his father to return home and when the old man did, he'd turned a blind eye.

Russ felt as though he had walked into a room to discover himself over the prone body of a child, a wet knife in hand. He craned his neck. The yellow teeth of the excavation machine loomed over him. He had to get out of the ditch. He staggered to his feet, facing out towards the sea and the open sky. His eyes sent messages to his brain, his brain spun, fighting the vertigo that had him fused with the infinite blue space in front of him. Some children stood at the parapet, skateboards in hand. They pointed at him and laughed. Then they dropped their boards to the pavement, their flamingo feet kicking up building dust as they skated away. He looked around at the building site. How much time had passed? Beck! He was supposed to be taking her to the airport.

When he stumbled into the bedroom, he was muddy from the dirt of the foundation trench, weak and dizzy, but insisted on driving her.

'Are you sure you're going to be all right?'

'Of course I'll be all right.' He laughed. 'I'll be fine, I promise.'

'You'll phone me.'

'Sure, of course.' He felt impatient. She treated him as if he were a baby, dependent upon her for his every need. Christ, even a child could last a few days without its mother.

His mother. He couldn't picture her face. Dark patches under the eyes came into focus, encumbered by vein-busted areas of skin. 'I've been trying to picture her face,' he said. 'All I can see are those blotches on her skin.'

'Whose face?'

'My mother's. I can't bring her to mind.'

'Why don't you look at that photograph you found? Russ, you'll call Dan Kahn if you need something?'

'Dan?' Dan Kahn was their GP.

'If you need some tranquilisers or sleeping pills.'

'I'll be fine. Stop going on about it.'

Beck's packed bags needed to be taken to the car. 'I'll take this,' she said. 'I can do some on the plane.' She had the Good Croxley in her hand.

They rode in silence to the airport. His body ached. The concrete barriers that separated the shacks from the highway were dull, solid, suddenly no longer there to keep the anger and despair from the road but flashing by over the gear shift that sat between them.

He thought he might tell her about his dream and the sickening memory it had unleashed. He might tell her about turning a blind eye. Ha! Is this why he'd become an optometrist? Had he been trying to make up for one horrific act of blindness? And remain blind to the whole endeavour while doing so? Fuck, yes. He had found a perfect way to pull off this mind-numbing feat: as long as he focused on aiding the sight of others he could remain insightless himself. Incredible.

The dream had brought back the memory of his crime and he felt overwhelmed by the shame of it. Why had he ignored his father? Why had he not flown off the bike into the old man's arms? Why had he not embraced Barak and taken him inside and given him food and succour? Was he too angry to let the old man back in? No, that was not it. Of course he'd been angry at Barak, even enraged – he understood this now – but it was not the death of his father he was trying to will into being, not at that time. Quite the contrary: his ignoring of the tramp that day was a desperate, mad act of love. He was trying to safeguard the image of the father he cherished and so he had displaced his love from the person of his father to the *idea* of his father's arrival. Waiting for Barak had become his state of desire. Fulfilment of that desire could never live up to its hope, was destined for disappointment. So it was better to live *in hope*. And for that, he had to remain in a state of waiting. If that broken man was Barak, then Russ would have to feel equally broken. He was as invested in the idealisation of Barak as Barak himself.

This is why he had to bicycle past the soldier-tramp that day. Barak in his wasted flesh three years after his disappearance could never return Russ's beloved, loving father to him. If that tramp was not Barak, then the real Barak may still come back and it would be as if the three years of sorrow never took place.

Rebecca was trying to tell him something. 'Remember that Beatrice is away for the weekend. There's plenty in the fridge. You'll have to take care of the meals. She'll be back on Monday. And don't forget about tonight's arrangement.'

'Huh?'

'It's Friday night at Tante Julia's. I said you'd go with the kids.'

'Yes, yes, I know. Did you ask her about the translation? Is it ready?'

'Sorry. I forgot to ask. I'm sure she'll have it. And don't forget to feed Dali. You could take him for a walk, or get Savannah to do it or you're going to have a very restless somebody on your hands.'

'Why's she getting restless? Did she have a fight with Temba? She's not pregnant, is she?'

He was thinking about his mother again, that she had been a little girl who found a way to satisfy both her intense hatred and her love for her father in one stinking foul swoop: by marrying Barak, a man as arrogant, entitled, and impressive as the Viscount. Then followed him to the ends of the earth – the colonies – bore him a son and playmate and stayed at home, the African sun and cheap wine freckling and lining her delicate English skin, while he roamed the continent sticking his rock hammer into crevices. It wasn't really surprising that Russ couldn't picture her face. He hardly knew who she was. She wasn't Jewish, that's for sure. In his experience, Jewish women were uncompromising, they demanded an acknowledgement of their presence. If you disappeared, they went to find you. Maybe that's why he'd married Beck.

'I meant Dali,' said Rebecca. They had reached the airport. 'Dali's getting restless. Savannah's fine. You can drop me off. No need to come in. Go home, have a shower, listen to some music.'

'Don't be ridiculous,' Russ said. 'I'd like to see you in.' In his marriage to Beck, there should have been no hiding from her, and yet he had eventually managed it.

At the check-in counter she asked for a window seat. Unlike him, she loved flying and looked forward to seeing the Western Cape from the air, especially at sunset. She kissed him on his dirt-streaked cheek. He must look like the soldier-tramp.

'I'll be all right,' he said. 'Don't worry.'

That sideways glance said it all. She had little choice. He was forcing her to worry. With a flicker of a smile she turned and walked up to the security checkpoint. She handed her boarding pass to the security officer and gave up her handbag to be swallowed by the x-ray machine.

He had told her he would be all right. But when he returned from the airport, walked through the front door into the house, Dali nagging hungrily at his heels, the hollow echo of the door closing behind him and the cold and darkness telling him that no one was home, he knew he was not going to be all right.

Where were Beatrice and the kids? Had Beck said something about it? Should he be making supper? He opened the freezer, his gaze settling on a glass Tupperware dish containing a vegetarian stew he had prepared only two months ago, in an age that now seemed lost. Like the age of the Round Table. King Arthur took Barak to lunch at the Savoy. King? Well, it must have been *Sir* Arthur, but which one? Keith? Smith Woodward? Conan Doyle? No, none of those Arthurs. *Professor* Clement Arthur Oldfield.

It must be quite remarkable, Russ mused, as he slipped the bolognaise into the microwave to defrost, to be a man of such influence.

'You all right, Dad? Mom phoned to see if you were okay. She said I should call her back to let her know.'

'I'm okay, Sav. Don't worry, I'll call her later. She must be on the plane by now.'

'Okay. Mom asked me to wet the towel on her sculpture. Will you do it? I've got to shower before we go.'

Russ looked up. Where had Sav come from? 'Where are we going?'

'Dad! To Tante Julia's.'

'Oh, yes, of course.' He could object to her request to wet the towel. He could tell Savannah that her mother wouldn't appreciate him doing that, that Rebecca had asked her, and not him, for a reason. But instead, guiltily, he said, 'I'll do the towel. You go ahead and get ready. Where's Luc?'

'In his room. I've already told him where we're going.' It was best to prepare Luc for change, no matter how small.

Inside the studio, there was just enough pink dusk light for Russ to forego switching on the fluorescents. To one side of the sculpture, which was covered in the towel he was to dampen and replace, he could see that the board upon which Rebecca mounted her preliminary drawings and notes was covered in colour photographs. He took a closer look. The pictures had been taken inside the dissection room Professor Naidoo had used. He couldn't recall anyone taking photos during the examination, least of all Rebecca. She must have asked Leila Naidoo for them. The pictures, some of which were in close-up, were of Barak's corpse – in particular, the head – and were arranged around a reproduction of *The Scream*. Russ stepped back and turned towards the sculpture. Beck had placed the bust on a plinth so that she could work eye-to-eye, so that Russ now approached it as he would someone a head shorter than himself. Russ's glimpse of the fallen sculpture had left him with a glimmer of what he would find when he removed the towel, what had been building up around the armature as a result of Rebecca's last frantic effort during the week she had excluded him from the studio. But it hit him as though he had no preparation whatsoever. Cast in the pink light of the setting sun, the head came alive. Rebecca had reproduced his father's mummified head, but with one crucial change: the sculpted clay model, unlike the real head, had the mummy gape of Munch's horrified figure in *The Scream*. In the seconds before Russ removed the towel he saw, or thought he saw, what he might have expected to see: his father's head, the mouth clamped shut. With the towel removed, the mouth suddenly appeared open, as if in that moment Barak had let out a petrified, soul-shattering scream. Russ stumbled backwards.

It was grotesque. 'Fuck you, Beck! Fuck you! This is *my* pain!'

He went up to the head, wanting to smash it to the ground, just as she had done to her earlier version, but it was as though she was there and she was too quick for him, placing herself in front of it like a mother bear protecting her cub. I could hit you, Russ thought. If you were here I could punch you in the face.

But she wasn't – and he didn't.

28

BECK'S MODIFICATION to the mouth and jaw had transformed the withered Barak into a man who has seen true horror, a man who had actually huddled in the trenches watching his comrades getting bits of their bodies blown off.

How long did Russ stand there, having turned away, unable to look at the face while the studio grew dark? How long before he switched on the lights in order to drag his stare back to that horrid head, and then how much longer still before he began slowly, reluctantly, to see something else in the expression, something that brought tears cascading down his face? It was archaically painful. Beck had captured something beyond the almost garish horror of war; she had captured the fossil hunter in Barak, the history man, the searcher of meaning, *self-awareness*, and so his look of suffering spoke of something more than that of a singular, flawed man, or a singular, flawed war. The work, Russ began to appreciate, suggested a great antiquity, as if it had always been there.

In *Digging for Darwin* Shaw had written about the evolution of primitive art. Russ had glanced through it. Palaeontologists and art historians used to think that artistic skill developed linearly, a chauvinistic belief that we had to get better over time. The Grotte Chauvet with its 30,000-year-old exquisite cave art exposed this view. Those Cro-Magnon artists not only painted in perspective but enhanced the contours of their work by carefully scraping away the cave wall, imbuing their animals' straining necks and sprung haunches with a nervous energy and grace equal to any artist of the last five hundred years. Rebecca's sculpture, Russ now thought, had something of those first artists in it. It could have come out of Grotte Chauvet, half-fossil, half-art. A rush of pride caught him off-guard.

It was this sense of appreciation, not the earlier horror, which still filled him when Savannah came to tell him it was time to leave for Tante Julia's.

'Wow,' she said, catching sight of the sculpture. 'That's –'

'Yes. My father.'

'Cool.' She joined him, staring.

'You look pretty,' said Russ, as if noticing her beauty for the first time.

'Oh. Thanks, Dad.'

On the way to dinner Luc was silent, sitting on the back seat reading one of his oversized joke books. Russ was reminded of Luc's mummy joke. It was, on reflection, a clever little joke. Luc's interest in jokes had always puzzled Russ: the boy seemed so devoid of a true, spontaneous sense of humour, and yet he spent hours reading joke books, an activity that was only occasionally punctured by a stilted, forced laugh. Luc seemed to be studying laughter, as if he had identified humour as the battleground for his normality. If he could crack the code, truly understand the jokes people made, he would be able to enter the real world. Maybe he has something there, thought Russ. Humour is one of those things that makes us human. Do elephants have a sense of humour?

Savannah said something about her plans for the weekend – her over-explanatory tone betraying her realisation that Russ was not supposed to have been privy to the sculpture of his father's head. It left them in the position of conspirators, with Rebecca, for once, the outsider.

Graeme Friedman

It was Luc who broke the silence that ensued, reading to his sister from his joke book.

'When is a car not a car?' he said.

'I don't know,' said Savannah.

Luc gave a tinny laugh. 'When it turns into a garage.'

'Ha, ha,' said Savannah.

They had reached Tante Julia's, and as they pulled into one of the visitors' parking bays, Russ wondered whether Luc had deliberately chosen that moment to share his garage joke.

Tante Julia unlatched her door and opened it. Leaning on her cane she looked up at Russ from her shrivelled shell of a body. Her cheeks hung limply from her face, her chin sprouted several long white hairs. The weakened muscles of her eyelids, under eyebrows drawn on with liner, had left them flaccid and droopy. Yet despite this decay, this evidence of her nearness to death, her brown eyes were alive, warm. He could see by their moistness that she had been using the ointment he had prescribed. Photographs he had seen of her as a young woman showed a face that was too full to be called beautiful, too strong to carry her features; but there was a sultry air to them, and it was not difficult to imagine the young Julia teasing the cameraman.

'You're early!' she said, kissing Savannah three times – the first cheek, then the second, then returning to the first – and bending down to smile at Luc. She made no attempt to touch the boy. How, Russ wondered, did everyone else become so expert at approaching him?

'We couldn't wait to eat your food,' Russ said as she kissed him.

She smiled wryly and wagged a finger up at him. It had taken him many years to graduate from the less intimate kiss on both cheeks to the third kiss which signified his acceptance into the inner sanctum of the tribe, and then only after he diagnosed her open-angle glaucoma – caused by a blockage in her eye's drainage system – and referred her for successful laser treatment.

The others had not yet arrived. Some were habitually late, one or two would be in shul, and others, involved in the textile trade, were probably still at work. All in all, there would be around twenty-five people there tonight, and until recently, Tante Julia catered at least two Friday nights a month.

The question was on his lips – *have you finished the translation?* His frustration over the veracity of the notebooks had sharpened into excitement around the Ladino translations. He couldn't wait to read Julia's notes. It wasn't simply that the last entry in the Good Croxley spoke of a confession and Russ's ordering of the books suggested the possibility of his father continuing in the Mummy's Notebook. It was the choice of language; a last hope that Barak might have secreted the truth here. Ladino, *La-din-ho*, even the name tasted rich: more of a dialect than a language, a blend of medieval Castilian and Hebrew with Turkish, Arabic and other elements thrown in, the Sephardic equivalent of Yiddish. The Hebrews called the Spanish *Sephardim*. The Spanish called the Hebrews *Marranos,* which means 'pigs' or, more to the point, the 'damned', for those who practised their religion in secret. This, Russ knew as he followed Tante Julia into the kitchen where he was assailed by the aroma of Sephardic history, is what was stirring his interest: Ladino's link with persecution and secrecy. Barak had to have used it for his big secret.

Russ knew better than to ask Tante Julia about the translation. He would have to ward off his agitation so that he could attempt a decent showing at her feast. Friday night dinners would normally have been a pleasure. It wasn't the spiritual meaning of the sabbath meal – he had, after all, taken on his Jewish-born father's professed atheism – but their ritualistic nature. Their predictability provided a pattern around which to weave the fabric of the families that upheld them and he had thrived on the noisy cohesion, the freedom and prominence given the children. Even when tempers became frayed there was a sense of togetherness he quietly craved. At first, witnessing these conflicts, he had felt sure they would result in a family schism. But the following week the warring parties would be nattering away as if the blows that had been narrowly averted had somehow glued the two even more closely together. He was slow to realise that moments of tension and those of tenderness weighed equally and as importantly in the balance that kept the family together. 'Balance is not the word,' Rebecca had explained, 'it's enmeshment. We're ready to kill each other one moment and kill for each other the next.' The family mesh from which Russ had come had been all too suddenly and easily ruptured and the family celebrations pared down to a sad, lonely Christmas lunch with the same tatty tinsel he and his mother had been using for years, a dead pine tree that had been lying in the garage from a Christmas neither of them could remember – and her becoming progressively, articulately, drunk.

With Tante Julia's family finally assembled and the prayers spoken, Russ sat listening to the talk wafting around the table. He stared helplessly at the dishes and platters laden with borekas, fasoulia, stuffed dates, tahini, humus, tabouleh, felafel, and Yemenite-style herring. Mounds of pitta bread to smear it all onto, or stuff it into. How was he going to eat anything, let alone enough to satisfy Tante Julia? If he insulted her by not eating enough, she would withhold the translation, her volcanic generosity could run to ice in an instant. But between busying himself with preparing a plate for Luc and giving advice to one young family member whom he'd recently fitted with contact lenses and yes, she did look pretty without her glasses, and nodding distractedly during discussions about property and spiralling crime (it was a good thing Beck wasn't there, given the racist tone the conversation was beginning to take on), he managed to eat a bit and dodge Tante Julia as he bustled his criminally half-full plate off to the kitchen. It was only with the arrival of his Turkish coffee that Tante Julia bent down and asked quietly, rhetorically, 'With your father what is this Piltdown business?'

It was then he knew that he would be given the translation as he put on his jacket in the hallway. And so he had to remain patiently on the red velvet couch with the kelim antimacassars as Savannah and her cousin, Gabi, begged Tante Julia to read the coffee residue that had slipped down the sides of their upturned cups to settle in their saucers into maps of their futures.

'Tonight is not your night,' she told them. 'Tonight is Russell's night.'

Vaguely aware of Julia and the two teenagers awaiting a response from him, he said, 'Mmm?'

'Nona wants to read your cup,' Gabi said.

Seeing his hesitation – in all the years he had been part of the family, he had only once before had this honour bestowed upon him – Savannah urged him, 'Come on, Dad, Tante Julia wants to read your cup.'

'Oh, yes, of course,' he said, 'that would be fantastic. *Merci.*'

He drained his demitasse, placed it upside down on the saucer and handed it to Tante Julia. She put it aside to let it settle and continued a discussion with her son about her kidney troubles. Two of Beck's female cousins, mouths full of words and semolina cake, were deeply engrossed in conversation, their hands touching each other's arms reassuringly and in the next moment flapping about argumentatively. Tante Julia was now in the depths of her kidneys.

Russ sat next to his upside down coffee cup, waiting. Not for the telling of his future, but for that of his past. Perhaps it amounted to the same thing. After all, wasn't he trying to know his past so that he may clarify his future? There was something exquisite about this painful anticipation. It reminded him of years spent in expectation of the oncoming dust cloud of the Ford, or of waking in the morning to find his father in the bathroom, as always up at first light, the ivory and silver handle of his shaving brush protruding from the heavy white mug on the basin's edge, beneath smiling eyes his cheeks, chin and throat already lathered, and Barak deftly sharpening his cutthroat along the strop he held out with his left hand, first one side of the blade, then the other. Coming home on his bicycle from school Russ would look for him in the garage, hoping to find him hunched triumphantly over a new find. Instead he'd come home to an emaciated tramp in filthy rags, a broken man, and ignored him. Russ's wincing glance fell on his upturned demitasse, as if the sludge he imagined settling in the saucer was viscous shame.

Tante Julia turned towards the cup, removed it from the saucer, turned it right side up and examined the dark, coagulated bog.

'Russell,' she said ominously.

'Yes?'

'Julia!' Marcel, Tante Julia's brother and the family patriarch, was calling her from across the room.

'*Oui?*'

Marcel said something in French, Russ catching the word 'aspirin'. Tante Julia pushed herself to the edge of her seat and, leaning on her cane, hoisted herself to her feet, walked a few steps, and then stopped and looked back at Russ.

'When does Becky come home?' Only Tante Julia got away with calling Rebecca 'Becky'.

'In a few days.' His mouth was dry.

'Good.'

'What does it say?'

She chuckled, waving her hand dismissively. 'It says clean me.'

Later, on Tante Julia's instruction, he waited at the door with the children as she walked stiff-legged to fetch the Mummy's Notebook and the writing pad he had given her, now filled with her untidy, shaky scrawl. He met her gaze for a fleeting moment, and saw again in her eyes the attempt to cast off whatever concern the coffee residue had aroused in her. It was raining hard.

'Here, take this.' Tante Julia thrust an umbrella at Russ. 'You can bring it back next time.'

He tucked the notebook and pad under his jacket, motioning to Savannah to keep the borrowed umbrella held over her and Luc's heads. Drops of water found their way down his neck as they plodded the course of slippery steps and pavement toward the car. *When*, he heard Luc's voice as his neck gave a little spasm in response to the cold rain, *is a car not a car?*

29

IT IS COOL INSIDE THE earth. Russ presses his little hands against the walls of the Elephant's Chamber. This is his daddy's sanctuary and it is becoming his sanctuary too.

'Look here, Red,' Barak says, touching the cave wall, 'this is dolomite. Lime seeps out of the dolomite. Look at the elephant. See his trunk? And there, his huge ears and tusks, and the large body behind him? He used to be covered in water. These caves are much, much bigger than we can see. They're mostly still covered in water. But the water table has dropped and it's left us with the elephant that it carved out of the dolomite. He looks as though he's crying but it's the dolomite that weeps. Those white tears are tears of lime. And these, my lad,' – Barak points around him at the structures protruding like spiky teeth from above and below – 'these are stalac*tites*, they hang from the roof. These are stalac*mites*, they come up from the floor. Do you want to know how to remember which is which? The stalacmite just *might* reach up to the tite.' And with that he hoists the boy onto his shoulders and Russ reaches for a stalactite. 'Now these caves have lost almost all their stalacmites and stalactites. The old lime prospectors cut them away. Well, that was how they made their living. The old boys also cut windows in the caves so air could flow through it. Feel it? There's a draught. Nice for us to have fresh air but not for the stalacmites and tites. Those fellows need things good and musty. But we shouldn't be cross with those prospectors: if it wasn't for them, we wouldn't be here. It's the lime, we owe everything to the lime. You see, it's like glue, it cements the infill to form breccia, and it's in the breccia that we find the fossils. If it wasn't for the lime quarries, we might never have found anything. Now look here. See the water. The only things that live down here are in the water. Don't be scared, I've got you. Here, look. See? Those are fresh water shrimps. They're blind. They have no use for eyes in this darkness.'

I looked for you! he wanted to shout. *I looked!* I searched the Elephant's Chamber. I even went into the water. I braved the shrimps. I crawled in the wet and dark to the Fossil Chamber. I kept thinking, were you in the deeper water? Had you returned home from the Cape, stopped here in your sanctuary before coming home to us, and slipped, and knocked your head, and drifted into the tunnel? I had to come up for air. On the edge of the quarry, I gazed out over the dry grassland. I imagined everything you had told me, that in the time of the ape-men three million years ago the caves were surrounded by riverine shrubs and liana, which grows only in tropical Africa. And that the dry grassland was out there, on the horizon, not here as it is now, surrounding the caves.

I imagined you on the savannah, walking towards me.

He shivered. He was standing in the kitchen, the notebook and pad again tucked under his jacket – only this time, needlessly, since the automated garage was attached directly to the house. He sat down at the kitchen table and turned to the first page of Tante Julia's translation. The notes did not run to many pages but then the Mummy's Notebook was in poor condition and, knowing his own struggle to read many of the English-language notes, he knew what an effort it must have taken the elderly Tante Julia.

He read with a sense of dullness, as if he was reading an academic text on a subject in which he had no interest. The language was stilted, accented by Tante Julia's idiosyncratic English. But no grammatical artifact or translator's error could obscure the contents. His instincts had been right. Barak had used Ladino, the language of the damned, for the confession of a most damnable crime.

He had been staring at the last sentence for some time before he became aware of Savannah's presence in the kitchen.

'Luc's asleep. He was calling for Mom but he's okay now.'

'What?'

'Luc's gone to sleep.'

'Oh, yes, sorry, I was off somewhere.'

Savannah smiled. Her sweetness was unsettling. He saw in it a fear that her usual contrariness might tip him over the edge.

'I'm going to bed too. Goodnight, Dad.'

'Wha-? Yeah, sure, okay, darling. Sleep well.'

Tante Julia's script contained shaky embellishments, extravagant loops, a hand brought reluctantly back to its purpose. It suited Barak's claim. Russ went over it again. He got up, began wandering around the house, finding himself, inevitably, in the studio.

The moon, just slivered off from full, threw its light through the portrait windows, blueing the contents of the room: the drawing board covered in the photographs of Barak, a worktop strewn with clay-encrusted tools, the cold tiles of the floor. The sculpture was covered with a towel, damp to the touch. Sav must have wet it, wrung it out and draped it over Barak's head – he couldn't recall having done so himself.

He stood in front of the large mirror Rebecca used for self-portraits and took off his clothes. Was it possible Julia got it wrong? She was almost ninety. But no, her *borekas* tasted as good as they did twenty years ago, maybe better.

And Barak's words, despite – or perhaps because of – their translation into Tante Julia's far less erudite English, flowed too consistently, too honestly, backing one another up as if to say, this next one tells the truth. There wasn't a chance in hell that an old Sephardic lady could have come up with that narrative.

Naked in front of the moonlit mirror, Russ was struck by the pattern of hair growth on his body, as if noticing it for the first time. In the photograph of his parents and himself on the beach, Barak standing with his hands on his hips, smiling wildly, the hair on his torso was patterned in exactly the way now showing from the mirror: the dark, narrow pathway from Barak's swimming trunks leading up past his navel, up to his chest where it fanned out in a broad mat that swirled around his dark nipples and beyond, up toward the neckline, strands reaching the shoulders, reaching up to that wild smile. Russ adopted the same hands-on-hips stance but the wild smile he tried to emulate was the forced, crooked smile of someone who has just been hit in the face and is trying to make light of it.

Had the old bastard been capable of love? Or was his interest in others merely that of a scientist examining modern *Homo sapiens*? Was his father so incapable of grasping family life, of bearing the domesticity, the *ordinariness* of love? Where did that leave Russ himself? Was he equally incapable?

He peered at himself. The base of his stomach issued forth from his pubic area and from there expanded upward in an impressively firm arc, barrel-like where it joined his chest. He pressed his fingers into his stomach, felt the meeting of tension between the muscles inside and the prodding tips of his fingers. His calves and thighs looked large, well-shaped, but the moonlight hid the excess of years and flab. His legs ached from the abortive run. He grabbed hold of his testicles, hefted them in the palm of his hand – they felt like brittle clay conkers – and then pointed his penis – circumcised not according to Jewish tradition, but circumcised nonetheless – at its own reflection in the mirror. Blind Cyclops! The mirror was angled upward, so that behind his image he could see the open system of beams and rafters that held up the roof, and the iron rod that many years ago he'd fastened below them as a support for a large piece Beck was working on.

Dali came in, head askew, his grey eyes holding Russ's with a curious regard. An ear twitched. He sank slowly to the floor, his tan and black body folding inward so that all four paws met in a gathering of weary pads. Suddenly Russ clambered onto one of the worktops and, taking aim at the iron bar, lunged. His grip held, and he swung there. Dali, frightened, raised himself to his feet and shuffled from the room.

Russ swung in front of the mirror, watching the strain of his biceps, imagining the tendons stretching, the veins showing blue with effort, the ridges forming in the workings of his wrist. Like a gymnast on the high bar he kicked his feet up together so that the momentum added to his swing. The bar trembled and gave slightly, bending down towards his weight. The sweat started to flow from his armpits, little streams marking the convex fans of his pectoral muscles. He watched his genitals swinging about, pictured more matting there, dark, curly, coarse, protective fur. If he was a European *Homo*, he'd have adapted to the climate by developing a squat body. An African *Homo* would be taller, more cylindrical, exposing maximum skin for cooling under the hot sun. He was neither. Tall and broad, he was a hybrid.

He dropped to his feet, heard the slap of damp flesh on the floor, felt the pain shoot up his bare soles, and came down hard on his hands and knees. *This is an experiment.*

I am experimenting. He lurched forward, bent at the knees, using his feet and the back of his hands, propelling himself across the floor in a knuckle-walk. He climbed clumsily onto work-tops, knocked over a pail of water, hardly noticed the spreading wetness, dug a knee into one of the cutting tools. Blood oozed from the wound. He swung from the bar, tried to reach the rafters but couldn't. His circuit about the studio took him past the duffle bag and the trunk – having been freed of its secrets it had been pushed into a corner like a sloughed snakeskin – and brought him face to face with himself in the large mirror. He tilted his head to one side, gazed curiously, drew his lips back from his teeth and let out an ape's bellow. And all the while the sculpture of Barak was there, hiding beneath its shroud, mutely observing.

Gradually Russ began to move about on his haunches, circling the mummy head, his chest tilted forward, and when he grew weary, dropping onto his knuckles again. He stabbed at his forehead with the back of his hand, the smeared blood matting his sweaty hair. There was design in his movements, a slow evolution as he lumbered about, changing modes, using more of this muscle group now, forgetting about this one, until eventually he no longer used his hands to walk, and he had become bipedal. Slowly, over what felt like hours, he gained an upright posture.

He faced himself and noticed the blood. With a grunt he moved over into a corner where an old blanket used by Dali lay crumpled. He huddled down into it, drew it about himself. As his body cooled, he began to shiver. From far away came a voice, edgy, like wet chalk on a blackboard. Savannah was standing in the doorway to the studio, talking to someone on the phone.

'Dad's gone ape.'

There was a very brief silence, the other person's chance to speak.

'Well, that too,' replied Savannah, a little more calmly. 'But I mean he's gone ape – he's been swinging from the beams, walking on his hands, he's acting as if he's an ape! And he's got no clothes on!' There was a hesitation. 'No! Well, he's lying on the floor now. I think he might have gone to sleep or something. What must I do? Maybe he's been sleepwalking. You're not supposed to wake people when they're sleepwalking.'

Sleepwalking? Perhaps that's what it was, this bounding about the studio, this experimenting with his body and mind, his inquiry into the metamorphosis of hominid shape and posture and locomotion. Why? What was motivating him? Maybe he should look it up. But where? In Barak's Ladino passages? He'd probably find more believable answers in the Bible, or the latest edition of *Vogue* magazine. Why was he so shocked by the revelation of the Ladino passages? He had anticipated the forged nature of the black skull Shaw had pieced together. But Barak had done nothing with *that* creation. Deceived no one. He had merely *experimented*, he'd been sculpting, having a bit of fun to ward off the boredom and tedium of the dig. Then he'd smashed it, surely to avoid anyone being deceived. He had undone his experiment. Can it be his responsibility if some inquisitive oafs decide to put his Humpty Dumpty back together again? Really, he'd done nothing more than Beck when she sculpts one of her heads. But this Ladino stuff! This was something else altogether.

He crouched under the dirty blanket, shivering, imagining the story, not as he had read it at the kitchen table and not in the third-language English of Tante Julia's written translation. No, this time he heard the words as his father would have spoken them, sitting at the old man's knee as he would have so many times as a boy, gazing up at his big strong face, aware on the fringes of his tingling consciousness of his father's large workman's hand stroking the corduroy of his trousers, the scratching of his bushy eyebrows, the sipping of his tea; and in the background, the seditious voice of the fire crackling and hissing as it consumes the wood, and the gentle tugging of the radiogram, music now where news had been, glowing from the brown numerals, the yellow knob, the mustard casing, the needle that traverses its well-worn path along the radio frequencies…

Why have I returned? For almost three years I have coaxed and cajoled, pleaded and threatened, but in its refusal to give up Early Man, this place has sapped my strength. It has teased me with all manner of beast. Except a single hominid. I despair. So why have I come back? Is it because I have nowhere else to be? Certainly not Krugersdorp, of that I am now sure. The boy wants nothing of me. And can I blame him?

The cave has won – and so it must have its spoils. I have come back to reflect and to die. So here it is, the shaft about which my life has turned, my shame, all too easily brought about. Here's the sting in my tale.

I got wind of Dawson's find and soon had a chance to examine the fragment. I matched his piece with others broken from a relatively modern skull. The mandible was indeed that of an orang-utan, with the head – the part that articulates with the base of the skull – snapped off, so as not to give the game away. It had to be an orang-utan, since the red ape's molars, unlike those in the jaw of a chimp or a small gorilla, are quite humanlike. All it took to make them very humanlike was a little filing and smoothing out with acid. I decalcified and stained (iron, chromium, etc.) some of the bone – not only so that they would look old, but that they would appear to be equally mineralised, to have been in the ground for the same length of time. For good measure, I threw in a doctored femur of an extinct elephant. Then I planted the pieces, and voilà: the world was introduced to Piltdown Man.

The hoax was meant to last only long enough to embarrass the upper crust of the British scientific establishment. I wanted them to see where their arrogance was leading us, that they were wrong about Man's

Graeme Friedman

place in the universe, and they were wrong about the Englishman's place in the human race. Man – and English Man – was nothing more than a highly evolved animal, not some special creature placed by God to lord it over all others. Where was that attitude going to take us? It was not scientific! For the sake of knowledge, they had to be brought down a peg or two.

I left clues that would surely lead to detection of the fraud. I filed the molar cusps flat. Surely any scientist worth his salt would see this as human artefact? Would know a molar subject to natural attrition should show concave dentine depressed below surrounding enamel, not the unnaturally flattened surface brought about by filing? And then there was the elephant femur, which I carved in the shape of what was correctly identified as a Pleistocene cricket bat! If they could see the bat, why could they not see the joke? Instead Smith Woodward called it 'a supremely important example of the work of Palaeolithic man'. Pah! Did Palaeolithic man play cricket?

My little fossil and his cricket bat had his critics, although these controversies were about the concomitance of jaw and skull, or the age, or the faculty of speech, rather than suspicion of forgery. It took Franz Weidenreich to recognise the jaw as orang-utan in origin, and the molars as having been filed down. But during the summer of 1913 I was as taken by surprise as everyone else when Dawson came up with some nasal bones and Father Teilhard found a canine – none of which were planted by me – and miraculously many of Piltdown Man's critics were silenced, and by the time Weidenreich called foul, Piltdown Man had entered into the fossil record.

So it seems I had at least one co-conspirator. Who, you ask? I have my theories. But enough fingers have been pointed for me not to add another. Let my finger point solely at the heart from which it draws its blood.

The whole enterprise had slipped out of hand. I tried to stop it. I requested an audience of the Royal Society, described earlier in these notes. I told them everything. These teeth have been tampered with! I shouted out. This is the jaw of an orang-utan, broken in just the

208

right places! I even gave them a demonstration of how the hoaxer had accomplished his feat.

The euphoria of my senior colleagues at claiming the missing link for England was too great to allow the debunking of the myth. And so Piltdown Man, the creation of the young and foolhardy Barak Codron, aided and abetted by a hidden hand, stood fast. I had set out to embarrass them into owning up to their arrogance and succeeded only, if you will excuse the military pun, in giving their faulty canon more ammunition. You would have thought the sad irony – the wrecked careers, the damage to science – would have haunted me over the years but they had humiliated me in my attempts to enlighten them and therefore, I reasoned, they deserved what they got. I knew that sooner or later Piltdown Man would be exposed. It is only now, some years after Weiner et al finally buried him, that the ghost of Piltdown Man has returned to haunt me. It is satisfying that after the pleas of Codron, an English Jew, and Weidenreich, a German Jew, the coup de grâce should be delivered by Weiner, a South African Jew.

Russ could bear it no longer. He knew what came next. He wanted to blot it out. Better to concentrate on the fraud itself, the revelation of which should not have shocked him. Isn't this what Barak had been telling him? Everything about the old man was forged, from the image of himself as a loving, trustworthy father, to the sculpted fossil that sent an entire scientific field off-course for forty years.

'Dad? Daddy?' Savannah stood in front of him, her dressing gown held tightly to her waist, in her hand the cordless phone, held out to him – as a lifeline? an accusation? – he couldn't tell which. It was hard to tell with Savannah. He used to understand her needs so well – food, nappy change, comfort. The toddler who needed limit-setting, the pre-schooler who could be calmed by the singing of a song. Now he smelled her fear.

'Mom's on the phone.' She handed over the instrument and stood back.

'It was an experiment, just an experiment, Beck. Knuckle walking. I'm trying to understand the relationship between locomotion and technical advances. Did we start making tools because we had freed our hands? Or did we free our hands from locomotion in order to make tools?'

She interrupted him to say something about him swinging from the rafters.

' – what? Swinging from the what? Lord, no!' He forced a laugh. 'Not the rafters, that iron bar I – '

'That's not what the bar is for. What's the point of this, Russ?'

'Dart used to do it.'

'So? You said Dart was a little crazy.'

'What? Well, yes, I did say that.'

'Are you okay, Russ?'

'I'm okay, Beck, really. Everything's all right, don't worry.'

'I am worried.'

'Don't you see? It's about bipedalism, that's what made us human. Such a silly little arbitrary change forced on us because the world lost too many trees. That's funny, isn't it? We're facing extinction once again and it's because the world is losing too many trees. That's – '

'Russ!'

'No, wait, just *listen* to me! That's why we got to our feet. We became upright first and developed brains later. It's all the fault of the damn trees. If they hadn't receded in the first place we'd never have developed the intellectual capacity to destroy the planet. It was obvious to Barak that the key to evolution was environmental change. The savannah was taking over from the jungle so we started walking upright. This freed our hands, we stumbled on the better use of tools. We scavenged from the real carnivores. We broke open bones to get at marrow. We cut flesh off the bone. Our brains were nourished. All that protein – just what a little *Homo erectus* brain needs to grow.'

'Russ, what's all this got to do with – '

'I'll tell you,' he said, cutting her off. 'The thing is this: It was so obvious to Barak that the bones he planted at Piltdown were ludicrous. He didn't expect them to fool anyone for very long. It was a joke, make them think how silly they were all being. Cricket in the Pleistocene, honestly! Only by the time they got the joke, most of them were dead.'

Rebecca's voice was shrill. 'Russell! You're not making sense. What did you say? What's Piltdown and cricket got to do with this?'

'Cricket – nothing, nothing.' Had he mentioned cricket? It didn't seem the time to be talking about cricket. 'How was the opening?'

'Ah, fuck, Russ,' she said, 'the opening isn't until next week.'

'Yes, yes, of course. I knew that. We had dinner at Tante Julia tonight, her *borekas* were as delicious as ever. They all send their love.' There was a silence on the other end of the line. 'Beck?'

'Yes, I'm here.'

'Your sculpture of Barak is unbelievable.'

Silence again. And then she said, 'I – I'm sorry.'

'No, no,' he said quickly, 'don't apologise. It's incredible. I mean it. You've caught a sadness I didn't know existed in him.'

'Maybe it's not his,' she said.

'No, I think it is. Well, it could be yours too. And mine. What the hell, it could be all of ours. Sharing is caring, right?'

He hung up.

Oh, and guess what? Had he told her? Barak claims he planted Piltdown Man – or, at least, parts of it. And Russ believed him. A live, wriggling worm of truth had burrowed its way up. At first the possibility of his father being involved in the biggest scientific fraud of all time seemed ludicrous. But then, why not? Whoever did it was somebody's father, why shouldn't it be his? Barak was there, a junior man at the British Museum, with the expertise, access, and, apparently, the requisite anger. And there was his use of Ladino. Russ's suspicions had been correct. It *was* the language of secrets. Throughout the three notebooks Barak had yet to use it, until that moment.

The life work of so many good men had been led astray, wasted. Poor Arthur Keith, taken for a fool. And Smith Woodward, dictating *The Earliest Englishman* on his deathbed in 1944. It is unimaginable: to be so passionate about one's calling, only to learn at the end that you have allowed yourself to be duped. They wanted so much to prove that our ancestors looked like us, that humans evolved *alongside* apes, that it was our brains that made all the difference, rather than our feet. The mind seemed a far nobler, God-given instrument than upright locomotion. What had Keith written in the *Antiquity of Man*? Russ recalled the words: *Concerning the Garden of Eden… even England was part of it – apparently an important part.* Barak gave Keith Piltdown Man; and so the Taung child, so ape-like, was lost to us for decades. Dart's find simply couldn't have been an ancestor. And so for decades the mad professor was ignored – worse, made an object of fun. And Barak had the gall to sit there with him, examining his fossils.

No, Russ shook his head, pulling the dog's blanket tightly about himself, it *can't* be true. He was bragging. He was delusional. Demented. Senile. Lack of oxygen in the cave. Too much sulphur in his cave of farts. But he knew he was protesting too much. His father's remorse said it all. A broken man reached out, and Russ had ignored him. If there was an antithesis of the noble man, then this was it, within both Russ and his father, this shadow with its bitter taste of shame. It had kept him trapped like Barak in the darkness, running out of air, waiting to die.

He must get out of the house, he must get away from this place of frustrated discovery, of books and words and theories. He looked down. The phone was still in his hand. He padded through the house to look up Shaw's number, keyed it in and held on for a long time, listening to the phone's incessant song.

The young scientist answered. His voice was muffled, breathless. 'Jesus, Russ, it's twelve-fifty a-bloody-m.'

He's fucking somebody, thought Russ, and for a mad moment imagined it was Rebecca, her spine flexing backwards as she straddled him, then curving down towards him like the graceful neck of a swan, her beautiful heavy breasts burying the phone as she pressed against that handsome English face, against Russ's own voice, ramming the voice of her husband into her lover's ear.

'I was just wondering whether you'd spoken to them about the permit?'

'Oh, Christ, Russ, I spoke to them today – *yesterday*, rather. They've yet to attend to it. Give it another week and I'll try again. I can't talk now.'

30

I WRITE THIS CONFESSION IN *the tongue of my forebears. I hide in it, yet it is the most painful place to hide. That is a paradox, just as it is to be a Jewish-born atheist obsessed with Jews. Franz Weidenreich, Joseph Weiner, Isaac Rosenberg. Isaac, who has walked the battlefields of my dreams for almost fifty years, again making his appearance last night, albeit in disguised form.*

I dreamed of the legendary snake park attendant Johannes, dressed in a tight-fitting brown blazer, polka-dot bow tie and white hat dating from the last century, standing in front of a sign that read 'THE POISON FANGS OF THESE SNAKES HAVE NOT BEEN REMOVED'. *He performed for the Prince of Wales when HRH visited the Union in 1925. He who had been bitten many times but continued to put on his shows for his European audiences.*

In my dream, covering Johannes's blazer from shoulder-seam to the lower pockets, are rows and rows of medals, presented to him by both King and Kaiser. He stands in the middle of a concrete pit, holding aloft a book containing pressed flowers. The skin of his face and hands are pockmarked and scarred. A black pond of sorts swirls gently about him to the level of his waist. I look more closely at the dark water, which is not water at all but a sluggish mass of snakes coiling languidly about one another. Johannes, smiling from ear to snake-bitten ear, holds open his book of dead flowers and gestures to the open page. There is one pressed rose in its centre.

I know what Prof. Freud's opinion would have been. I am the calm snake-attendant, someone who smiles for Europeans while thinking other thoughts. But I have been bitten — and poisoned. And I collect

*my wounds in a book of pressed flowers. And the most important is a
rose. It is the attempt to preserve a life ended in its prime.*

*The rose is Isaac Rosenberg, whose name means mountain of roses,
or red mountain, from 'rot' and 'mountain', and Isaac is all lost young
boys. He stands for the loss of innocence, of truth. Only now do I realise
that I unconsciously named my third son, Russell, after him. Russell,
whose name comes from the same Old English root: 'rut', derived from
'rot', meaning 'red'.*

Russ fumbled for the talk button.

'Trevor?' he said. It seemed to Russ that he might still be
on the phone to Shaw.

'No, this is Leila Naidoo.'

'Who?'

'Professor Leila Naidoo. I seem to have awoken you.
Shall I call back later?'

'No, sorry, I – what's the time?' The numerals on the
bedside clock made no sense, red pinpricks in the half-light.

'Seven o'clock,' she said, then added, 'in the morning. I
am sorry, it is a bit early.'

Russ grunted. There are moments when, big brained or
not, Man is as inarticulate as his australopithecine forebear.

'I didn't have time to telephone you yesterday,' said
Professor Naidoo. 'I have the DNA results.'

The professor need not have continued. Russ was
suddenly wide awake, confident of his thoughts. He was on
a roll of discovery, second-guessing Barak at every turn, as
though he was completing a Jackson Pollock puzzle and with
each piece his certainty of its place in the whole increased.
He had accepted Toka's inference that his father had not
met with an accident shortly after leaving Krugersdorp
in November 1963 and, in fact, that he was alive as late
as 1966, the time of his spurned re-appearance. He had
recognised the black skull for the composite it was. And he

had come to understand enough about his father's familial relationships to know the truth about the foetus's paternity. Piltdown alone, and the painful self-reflection unleashed by the confession, had blindsided him. His father's involvement in the fraud should not have caught him unawares. He knew that now.

'The DNA is a match,' said Professor Naidoo. 'The foetus's father is Dr Barak Codron.'

'Yes,' he said, 'I thought as much. Dr Barak Codron, I have discovered, has been rather adept at fathering children. He's had children with three women. One Jewish, one English noblewoman, one African. An eclectic mix, you'd say, but I'm thinking even his wives represented an anthropological study. Do you know, it has just struck me that by the time my father took up with Nombeko, he had long since removed himself from his relationship with my mother. And maybe me too. Those two years after he was banned from working Sterkfontein, he must have felt a growing distance from me that I never noticed. I guess I was like any teenager – you expect your parents to stay constantly loving while you go off playing rugby and running around with your friends. But he was holed up in his study, working on his theory. We weren't digging together anymore. Maybe it made it easier for him to leave me. Maybe he thought I'd left him.'

'You have been finding out many things about your father that you never believed possible,' said the professor. 'This is the trouble with children who lose their parents at a young age. Our minds are not developed enough to hold onto the good things in the face of the bad. So we try to forget the bad and remember only the good. We have to obscure things. And then because we can never really know them, we cannot know ourselves.'

There was something in her gentle tone that made him think, not of his own difficulties, but of hers. Her words had an undertow of a sadness owned. He felt his shoulders loosen, his neck and head relax against the pillows. Leila Naidoo was speaking to him now, not as the exuberant professor of physical anthropology, the foremost expert in mummy studies in a country whose known natural mummy population had just doubled, but as a woman who had early in life lost a father, or a mother, or perhaps both.

'Have you heard,' he said, aware of his body in the warm bed, already knowing that she would answer his question in the affirmative, and that that would allow him to go on talking, to spill his thoughts into the phone, 'of Piltdown Man?'

31

UNDER A LOW SKY HE drove along the beachfront, Barbara Robertson's voice drumming painfully in his ear as if it was an infection. A wind came in from the sea, cuffing the palm trees.

Talking to Leila Naidoo had exhausted him, and he had fallen back to sleep. When he woke for the second time, Luc was standing next to the side of the bed, an extended arm holding the telephone to Russ's ear. Russ had been dreaming of four blind men leading one another over the white cliffs of Dover. The men, linked by outstretched hands and wooden staves, stumbled along a path that wound its way through brilliant green shrubbery. They were hoping to reach a village before nightfall. Each man suffered from a different ophthalmic problem. The corneas of one were covered in a white filmy growth which he recognised as a case of leucoma. Another had optic nerve damage caused by advanced glaucoma – the man stared blankly at the sky with atrophied eyeballs – and the third, the inheritor of some horrific genetic mishap, had patches of skin stretched over hollow sockets where his eyes should have been. Russ was the last in line. He was not blind like the others but could see dimly, and what he could see was that the blind men in front were about to step over the cliff. Russ's sight was impaired because his organs did not fit his head: he had the eyes of a pig. And he could not warn those in the lead that they were about to tumble over the cliff because he had the mouth and snout of a pig, and his frantic, unintelligible squeals were ignored.

Out of the handset came the sibilant tone of Barbara's voice. Her bowel must be playing up.

'Russell!' He had imagined her standing in a classroom, hands on hips, in a severe black two-piece suit, the white ruffles of her blouse showing abundantly about her neck, having squeezed and finally popped her head out from the constraints of the suit. 'You're expected today. I simply can't put these patients off any longer. Your first appointment is at nine-thirty. That's in ten minutes, Russell. Mr September, contact lenses. There's another fourteen after him. I've had to accommodate them because of your unscheduled breaks this week. It's Saturday morning, we're going to be as busy as hell, *and* it's Anthea's weekend off, remember? Don't be late!'

Propped on an elbow, alone in the bed, feeling the cold sheets of Beck's absence, he reached over to return the handset to its base. The aches in his body brought back a memory of his experiments of last night, and he groaned.

And then the horror of the dream returned. Christ, how was he going to function with a pig's head on his shoulders? His hands went up to his face, fingers feeling for the familiarity of his eyes and nose and mouth, blinking to bring the world of the bedroom into focus. He flopped back onto the pillows, laughing in relief. People would say of him, Russell Codron woke one morning to discover that he was pig-headed.

Now, driving parallel to the metronomic row of unsettled palm trees, he wondered about the dream, the inspiration for which could only be Bruegel's *The Blind Leading the Blind*, painted not long before the artist died. Yes, one of the men in the dream had even been wearing wooden shin guards, such as some blind people in Bruegel's time wore to protect themselves from coming up painfully against sharp objects.

Russ had recently – it now seemed, in a former life – read an article in an American ophthalmic journal on Bruegel's understanding of eye problems. The painter seemed to know far more than the average Flemish doctor of the time, who would typically have seen toxic stomach vapours as the cause of these difficulties. The good Flemish doctor's prescription would have been to have someone blow gently into the eye with a breath sweetened by chewing cloves or fennel.

He stopped at a traffic light. During the week, at this time of the morning, the promenade was populated by the unemployed, or mothers pushing their babies in prams, or the retired white folk of Sea Point hobbling along on the arms of their black retainers. Today being a Saturday the beachfront was busy, despite the chilling wind. Teenagers on skateboards and children, their little legs pumping at tricycle pedals, wove around strollers, around benches, around blue plastic rubbish bins attached to stakes on the lawns that ran between the promenade and the beach road.

Don't be late! Barbara's words were clear, brittle, despite the fact that the handset was already a long way from his ear. And now it struck him: the significance of receptionists. After all, who were they but waiting room attendants? And who was he but a habitual waiting room occupant? He had an image of himself having spent the past decade in a waiting room as its sole occupant, watched over by a bored receptionist, flicking through magazines or refilling his plastic cup from the water cooler or looking at his watch in the hope that this may hasten the appearance of the doctor who will never come. What a waste. At least Arthur Keith kept himself busy. And now Shaw wanted him to stay in that waiting room. Not bloody likely. *I can be just as fucking pig-headed as my father. And I will lead myself blindly on.* Suddenly realising the effortlessness with which he had interpreted his own dream, he laughed.

A hoot from behind startled him. The light had turned green. All this thinking, Russ smiled to himself, is making me hungry. He turned off the beachfront and into the main road where a parking space beckoned. A man was labouring at his informal barber's shop, set up on the side of a driveway that led into a loading dock behind a row of shops. Both he and his client had to shift over to the side when a large delivery truck turned in. A long extension cable that disappeared into a second storey window powered the electric haircutter sweeping the client's head. *Why not?* thought Russ. No better way to examine the anatomy of his skull. He waited his turn, sat while the locks of hair fell, paid and walked away from the pavement barber, the cold catching his head. With a thrill, he ran his palm over it. His hunger forgotten, he wanted now to go home to examine his skull.

He peered into the bathroom mirror, turning his head so that the light bounced off the freshly shaved skin, investigating the ridge that ran along the top of his pate – it felt like a small sagittal crest, and he could imagine it expanding upward, a bony plume to hold the giant chewing muscles required of a leafy diet – when he heard Savannah's voice outside.

'What's that?' he said.

'Mom's on the phone. She's been trying to track you down. So has Barbara. Why didn't you have your cell phone? Jesus, what happened to your hair?'

He took the phone. 'Beck, you won't believe this. In the Ladino translation… my father says he did it.'

'Did what?'

'Planted Piltdown.'

'That's what I thought you –'

'In 1908 Dawson was given a piece of cranium by a

labourer who was working in the gravel bed at Barkham Manor. That's the place in Piltdown. Sussex. Left parietal, I think. He looked for more but found nothing. A few years later he went back, found a piece of hippopotamus tooth but no more hominid remains. So Barak gave him more. And the doctored orang-utan jaw. And a fucking elephant femur carved to look like a cricket bat. That was enough to get Arthur Smith Woodward fired up. And the rest – the rest's history, so to speak.'

'Russell.'

'Yes, Rebecca.'

'Barbara's been calling. You're supposed to be at work.'

'Sure, sure. I'll get there. I'm just a little excited, that's all. It feels like it's all coming together.'

'Do you want me to come home?'

'No, no. I'm fine. Really. I'm okay. Just a little hyped up. Wouldn't you be if you just discovered that your father committed the greatest fraud of all time?'

He said goodbye.

Savannah was looking at him strangely. 'Dad…' Whatever she was going to say, she seemed to think better of it and instead continued, 'I'm going out with Temba. I'll be back later – don't wait up for me. We'll be *really* late. Luc is in his bedroom. Are you going to take him with you to work? You do remember Beatrice isn't here?'

Really late? What was she telling him? She was going to sleep out? Somewhere far away, a phone rang, and rang. Why wouldn't they leave him alone?

'That's probably Barbara again, Dad. Don't you think you should get it? It's in your hand, Dad, just press the talk button. The green one. Just press it. We've got to go. Okay, Daddy? Okay?' She kissed him on the cheek.

Russ nodded and raised his hand in a vague return of Savannah's wave. The hand hovered. He looked down at it.

When you're conversing with an African, my boy, remember to indicate a person's height according to African custom: you must hold your hand upright. If you hold it flat, with the palm down, you are describing an animal that goes about on all fours.

He wandered into the lounge. The black skull stared up at him from the coffee table. How the hell did it get there? He couldn't remember. Its lack of integrity seemed obvious. There was indeed a time when his father might have made something like it for him, like other fathers might have constructed model Spitfires or Heinkels with their sons. But by 1966 or whenever Barak created his little composite, that time had long since passed.

There was something he had forgotten to do. He couldn't bring it to mind. It nagged at him. What was it? Out of habit he went to the studio, but where formerly the elements of Beck's art would have calmed him, he now found himself face to face with Barak's screaming clay head. He opened one of the side doors and rushed out into the front garden. Beneath the ossified gaze of the house, he began to pace about. He ran his hands over his bare head. He stopped to pee, aiming the stream at the Medusa's head. The plant quivered. They were building a relationship, the Medusa's head and he, albeit an abusive one. He attacked it with another volley of piss. The plant trembled momentarily and then resumed its unassailable air. He turned his face to the sky. A light drizzle fell. God was pissing back at him. He felt the soft pinpricks of the rain but it was like being massaged by butterflies, and he wished for a downpour. Finally he sat under the loquat tree in the corner. He leaned over and picked a leaf off a nearby bush and began to chew it. It had a bitter, hard taste. He picked another, from a different shrub, an African dog rose. It too was bitter. He crawled across the garden and chose something else, the stem of a succulent. This one was moist, and if he sucked on the coarse, knobby stem, sweeter. He tore more of the stems away from the plant and crawled back under the shelter of the loquat tree. His jaws had begun to ache. As he bit into the stems a milky sap oozed into his mouth. His tongue and lips began to burn. Confused, he gazed back over the lawn at the plant from where he had plucked these odd delicacies and saw that it was the Medusa's head. Work! He suddenly remembered work and the string of appointments. *You're expected today. Don't be late!* Got to get to work.

'What rot!' Barak would've said. 'Work on your own, Red. Why have to rely on others?'

But should he take advice from a father who had abandoned his child? Why was it that those least qualified to teach were the ones who most assumed the teacher's authority? The skies grew darker, the clouds thickening. Russ felt cold, his mouth burning fiercely now. He looked about the garden, across to the stone walls that surrounded the house, to the pathway grown wet and dark from the rain, to the beds of ginger bush, wild garlic, rat's tail. The fire in his mouth had brought him back into his body. He crawled out from the cover of the loquat tree and opened his mouth to the rain. It wasn't enough.

'Fuck it!' he said, but the words that emerged from his tensed-up face were distorted, hardly audible. His jaws were stiff with pain. He ran around the side of the house and back into the studio where he turned on a tap and sucked at the cooling flow. He splashed water over his face, rubbed at his stinging lips and cheeks, bringing tears of pain to his eyes so that the tears and the water and minute traces of sap from the Medusa's head co-mingled and found their way beneath his eyelids. It felt as though someone had poured sand onto his exposed corneas, his eyelids clamping shut in protest. He forced open the lids to allow the water to wash away the sting. The pain subsided a little, and he tentatively opened his lids, his vision restricted to blurred outline and colour. He lumbered towards the door to the passage, stopping suddenly as he saw a fuzzy image of someone in front of him, the dark balaclava-clad figure of an intruder.

'Where the fuck did you come from?' His voice cracked. 'How did you get in?'

Who was this now? Was he amidst all this turmoil simply to become another South African statistic? He lunged towards a counter where some of Beck's tools lay idly, grasped a mallet and advanced on the silent intruder. When he later reflected on his actions, he was sure that he meant only to scare the intruder, who was clearly the smaller man. But as he moved forward he lost his footing. It had been his shoes on the smooth tiles, he would reason afterwards, slippery following the desperate showering of his face and eyes. He put his hands out to steady himself, grabbing at the figure of the intruder, the touch of the damp towel coming away in his left hand telling him in the same appalling instant they both toppled to the floor that it was no intruder at all but Rebecca's bust of Barak. He came to rest on top of the sculpture's plinth, the clay head's towelling shroud still clasped in one hand and the mallet in the other. The armature had come loose from the plinth and skidded across the tiles. He disentangled himself from the plinth and crawled over to Barak's head. Once again Russ found himself peering anxiously at a sculpted mass of clay, only this time he had caused the damage and there was no Rebecca to hasten him away.

He started guiltily. Was that the sound of the front door slamming? Rebecca? Was she due back? He heard Dali clambering down the passageway. Frozen in the position of a murderer hunched over the body of his victim, Russ could only wait as Dali came clattering across the tiles and jumped up against his back, his paws wet and muddy.

'Down, boy.' Russ looked up to see Luc at the door. 'Luc, it's… I… had a little accident with Mom's sculpture, that's all. Just a little accident. It'll be okay.' The sculpture was now in danger of being trampled under Dali's paws. 'Dali! Down! Get away from here!' Russ elbowed the dog away and gingerly picked up the head. It didn't look too bad. A dent in the parietal region, that was all. That was funny. Wasn't Dawson's original piece parietal? He turned to Luc, grinning.

'I cut my hair,' he said. 'Well, shaved it, actually. D'ya like it?'

Luc's eyes were wary. 'No,' he said. 'Come, Dali.' The dog followed him out of the studio.

Russ put the sculpture down, pulled the plinth upright and reset the base of the armature upon it. Emboldened by his assessment that the damage had been only to the side of the skull, he studied the head more carefully, and then wished he hadn't. The impact of the sculpture on the tiled floor had transmitted itself like an electric pulse along the set of interconnected wires that made up the armature, bending the framework and throwing the entire face a few degrees out of kilter. Small fissures showed where the face had been skewed and the layer of clay stretched.

He began to whimper. 'Fuck, fuck, fuck.' He dragged his thumb across the damp clay, trying to close the wounds. It only distorted the face more. Barak's eyes stared at him, hurt beyond measure. *What have you done to me?* they said. *You have done me in.*

Beck would never believe it was an accident. She would think he had done it on purpose. She would accuse him of malice, of having ruined her best piece on the eve of her exhibition. But worse than the anticipation of Rebecca's recriminations, perhaps even worse than the slaughtered eyes of his father, was a sick, vertiginous feeling that flooded him as he recalled how much the work had moved him, how beautifully she had caught the universal suffering of Man. I have destroyed a real work of art, he thought.

He covered his own face so as not to see the other. How long he stood there, his self split again into a hovering consciousness above a body caught in the aftermath of disaster, he would never know. And when finally the parts of him were reunited, it was of Luc he thought. He imagined he and Luc were embracing as father and son, his hand pressed against the boy's head, holding him against his chest, swaying with him in his arms, the father's cheeks wet with the son's tears, and the son's cheeks wet with the father's tears. But Luc had gone back to his room to be assailed by dead physicists emerging from the computer's screen saver, and Russ had remained motionless in front of his own crime of the century.

He thought to call a friend, but there was no one. All his friends were their friends, the only places to go were those where intimacy had been diluted by dint of numbers. Apart from Rebecca, there was only one person he could think of and that was Trevor, who didn't believe in Barak any more. There was only one thing to do.

He went over to where Barak's duffle bag sat on top of the trunk in the corner, loosened the drawstring, smelled again the mingling of earth and metal and decaying canvas, and rummaged about inside. The tools were back in the bag: rock hammer, brushes and brooms, chisels and awls, and the mouldy bag of scalpels and dental picks. He hadn't remembered replacing the tools after he had first scattered them about the studio floor. Rebecca or Beatrice, or perhaps the two of them together, must have tidied up. He tightened the drawstring, the blue-white eyelets of the duffle bag's mouth coming together like the pursed lips of a toothless old codger, and hefted the bag over his shoulder.

32

HE WAS BACK, DRIVING along the beachfront, past the leaves of the palm trees made wild by the wind, the deserted red and grey paved promenade, and a memory of finishing a 10km fun run in a burst of speed and blurred Adidas stripes and the gasping joy of an endomorphine high.

The Piltdown bones – his father had written – *were meant to be a mere comma, a pause for self-reflection, not a life-time sentence. I had to push their faces into the mirror of their own stupid prejudice, those pompous imbeciles with their walrus moustaches and high collars and their little Edwardian minds. I had to awaken them to the fact of their short-sightedness. Do you understand this? They kidnapped science and I had to free it. I was simply trying to nudge those great men of science towards a more honest course, to give them a lesson in the follies of scientific imperialism. A short lesson, not one that lasted over forty years! But I under-estimated their nationalism and over-estimated their intelligence.*

I was simply… But there was nothing simple about Barak. Russ stretched a hand out to the duffle bag on the passenger seat, feeling the rough weave of the canvas. What was forgotten? Had he left something behind? Beck had the Good Croxley, and he'd finished reading the Bad Croxley, and so it was only the Mummy's Notebook, wrapped in a clean chamois he'd found in the garage, that was making the journey with him. There were unread sections of English he hadn't been able to get to since Tante Julia had been busy with it. Apart from Barak's tools, he had grabbed torches, two gas lamps from the old camping days – he would need to pick up fresh canisters – and a sleeping bag. He'd forgotten his toothbrush, spare clothing. No matter. Those were things his father might have forgotten...

'Name them, my lad!' Barak would bellow. 'Come on, son!'

'Rock hammer! Whisk broom! Twopenny nails! Twine! Sieve!'

'Good God, Red, you've gone and forgotten an essential item. What are you going to do when you're out there in the field, millions of miles from the nearest village – what will you do without it?'

The boy would think hard. It was that funny sounding one. And then all of a sudden it would jump off his tongue: 'The *Karai!*' Karai, Swahili for metal pan.

'And what else?' There'd be a sly smile on Barak's face.

'Your Johnnie Walker, Dad.'

'And?'

'And my Cadbury's Bourneville cocoa, Dad.'

And his father would lay his big loving hand on Russ's shoulder.

Russ stopped at a hardware store, rubbed his eyes, still sensitive from their encounter with the Medusa's head, and stepped out of the car. He bought canisters for the gas lamps, batteries for the torches and, just in case, two new battery-powered lamps with extendable stands. He wasn't going to risk arriving at the cave without enough light. Back on the road, the windscreen wipers swept the rain before him. He drove by the turnoff to the Mouille Point lighthouse – if he could bring that bloody great shore light along, he would – the Putt-Putt course, the garage and liquor store and blocks of flats, and then across the level ground of the Green Point common that was so long ago reclaimed from the sea's greedy grasp, and past the flyover which is never going to be finished, which hangs in mid-air, a barren ramp aimed ever-hopeful at a distant terminus across the foreshore; and then the car climbed onto the highway, rising above the harbour, now rehabilitated by the Victoria & Albert Waterfront, chrome and glass, shoppers and tourists where there used to be foreign seamen and whores and the smell of burnt oil and a young artist battling to understand why her painting of a little coloured girl at the docks was failing. In the slant of the rain and the pale coldness of everything, he went past everything.

All he could see was the cave entrance exploding in a rock-shower beneath the direct hit of an artillery shell, crumbling, crumbling, and Barak and the pregnant woman inside and the air, the finite, poisoned air, trapped in there with them, and Barak tearing at the rocks that blocked them in or fatalistically lying back and waiting for death, musing on the conjoining of imagination and reality, the closing of a circle, a journey from imagined trench to real cave: having inserted himself into the history of the Great War, conjured tales of crouching in the mud, frightened, despairing, his mask filtering out the mustard gas, wishing he could bundle himself inside the earth, and then fifty years later finding that he was, this time for real, bundled inside the earth choking on another army's poison gas.

Luc! Fuck me! Russ braked suddenly, as if the thought he had hit was a solid barrier in the road. *Jesus!* He was on an underpass. He couldn't turn around. He picked up speed, frantically scanning ahead. He was in Paarden Island already. A gap opened up in the oncoming traffic and he did a screeching u-turn across the solid white line. He felt his armpits sticky with sweat, his mind full, not with marauding house invaders, as many South African parents' minds might have been, but with the lonely distress of his delicate son. In the pale coldness of everything, he had unthinkingly left Luc alone in the house for the rest of the weekend or whenever it was that Savannah was going to come home. Twenty fretful minutes later, he was back at the house.

Luc was sitting at the computer in his room, unperturbed.

'Luc,' said Russ. 'You're coming with me. We're going for a drive.'

While the child made some decisive sounding clicks with his mouse, Russ packed spare clothing and jackets and grabbed another sleeping bag. With Luc strapped securely in the back seat, and the car now passing the point at which he had turned around, Russ smiled. He was back on track. Soon they were on the coastal road with its dunes and sea and wind-blown tall grass, and heading past Koeberg. All that man-made energy in this place of stark nature.

'There are oyster graveyards out there,' Russ said, pointing towards the lagoon. 'Enormous colonies of oyster shells that run seven metres deep in places. They died after the water temperature changed.' There was no acknowledgement from the back seat. 'You could see southern right whales off these shores, and some people think that on those beaches out there' – once again he stretched his left arm out to indicate a place beyond the dunes – 'Phoenicians from the sacked city of Carthage landed long before the birth of Christ.'

This was the way to communicate with Luc. Respect his intellect. Don't try to connect directly. Choose a topic and speak to it. A surge of excitement shot through Russ. For the first time since he held Luc as a toddler and looked into that unreadable face, only to see his own disappointment, he felt that he may have found a way to be the boy's father. He swivelled in the driver's seat so that he could look into Luc's eyes, certain he was going to see something different. But the boy was slumped across his seatbelt, asleep.

There was a ringing from the car's glove compartment. His cell phone – he couldn't remember putting it there. He let the phone ring out. A moment later it started up again, and this time he leant across to grab it.

'Russ?' Rebecca's voice was strained.

'Hi,' he said. Jesus, had she found out about the sculpture already?

'Where are you?'

'In the car.'

'Is Luc with you?'

'Yup. How's it going up there?'

'Are you on your way to work?'

'Yeah.' Well, he was – sort of. Fossil hunting work.

'Barbara's cancelled your appointments. Maybe you should go home and rest.'

'I don't need rest.'

'Look,' she said, her voice tentative, sounding him out, 'I've been thinking I need to come home today. All that stuff about swinging from the bar –'

'My bipedal experimentation.'

'Yes, well, sounds manic to me.'

He could hear Ulrike's voice in the background, insistent, 'He's not interesting enough to be manic.' The agent would have a lot more to say when she found out he had destroyed Rebecca's finest work ever.

'Is Luc okay?' said Beck.

'He's fine. We had a good time last night. Sav's out with Temba.' He had found his steady Russell voice, could sense her calming down.

'Russ –' Beck's voice was tentative, 'I wasn't going to tell you this until I got home but I've been busting to, so if you promise not to get over-excited…'

'Sure. What is it?'

'I was reading some more of Barak's notes on the plane. Not so bloody easy, the way it's wedged between the lines of English. Who knows whether he's right but if he is, Jesus,

Russ, this could really be something. I mean, he sounds pretty manic himself, but then, if he'd really thought he'd found the Garden of Eden, who could blame him? I've written out the translation. Listen to this.' He could hear the unfolding of a sheet of paper, and then she continued: *'This morning I made the most important discovery in the history of mankind. The cave floor opened up, the two specimens at first emerging in the form of the man's jaw and the woman's clavicle and then, as I worked, I could see I was going to uncover the remaining parts of their skeletons, lying there as if sculpted by God – yes, it was then – that sublime moment – that I knew of His existence. "You beauties! You beauties!" I shouted at the fossils. I was looking at the scene of an ancient accident, the collapse of a cave ceiling on a couple of early modern Homo sapiens, perhaps the very first: Adam and Eve themselves. I began to weep, and could not stop. Like the caves at Lascaux where our ancestors painted in the dark such exquisite work that no one would ever see. Did they paint for God? Yes, yes, I know they did, just like art inside Egyptian tombs, never meant for human eyes. Men painting for God! And here – dare I say it? – here was God painting for me!'*

Rebecca and Barak's voices seemed to be speaking in unison, and rising up in counterpoint was Russ's own, strident and preoccupied with the horror at having destroyed Beck's sculpture. It was a clash of intensity that proved too much for him. If this was the Garden of Eden, then he was the snake.

Rebecca went quiet. Finally she said, 'Russ, are you still there? What do you make of it?'

'Christ.'

'No,' laughed Rebecca, 'not Christ. Adam and Eve.'

Russ didn't know what to say.

'Should I come home?'

Beck's question was quickly followed by Ulrike's interjection. 'Zis client is getting his pecker up to spend

$50,000 on your vork. And he vants it because he vants to fuck you. At least let him zink he's going to get both.'

'What's her fucking case?' said Russ.

'Relax, Russ, she's just looking after business. Look, I need to know whether you're okay. There's a Hungarian businessman who's insisting on seeing the pieces. He has to leave before the exhibition opens and Ulrike's heard that he wants to spend upwards of $50,000 on my work. More importantly, he's a patron of the Museum of Modern Art in New York. They reckon he's more likely to buy the pieces if I flash a bit of cleavage at him.'

'I... well, that's fantastic news,' said Russ. 'I mean, not about flashing your cleavage but... Look, there's no question about it, you've got to stay. It's ridiculous to even think of coming home. Why don't you stay until after the exhibition?'

'I've got to come home to cast the silicone of the mummy piece,' she said.

Fuck me, he thought: *the piece that's in pieces.* 'I'm not sure you're going to need to do that,' he said.

'What? Russ, I can't hear you, you're dropping out.'

'I'm here.'

'Hey, what do you think your father would have to say about his head ending up in the Museum of Modern Art?'

'The mummy of MoMA,' Russ said, hoping Beck wouldn't be able to read his laboured laugh. The back of his throat was snatching at pockets of air.

'Russ? Russ? Say again?'

'The mummy of MoMA,' he said. 'I accidentally knocked it over.'

As if on cue, the reception on his phone cut out. Had she heard his last comment? He'd said it, of that he was sure. But had the line gone dead *before* or *after*? And would he have said it if the reception hadn't been fading out? This way he could at least claim to have told her. He turned his phone off.

As the car sped towards the cave, his thoughts gradually disengaged from the damaged sculpture at home. Breathe, breathe, he told himself.

The mummy of MoMA, ha! What would Savannah have said? Good chirp, Dad! Or, as Luc would have it, the Egyptian boy was upset because his daddy was a mummy. No, that's not quite how Luc had phrased the joke. Luc had used the word 'confused' – why was the boy confused? But of course, it was the word 'upset' that more aptly described Russ's state of mind since the discovery of the mummies. He was at last mourning his father. He would have to contact Rabbi Levy of the *Chevra Kadisha* again. He needed to bury his dead. Professor Naidoo wasn't going to like it. She would want to keep the mummies. Put them on display in a museum. But surely his right to burial took precedence? Why this strong need for a burial, he could not say. Why had human beings taken up this practice in the first place? Monkeys mourned. So did elephants. But only *Homo sapiens* found it desirable to bury its dead. Was it an appreciation of a deity, a soul, an afterlife, some other nascent sense of the spiritual? He knew the evidence from Europe – where the earliest known burials were at most around 50,000 years old – had been surpassed by the find of a child's 80,000 year-old burial site at Border Cave in Kwazulu-Natal, the little body having been covered in ochre before it was laid to rest. Barak would have held this up as another mark in favour of an African location for the Garden of Eden. But then, if the passage Beck read to him was accurate, who would need to bother with circumstantial facts? Barak might well have found the mother of all evidence.

Even Sir Arthur Keith knew that in the tale of evolution, there were many Gardens of Eden. The one Barak sought, had singled out as *the* Garden of Eden – and says he found – concerned the origins of humanity as we know it, the Adam we could look at and say: there goes Great-Grandpa. The man who had moved on from archaic *Homo sapiens'* production of primitive stone implements – choppers, scrapers, hafted spear points – to the far more sophisticated bone harpoon; the cache of ochre, surely used for make-up or paint. This is what Barak was seeking: a self-reflective being in search of meaning, the first of our kind with thought processes complex enough to undertake a spiritual journey, the first to expand humanity's horizons beyond the craft of everyday survival into the realm of the imagination, the world's first artists: there, he reasoned, we'll find Eve and her man.

Russ pulled into a petrol station – two old-fashioned pumps alongside a bare-bricked little office – on the outskirts of a small town. He glanced over at Luc, who was still asleep on the back seat, and got out to stretch. The attendant stared at Russ's shaven head. Across the street there was a bar, its windows painted over with a faded beer slogan – 'CASTLE: THE TASTE THAT'S STOOD THE TEST OF TIME' – and its outer doors open to reveal saloon doors within. Russ got back into the car and paid the attendant, who still seemed unable to take his eyes off his bald dome. Christ, what was so unusual about it, men shaved their heads all the time? How was this man to know he, Russ, had never done it before?

Luc was sitting upright, staring ahead. 'Are you hungry? Thirsty?' Russ asked him, peering down the street. Seeing no sign of a café or restaurant, he turned to the attendant. 'Anywhere we can get something to eat?'

The attendant flicked his head towards the bar across the street. 'Only there. Nothing else open now.'

Russ drove the car across the silent street and parked outside the bar.

'Not exactly a family restaurant, Luc, but let's see what they have to offer.'

There were no surprises behind the saloon doors. Three beer-bellied, rugged-faced men at one table: a grimy brown moustache on the one, long, greasy blond hair on another, a third who watched Russ and Luc with the disguised interest of a crocodile's lazy eyes. They were viewing a rugby match on a television set placed at a downward angle high above the counter.

The stucco walls were grey with dirt. 'These walls, Red, are covered with lime,' Barak had told him when they first walked into their new Krugersdorp home, 'know what that means? Fossils! In the plaster! All over the show. Bits of hippo, sabre-tooth, hominid. In the bathroom, kitchen, here in the lounge! We're surrounded by minute bits of our ancestors and the animals that preyed upon them. What a puzzle, eh, Red? If we could put those little pieces together...'

There was a quarter-size pool table in the corner, its green baize top worn bare in parts. A thin man looking equally worn hunched over it, his trousers falling down so the top of his bum-crease was visible. Another's face disappeared in the smoky gloom of the corner. *White trash*, Russ's mother would've called them.

No one, including the bartender, a black man in a red waistcoat shiny from over-ironing, raised any objection to the shaven-headed man bringing a child into the bar.

A blackboard with a menu written in chalk was propped up on the bar. Russ could just make out the two items on offer: burger & chips; oxtail stew. Figuring the hamburger would be the less likely to have been nurturing salmonella for the past week, Russ ordered two, along with a glass of milk for Luc and a Castle for himself – perhaps he, too, would stand the test of time.

Luc clambered onto a bar stool. Russ caught sight of himself in the rusty mirror behind the counter: his eyes, shocked, puffy and purple, like his mother's before her death, stared back at him behind a row of bottles that lined the shelf at the bottom of the mirror. Viceroy, Count Pushkin, Campari, Codron. Maybe the petrol pump attendant had good reason to stare at him. The television crowd erupted in response to the scoring of a try. One of the pub's patrons made a remark which was swallowed up by the neck of his beer bottle. The pool balls clicked against one another. The bartender disappeared through a door, presumably to place the hamburger order with the kitchen staff, such as they might be, and returned with a glass of milk. He gave Russ a beer.

An old man shuffled in. No, it wasn't an old man. Rather, a young man with a dog-weary demeanour. He looked drunk but Russ decided that he wasn't this either, it was something else, something more permanent. He had given up. He didn't belong in this world. His body dragged him around. He slunk over to the end of the bar nearest the saloon doors and sat down on a stool, some four feet from where Luc sipped his milk. He mumbled something monosyllabic to the bartender. The barman drew a draught and brought it to him, wiping the counter with a damp cloth before setting the beer mug down. The man looked up. His face was tattooed. Russ recognised the markings as those of a prison gang. The man closed his eyes, showing the tattoos on his eye lids. The wrinkled brown bulging skin of each lid was inked with a four-letter word, and Russ imagined he saw the inscriptions LOVE and HATE, but he was too far away and the light too poor for him to really make them out. The man's hair was a carpet of tight, dry black curls, his teeth rotten, his fat lips cracked, bloodied, fever-blistered. Your face and mine, Russ thought, the foul odour of the man reaching his nostrils. This, he supposed, would be *coloured trash*.

The white trash checked out the coloured trash. The

smell of violence drifted slowly into the air. The dogs were marking their terrain. There was something that utterly shocked Russ: he had a vision of himself getting up, walking the distance between his table and the tattooed man, taking the man's face in his hands, his palms gently but firmly holding those marked cheeks, bending down, and pressing his lips in a full embrace to that fever-blistered mouth.

No! No! No! He gulped down half his beer, some of the liquid spilling out of the sides of his mouth and flowing in a little golden-brown stream down his chin. The vision would not go away. He could taste the man's fever blisters. This is no place for Luc, he thought. He tried to remember whether there were any tables outside the bar, where they would be able to eat their hamburgers.

One of the white men had taken himself away from the rugby match and was standing over the coloured man, his hands on his hips. The tattooed man refused to look at him. Russ and Luc's exit was now blocked. They would have to weave their way around the tables to get out.

The white man said, 'What d'ya want here, you rubbish? *Sies, jou vuil bliksem,* you stink! Now *voetsek*!' His arm pointed towards the door. 'Come on, *fok* off!'

The ex-prisoner stared into his beer mug. He hadn't flinched. The barman disappeared hastily into a back room. Was this a Western? Russ must be at the Krugersdorp drive-in, in Barak's old Ford. Barak, bored with the film, might be expounding on the inherent aggression of man, agreeing with Dart's theory that man was instinctively violent but dismissing the evidence the Aussie had gathered to support it. Dart noticed holes in some *africanus* skulls and blamed them on a murderous neighbour. Barak saw them as the marks of a leopard's teeth, or an eagle's talons. But just because man's ancestor was more prey than hunter didn't convince Barak of his peaceful demeanour. The australopithecine *would* fight to conquer new territory, maintained Barak, but he'd pick on someone he thought was weaker. 'Man as Noble Creature!' Russ's father would scoff. 'Merely a fiction put forward by those wishing to see us as morally superior to the apes.' He saw the history of humanity as a slaughterhouse of cannibalism, human sacrificial practice, and genocide. If he'd been in this bar now he would have swept his arm like a showman, as if to say, watch how this unfolds, it's the way we've been doing things for millions of years.

'Hey, you, bushman. *Boesman*! I'm talking to you.' The white man pushed the other on the shoulder. 'What's this *kak* on your face, uh? Let me see, man…' He peered in mock examination of the blue markings. 'Hey, *ous*!' – he looked over his shoulder – 'I know what this *blerry* picture is, man! Hey, *boesman*, what's this, hey? Your mommy's pussy?'

The tattooed man stiffened.

Russ leaned towards Luc, whispering, 'Come, we're going to leave now!' He helped the boy off the bar stool.

'*Dis my reg om hier te wees,*' said the tattooed man sullenly. There was no mistaking the aura now; if violence had a perfume, this is what it would smell like.

The white man guffawed. 'Rights? *Jou bliksem*! You've got *fok-all* rights here, *kaffirtjie.*'

Luc had his hands flat over his ears and was beginning to curl over, on his way to a crouch beneath the overhang of the bar counter. As Russ bent down to pick him up, the tattooed man rose from his stool and in one fluid motion grabbed the white man behind the neck, brought the man's head forward and thrust a fist into his face. The man's blood flowed from his nose like a teenager's stream of piss. His hands clutched at his face as he turned and staggered goggle-eyed towards his friends' table, where he sank to his knees. He looked, from Russ and Luc's viewpoint, as if he was praying. Narrow streams of blood coursed between his fingers, coming together at the base of his palms in rivers that flowed down the stalks of his forearms toward his elbows. His friends' eyes darted between him and the man at the bar. The barman appeared and jumped back out of sight. The men playing pool rested on their cues. A more interesting game had presented itself. The television crowd erupted again.

The tattooed man seemed confused, as though he wanted to sit down and finish his beer but couldn't. He remained standing, rubbing his knuckles. Russ knelt down, gently scooped the trembling figure of Luc into his arms, and turned towards the door.

The tattooed man became alert, suddenly, as if Russ's motion had flipped a switch in his brain. He stepped into Russ's path. His eyes, aroused now, excited, drew Russ's.

'What do *you* want?' he said in Afrikaans.

Russ had been right, after all. LOVE and HATE each had its own eyelid. The man's question caught Russ, as with everything else since his appearance, by surprise. The man was right, though, he did seem to want something. An explanation? But he was now engaged in something time-old, a joust of manhood. He was meant to turn his instinct to what all the other men in the bar were doing: assess the risk, mobilise for fight or flight. Was he strong enough to take this man? Would the wounds render the venture too costly? What was this territory worth? But it wasn't Russ's fight and he had Luc in his arms. Besides, even if it was his fight, he would have placed himself on the tattooed man's side.

The man took a step towards him, his breath now warm against Russ's face.

Russ felt becalmed. He turned and placed Luc on the bar stool so recently vacated by the tattooed man. For once he felt the imposing nature of his own size and as he straightened, something in the man's eyes told him he was in no danger.

It wasn't that the tattooed man was intimidated by Russ's bulk and couldn't hurt him – he had already provided ample evidence of his skill – it was more that this man seemed to recognise Russ's total lack of animus towards him.

Russ did want an explanation. What was it that allowed this man to live on the edge? What allowed him to stand up to his persecutors? It was not simply that he had nothing to lose. That he had nothing to lose, in any case, was a construction of Russ's.

'I want,' Russ said tentatively, 'to know what it is that makes you feel alive.'

The eyes closed for a moment, exposing their indelible-ink message of LOVE and HATE. It was the answer Russ sought, of course – the ability and willingness to feel across that spectrum between love and hate – but it was not the ex-prisoner's answer.

'I do not live,' he said. 'I am a dead man.' He looked over Russ's shoulder towards the other men, who appeared to have thought better of tackling him. One of the pool players returned to his game, and steadied his cue behind the white ball. The tattooed man shrugged his shoulders and walked out of the bar.

When Russ turned, Luc was not on his stool. In panic, he charged about the bar, stumbling over chairs as he skirted the injured man, who was now having his nose looked at by his friends, a handkerchief stemming the flow of blood. He was trying to tell his friends to get the fucker.

'Ag, leave it alone, man,' said one.

Russ found Luc huddled with his back wedged into a corner and his knees drawn up under a quivering chin, his elbows clamped about his knees, hands over his ears, eyes fixed on the injured man.

'It's okay,' said Russ. 'It's okay. We're going to go now. I'm going to pick you up now.'

The boy's arms reached for his father's thick, powerful neck. Russ lifted him up, and with Luc's head resting on his right shoulder, threaded his way between the tables and chairs and out into the daylight.

33

LUC WAS WHINING NOW, a high-pitched squeal. 'Becca, Becca!'

'Your mother's in Jo'burg, Luc. And we've come to see what's in the cave. When that's done, we'll meet her at home.'

Russ tried to insert the keys in the ignition but his hands and fingers wouldn't play along, so he gripped the steering wheel instead, the keys still wedged in his right hand. It seemed every nerve ending from the shaved crown of his head to his toes had joined in a chorus of violent trembling.

They had stopped off at a sleepy country town and witnessed a simmering violence find its voice. Was he attracting these things? Now that he had decided to emerge from the waiting room, was his life to be action-packed? He had gone into the bar, a rough-looking environment, but surely even in there, on a lazy Saturday afternoon such as this, violence was not to be predicted? He felt like a rape victim wondering needlessly what she might have done to invite such attention. But then, he hadn't actually been the recipient of the attention – he wasn't the one with blood spurting from a broken nose. The one with blood spurting from his nose had, in fact, invited *something*, although Russ was sure it was supposed to be a feeling of power and the admiration of his friends, rather than a swift fist to the face. They – he and Luc – might cleanse their minds of that preposterous figure, if only they could get to the cave. It sat waiting for them on the south side of the peninsula, the tumbled-down entrance hidden amongst boulders and shrubs. Dassies moved in and out, seagulls drifted their cumbrous bodies over the rocks, and the wind lashed the bushes, and, down below, chopped up the sea. The tableau was set. All he had to do was enter it. But he couldn't go, his bodily tremors held him in their vice. He wasn't going to this cave at all, he was going to another one entirely. He was going to find his father in the Elephant Chamber at Sterkfontein. He would leave his bicycle at the top, walk down the path to the cave entrance, feel the coolness of the earth against his face and bare legs and arms, and find Barak drinking tea in front of the great lime pachyderm. What was he going to say to him?

It was the arrival on foot of two policemen that prodded him into action. It seemed to have taken them forever – perhaps they'd had to be roused from their afternoon naps or dragged from their television screens – but no, they would be only too excited to be called to a fight scene and between the doling out of injury and the arrival of the investigators was probably less than five minutes. With one hand holding the other steady, Russ fed the key into the ignition, started the car and drove slowly away. Fifty metres down the road he saw the hotel on the right and pulled over opposite it. He took the duffle bag from the passenger seat, slung it over his shoulder, picked up Luc – who did not resist him – and headed across the road.

A two-seater faux leather sofa did duty as the hotel's lounge. Russ deposited Luc onto it and stepped up to the counter behind which sat a pubescent girl with a waxy, taut complexion, her brown hair tied back in a ballerina's knot. She was reading a *You* magazine. The daughter of the owners? She looked up, composing herself as she rose to her feet and smiled with a welcoming formality.

'*Kan ek u help, Oom?*'

He felt her tentative warmth lift him immediately. He

wanted to stretch out, take her hand in his, and pull her towards him so that he might kiss her on both cheeks. Her cheeks were concave, yes, like little caves to receive his kisses.

'I'd like a room – just for a couple hours,' he said. What was this new urge to be kissing the faces of strangers?

She seemed to relax, and smiled sweetly at him. A beautiful girl. Well, perhaps not all that beautiful – in fact, her waxy skin and sunken cheeks placed her more in the Addams Family compound than on the rugged, wind- and sun-beaten West Coast. But from his side of fifty, youth in itself was beautiful.

'Oh,' said Russ, 'it's nothing funny. Really. My son's just tired. So am I. We've only got an hour or so to drive but I just can't do it. I need to sleep for a short while. I should've come tomorrow really, after a good night's sleep.'

'Yes, that is okay,' said the girl. 'Sorry you must pay for the whole day. We make rooms for the day. You can stay more, but no persons stay here for more than one day.'

Did she mean that the town had nothing to recommend a stay of more than a day? Or that a day in the hotel was enough to nudge everyone along their merry way? He was of a mind to clarify this.

'Is there something wrong with the hotel? It looks like a fine family hotel to me. Well, I'm sure you get lots of salesmen here. I suppose even that they're your main customers.'

'Oh, no, it's not that,' she said, ready for his query, 'it's this town. There's nothing here. Nothing ever happens here.' She held out a pen, indicating an old-fashioned guest register. 'Make your signature here please.'

'Oh, I wouldn't say *nothing*,' he said. He took the pen from her dry fingers, thought of telling her about the skirmish in the bar but decided this wouldn't count in her lexicon as 'something'. He signed his name 'Eugène Dubois' and laughed to himself, his little joke having a steadying effect on his hands.

The girl pirouetted towards a wooden rack containing every one of its room keys, and gracefully unfurled an arm to pluck one from its hook. Her neck was long and elegant beneath the bun of her hair, the shoulder bones protuberant, the reaching arm pitifully anorexic. This girl trapped in her parents' one-horse-town hotel seemed to have acquired – in a grab at sophistication? – a big-city girl's disease. When she turned around, she peered over the reception counter and, eyeing the large duffle bag and the immobile Luc, shifted her focus back to the counter, where she looked about, searching for something.

'*Dit was hier*,' she said to herself.

She was looking for her bell.

'Oh,' said Russ, 'maybe…' He lifted the long rectangular cover of the guest register.

She beamed two rows of yellowing teeth at him – those clandestine vomits were already playing havoc with her dentition – and exclaimed, as if Russ had found a hidden escape tunnel, '*Dankie, Oom!*'

The bell was an old-fashioned one, in keeping with the antiquated guest register. It had a polished brass chamber with a percussion cap. He shifted the register away and with a springy movement the girl tapped her palm against the cap of the bell. A pure *ding!* resonated around the foyer. They waited, the shaven-headed man and the reduced-fat girl, smiling at each another. She tapped the bell again and, tilting her head to one side, her eyebrows slightly raised, smiled apologetically. She leaned out from behind her counter, but this didn't do the job either. A third *ding!* – accompanied this time by a slightly panicky 'Stoffel!' – had as little effect as the first. She looked helplessly at the duffle bag, which Russ had begun to hoist over his shoulder.

'Don't worry,' he said, scooping Luc up in his arms. The boy's eyes were closed, although Russ doubted he was asleep.

'Turn right at the top,' the girl called out as he mounted the stairs.

'Thanks,' he said in a stage whisper.

'*Oom!*' She laughed, holding out the key to his room as he retraced his steps and accepted the key from her lemur's fingers.

He thanked her again and carried Luc up to the room. There was a musty smell inside and the furniture and fittings were sun-faded and old, but it was clean and neat. He laid Luc down on the bed and gently undid the boy's shoelaces and slipped off his shoes. Russ took off his own shoes and lay down on the pink bed cover. But sleep eluded him; Beck wasn't there for him to hold, to cushion his body against, to make him forget, and, unlike Beck, he was unused to the comfort of cradling Luc.

They spent the rest of the afternoon in the room. At some point Luc seemed to pass from his deviated state into one of genuine sleep. Russ drank water that had been standing in a carafe on the bedside table and tasted of the room, a place that had absorbed the bodily emissions of hundreds of travellers, taken them into its walls so that bits of them were ingrained in the room like the fragments of fossil in the plaster of the old Krugersdorp house. He kept a vigil at the window for the comings and goings of the bar down the road but there was no sign of the injured man, his friends, or the cops. Maybe they'd already gone after the tattooed man, or taken the injured man for treatment. Russ was left with a still, dusty street and the realisation that it wasn't rest he had wanted after all, but a bird's-eye view of these proceedings, so macabre and yet so everyday: a bully picks on a seemingly weaker man, and gets it wrong. Should Russ contact the police and offer to make a statement? Did the tattooed man need his evidence? His middle-class concern seemed out of place, and with a twinge of guilt Russ dismissed the idea, turning instead to his own investigation. He opened the duffle bag and withdrew the Mummy's Notebook, picking his way along an unsteady path that told a story of Barak's visit to the father of psychoanalysis:

I visited a doctor once. We spoke in his rooms at 20 Maresfield Gardens, Hampstead, until he grew tired. It was late in 1938, not long after his flight from Europe. He was still full of the miracle of his escape, and of the fact that his antiquities had arrived intact. He had his sister-in-law bring us some tea. He revelled in the objects with which he had surrounded himself. There were Egyptian heart scarabs and mummy portraits, Ming dynasty heads, Athenian lekythos, *Syrian clay figures from the middle bronze age, a magnificent example of the Egyptian Baboon of Thoth, in marble.*

I think he was rather fascinated by my case because of his own interest in the origins of mankind. He wanted to uncover the unconscious motivation for my searching and saw in my digging in the earth more than a metaphor for his digging through the strata of his patients' minds. I went to see him about a family problem. My wife, you see, my wife — I was having nightmares, bloody awful nightmares. I was afraid to go to sleep. I kept dreaming that I was back in the trenches with Isaac reciting poetry from a head blown clean off his shoulders. The Professor said that my childhood had given me shell-shock, that just as Isaac's head was separated from his body, my intelligence had become separated from my emotions, that what I had to say for myself sounded very poetic, but without the rest of me they were just words.

Russ read on for a while, trying to understand the story of Barak's visit to Freud, not so much as an account of a real event, which it may or may not have been, but, more importantly, for the dialogue between two parts of Barak. After all, if Russ had his Inspector Toka, then perhaps Barak had his Professor Freud.

He told me — I had to strain at times to make out the words coming from his mouth, or what remained of it after all those operations to remove the cancer – that his antiquities looked even more impressive than they did at Berggasse 19. I remember thinking that he was trying to sponge away his grief at having to leave his beloved Vienna. His collection had begun with plaster copies of Florentine statues, his favourite being a reproduction of Michelangelo's Dying Slave. *We discussed the nature of collecting, which he held to be a child-like activity aimed at preserving early erotic pleasures. In her state of insightful naiveté, Nombeko has passed similar comments. 'Why do you collect these bones?' she asks. 'You are not a sangoma. These are child's games you play.' But she loves me and stays with me nonetheless.*

Collecting, the Professor said, gives one a sense of power, a way of controlling the world. Looking at and touching his pieces gave him a sense of renewal – he used the word erquickung *(we conversed in German) – which also means potency. He said that his purchase of* The Dying Slave *had to do with his relationship with his father. The older Freud had told him of an incident in which a Christian knocked his new fur cap into the mud and shouted, 'Jew! Get off the pavement!' When the boy Sigmund asked his father what he did, his father replied, 'I went into the roadway and picked up my cap.'* The Dying Slave, *he told me, was an image of the father he would have liked to have had: the powerful, sensuous, ideal man, dying peacefully.*

'Look,' Freud said, taking out a picture of the statue, for he no longer had the cast, 'ars simia naturae.' He was pointing at the crouching, primitive ape Michelangelo had carved behind the slave. 'Art imitates the nature of apes.'

'Beautiful,' I said, feeling only sadness.

I declined his offer of treatment. It seemed to me he had in mind that I should suffer, that he was going to help me to suffer. 'I prefer to look for my past in the ground,' I told him. In any case, it did not appear that he would live to see me through it.

Mindful of the discomfort caused by his dismembered face – by this time his entire jaw had been removed – I thanked him for the interview, settled my account with his sister-in-law and took my leave.

Russ stopped reading. He ran a bath, clambering in while the tap spattered and chugged rusty water into the tub. He had brought the glass of water with him and rested it on his chest. It sat at an angle, cold and clear in contrast to the fulvous warmth of the bath water. He drank from it, then raised himself up and dropped the glass onto the surface of the water. It sank between his legs and clanked against the bottom of the tub, remaining intact.

If the glass had broken and cut him, the water would have turned red. The image triggered a memory from the early days of their relationship. They were so young – or, at least, she had been young (no starved, concave cheeks on his Rebecca) and had made him youthful. They made love for hours, him marvelling at his new-found ability to stay with her, emotionally and physically, and at the way she looked at him, as if drugged, not knowing what to do with her hands, as if whatever she touched would be too sensitive for her fingertips, would burn them or turn them to ice, and so her hands moved about in the air, clenching into fists, then the tense release, only to clench up again, and all the while her mouth searching out his, her tongue probing restlessly, her teeth hectoring between pain and pleasure on his chin, his neck, his shoulders. Later they would discover bruises on each other's bodies and wonder how they'd got there. Sometimes he would find one on her days later and half-jokingly accuse her of betrayal. She enrolled him in her own very private course of study – 'Fluids 101' – introducing him to her bodily fluids; there were seminars on the joy of saliva on the tongue and lectures on the merits of pussy juice. But that one time it had grown dark and afterwards they lay in the bath, playful, sipping up the bathwater and spraying it from their mouths, giggling, swallowing some by mistake, then laughing more. Finally, they rose from the bath and dried each other. Returning to the bathroom for some reason, he switched on the light. The bathwater was the colour of a light red wine. She had come on during their lovemaking and they had unknowingly bathed in her menstrual blood. Excited by this, she wanted to repeat the pleasure, only this time being conscious of it. But they had bumped up against the limit of his new-found freedom.

And now I am here, desire-less, he thought, unless one counts as desire the wish to kiss a gangster's scummy lips or the sepulchral cheeks of an underweight girl – and Rebecca, my Rebecca, is a thousand miles away.

There was something important he had been trying to grasp, that had been on the tip of his tongue since speaking to Professor Naidoo that morning. He had read the Piltdown confession over the phone, her silence so rapt he'd needed to check every now and then that she was still there. It was the tip of Barak's tongue he'd been trying to find, hidden as it was behind that rag-tied mummy's mouth.

'My God,' Leila had said, 'all that wasted effort. All those people spending all that time. Well, he certainly made them pay. And then when the fraud came to light, all those false accusations, aspersions cast upon men too dead to defend themselves!'

'Yes,' Russ had said. But he wasn't so much interested in that as he was in the heart of the forger, and he had quickly picked up his reading again, eventually coming to the conclusion of the old man's confession, again needing to check that Leila Naidoo was on the other end of the line before relaying the part that was, perhaps even more than the revelation of the fraud itself, Barak's most profound volte-face.

Piltdown Man failed to speak up for himself because he could not. After all, the conformation of his jaw precluded it, especially in Woodward's reconstruction! (There I go, making light of things again.)

But if he could speak, he would reveal his creator's deepest shame. He would say that I did not create him in the name of science. He would say that I created him in the name of a childish revenge.

On Rhodes Papa would have attained the status of elder, teacher, rabbi. In England he was a kike who broke his back baking loaves of bread so that his children would have a better life. But I, his unhappy son, would toil in the field, breaking my back, a kike labourer to be used by the Great Men, His Majesty's scientists, with their arrogant pens in their hands, their dangerous, poison pens.

As you see, I have been reflecting on my actions as a young man. In the short time I worked under him at the British Museum, Smith Woodward treated me with disdain. I could see that I was always going to be his flunky, his spic assistant, my own scientific mind given no credence at all. A scientific eunuch. I saw in myself my father, obsequious, bowing before a Gentile who was handing out his judgment of me, who saw me not even as a lesser man but a lesser being. I was my father that day outside the bakery, and every day of his life, taking off my hat, shamed into bowing my head before the great Keeper of Geology. How I wished to restore my pride!

And now I see that my actions achieved the very opposite. I was unfaithful to Science. I was unfaithful to Truth. I shamed myself more than a thousand Smith Woodwards could have shamed me.

My God, is this what hung over the old man when Russ rode past him that day? Is this what had so reduced him? This, together with his failure to find the Garden of Eden, the discovery that was to exonerate him? Leaving his life book-ended by fraud and failure.

Russ had understood his own reluctance to recognise the soldier-tramp, but until now had not appreciated Barak's deep sense of shame, had not known him capable of it. Fuck, they were both buried so deep in it, the two of them caught in quicksand ten paces from each other, unable to touch, both sinking fast. They'd had their chance – and they'd fucked it up.

He pushed his legs over the end of the bath so that his head could slip under the water, along with the wave of remorse washing over him. In one motion he came gasping to the surface, the glass flying in anger from his hand. It shattered against the lip of the tub, the shards scattering onto the floor and into the water where they drifted down around his thighs and groin. His body felt too heavy to move, his breathing recklessly out of control. Bathrooms had been the site of too much humiliation during his teenage years, lifting his mother from the toilet where she had passed out mid-ablution. And now here it was that he, Russ the regretful, had finally understood the pathos of a broken son cycling past a broken father.

The bathroom, that most civilised of human achievements. Maybe this is what makes us human after all – not the upright gait, or the big brain, or the spiritual awareness that will have us ritualise our mourning by burying our dead, but our ability to wash away our shit as if it never existed.

Finally he lifted himself from the tepid bath.

He stared around the room. How had it become so messy? The only neat part was the boy lying on the bed; for the rest, the contents of Barak's duffle bag were strewn about the floor. Russ must have been looking for something. And now there was a trail of bloody footprints. He had cut his foot on a piece of broken glass.

He lay on the bed next to Luc, treading his way slowly through the remaining unread sections of the Mummy's Notebook, knowing all the while these passages would haunt him for years to come, his father's urge to record his remaining hours of life seemingly more precious than the need to continue it. With each sentence deciphered, Russ's urgency to get to the cave grew. Barak's words were like a bugler's battle cry, a call to action. But Russ was thwarted. Luc was asleep, the night had only just begun, and expeditions *always* began at night's end, just before daybreak, with Russ's child's arms laden with equipment, struggling down the steps of the Krugersdorp house, out to the tray of the Ford pickup truck. He let the notebook slip from his fingers. Shut up, he moaned, shut up, shut up. I'm coming. In the morning. I'm coming.

He curled himself around Luc in imitation of the pairing of mother and son he'd seen so often. The child shifted, laying a pale hand over Russ's hairy forearm, pulling him into sleep. They would, after all, be spending the night, Russ dreaming of a house on the savannah where, from the vantage of the veranda, he and Barak sit on wicker chairs watching a herd of wildebeest stampeding past. Suddenly thunderous hooves give way to a vast, dusty quietness, disturbed only by the hesitant trotting of a few stragglers trying to catch up. When these laggers also disappear, Barak, who in the language of dreams is now a blanket-wrapped invalid in a wheelchair, turns to a nurse – an older black woman in starched white uniform, a beatific smile on her grandmotherly face – to speak, stuttering, before he's able to spit out, '*N-N-Nurse!*'

As the nurse wheels Barak away, Russ calls out after him, 'You and I are the keepers of our father's wounds!'

34

THEY HAD BEEN TRAVELLING for more than an hour by the time Russ steered the car onto the dirt track. The elusive Stoffel had appeared to serve them breakfast in the hotel dining room, Luc eating enough to make up for the missed meals of the day before. He had been talkative – for Luc – but as soon as they were back in the car had lapsed into silence. Now the transition from tarred road to bumpy gravel seemed to stir him, as if he'd been waiting for it to prompt him.

'Your mother was wrong,' he said. 'Grandfather Barak did fight in the Great War.'

Russ was looking out for the Defence Force's 'DANGER! GEVAAR!' signs, where he would have to turn off. 'What's that, Luc?'

'Your father fought in the Great War.'

'Really? How do you know?'

'I looked it up on the Internet.'

'Oh. Of course. But where would –'

'On my computer.'

'No, Luc, I meant, where did you look for this information?'

'Your father said he was in the Royal Lancaster Regiment. He said they fought on the Western Front. That means he must have got a campaign medal. All the men who fought got campaign medals. There is a list. You can see it in the National Archives in England. You don't have to go to

England, you can see it on the Internet. I put in his name and found it in the index. They wanted three-and-a-half pounds for a copy of the record. I paid with your credit card. The Visa card. The gold one. I don't know how many rands that is. I was going to look up the exchange rate but I did not have time. That is what I was doing when you came to take me away in the car.'

'Jesus, Luc, I don't know what to say.' The extent of Luc's computer literacy and ingenuity was not the surprise it would have been a few short weeks ago; his research topic was something else. Russ had been so sure Barak's World War I passages were bullshit, the unreliable memoirist doing what he did best: rewriting history. That his mother turned out to be wrong about this most crucial aspect of his father's past came as an overwhelming, shattering relief. The man *had* been to hell. The hand tremor Russ had felt after the fracas in the bar set in again. Unable to trust his driving, he pulled over to the side of the road.

He glanced at Luc. A vein throbbed delicately in the hollow of the boy's temple. His almost translucent skin gave the illusion of emotional transparency, as if one could look directly into him. Only, under Russ's gaze, this thin skin hid Luc's thoughts and feelings as if it were a rhino's hide. And yet Russ now had a sense of coming to know his son better. Luc felt and understood so much more than he had realised. The boy had understood Russ's difficulty with his father's credibility, and gone looking for corroborative evidence. He was like a selective amplifier of the mood around him, not mad at all, simply hyper-responsive in some instances, and non-responsive in others. Pride wallowed up within Russ.

'Thanks, Luc,' he said. 'That really means so much to me. Thank you.'

Luc's eyes darted away, but the corners of his mouth

twitched into satisfied little creases.

It was the spring offensive of 1918. The Germans launched a blistering attack against our part of the Front. We held our ground. Our battalion was due for a respite, and so we retired to the reserve line. The situation was dire: we were ordered to maintain battle readiness and stand to at four-thirty every morning. Isaac was complaining a great deal about the delay in his requested transfer to Jabotinsky's Jewish Battalion, which was then serving in Egypt and Palestine. He had been trying to join his fellow Russian Jews for over a year, only army bureaucracy being what it is, nothing came of it. I can picture him so awfully clearly, reclining in his battle dress, his rifle at his side, trying to work on his poem, Through These Pale Cold Days, *while I interrupted him to give a bitter rejoinder in our ongoing debate about Zionism. He had once again misplaced his gas mask.*

In the dying months of the war the corpses were piled so high even the generals could see them, forcing them to acknowledge the triumph of machine over man. We were given more Lewis gun crews. We watched those gunners in their ugly beauty, making love to their machines, one man with his arm looped around the muzzle to steady it, the second holding the butt to fire, the jolting rhythm of their bodies as the bullets flew.

We were ordered forward and our commander, Major Hamilton, a dashing chap, monocle in his right eye, sword in hand, led us out. This was not unusual. I saw colonels striding forward with walking sticks in their hands. We were caught in open country by enemy cross-fire. I fired wildly. I turned to see Major Hamilton go down and then the Boche overran the front line. The man next to me was bayoneted in the chest, the German who held the rifle sticking into him was spurted with his blood. He put his boot on my comrade's chest and yanked his bayonet out. I shot him. The bullet hit him in the face from such close range it took off his lower jaw. He was no more than a boy, really.

I slipped down the muddy side of a nearby trench. My helmet went flying and spun along the duckboards. I slumped back against the wall of the trench. Many trenches were little more than furrows in the ground but the one into which I had fallen was deep, and had been widened by the burst of a shell. Moments later another form tumbled over the lip of the trench. It was the German boy whose mandible I had shot off. He must have somehow crawled to the edge and fallen in, his sweat-matted hair stuck to his forehead, his lower face torn away, his nostrils above a nude palate forming two perfect 'O's, then collapsing again as he struggled to gain breath. The noise of gunfire and the cries of the wounded floated with the smoke of battle over us. The soldier's fingers were poised in tense, awkward positions, frozen in the frenzy of conducting an orchestra of men playing for their lives. Finally I realised what he was doing. He was trying to reach inside his tunic. I crawled over to him and guided his palsied fingers inside. They came away with a compact book. In the time it took for him to die, we stared at each other, speechless. The book in his hand was a Hebrew Bible.

By the Sunday of that week, the surviving members of our Battalion were ordered, under cover of darkness, to the rear. I had lost contact with Isaac but then with the parting of cloud cover allowing a weak moon to splinter through, I saw his silhouette in the blue light just ahead of me. We had not gone far when a runner caught up with us: the enemy had renewed his attack, and volunteers to return to the line were called for. It was not an order since we had long since earned a rest. I was beyond exhaustion and had in any case a flesh wound to my torso, which I had only just discovered after a corporal pointed it out to me.

Isaac went back, I don't know why. I tried to catch his eye as he brushed past me, but he was unseeing. Within an hour he had fallen in close combat. It was April 1, All Fools' Day. Savage fighting continued for days and Isaac's body, along with thousands of others, lay unburied on the battlefield. He had become one of the 'older dead'. Pale Cold Days *turned out to be his last poem. 'They leave these blond still days,' he wrote, 'In dust behind their tread/ They see with living eyes/ How long they have been dead.'*

Inseparable from my image of Isaac lying long dead on the battlefield is the half-face of the German Jewish boy, bared upper teeth and horrified eyes pleading across the trench we shared for me to end his suffering. It took me a lifetime to put that second bullet into his head.

And all those years later, on the eve of another great world conflict, I should have accepted Professor Freud's offer of treatment. I know, I know. But can you not see? I had already shared a trench with a jawless German-tongued Jew. I had no stomach for a return to it.

Russ started the car down the dirt track again, eventually slowing to a halt in the same place as he, Rebecca and the coloured boys had done weeks before. This time there was no one to help him – Luc stood waiting to one side – as he wriggled through the hole in the fence, reaching through and pulling the duffle bag and the two battery-powered lamps that he hadn't managed to cram into the bag along with all the other equipment. Luc crawled through easily enough. Russ slung the duffle bag over his right shoulder and, looking around for the two lamps, found them gripped by the handle, one in each of Luc's hands. Under a heavy grey sky that had bleached the yellowness from the sun, the two set off.

Being in the wild was not new to Russ. He had slept out in the open, helped Barak as he went about finding supplies and tools from their surroundings in order to prepare meals, sleeping places, working facilities. Barak had shown him how to eat protein-rich termites by inserting licked blades of long grass into holes in reddish brown ant mounds. He had watched as Barak laid traps, hunted with spear or club, not simply because they needed to eat – Barak could have used a gun and a carving knife for that purpose – but because the anthropologist was attempting to understand the transition from scavenger to hunter, and the development of tools within early hominid culture. He was trying to match up the marks left on bone by different tools and cutting methods with the striation patterns he'd found on animal fossils discovered at hominid sites. He would hold two rocks in his hands, examining the edges, thinking about form and shape, then crack them together, work away until he had a flint with which he could skin and carve the animals that fell afoul of his devices. By comparing scratches on ancient bones with his newly skinned remains, he could tell what kind of tool the hunter used. 'Making a stone flint is no easy task, Red,' Barak would say. 'Stone is not like bone. Bone is suggestive of form and of function. Stone is not. The toolmaker must impose his wishes upon it. He must think creatively, he must imagine the shape and then release it from the nebulous form of the rock. When our ancestors started doing that, they became artists, and *that* forged their humanity.'

Now as he made his way to a fossil site with *his* son in tow, Russ smiled. He was thinking of Rebecca. He must remember to tell her. Sculpture, according to Barak, made us into human beings.

But, Father, Russ wondered as his delight quickly soured, what made you human? You deserted two families and wiped out a third. What happened to your humanity? Did you misplace it somewhere? Lose it in a cave? No, of course not, that's where you'd been looking for it. Luc had found the more likely site of Barak's misplaced humanity. It had been lost in a French trench, along with that German Jewish boy's jaw.

Russ stubbed his toe on a rock. He looked around. Luc had fallen behind by a good twenty metres. He was battling with the lamps. 'Shit!' Russ said, waiting for the boy to catch up. He was not the outdoorsman his father was and Luc not the predictable, physically capable son he had been – and this time he was without the guidance of the sure-footed, whizzing bare feet of the brothers Petrus and Bartholomew. What had he been thinking, bringing Luc on this expedition? Beck would be furious. He had destroyed her sculpture and now he was endangering her son. He held out his hands to relieve Luc of the lamps. We don't have to stay, Russ told himself, fighting off the loneliness of his poor judgment. We can go back to the car and drive home –

No way, no fucking way. He was needed here. Flooding his mind was an excerpt he'd read last night in the hotel room, towards the end of the Mummy's Notebook.

Nombeko wants us to leave but I see no point. 'Don't worry, my dear,' I told her, 'Verwoerd's guns will soon fall silent.' With her eyes she accuses me of arrogance but I know their pattern. They test Monday to Friday, never on a weekend and never after four-thirty in the afternoon. They have always aimed wide of the peninsula. It is too close to the sea and shells landing in the water leave no dust clouds to mark their point of impact. No shadows at noon. Boom, boom, boom! I have decided to put up with it. Why not? Stanley had to contend with hostile tribesmen and wild animals, Darwin with scathing, mocking critics, why should I not carry on in the face of some loud noise? How can I leave before excavating these fossils? It would be madness to turn my back on the apotheosis of my life's work. It is here. At long last, after almost three years, I have found the first humans. I have gone back in time, to a stratum dating between 120,000 and 200,000 years ago! I have found where Man began and I shall not stop digging until I have their bones free of the earth.

Ha! What a difference a week makes. I pick up my pen to note that I am right, I have been vindicated. On Friday the guns fell silent and now Verwoerd himself has been silenced. We have heard the news. There has been a celebration in the village. They are calling Dimitri Tsafendas a hero.

To be honest, I was more bothered by Nombeko's nagging than the guns. She was afraid the mountain would fall in.

'It is because your people grew up on the savannah,' I told her.

'No, it is not true,' she said. 'When we were children we played in the caves. We consulted the Inyanga there. I am not scared of this cave. I am scared of those guns.'

This is not the first time we have spoken thus. Each time they

*announce a new series of tests with a burst of shell-fire, she badgers me.
Sometimes, if she is on the beach, or checking the traps, or collecting
bulbs or berries, she rushes into the cave in a sweat.*

'Barak, Barak! They are back! They have come back!'

*We do have to be careful then. They watch with binoculars for the
explosions. And even though they will not have the peninsula in their
sights, who is to say one of them will not sweep his glasses across the
fynbos and pick us out amongst the proteas and daisies? We have to be
careful they do not catch sight of an old white man and his native woman.*

Russ's recollection of the passage was interrupted by
Luc. 'The word *cheetah*,' the child said, as if they had been
conversing and he was simply responding to a comment of
his father's, 'comes from the Hindu word for spotted one.
Only no one's spotted one in India since 1952.' Luc's thin,
stilted laugh burst over the vegetation.

Russ chuckled. 'That *is* funny, Luc. No one's *spotted one*,
yes. Good joke, sweetheart. But we must try to hurry.'

A herd of zebra, unsure of the threat posed by the
intruders, began to wander off. They weren't going to waste
energy on running if they didn't have to. The morning,
despite its lateness, was still chilly, and the zebra, having
made a collective assessment, settled back into their grazing
pattern, showing their flanks broadside to the sun, their
black stripes soaking up the warmth. Something else was
moving close by and Russ, glancing to his left, saw a baboon
advancing parallel to him. Then there was another, and
another, big, dark grey shapes dawdling along on all fours
while the smaller ones, the children and the adolescents,
bounced about with the agility but not the grace of chimps.
The leader stood out amongst them: the most powerful
of all African monkeys, much larger than the female of
his kind. 'His is a society that runs on threat,' Barak more
than once told Russ. 'Look at those teeth! They're part of
his weaponry, rather than his cutlery. They're supposed to

be vegetarians, don't really need blades in their mouths for eating. Still, I have to say I've seen the odd baboon dig into a piece of meat and even one rare troop that has worked out how to hunt flamingos, hurling their brutish bodies at speed into shallow water and coming away with a bent pink bird.' So many of Barak's lectures turned on the theme of aggression. 'The bigger and tougher the baboon, the higher up the pecking order he'll go. Not that a baboon is averse to using his head. He'll swagger about, show his teeth, bluff his way to the top if he can. Not unlike the human male, eh?' Russ's thoughts flashed back to the fracas in the bar.

If Edwardian society had been a baboon troop, Barak's father would have been the most subservient of the males. Barak was ashamed of that.

The leader's eyes were searching the ground, his jaws working away, storing food in the portable grain silos that were his puffed-out cheeks. His eyes were brilliant for foraging scraps of food, but set too close for long-range vision; for this, the animal had to move his eye base from side to side. Trying to imitate the confidence of Petrus and Bartholomew, Russ kept walking. But in front of him, converging with him, was the large alpha male, its tail arched as if in a question mark: what are you doing here, trespasser?

Russ tucked one of the lamps under his arm and reached for Luc's hand. The boy let him take it. The baboon disappeared behind a protea bush. Relieved, Russ said, 'Do you know that in Saudi Arabia men and women have to visit the zoo on different days? On the women's days, the male primates are dressed in nappies – to hide their privates.'

Luc didn't reply. He was staring past Russ at the alpha male who had re-emerged, baring his teeth. Russ stood still. Again he fought the urge to turn back, to go home, walk the dog, watch TV until it was time to fetch Rebecca from the airport but it was too late, he and Luc were trapped here with these fucking animals, with this angry looking leader, with his dark hairy face and beady brown eyes. At the very least, he wished for the presence of the brothers Petrus and Bartholomew to provide safe passage. The baboon barked. *We can't outrun it. Can I fight it? I could swing a lamp but...* He stared at it, watching those eyes, and then remembered his father's admonitions about eye-contact and body language. *Don't look. Don't smile. Smiles appease humans but incite baboons.* There were barks from the other members of the troop. Russ was aware of a flurry around him but couldn't take his eyes off the leader. Were the others moving in on them or away from them? The leader opened his large jaws in a yawn that was anything but benign and sleepy, his massive canines looking every bit the cutlasses they were, the twin black nostrils at the end of his dark, elongated snout aimed straight at them. The male went into a swagger, pacing from side to side in front of Russ and Luc, rolling his shoulders forward in the stage routine of a posturing body-builder. Russ forced himself to walk backwards, dragging Luc with him, and managed to go some distance on his weak legs before he stumbled over a shrub, the lamps and duffle bag pulling him further off balance. He landed on his back, caught by the fleshy softness of a large succulent and with Luc coming down on top of him. The male stopped his posturing, his great head shifting on his shoulders from left to right, right to left, focussing those eyes. He looked like a hairy metronome. Russ stifled an anxious laugh. Maybe if he fitted the fellow with prisms it might get those eyes to focus long. Satisfied, the baboon let out a bark, turned around and loped off after his family, his big pink bottom sauntering out of sight.

Luc was rigid. Russ rose to his feet, wiped bits of soil and scrub off his palms. He leant over Luc, picking him up, readjusting his grip so that he could lift him onto his shoulders. But the boy would not move his body in concert, would not adjust his legs to land on the saddle of his father's neck. For a moment the two of them were frozen in an awkward pose, Russ's hands beneath Luc's armpits, his arms outstretched so that he seemed to be offering up the body of his son to the heavens.

'If you'd rather walk, that's fine. But if you'd like a ride, you need to open your legs.'

'The baboon was barking,' said Luc, still rigid.

Russ put him down. *Just like Barak's father,* he thought, *I'm just like Barak's father. Fucking petrified of an anti-Semitic baboon.*

'Yes,' said Russ, 'they bark. Not quite like dogs, but they bark.' He sat down on the duffle bag. Luc's eyes were flicking from the ground in front of him to the surrounding bushes, his head jerking in parallel. He was looking for the baboons. There was no point in rushing him. His fragility was even more exposed out here in this stark, male place, without the love of women.

And what of Russ's love? His love for his little boy had fallen to an enemy within him. He had not been man enough to love. As he grasped the extent of his own ineptness, the tears for this loss broke silently from between his lids.

Luc stared at his wet cheeks. 'Those are tears,' he said.

'Yes!' said Russ. 'I'm crying for us.'

'Why?'

'Because I love you and I haven't told you that in five years.'

'Oh,' said Luc, looking away. 'Are you supposed to tell me?'

'Your mother does, doesn't she?'

'Yes. But not always with words.'

They fell quiet, and for once Russ was feeling too much to be discomforted by it. He was feeling painfully alive.

After a while he took out one of the bottles of water he had stowed in the duffel bag before they left the hotel, opened it and offered it to Luc, who took a few sips. Luc passed the bottle back and Russ drank.

'Do you want me to tell you another story about baboons?'
Luc shrugged.

'It was during the genocide in Rwanda,' said Russ.

'Rwanda is a country in Africa where one tribe attacked another,' Luc said.

'Yes, that's right, Central Africa. The Hutus attacked the Tutsis. Or was it the other way around? I get confused.' He searched Luc's face but if the boy had an answer, he wasn't sharing it. 'In any case, at the time this was happening a troop of baboons took over one of the posh tourist hotels. All the people had fled because the Hutus were coming. Or the Tutsis. Jesus, you'd think I'd remember who was who. I mean, I don't get the Nazis and the Jews mixed up, do I? Anyway, the baboon takeover was discovered by some journalists who arrived on the scene. They found one baboon floating face-down in the swimming pool, others grooming on the stairs, younger baboons playing on the couches, baboon droppings on the roulette tables.' He stopped. He wasn't sure why this anecdote had come to mind. Was he simply grabbing at any old baboon story he could think of? Or was there a point to this one? It didn't seem to go anywhere. Or maybe it had something to do with Nature's pull for things to return to their natural state. You build a luxury hotel in the bush but the bush claims it back. And along the way we are greeted with the bizarre image of our own primitive selves crapping on the craps table. He smiled at the pun, but was then reminded of his earlier, sober feeling that he had no business bringing Luc here. They were as out of place in this wild land as a luxury hotel in the Rwandan bush.

'That male baboon who confronted us,' he said 'he's not like us. He's more prudent when it comes to spending his aggression. He won't fight if he doesn't have to. So when we fell over, he could see we weren't a threat to him, and he left us alone. It's only if he thinks we're going to muscle in on his territory, or threaten his family, that he'll use up energy on attacking us. Most animals are like that.'

A grey rhebok came into view, its long, pointed ears on either side of a pair of parallel horns, and then moved off with a stiff-legged gait.

'See how he moves,' Russ said, 'almost like a rocking horse.' They caught a flash of the white underside of the antelope's tail and then it was gone. Verwoerd's shells must have scared those graceful creatures witless.

'Lions use their energy to attack,' said Luc.

'True. Carnivores attack out of necessity. They need to eat. Killing a kudu is no different to them than those baboons pulling berries off a tree. Humans are unusual animals. We attack out of hate or prejudice. Like those men in the bar.'

Russ picked up the duffle bag and lamps and, judging Luc's mood to be ready, moved off slowly in the direction of the cave. The boy walked after him. It was an act of simpatico that made him realise how superfluous so many of his instructions to Luc over the years had been.

After half an hour they had almost reached the spine of the peninsula and with the closeness of the cave came the sound in Russ's ears of the falling shells. Barak had written of Hendrik Verwoerd, stabbed to death by Tsafendas. The assassination had occurred on 6th September 1966, soon to become one of those dates drummed into South African children of the apartheid era. Russ had been in Standard 9 at the time. Now the date had a different meaning. Barak's reference to it was only pages from the end of the Mummy's Notebook. His story, along with his life, was coming to an end.

Verwoerd's assassination placed a date, more or less, for

the last time Russ saw his father. It was September 1966, almost three years after Barak had left for the Cape. Russ had turned 16 on 7th August 1966, one month before. The bicycle he was riding as he cycled past the soldier-tramp had been a gift from his mother for his sixteenth birthday. It was the second bicycle he had owned, bought second-hand from a neighbour. The frame had been spray-painted, the manufacturer's name hidden beneath blue paint. But it was a special bicycle, a racing bike, and the envy of his friends. And on that special bicycle he rode past his father without so much as a nod of the head.

Remembering where the notes had picked up, Russ was filled once more with regret for his own crime, and an urgent desire to get to the cave, because while Verwoerd had been silenced, the Nationalists' artillery programme had not. When they resumed their shelling, they were accurate enough not to worry about shooting into the sea. They could aim at the peninsula, at that patch of deep shadow that hid an overhang or perhaps even a cave.

Of course I am concerned that they will blow the dune middens to bits and with them a fossil record that runs seamlessly from primitive to modern man, and alongside him the beasts with which he shared this patch of earth: lion, rhino, leopard, antelope. They are destroying all that I hold beautiful.

But who would have thought they would begin shelling the peninsula itself?

Nombeko wants to prepare a meal but what is the point? The only meal our bodies desire is made of silence. We think we can hear the frightened yelps of the baboons. In truth there is little to hear but the barking of the guns, the ear-shattering impact of the shells, the trembling earth. Nombeko is frightened they will score a direct hit on the cave. I have told her the chances of this are a hundred to one but she does not understand statistics and I have to restrain her from rushing out into the open.

'What about your child!' she shouts, holding her belly.

'He will grow strong in his body and mind. He will be educated. He will become a lawyer and in fifty years time, the Prime Minister of South Africa!'

She smiles wanly. The baby kicks against her skirt. 'He wants to go out!' she screams.

'We will be safe here,' I say, doing my best to lighten her mood. 'Listen, if those buggers knew what is happening under the noses of their guns, they would aim them directly at us. Can you imagine what they would think of us? A white man living with a native woman searching for the remains of a native man and woman? Don't look at me like that! You've had too many missionaries showing you their naïve pictures of Adam and Eve. Pah! Adam and Eve were not some pale couple who lived a few thousand years ago. They are 120,000 years old and they are dark-skinned. Negroid! African! They looked like our child will look. Tanned, like the Bushmen. Those bloody gunners would drop a shell on us in an instant if they knew who we were looking for!' I have to shout this last sentence because the impact of a shell bursting not far off has temporarily deafened us. The ground shakes and earth rains down from the roof of the cave. Nombeko is looking at me with wide, frightened eyes, and so I add: 'Fortunately, they don't know who we're looking for.'

Russ stopped. 'It's been a long walk. Would you like to ride on my shoulders?' This time the boy accepted.

Carrying Luc would allow him to move faster. He could see his father and the pregnant woman crouching inside as the shells burst around the cave entrance. What if he could reach the cave in time? Lead them out before that fateful shell drops directly on the entrance and closes them in, before they become trapped in the airless dark, ghostly souls with fingers scratched and bloody from years of trying to get out into the sunlight, of trying to escape their cold tomb. But this was madness, this hurrying along under the burden of the duffle bag, the lamps, the increasing weight of the boy on his shoulders. They couldn't still be there. Russ was decades too late.

They reached the spine of the peninsula, walked along and then cut down towards the beach following Petrus and Bartholomew's route. He clambered carefully – Luc was still on his shoulders – across the rocks, cold spray from the waves wetting their exposed arms and faces, the turbulent sea with its head of foam, the swaying kelp beds sometimes inches from his shoes. The proximity of the cave energised him and he began to move over the rocks with some agility despite Luc and the equipment. Sweat dripping from his face, he stopped to get his bearings. A cormorant rode a thermal above their heads, gaining height as it moved out to sea. He looked up, spotted the rock avalanche that covered the cave mouth. It was time to cut up the side of the peninsula.

'Do you think you can walk this last bit?'

Luc slipped off his shoulders. Russ took out the water bottle and after they had both quenched their thirst, offered his hand to Luc.

35

THERE IS A STORY CONCERNING *an Indian fellow, Abdul Saloojee, who ran a restaurant in Krugersdorp. His wife made magnificent curries. Abdul had something of a mixed clientele and took great pride in greeting his customers in their native tongue. 'Môre!' he'd hail his Afrikaans patrons. 'Shalom!' he'd say when a Jew entered his establishment; and when they left Abdul Saloojee would shout after them, 'L'hitraot!' which means 'See you later!'*

But if you listened carefully you would hear him repeat what his own ears erroneously heard and what he took to be the way in which Jews parted from one another – not 'L'hitraot', but: 'let Hitler rot!'

Yes, yes, I know. I am rambling. I should be apologising to Nombeko. I should be saying: you were right and I was wrong. But how was I to know they would score a direct hit on the cave?

I have no idea how much time has passed. Ten Minutes? An hour? A day? I feel that I am back in the trenches, not with Isaac Rosenberg's decapitated head reciting poetry, but with Nombeko's hysterical crying, which some hours ago gave way to ululating in the manner of her people, as if someone has died.

Now her lamentations too have subsided and in their place, every few minutes, she lets out a soft whimper. There is a sharp, piercing sound in my ears – damage from the explosion – but I can hear her nonetheless. She has made a resting place for herself. By the light of the lamp I see how drenched she is.

I am sitting here writing. She says something I cannot make out. 'What is it?' I feel compelled to ask her.

She thinks this is some form of divine irony. That even when we

272

Europeans wish to do good, nay, even when we love, we kill. I told her long ago about Piltdown Man. I told her she is the third woman I have taken for a wife and that the other two also bore me children. I told her I was not a man who was made for enduring love. I told her I was a man who lost his heart in a great conflict in Europe, who has been searching for it ever since. I told her, quoting the great Professor Freud, that my childhood too had given me shell-shock. That one shell-shock had compounded the other. That I trusted only in the inherent aggression of the human race and therefore in the inherent untrustworthiness of the human race – and that I was trying to find the source of this aggression and untrustworthiness. That if only I could find it, perhaps I might be able to fix the rupture within me. She does not know why she loved an untrustworthy old white man. It is hard to write with her staring at me, her big dark hands rubbing her belly. 'What about this child?' she wails. 'What will happen? You are not a man. A man must think of something to do. A man must think of moving these rocks.'

But I tried. Believe me. I tore at those rocks. I hacked with my hammer and chisels. My hands are bleeding. I dislocated the index finger of my left hand and even though I have pulled the bone back into the socket, it is swollen and useless. The smaller rocks are easy to move but they are merely the fill around the boulders that hem us in. It is a pity we have no dynamite. Where is Robert Broom when I need him?

I could see my efforts would come to naught before I had even begun to apply them, but I continued for hours, like a fossil trying to tear its way out of the rock. I did it for her and the child. For myself, I have no need. I have seen God staring up at me from a grave of ancient bone. But I must not think of that now. Plenty of time for that. We will be here until released by wind and water. We will lie on the floor of our dwelling-place, amongst my tools and Nombeko's possessions. I hope I have the presence of mind, at the moment before the end finally comes, to adopt the posture of the ancient dead. It is a matter of exquisite irony, given the fact that Homo sapiens *arose here on the West Coast, that we should end our lives in the very place our species began its existence. We have come home.*

The guns, at least, have fallen silent for today. It must be after 4:30p.m.

The slope was grower steeper, the space between the boulders opening up to form small chasms. He hadn't remembered the last section being this arduous, but then he wasn't as encumbered on his previous visit. He kept a grip on Luc's hand. He had been aiming for the spot he imagined the cave opening to be, perhaps twenty metres above them.

Russ stopped to allow Luc to catch his breath. Some seagulls took to the air, squawking. He felt like a meerkat on sentry duty, aware of his height. If those SADF gunners who pounded the peninsula were here now, they would spot him in a second.

Father and son clambered upwards, Russ now training his eyes on the ground so that he came across the opening sooner than he had anticipated. 'This is it.' He let the strap of the duffle bag slip off his shoulder, fumbled around for the matches and lit the gas lamps. 'I'll go in first, then you follow. It'll be light inside, and cool.' He passed through the narrow opening, reached up to where he had left the two lamps and placed them at his feet. 'Okay, Luc, you can come inside now.'

From where he stood inside the cave, he could see only a threatening sky. It was going to rain. Luc did not appear. Russ gave him a minute, then the boy's one leg came into view – and the other. Russ peered around him, the light of the gas lamps illuminating the space so that he could see it properly for the first time. The cave was about fifteen to eighteen metres in length and ten at its widest. Barak's slackened, tangled twine criss-crossed the floor. In several places the footprints in the dust trampled the twine, as if the shoes that made those indentations were still there. Shadows, here jagged, there ill-defined, were thrown up by the irregular surfaces of the walls, floor and ceiling. The place smelled dank. Russ positioned the one lamp on a natural rock table and with the other in his outstretched hand, went over to the fossil that jutted its way from the cave wall, above the sagging spider web of the second twine grid. He could see now what he could only feel before, in the near dark, when Petrus and Bartholomew had brought them here.

'Luc, come and have a look,' he said. 'This is what my father has been telling us about. Can you see the curve of bone? The socket here where a tooth would have been? It's filled in, but you can see the different colour. I'm pretty sure it's the front part of a lower jaw.'

He ran his eyes and hands over the surrounding rock. It was ridged and striated by tool marks, the bite of steel on rock. He felt certain there were at least four or five distinct pieces of fossilised bone, but only the jaw had been excavated enough for him to begin to appreciate its shape. Even an experienced palaeontologist would have difficulty identifying the other pieces until they were better exposed, and Russ's learning, thorough as it had been, had terminated when he was thirteen years old.

'Is it a man's jaw?' asked Luc.

Russ felt his stomach lurch. 'I hope so, but we won't know until we get more of it out. Do you think you can wait here while I fetch the rest of the stuff?'

Luc nodded.

A light rain had begun to fall, the duffle bag beginning to coat up with small droplets. He was trying to ignore an urge to defecate – he didn't have time for that – but he barely managed to step away from the cave entrance and yank his pants down when the watery excrement passed from him. He squatted in the rain, remembering the last time he had relieved himself under an open sky. That time he'd pissed on the Medusa's Head and ended up chewing on it. He felt queasy. Was this really the greatest discovery ever made? Surely the fossil pieces weren't freed enough for even Barak to make that claim? Maybe the old man had gone mad after all.

Barak had been so desperate to right the wrongs of his world, to triumph over a system that despised him for his otherness but didn't flinch when it came to sending him to war on its behalf. But he was wounded even before the Great War got hold of him. In the name of truth the brilliant young Jewish employee of the British Museum had perpetrated a falsehood that put nothing right, only left him and those he was to touch with a problem of authenticity. Perhaps this is why Russ had been drawn to Rebecca, who seemed so earnestly to be struggling to be authentic. Even her vagina sculptures were a desperate grasp at it. These, he now thought with great clarity, confused authenticity with transparency. It wasn't the same thing. But at least she had been giving it a shot – and look at the great art she was capable of now.

Despite the tinnitus, we hear tapping sounds, they seem to come from the rocks that block the entrance. First a loud tap, then a little one, and another, then silence, and the whole pattern is repeated again. I thought perhaps it was a rescue party at work. It took me a little while to solve the puzzle, but then it seemed so obvious. After all, it was hardly the first time we had heard these tapping sounds, albeit the first time from an enclosed echo chamber. It is the sound of the gulls flying above with molluscs in their beaks, and dropping them onto the rocks above our heads.

'Do you know what Nombeko means?' she asks.

'Of course. It means "respect".'

'Then why,' she grunts, waiting for the pain to pass, 'do you not respect me?'

Russ grabbed wildly about him, coming away with tufts of slippery grass, wiping at himself, rising unsteadily to his feet, pulling his trousers up even as he hobbled over the rocks at the entrance to the cave. It had become *his* cave too, the cave he shared with Barak and Nombeko. He wriggled through, dragging the duffle bag after him. He pulled open the cord and spilled out the bag's contents into an untidy heap. Going back to the wall, he set up the battery-powered lamps so that the wall now blazed with light. And then it struck him. In the Good Croxley passage Beck had translated, hadn't she said the fossils were embedded in the cave floor? *The cave floor opened up, the two specimens at first emerging in the form of the man's jaw and the woman's clavicle.* He was looking at a jaw, but surely none of the other pieces were visible enough to identify them as a clavicle. And these were in the *wall*, not the floor. Had Beck mistranslated the French? What was wall and floor in French? He had no idea.

'Luc, what is the French word for "wall"?'

'Mur.'

'And "floor"?'

The child thought for a moment. 'Plancher.'

Mur. Plancher. Not close enough to confuse but there'd be other forms of the word. 'Any other words for wall and floor in French?'

'Yes.' Luc pondered the floor, then the wall. 'I don't know the other words.'

Russ grabbed the most powerful of the torches and began to scan the ground, holding the beam low to enhance the shadows. Barak had worked the surface for months on end, probably taking layer upon layer off it, lowering the twine grid as he dug deeper into the earth. There were no bones sticking out of the floor. Russ was losing precious time. Beck must have got it wrong. He went back to the bulge of fossil in the wall, closed his eyes, trying to separate the image of the furious Nombeko from the face that lived on the fossilised jaw all those eons ago. How far back into the rock did the jaw line go? What did the teeth look like? Whatever it was, it was definitely mammalian. He opened his eyes and began to chip away with the rock hammer at the sandstone, every so often using the whisk broom to brush away the loose sediment. He blew into the little nooks that he had chipped out, wiped at his forehead, at his eyes that became gritty with dust, tried to blow his clogged nose, to free it so that he wouldn't have to breathe through his mouth. He was perspiring hard. He didn't trust the accuracy of his blows, and aimed the hammer's sharp edge at the surrounding rock, giving the fossilised jaw itself a safe berth. Out in the light he'd be able to free the remaining conglomerate and examine the specimen.

Nombeko has an ominous expression in her eyes, her hands hold her bulging tummy. She coughs, but her hands remain on her belly. She wants to tell me something. But what can she say that will make any difference? That she hasn't already said? I would have thought her screams had played themselves out.

There is still dust in the air from the falling of the boulders. I am burning the lamp even though it eats up our little supply of oxygen. It seems to me that writing is more important than breathing.

I thought at first that Nombeko had defecated but the smell has grown too strong for that. It is most pungent at the section of roof that has collapsed, as if it is leaking through the rock from the outside. I have wet a shirt and instructed Nombeko to breathe through it. I wish we had gas masks. The lamp flickers. It, too, is being starved of oxygen. Soon we will be in darkness.

Nombeko cries out. It is the contractions. Her dark face sweats. I cannot look into her eyes. I sit here writing, my palm sticking to the page. When she calls out again I look up. It is because of the note in her voice. I recognise it, although I have not heard it for half a century. The boys lying wounded in the trenches would reach the same note.

'Is there something I can do?' I ask. She curses me in her own language.

It is rather queer. One never thinks about one's breathing until one is deprived of it. This new smell is stinging in the air, it whips at our lungs and eyes and noses. It is the overpowering smell of mustard. I thought it a hallucination of the olfactory senses. It is a joke, for what else would I hallucinate? But now I am sure of it, since I see Nombeko's reaction: her gagging, her bloodshot eyes, the scratching at her burning skin. This is no hallucination. It is also not the effects of oxygen starvation. Something else is leaking into the cave. It has a foul stench that is overpowering, it has us in spasms. It has us. I think it is sulphur. Brimstone. What else would it be? My death has been prepared with the poisonous ingredients of my life. Perhaps Nombeko is right and the place I have identified as Eden is really Hell itself.

He had made it to the cave, but he was losing them. He could see them inside, scratching at their skin, gasping for air and instead taking in the slow poison of the gas as it begins to mummify them alive. Barak is hunched over the Mummy's Notebook, writing frantically, as if the transfer of ink to paper will stave off death, as if this flow of ink is something other than the leaking of his life's blood. Nombeko's hands race between skin and throat and belly and eyes, unsure as to which is the greater source of pain.

The careful, steady blows of his father's hammer in his hands were as useful a rescue attempt as the dropping of molluscs onto the rocks above the cave. *Tap-tap... tap-tap... tap-tap...* Russ had been so afraid of loss that he had lost exactly what he was so afraid of losing. He had backed away from life, from Rebecca's passion, from Luc's strange curiosity, and from Savannah, so much her mother's daughter, grasping Africa with an unafraid hand. He flinched at the unbidden innuendo and its unbidden image: Savannah's pale fingers furled around Temba's brown cock. My god, was there no place his mind would not go?

I gasp as I write and yet my hand is steady. The light grows faint, dull shadows dance weakly against the walls. I have never concerned myself *much with my body. I was blessed with physical strength. Now look at me. I have wasted away. The skin of my stomach lies in empty folds. It is no wonder my own son never recognised me. Or, should I say, not at first. There was something more than mere curiosity in the slowing of his bicycle, in the backwards glance. I raised my shameful hand to him. I could not make him take it. My hand was empty. Perhaps it had always been empty. I had thought it so replete with my passion for this digging life. But that day I had not yet found them, my Adam and Eve, and my hand was empty, and I could see it had always been empty. I had failed those who called themselves my family, given them nothing. But then, of course, to give nothing to your family is to give them much sorrow. And I was back in Krugersdorp, standing in the street. For what? I had arrived as I had left, empty-handed.* Arriver comme un cheveu sur la soupe.*

What is this life I have chosen? My skin, my skin. We lay down dead cells to protect ourselves from damage: too many, you die of a thick skin. Death by scleroderma. Rocks block our air supply and keep the wind from blowing away the gas. Look at my fingers. Can't tell the blood from the dirt. What was I doing, scratching at the boulders like that? Better to have scratched at the thick layers of my skin.

'Dad.' Luc's voice came from behind him. Russ turned. The boy was sitting next to the lamp on the rock table, the light illuminating one side of his face and body, so that he looked like half a child.

'Yes?'

'I'm hungry.'

'No problem.' Russ looked around for the sandwiches he'd had the hotel make for them but the old hamper – 'only R120 for the basket, Oom' – in which the waxen-faced ballerina had placed the food and tea flask, was not with them. He had stupidly left it in the car.

'Can you wait a little while? Come and look here, I've almost got enough of it out to see what it is.'

Luc came to stand beside him. Russ began to hammer away more recklessly until he was again snapped away from the rock face, this time by a low moan coming from Luc, who was now crouching back on the rock table.

'Becca, Becca, Becca.'

'No, Luc, please, don't. Don't. I'll get you some food. Just give me a few more minutes.'

Her labour has moved into the next phase. Can't pretend I don't know what to do. Assisted at the birth of chimpanzees whose mothers were reared in captivity. She's taken off her clothes. Drenched.

She squats. Her swollen genitals pulse with the life pressing at them. The baby's head has long been engaged in her pelvis.

It will not emerge. The problem is easy to diagnose: it is a failure of evolution. To survive on the savannah, we had to move more efficiently. The loping, swinging walk of the Australopithecines was too enervating. We had to change our centre of gravity, bring our knees beneath our torsos. The cost of this change in shape was to be carried by the female of the species. We became more cylindrical, which meant a narrower pelvis and that, as Nombeko is finding out, results in birth difficulties. There is no use in explaining this to Nombeko. We are trapped here. What meaning has it whether the child is inside her or out?

From somewhere far away I hear her screaming at me, like the thunder of distant guns.

There's no point in me helping her. Evolution has failed her.

Russ could hear Nombeko whimpering. He wiped his forehead for the umpteenth time, pushing the sweat away from his eyes. 'Fuck!' he shouted hoarsely, hacking away at the rock.

'Becca! Becca!' came the high-pitched wailing, not of the woman with the child stuck inside her, but of the scared, hungry boy on the rock table.

Russ brought the lamp up to the fossil. *'Fuck! Fuck! Fuck!'* He could finally see what it was. Or rather, what it wasn't. The jaw didn't belong to Adam, or Eve, or anyone even closely related. It wasn't even a primate. It was – Russ was sure of it – the jaw of a wild pig.

He had been looking in the wrong place. Beck was right. It was the floor. Barak had known this fossil in the wall was a pig, which is why he hadn't bothered to excavate it further. Russ began to move about the cave, one skewed grid block at a time, like a pawn moving illegally across a chess board. He scratched at the dirt, sweeping with the whisk broom, poking at the ground with a chisel, the shadows cast by his own body shimmering madly against the cave walls. He found a pile of stones and soil and rock dumped in a corner. Luc was quiet now, watchful. He had found a muesli bar in the pocket of his jacket and was eating it slowly. An open bottle of water was sitting next to him, the lid alongside it.

'I'm just looking...' Russ said, but his sentence trailed off. 'Good, you found something to eat.' He crawled over and took a sip of Luc's water, then went back to his frenzied search.

In one place, embedded in the centre of a square of Barak's slackened twine, Russ identified, with some certainty, the cranium of a zebra, or possibly zebra ancestor, a primitive horse. Was Nombeko squatting here? If the baby had been able to leave the birth canal, would it have been birthed on top of this horse's head? And in the presence of Nombeko's plight, Barak resorted to theory, Science rescuing him in death, as she had in life. It had always been his one true love. Not a woman or a child. Barak's lover was enquiry, the use of his own mind. Digging in the earth kept him from searching inside his painful self, had kept him from a sadness he perhaps once showed, dancing with Russ in his arms, his tears wetting his boy's cheeks. He was enraptured by Science and the more she spurned him, the more he wanted her, until he had elevated his enquiry to what some might say is a search for God in the Garden of Eden, but that he disguised as a search for the first ancestors of modern man. But by August 1966, Science had finally run out on him. Abandoned at last by his lover, he had attempted a return to his family. Perhaps if he had come back in triumph, that day might have turned out differently. But Barak had come back a failure, his theory unproven, his pride shattered, his life's work come to naught. Instead of Adam and Eve, Russ now thought, he'd found a pig and a zebra.

Russ slumped down and put his face in his hands. He felt a wispy figure sit down next to him, but he was too frightened to look. So he sat frozen for ages, until he could no longer feel his body. Like the man who wakes to find a snake sharing his sleeping bag, or the soldier who hears the click of an anti-personnel mine as his foot goes down and knows if he raises it, he is dead, Russ could do nothing. The spirit only waited for him to look and, once he did, it would do its dirty work. Dread. There will be retribution, if only he looked.

In amongst the tools at his feet lay the Mummy's Notebook, Barak's storybook. The old man with his hand on his boy's shoulder, looking out over the Krugersdorp veld from the stoep of the house with the limed walls that contained the remains of our human ancestors – telling, at the end of the day, stories, only stories. 'These are only fictions,' Rebecca had once said of her work. 'Fiction, from the Latin *fingere*: to fashion in clay. We make them real because we need reality. But it's really only magic, an illusion.' Russ had been the Keeper of the Chocolate Cupboard, of these delicious, wounding fictions belonging to his father.

He needed some magic now, good magic, to get away from this atmosphere, this place, this spirit waiting to pounce. He understood it all. His father had fought a personal war in the trenches of Piltdown, then a terrible war of imperialism in the trenches of France – and whatever capacity for love he might have had prior to these flagrant conflicts had been left forever perverted. The 16-year-old Russ's misapprehension of his returned father as a soldier-tramp was a kind of truth. Barak's Hindenburg Line had been overrun. He was broken. The man of arrogance had given way to the man of shame. He *was* Piltdown Man, a being held up as the first noble Englishman, now exposed to himself as nothing more than a cobbled-together fake. That is why he looked so diminished. And that's why, when Russ ignored him, the old man didn't force the issue. He left quietly with his shame in tow, to return to the cave for one last desperate look.

N. lies back, exhausted, breathing laboured, fitful. Baby's stuck. My dear N., evolution tried to help by giving women wider hips & by having the baby's brain premature at birth. But then the human brain kept getting bigger. We got too brainy.

Brimstone fills the cave. The artillery shells have delivered it to us and my scrabbling at the rocks opened up a channel for the gas. Perhaps it will preserve our bodies. Have torn a strip off my shirt, twirled it around to make my jaw fast. I do not want to be found with my mouth hanging open.

What good is this writing? Where is the oilskin in which to wrap these words?

Have I adopted the posture of the Dying Slave? At least my death will be ideal.

Cannot see words on page. Is there ink?

Beck had been right. The rag tying his mouth closed was Barak's vanity. In his struggle with an inner truth that left him humbled and despairing, vanity had won out. It left a picture of Nombeko dying in terror alongside Barak in an ideal contemplation of the universe. It was the way in which he had lived, with all those around him taking up the emotional slack. He'd had to leave Krugersdorp because the life left to him there was ordinary, filled with the everyday matter of getting older with a drunkard wife, a son who was growing up and would leave home – and a life-ban on excavating Sterkfontein. He had to find a new site for his struggle for glory and his theory about Eden existing in the Cape was it. He would return Adam and Eve to God and be covered in the greatest glory ever.

For the first time, Russ felt sorry for his father. Barak was too hurt for any other kind of love. And now Russ was too cold, too numb, too tired to care. He turned his head from the cover of his hands, turned to look at the ghost of his father, this sad shaper of fossils and stories. He cried out in relief. There was no ghostly creature, only Luc sitting next to him, waiting, their thighs a hammer's length apart.

'Why didn't the fossil want to go to the symphony?' Luc said.

'What?'

When Luc repeated the riddle, adding that he had made it up, Russ smiled tiredly and this time responded. 'I don't know. Why didn't the fossil want to go to the symphony?'

'Because,' Luc said, 'he preferred rock music.'

Russ felt dulled. He forced a smile to please the boy. But then suddenly, as if he was in a lift that was stuck in his head and then abruptly fell to gut level, he got it – and a laugh burst from him, a genuine guffaw. Luc laughed too, at first his usual high-pitched squeal, a tittering siren, then, slowly, as their laughter mingled and bounced off the cave walls creating its own little rock symphony, the sounds from the boy's mouth dropped an octave – and another, rounded out, the tone becoming more fleshy, the resonance full, then joining Russ's, then both their voices notching up into a hysterical pitch until father and son were shrieking uncontrollably, gales of joy pealing from their throats, tears squeezed from eyelids creased shut by their smiles, their bellies sore from the effort. Russ farted and that made the two of them laugh even harder.

And when finally they grew quiet, Luc said, 'I'm still hungry.'

36

THEY EMERGED FROM the cave. The rain had stopped, leaving the ground spongy and pungent. A strong off-shore wind blew moist air into their faces. They had arrived at the cave late morning. Russ looked at his watch. It was now close to five o'clock. He had been chipping away at a useless fucking pig for over five hours, while Luc sat patiently waiting.

Trevor Shaw's choice to pursue his East Coast excavation rather than rush out here was the correct one. Shaw, the student of palaeo-anthropology, had followed the same course in his attachment to Dr Barak Codron as Russ the son: idealisation followed by a profound disappointment. Only Russ had contrived to keep some faith alive in order to finish his boyhood search for his missing father. Now that was done.

He looked up at the sky, the thinning clouds turned blond by the sloping sun, and wondered whether there was enough daylight in which to make it back to the car. He wasn't keen to risk a trek back in the dark, even with the torches and what little moonlight might shine through the cloud cover.

They could spend the night. Only he had forgotten the sleeping bags in the car. And since he had also forgotten the picnic hamper, they would go hungry, unless he could rustle up some food from the environment. Rustle up. An eponymous pun – strange he'd never thought of it before. There were plenty of berries, but he didn't have a clue which might be edible. If they gave Luc diarrhoea, he would follow the example of the baboons, who knew that chewing on deposits of kaolin clay would cure an upset tummy. He could try to hunt a rhebok or zebra. Could he leave Luc in the cave? He thought of his panic in the car when he'd set off from home having forgotten Luc. The danger of intruders in the city. What of the dangers of this other wild place? Which place had the wilder, more ruthless animals? But his chief worry then had been Luc's internal world – and Luc still had Luc to contend with. If he went hunting for food, he'd have to take him along. And why not? Was this not what fathers had been doing with their sons for millions of years?

A small darting shape caught his eye. He turned to Luc. 'Fancy dassie for dinner?'

Barak had passed on the hunting techniques he had learned from tribespeople – Masai, Sotho, Khoisan – who had given him hospitality over the years. When Russ was a boy, he and Barak would hurl missiles at raptors in the hope of startling the birds into dropping whatever it was they'd caught in their talons – mice, small birds, hares. But it was late in the day and the raptors mightn't be on the hunt. He knew how to catch a dassie, though, without relying on an eagle or falcon to do the job: fashion a spear out of a tree branch and wait on top of one of their dens. As soon as the timid little rock rabbit emerged, plunge the spear down into the fur. But the heat had gone from the day and by now the animals would be huddling underground for warmth, unlikely to re-emerge.

Luc was looking at the spot where the dassie had disappeared. 'I don't eat meat,' he said.

'What?'

'Meat comes from animals. I don't eat animals. Therefore I don't eat meat.'

'But... you ate the hamburger at the bar.'

'No, I didn't. The hamburger did not come because one man hit another man in the face.'

'Oh.' Bloody hell, why hadn't he remembered something as simple as Luc not eating meat? Of course he didn't eat meat. He was barely two when he picked up a chicken leg, examined it carefully and announced, 'Chicken Licken. The sky fell on his head.' He hadn't eaten chicken since. And if he wasn't going to eat Chicken Licken, he'd be bloody unlikely to tackle Peter Rabbit.

'The picnic hamper is in the car. But we're running out of light. We're going to have to hurry. We don't want to get lost in the dark. Do you think you can walk quickly?'

'Yes,' said Luc. 'I'm hungry. The food is in the car. I'll walk quickly.'

Russ smiled. 'Makes sense. Come to think of it, I'm hungry too.' He hoisted the duffle bag over his shoulder.

As they were walking off, Luc tugged Russ's shirt. 'Your father's tools are still in the cave.' He was right. Russ had put the lamps and torches and the Mummy's Notebook in the bag, but left the tools behind.

'That's okay, Luc. I think we're done with fossil hunting.'

Scrambling down the side of the peninsula they could see the kelp gulls circling above the beach, coming in to land on the sand where they settled in a shadowy group. A light fog was drifting in off the sea and hung over the beach. Russ looked up, hoping they would climb out of it, that the wind wouldn't have pushed it off the beach and over the top. The Bruegel dream came back to him, chilling him. Walking blindly over cliffs, the pig's head replacing his own.

But he was not following three blind men over the cliffs. He was now leading Luc, his son, and the boy required protection. He had told Luc that he too was hungry, but in truth he wasn't hungry at all. He was beyond hunger, beyond tiredness. There was only one rest he required, one appetite to satiate and he had had his fill in the cave, laughing unabashedly with Luc for the first time. There would be no blind walking over the edge. He would find the car.

He had also told Luc that they would have no more use for his father's tools, that they were done with fossil hunting. On this subject, he'd meant every word. Unlike Barak, he hadn't come back to find Adam and Eve. He had come to find a father. And in that one sweet moment of laughter with Luc, that rolling, rollicking, beautiful moment, he'd found the father he'd been missing all these years.

Rising out of the mist, the wind at their backs, they made the plateau of the peninsula. The baboon troop was there, as if waiting for them. An infant clung to its mother's chest, its pink, translucent, pixie ears catching the late afternoon sun. Russ had begun to smell like an animal now, like one of them. He lifted Luc onto his shoulders and walked assuredly amongst them. The big male glanced up from his foraging, gazed around, then began to move off, parallel to Russ, the rest of the troop following. This time, though, it seemed to Russ that the leader and he knew each other, had satisfied their parlaying requirements. He imagined the troop forming some sort of guard of honour as baboon and human, for a short while, walked in the same direction. He looked up into the fading sky.

They made the car in the lingering light after sunset.

Luc, who had walked the last half hour under his own steam, ran towards the hole in the fence and slithered through, Russ coming after him. Russ deactivated the car's security alarm, which squealed a welcoming hello. He retrieved the picnic hamper and handed a sandwich to Luc, who had settled in the back seat. Russ got in beside him and poured two cups from a flask of rooibos the ballerina had prepared for them. He handed one to Luc, watching with pleasure as the boy gulped the lukewarm tea. He caught sight of himself in the rear-view mirror, laughing as he did so. He looked a little like the soldier-tramp, his eyes rheumy, his face cut, his bald head sweaty and grey with dirt. Luc finished his sandwich.

'Should I slice an apple for you?'

Luc nodded, draining his tea. Russ leaned over the front seats and opened the glove compartment, thinking he might find a Swiss army knife he usually kept there. His cell phone pointed its face at him with an accusing stare. He took it out and turned it on. The display told him that there were 12 missed messages. He examined the reception indicator. One bar. He speed-dialled Beck's number.

'Wait,' he said, interrupting her angry *where the hell are you?* 'I'm putting the phone on loudspeaker… Luc has got a joke for you. He made this one up.'

'Becca!' Luc said. 'We've been hunting for fossils!' He told her the joke about the fossil preferring rock music. Russ was chuckling, Luc too, then Rebecca joined in, the warmth of her laughter and relief coming through the phone's loudspeaker, setting Luc and Russ off again.

'So,' said Beck, 'did you find any fossils?'

'No,' said Russ, 'not any hominids anyway. A pig jaw and a zebra ancestor, I think. No Adam. No Eve. I checked all over. I think my father became delusional towards the end.'

'Where was the entrance to the inner chamber?'

Russ was silent. It was Luc who asked the question, 'What inner chamber?'

'Where the fossils are. The inner chamber. Must be another cave off the main one.'

'You didn't say anything about an inner chamber,' said Russ.

'Yes, I did. Your father's notes say he had only been

excavating in there for a week before he found them. Hadn't even known of the inner chamber's existence until he saw a centipede crawl out of a hole. Barak says the centipede was sent from God to show him the way. Didn't I read that part to you yesterday? Shit, maybe that's the bit I hadn't translated yet. I did some last night.'

'It was a difficult conversation. The phone was cutting out, too.' Russ thought that perhaps she too had not heard something *he* had said – about the damaged mummy head. 'I'm sorry about your sculpture. I – I don't know if you heard what I was trying to tell you about Barak's head. An accident. Bumped into it by mistake. Best piece you've ever done. I'm so sorry, Beck. I'm so sorry about everything.'

'Ah, Russ, I heard what you said. Don't be an idiot. Do you really think I'd leave without making a cast? Couldn't you see that from the state of the clay? The cast is in the studio, so unless you've set fire to the steel cabinet, it'll be safe enough.'

'No, crikey, I haven't set fire to anything!' he said. 'But then why did you want Sav to keep the clay moist?'

'Oh, I don't know.' She fell silent. She usually disposed of the original clay sculpture, as if it was afterbirth. 'Maybe I wasn't ready to say goodbye to it. Or maybe I left it there for you to see. I did fix it up after the cast came off. I don't know why. I guess I didn't know how to tell you what I'd done. Better to leave you to see it for yourself.'

He peered out of the car window, towards where he imagined the cave would be. It was now pitch black outside. The passage Beck had read him over the phone from Johannesburg now had meaning once more. What had Barak written? *You beauties! You beauties! Here was God painting for me.*

Russ felt the tug of excitement. An inner chamber. Well, no wonder he hadn't found anything. They could be there, after all. Adam and Eve.

As if reading his thoughts, Beck said, 'What do you want

to do? Are you going to go back?'

They could spend the night in the car. The sleeping bags would keep them warm, they had enough food. They could simply go to sleep, wake up in the morning, and walk back. The duffle bag would weigh less and he was no longer frightened of the baboons. They could find the inner chamber, now that they knew to look for it. They too could stand over the scene of that ancient accident.

But the image of Barak's ecstasy as he stood over the fossil family quickly gave way to one of the old man standing over the crushed remains of his own family, his wife and son, and his first family in London, and his third family in the cave, dying as it birthed itself. Barak had tried to turn his incapacity for reliable love – and his subsequent abandonment and destruction of his families – into a virtue; and in his last few weeks he had come, finally, to understand how much sorrow he had caused them all. He had only one defence against the shame this caused him. That was to turn back to his cave.

Perhaps he knew, with the memory of Russ cycling away from him, that he had spent his life fleeing the terror of love and that he had done this by searching for his ideal self, that the rock faces he gazed into were mirrors in which he wished to see something uniquely beautiful, something so special that it would obliterate all the pain and longing in his world. The remains of Adam and Eve would be truly beautiful.

Then he had found them. Russ knew that now. They were there, in the inner chamber, waiting to be marvelled at.

Russ gazed at Luc, sitting on the back seat beside him. He had told Luc they were done with fossil hunting. If he took the boy back to that cold place, what would it mean? Barak would have done it. If Russ did it, he would be his father's son, following in the old man's single-minded footsteps. He had had enough of that. He had found his own beauty in the cave, in the marvel of his and Luc's shared laughter. The fossils could wait.

'It doesn't matter,' he said, finally, to the patiently waiting Rebecca. 'Trevor Shaw can come back when he gets the permit. I think I found what I was looking for.'

He knew he hadn't quite found Luc. He was feeling too sad, too regretful about his own flight from love. There was no fooling himself into believing that everything would now be all right. What he had found, though, was the grave of his own lost boyhood – and that was a start. Trevor would get his permit and excavate properly, perhaps in a month or two when spring would throw a carpet of flowers across Namaqualand to the north, its floral fringes reaching down to the West Coast. But for now he and Luc would go home in the dark with their new herd of memories. The Merc's headlights would pick out the road ahead, the dunes to their right and somewhere out there in the darkness the oyster graveyards in the lagoon, with the cormorants and gannets huddling on beaches where centuries ago fleeing Phoenicians had landed and a hundred thousand years before that human beings began scavenging and hunting food from the sea.

Tomorrow he would call Leila Naidoo and tell her she could have his father's body. He might even call Inspector Toka and tell him he was right, that Russ hadn't known his father, but that he had now come to know him better.

He thought of Isaac Rosenberg looking out over False Bay, toward Hangklip, at the cobalt tumble of the Hottentots Holland mountains, and of Isaac a short time later on a muddy French field, turning back to the frontline while Barak trudged to the rear with the rest of his battalion. That's what Barak's cave had been: Russ's frontline.

Perhaps he and Beck and the children could now take a

trip out to Muizenberg beach, wrap themselves in blankets and sit on the deck chairs they would bring with them. Savannah could invite Temba. Tante Julia might want to join them. They would go by train and after their arrival sit in the weak winter's sun, sipping hot chocolate and gazing across the bay at the poet's piled-up mountains of Africa. And later, when the wind picked up, making it too uncomfortable to stay on the beach, they would take a slow walk to the station. They would climb on board the next train for Cape Town, struggling with the deck chairs, take their seats and, in silence, watch as the stations passed by: Retreat, Diep River, Wynberg, Observatory, Woodstock. Benches and concrete shelters and station names on poles. Women with recyclable shopping bags. Pensioners. Schoolchildren climbing aboard, their hands slung casually over the straps of their rucksacks. Russ would look past the young mixed-race couple sitting opposite him on the torn blue vinyl of the train's seat – his daughter and their neighbour – towards the jostling bodies of the school-children as they clamber over one another for seats, their boisterous chatter coming down the aisle like ice tinkling in the golden-brown of a whiskey glass.

The End

Author's Note

The Codron family, and the friends, relatives, scientists and police officers with whom they are directly involved, are all fictitious characters. However, several of the fossil finds, events and figures in this novel are taken from history. Raymond Dart, Robert Broom, Eugène Dubois, Sir Arthur Keith, Sir Arthur Smith Woodward, and Sir Grafton Elliot Smith, amongst others mentioned in the novel, were all real people central to the early exploration of human origins. Professor Clement Arthur Oldfield, on the other hand, is a fictitious character. The Piltdown forgery did occur and, as described in the text, had a devastating effect on the field of palaeo-anthropology in general, and the acceptance of Dart's Taung Child in particular. A finger has variously been pointed at those most closely associated with the 'finds' – Charles Dawson, Sir Arthur Smith Woodward, Sir Arthur Keith, and Sir Arthur Conan Doyle amongst them – generating a field of study in itself. In the 1970s a trunk came to light, bearing the initials of Martin A.C. Hinton, a zoologist at the British Museum (Natural History). It contained assorted carved and stained bones, identical in colour to the Piltdown pieces, and together with Hinton's known fondness for hoaxes and antipathy towards Smith Woodward, suggests that he may have been the forgery's mastermind.

The Cape's West Coast is indeed a fossil hunter's paradise and, as posited by Dr Lee R. Berger in his book, *In the*

Footsteps of Eve (National Geographic, 2000), may well be the Garden of Eden referred to in the novel. Defence Force weapons testing sites have been located at De Hoop and Rooi Els in the Western Cape. However, the descriptions of the artillery testing range and the local area in which it is located, including the village, the peninsula and Barak's cave, represent amalgams of West Coast geography and history.

The State mortuary in Salt River exists and, while my description does not nearly cover the true horror of the place, the physical setting is partly imagined.

The poet Isaac Rosenberg did become one of the 'older dead' in the manner described here. Quotes from his letters and poems are from Joseph Cohen's *Journey to the Trenches: The Life of Isaac Rosenberg 1890-1918* (Robson Books, 1975).

Sigmund Freud wrote about the anti-Semitic incident involving his father in *The Interpretation of Dreams* (Penguin Books, 1980).

Many other books have been invaluable in my research, chief amongst them being Frank Spencer's *Piltdown: A Scientific Forgery* (Oxford University Press, 1990), Richard Leakey and Roger Lewin's *Origins Reconsidered* (Abacus, 1992), Donald Johanson and James Shreeve's *Lucy's Child* (Penguin, 1989), and Alan Walker and Pat Shipman's *The Wisdom of the Bones* (Knopf, 1996).

Acknowledgements

The Fossil Artist first came to life in the writers' workshop run by the wonderful, late Lionel Abrahams; I am deeply grateful to him and to the members of his group. Stu Woolman brought to bear his acute literary mind on at least two different drafts of the book: thank you, my friend, for your insights and your support. Ivan Vladislavić read an early draft and David Medalie a later one; both are writers whose work I greatly admire and whose astute comments helped shape the narrative of *The Fossil Artist.*

Michelle Aarons's close reading and open-hearted backing has once again played a big part in keeping me on track. For their fervent encouragement after reading various drafts, I wish to thank: Helen Bliden, Peta Friedman, Jeremy Friedman, Jacqueline Nel, Kim Segel, Deb Gould, Alan Colam, Keith Kearney, and Alison Churchill. Incisive feedback from Jonathan Edelstein, Heather Jersky, Michelle Jersky and Lesley Weiner (whose uncle, Joseph Weiner, coincidentally appears in *The Fossil Artist*) helped inform elements of character and structure. I would also like to acknowledge the interest and support of Martin Bliden, and Beryl and Lew Segel.

Joanne Fedler was there when the first words of *Fossil* hit the page – in Lionel's writers' group in Johannesburg – and at the end, in Sydney, where the paths of our two families have converged. As writer, collaborator and good friend, Jo – along with Myron Zlotnick – has championed the cause

Graeme Friedman

of this book. The faith you kept made the final part of the journey possible.

My heartfelt appreciation to Maggie Davey and Bridget Impey for believing in *Fossil* and for placing it in the editorial hands of Hugh Lewin, who approached the text with sensitivity and care.

I am indebted to Morris Stoch and his family for having decades ago shared the warmth of their Sephardic home, one which provided the inspiration for the Sephardim of *The Fossil Artist*. While the characters in the novel share a family surname (with the kind permission of Morris), they are not intended to resemble any persons (named Codron or otherwise) living or dead.

The final expression of gratitude is owed to my family. All these words would mean nothing without the love of my first reader, Tracey, and of our gorgeous, creative children, Dave, Matt and Ash, who have had to make place in our home for the far too intrusive characters of my imagination.